The Shadow That Finds Us

ANDY DARCY THEO

GALLERY YA

SIMON & SCHUSTER

London New York Amsterdam/Antwerp Sydney/Melbourne Toronto New Delhi

First published in Great Britain in 2026 by Gallery UK,
an imprint of Simon & Schuster UK Ltd

Text copyright © 2026 Andy Darcy Theo
Cover illustration © 2026 Katt Phatt Studio

This book is copyright under the Berne Convention.
No reproduction without permission.

All rights reserved.

The right of Andy Darcy Theo to be identified as the author of this work
has been asserted by him in accordance with sections 77 and
78 of the Copyright, Designs and Patents Act, 1988.

1 3 5 7 9 10 8 6 4 2

Simon & Schuster UK Ltd
1st Floor, 222 Gray's Inn Road
London WC1X 8HB

For more than 100 years, Simon & Schuster has championed authors and the stories they create. By respecting the copyright of an author's intellectual property, you enable Simon & Schuster and the author to continue publishing exceptional books for years to come. We thank you for supporting the author's copyright by purchasing an authorized edition of this book. No amount of this book may be reproduced or stored in any format, nor may it be uploaded to any website, database, language-learning model, or other repository, retrieval, or artificial intelligence system without express permission. All rights reserved. Inquiries may be directed to Simon & Schuster, 222 Gray's Inn Road, London WC1X 8HB or RightsMailbox@simonandschuster.co.uk

www.simonandschuster.co.uk
www.simonandschuster.com.au
www.simonandschuster.co.in

The authorised representative in the EEA is Simon & Schuster Netherlands BV,
Herculesplein 96, 3584 AA Utrecht, Netherlands. info@simonandschuster.nl

Simon & Schuster Australia, Sydney
Simon & Schuster India, New Delhi

A CIP catalogue record for this book is available from the British Library.

PB ISBN 978-1-3985-5331-6
eBook ISBN 978-1-3985-5339-2
eAudio ISBN 978-1-3985-5338-5

This book is a work of fiction. Names, characters, places and incidents are either
the product of the author's imagination or are used fictitiously. Any resemblance
to actual people living or dead, events or locales is entirely coincidental.

Printed and Bound in the UK using 100% Renewable Electricity at CPI Group (UK) Ltd

PRAISE FOR THE SERIES

'Explosive, action packed and full of twists I didn't see coming, all while bringing together my favourite found family and sweeping romance – truly everything I love all in one book.'
Bea Fitzgerald, author of *Girl, Goddess, Queen*

'Absolutely enchanting and nothing short of epic. Andy effortlessly transports you back to the golden age of YA fantasy.'
Bill Wood, author of *Let's Split Up*

'Andy Darcy Theo is such an exciting new voice in YA. This series is truly thrilling.'
Juno Dawson, author of *Her Majesty's Royal Coven*

'Breathtaking and exhilarating.'
Rosie Talbot, author of *Sixteen Souls*

'This series establishes Andy Darcy Theo, not only as one of the freshest voices in YA literature, but one of the most vital. I couldn't put these books down!'
Sasha Peyton Smith, author of *The Rose Bargain*

'With prose that is lyrical yet accessible, Theo evokes a sense of nostalgia which reminds you of your love for classics in the fantasy genre, whilst still feeling fresh and modern.'
Busayo Matuluko, author of *'Til Death*

'A full-throttle roller-coaster ride complete with swoon-worthy romance, vibrant magic and sharp insights into mental health. Above all, this book understands what it is to face your fears and come of age – my teenage self would have gone absolutely feral for it.'
Ella McLeod, author of *Rapunzella, Or, Don't Touch My Hair*

'Exhilarating, electrifying and unputdownable. I devoured it in one sitting. A breathtaking debut from one of the most exciting voices in YA!'
Danielle Jawando, author of *And the Stars Were Burning Brightly*

For those who dream to love, and dare to live.

AUTHOR'S NOTE

They say that parents and teachers shouldn't have favourites, but for me, this book has always been closest to my heart. Maybe that's because it's the truest reflection of me.

Grief runs throughout this story, discussed in all its raw, incomprehensible intensity. Grief for loved ones we have lost, grief for things that could've been. Alexis's mental health journey takes centre stage, and while this is a world of powers and prophecy, his experience of psychosis is very much grounded in the lived experiences of my past patients and family. Caeli's unapologetic journey of self-acceptance and self-actualisation also serves to remind us that our worth is not contingent on anybody's recognition of it. For this reason, book three is as devastating as it is hopeful, as vulnerable as it is powerful. Ultimately, it's a reminder that power – true power – comes from unity and connection, regardless of whether those people are still with us or not.

While the shadow may find us, it is the angel that guides us. So keep your head up; you won't find them on the ground.

PROLOGUE

Eleven years ago

Caeli Doran's mother was certain her daughter was the most independent, self-sufficient girl there ever was, that she loved being in charge.

She was wrong.

Caeli hated being in charge, but someone had to do it, and she had long learned that she couldn't rely on anyone except herself.

Independence, it seemed, was not a trait she had developed of her own accord. Rather, it was a vice that had been thrust upon her. She had no choice. It was that or risk starving at the empty hands of a mother who struggled to provide and a father who didn't care enough to stay.

Caeli's mother truly believed that she was capable of anything, that she was wise beyond her years and could take charge of any situation, no matter how dire or desperate. Why else would she ask her six-year-old daughter to watch over her one-year-old while she went out on a date?

Caeli didn't mind, though. She loved spending time with Celina, especially now that she was able to sit up and crawl, which she seemed insistent on doing at all times. It meant that Caeli could leave her for short periods to see to the other chores – washing plates or vacuuming.

'So pretty with your silver hair, Cel,' said Caeli, stroking the short tufts of ashen hair that wisped around her sister's head as she wriggled on the spot. Celina blew bubbles at her in response and Caeli pressed the tip of her finger against Celina's lips to pop them. 'Eat your food. I'll be right back. Mummy asked me to do the dishes.'

Caeli replaced the picture book in front of Celina with a princess-decorated plastic plate of chicken nuggets. Her sister's grey-blue eyes fixed on them and she put a cut-up cube into her mouth while Caeli rose to her feet.

As she padded across their two-bedroom flat, she wondered what time her mother would be home. She said that she was out with a man-friend and had been fretting when the babysitter had cancelled last minute, but Caeli reassured her that the two of them would be fine. That she was there to help her, so much so that her mother no longer needed to ask. It had been like that even before Celina was born.

To help with the washing. To help her sweep the hair at the hairdresser's on weekends, and even on schooldays when the salon was especially busy. To help her add the numbers written on the letters that came through the post, letters about bills and rent and final notices. Even to help her smile when tears stained her cheeks after Celina's father left, just as Caeli's had.

Caeli was always there to help put the pieces together.

'*Us two against the world*,' her mother always said.

And then one day Caeli noticed her mother's belly had grown bigger. She didn't eat much, so it couldn't be that. When she told her that she was growing Caeli a new brother or sister in there, that Caeli would get to meet them in a few months, Caeli couldn't stop herself from bragging about it to everyone at school.

Finally, another person to help me, Caeli had thought.

In reality, Celina was more of a burden than anything, but she was a burden Caeli adored, another responsibility she knew she could take care of.

Caeli stepped up on the stool to reach the sink and began scrubbing the fancy glass her mother drank her special juice from. She began humming the nursery rhyme her mother used to sing to her and now sang to soothe Celina. Glancing over her shoulder, Caeli couldn't see her sister over the sofa that separated the lounge from the kitchen.

'Remember to chew – I'll be back in a minute,' she called when she heard her cough, knowing her sister had a propensity to shovel things into her mouth without a care and also to cry whenever she or their mother were out of eyesight. Caeli was surprised she couldn't hear her wailing now. She continued washing, wanting to get it done before her sister crawled off somewhere or realised she'd been left alone.

A year ago, when water had pooled between her mother's legs while she was brushing Caeli's long silver hair in the mirror, Caeli had called the ambulance. They went to the hospital together and she knew, based on the books she had read, that her sibling would soon be leaving her mother's big round belly.

No annoying boys, she had replied when the kind elderly nurse asked her what she hoped it would be.

Whichever it was, Caeli would like them to wear a necklace like hers. With an amulet, a small stone in the shape of a triangle, they could be matching, but maybe a different colour to her grey one.

Once all the dishes in the sink were cleaned and dry, Caeli made her way back to the lounge.

'Cel?'

Caeli drew closer, wondering if she had somehow fallen asleep. Celina wasn't fidgeting or wriggling, which was weird because she always wriggled when she slept, and her chubby cheeks and lips were an unnerving blue.

Caeli dropped to her knees, her heart racing so fast that it hurt in her chest. Something invisible coiled round her neck and made her breathing rapid. Her eyes darted around.

'Celina?' She heard the fear creep into her voice as she tried to shake her sister awake. Then panic as she said her name again, louder this time, demanding her to open her eyes. 'Celina, wake up!'

Still, no matter how many times she shouted her name or how hard she pressed her baby sister to her chest as she rocked her back and forth, Celina remained asleep.

It was only when her mother returned home, when the sound of Celeste Doran's shrieks shattered all the windows of their flat, did it dawn on Caeli that everyone was crying except for Celina.

Eleven years later

Caeli's independence had solidified in the years that followed. After losing her husband and her baby daughter, her mother Celeste could only manage her own grief, leaving Caeli to run the house. Caeli cooked and cleaned, kept up with school, helped her mother at the hair salon. She wiped her mother's tears when she couldn't get off the sofa on the anniversary of Celina's death, and then helped her get dressed for dates when she was tired of being alone. Caeli mended her own heart whenever she let a boy break it, and her mother was happy to allow her to do so.

The devil works hard, but an eldest daughter works harder.

Celeste thanked her, of course, profusely, and had never once blamed Caeli, but she made no attempt to intervene either. She became more of an older co-dependent sister rather than a mother.

Irrespective of whether or not she liked being in charge, Caeli had always known that she *needed* to be. Only that became all the more difficult now that she was disabled in a way she'd never had to consider before.

'Cae, do you need a hand?'

Blaise Ademola leaned against her bedroom doorframe in her mother's flat, sporting a T-shirt that was tight on his arms and a pair of loose shorts, impervious to the evenings that grew progressively colder with each passing week. He scrunched his face, realising what he had just said after Caeli gave him a gruelling look. 'Shit, sorry. Bad choice of words.'

Caeli acknowledged his apology with a nod as she tugged on the grey-gloved sleeve that went up to her elbow, concealing the end of her arm. Blaise told her that she didn't need to wear it, at home or in public, but she wasn't ready yet for anyone to stare, not when she was still coming to terms with it herself. She continued trying to fold the bedsheet with just one hand. It kept wrinkling in the middle. She'd restarted four times but still the creases returned.

'Let me or your mum help—'

'I don't need your help,' she snapped, using her right arm, the arm that no longer had a hand, to push him away. From its end came a blast of wind that knocked into Blaise and threw him against the far wall.

'Blaise, I'm sorry –' she began, tucking her arm behind her back as it began to itch. 'I didn't know I could still use my powers with . . .'

'Caeli?' Celeste Doran rushed into the room, wobbling on heels she had borrowed from her daughter, her hair up in curlers. She helped Blaise up as he rubbed the back of his head, examining the broken plaster behind him. 'Everything okay?'

'Not really,' said Blaise.

'Yes,' Caeli insisted at the same time.

Caeli felt her mother's gaze drift to her right arm.

Celeste had barely taken a step towards her before Caeli protested. 'I'm fine. Any time either of you offer to help, you end up just doing it for me. I need to learn to do this by myself.

Go on your date, have a good time with Lucas, and don't forget to take a key.'

'I can cancel?' her mother offered, wringing her hands awkwardly. 'He knows you've been having a hard time adjusting since the crash.'

The crash. That was the lie. That a reckless driver had taken a corner too soon and hit her, leading to her hand being amputated and her car being towed. The High Order had sent an Eraser to embed that false memory in Celeste's mind.

Caeli caught Blaise's glance and threw him a withering look. *What? Should I tell her my hand was sliced off on a battlefield by a man who smiled while doing it? That I lost it defending you. That I'm one of the most famous Elementals in history and she has no clue – as oblivious to the powers I inherited from her as she is to everything else?*

If anyone could get all that across in one fleeting look, it was Caeli. Blaise relented with a shrug. He had been backing down a lot lately, even when Caeli was in the wrong. She hated him for it.

'Go,' Caeli said, offering her mother a weak smile. 'Blaise is here if I need anything.'

It had taken Celeste years to date again after losing her youngest daughter, but Caeli was glad she was. It meant her mother would become less dependent on her.

Celeste knew better than to argue with her. 'Such a good boy, you are,' she said, squeezing Blaise's cheeks. 'How do I look?'

She did a little spin when he twirled his finger.

'Beautiful dress, Ms Doran,' he said with a smile.

'That's because it's mine,' Caeli muttered.

'People sometimes think we're sisters.' Celeste beamed. 'You know I was only your age when I had Cae. You should've seen me then, Blaise.'

'Stop flirting with my boyfriend, Mother,' Caeli teased.

Blaise's eyes lit with a spark of mischief. 'There's plenty of me to go around,' he said, his eyes sliding over Caeli in a way that made her body prickle with arousal, a rare and deeply missed sensation these days. She needed her mother to leave – urgently. For the first time in a long time she felt something other than anger and she didn't want to suppress it.

'Mum—'

'Yes, I'm going!' Celeste replied with a knowing smile. 'Be *safe*.'

'Oh, please get out! And, Mum,' Caeli called as she heard the front door open a moment later, 'you still have your rollers in.'

Celeste swore, her heels clicking back to the bathroom. As Caeli waited for her mother to leave, she stared across her room at Blaise, and he right back at her. Neither of them moved yet, but she could feel herself growing excited at the prospect of being alone with him. Of feeling his hot muscular body press down on her, thawing the coldness that had settled within and around her. She imagined her fingers raking down his broad back, his hands tightening on her waist. His full lips on hers as they wrapped themselves around each other. She tried to steady her breathing and cage her lust, but with each passing second her patience was weakening.

After what felt like an eternity of hair brushing, the front door clicked closed and Celeste was gone. Caeli and Blaise collided a second after. His arms lifted her off the ground effortlessly as she wrapped her legs round his waist, grinding herself against him. He carried her to the bed where he lay her down, creasing the sheets she'd spent the last ten minutes folding.

'I've missed you,' she moaned as his lips sucked on her throat.

'I've missed you,' he growled back.

She ripped his shirt open, making him laugh, the lines of his stomach flexing as he did. She then tried to take off her own T-shirt, not wanting to tear it as she had only bought it the week before. The collar caught on her head, and she wriggled to remove it.

'Let me—' Blaise began.

'No,' she said, her voice muffled. 'I can do it.'

The fabric tightened round her face, making her feel claustrophobic. It was all getting too much. How long it was taking. How unsexy Blaise must be finding her.

You're ruining the moment, Caeli screamed at herself.

Her nails tore the shirt in half and it fell to the floor, ruined beyond repair. Her chest heaved as she tried to calm the storm of her thoughts, convincing herself it wasn't a big deal. But Blaise was no longer looking at her with lust, but instead with a sad sympathy that made her stomach lurch.

She slapped her arm against her hip as she sat up, trying to banish the itch of her missing hand.

'Is it hurting again?' he asked gently.

'It's fine. Where were we?' She pulled him on top of her again, kissing him with the same eagerness and ferocity that he'd been kissing her with just seconds ago, but the moment was gone. He was kissing her out of service, not desire. Out of pity.

'Get off me,' she said, pressing her hand against his chest.

Blaise instantly backed away. 'I'm sorry,' he muttered. 'Just ... don't feel like it.'

'Can't blame you,' she said, snatching her ripped T-shirt from the floor. She waved her right arm in the air. 'Look at me. Not exactly what you signed up for.'

Blaise stood up straighter. 'No, it's not that! I promise. You're beautiful, just as much as before.'

Liar, she thought, fixing her gloved sleeve. *You only feel guilty that it was your fault.*

'We can do something else,' Blaise suggested. 'I can help you with the Scholar research Ziya assigned you before we go back to Haven tomorrow? That's the speciality you've chosen, right?'

I don't need help – but Caeli couldn't bring herself to say it without feeling pathetic. 'Find us a film,' she said instead. 'I'll be there in a bit, just need to tidy up.'

'I'll help,' Blaise offered.

Caeli wanted to scream, but her mental breakdown was scheduled for later in the week and she hated when things didn't run to plan. She forced herself to take a steadying breath and shook her head. With her left hand, she manipulated the wind beneath Blaise's crumpled T-shirt on the floor and flew it towards him. 'Heat up the popcorn. I know you like popping it with your hands. Salty only. No action films just because you fancy the female lead. Or ridiculous comedies.'

'Better than a boring documentary.' There it was. A hint of them again, the old them that bickered, confident that the other could take it. 'Fine, but no serial killers.'

'Fine,' she said with a smirk.

Blaise left, and she pulled out one of his old sweatshirts that was oversized on her – a grey one he'd lent her years ago at a dance competition when he'd been dating her friend. It had caused drama but she secretly loved it – even back then he'd chosen her.

Now Caeli loved it because the sleeves were long enough to cover what was gone.

She resumed folding the bedsheet, smoothing creases, striving for perfection as she always had. Only that need had multiplied somehow. It consumed her most days, this deep desire to iron out creases.

Perhaps that was why she despised herself so much now. Instead of admiration, people looked at her with pity.

Poor Caeli Doran, they must think. It made her feel sick.

She checked over her shoulder to make sure Blaise couldn't see her, then slipped off her glove and stared at the end of her arm. It had healed cleanly: no sign of infection, ready for a prosthetic should she ask for one. But Caeli didn't see the potential in her recovery or feel appreciation that it had been her hand and not her life that had been taken.

She could only see blood. The blood that had poured from it that day on the battlefield under the eclipse, bodies littered all around her.

She'd once read that the loss of a loved one was like losing a limb. *What a sick, twisted analogy that is*, she thought, her mind flashing with the hazy memory of what it felt like to hold her baby sister's cold body against her chest long after she had taken her last breath. Now phantom pain haunted her, a tingling, pinching sensation. She'd researched it extensively, of course:

nerves misfiring, neurons rewiring around the amputated area. Imagined pain but it hurt all the same. It worsened with stress, fatigue, anxiety, which were ironically her three closest companions of late.

She had tried everything at the Healing Sanctuary, often going with Demi for support. Mirror therapy, massaging, acupuncture, healing crystals, energy redirection. Nothing had a long-lasting effect. The pain always returned.

'You coming, Cae? Think I've found something.'

Caeli rolled down her sleeve and joined Blaise, curling into his open arms as he welcomed her.

'Didn't know you still had this?' he said, tugging at the sweatshirt, his mouth upturned in a slight smile. 'It's grey, sure, but it doesn't match the rest of your wardrobe.'

'It's autumn,' Caeli replied. The smell of burnt popcorn hit her and she was reminded of the smell of cauterised flesh. She no longer fancied it. Instead, she buried her nose into the crook of Blaise's neck and inhaled the scent of him. 'I'll make it work.'

Blaise kissed the top of her head and started the documentary on the top-ten unsolved murders of the last decade. 'Next time, it's an action film,' he said, and she nodded. He pointed at the screen with the remote. 'Guaranteed that if you were in charge of these cases, you would've cracked them all. No wonder you've decided to specialise as a Scholar.'

Caeli smiled for him. There it was again. That belief that she could do it all alone. That she knew everything. That she liked being in charge.

But none of those things had been true when she needed them to be. It was why she chose to focus her studies at the

Haven as a Scholar and not a Fighter, though she was equally adept at both. She hated to admit it, but there was so much she was ashamed that she didn't know. Whether she would use the prosthetic her Healers at the Haven had made for her. Who her father was. Why her sister had deserved to die, choked on food and deprived of air. Another cruel joke. Why someone else haunted her mind, someone opposite to Blaise: pale where he was dark, feminine where he was masculine. Someone like her. What it meant to have feelings she didn't understand about a girl she thought she hated? No, that she *did* hate. But also that she couldn't stop thinking about.

Regardless of how it may impact Blaise or Valentina, Caeli wondered what those feelings meant for *her*?

Above it all, Caeli questioned whether she would ever adjust to this new normal. She tried to be who she used to be, the same headstrong, self-sufficient girl. But, in truth, Caeli had long felt dependent on many a thing. On her academic merits and grades for validation, on the attention from others for self-worth, on her friends for family.

Blaise fell asleep before the documentary reached case number nine. He slept a lot now and she was jealous. After the battle, his mind had slowed while hers now raced.

She slipped from his arms, her restless body compelled to satisfy the demands of the thoughts that couldn't be ignored. The bedsheets weren't perfect, and if she let her standards slip, then she was sure she'd unravel and everything else would fall to ruin too.

Back in her room, Caeli folded the sheets over and over again, chasing perfection, all the while introducing as many new creases as she fixed – trapped in a never-ending, terrorising loop until she eventually succumbed to exhaustion.

Then, as it had every night since the Battle of Stonehenge, the darkness that she didn't know lay hidden within her came to steal her sleep away and terrorise her some more.

1
RUDENĖJA

Rudenėja (n.) *Lithuanian origin*
The transition of the world into autumn

Autumn's come early this year, thought Alexis Michaels as he readjusted his grip on his sword, cursing the reddish-brown leaves that crunched beneath his bare feet and threatened to give him away. He kept to the shadows where possible, his lean sweat-slicked body pressed against the rough tree trunks as he advanced deeper into the woods.

I know you're in here, he thought, scanning his surroundings.

Leaves scattered behind him and Alexis spun. He caught himself just before his sword severed the head of a stocky blue Staffordshire bull terrier.

'*Reina*,' he hissed, forgetting to whisper.

The Michaels family's newest addition, a two-year-old adopted Staffie, tilted her head at Alexis curiously. She let out the slightest of whines, her only complaint after hours of standing guard beside Alexis as the night turned from pitch black to a blossoming orange.

'We're on serious patrolling business, princess.'

Reina yawned and sat dutifully.

Alexis looked through the canopy at the sky, where the sunrise struggled to break through the sea of low-lying clouds. He had come soon after midnight, as he had the night before and the night before that, sword in hand and powers at the ready to search the entirety of Protegere Forest if he must. But there had been no sight of the man who he had seen weeks before, after he heard his mother say, '*They know who we are. They know what we've done. Alexis can never find out.*'

A shiver ran down Alexis's spine as he recalled the fear in his mother's voice and the look of worry on his father's face. It took a lot to shake up the surgeon and detective, but the new state-of-the-art home security system and the dog pointed to something bigger.

Alexis would have to try his luck again the following night.

'Come on then, darling. Let's go home.'

They reached Valerian Lane, bypassing the new alarms at the gates and entrance of the Michaelses' home. Alexis used his powers to wash his feet and Reina's paws before floating them up to his window on a cloud of water vapour, where Reina padded off to his parents' bedroom while he hid the sword under his mattress and crawled into bed.

Not finding anyone is a good sign, he reminded himself, coaxing his nervous system out of fight-or-flight. *Maybe they left once they saw me. Maybe I scared them off.*

It was a lie, perhaps a delusion, but it helped him to rest.

Sleep, however, brought no peace. It was as if the shadows were waiting for him there, its talons that much sharper when his mind was unconscious and body was paralysed. In sleep it could reach him. In sleep Alexis was at its mercy.

The nightmare returned. The cliffside. The searing pain of his body ripping apart. The surface of the black ocean rushing to meet him, showing his reflection just as he closed his eyes and waited for it to all end. The memory that belonged to his father still haunted him, even months after Mortem had died on the summer solstice.

Usually he woke up then.

But not tonight.

What had usually broken him free from the nightmare, the touch of his body to the element of water, a power only he could control, no longer liberated him. He reopened his eyes in the dream to find himself, seventeen-year-old Alexis, floating in a vast onyx sea.

What should have made him feel strong, powerful, now felt foreign. The water was heavy and threatened to pull him beneath the dark surface. He kicked, thrashed, imagining that it was Demi he was swimming to, Demi that he was fighting for. *Sink or swim*. He couldn't sink.

A voice whispered in his mind: *Give in.*

He fought harder, but all his strength had abandoned him.

Darkness filled his vision as he was dragged underneath the surface. His amulet vanished. Demi disappeared. *It's just a nightmare*, he told himself, another nightmare, born from anxiety and stress.

Just because it isn't real, doesn't mean it can't hurt you, the *Shadow Man* was quick to remind him, its voice echoing through the black ocean.

His powers had betrayed him. His lungs burned and limbs stilled. Against every impulse in his body, Alexis finally inhaled the sea of darkness.

And woke.

2

SKINSHIP

Skinship (n.) *Japanese origin*
Bonding through the intimacy of touch, especially
the closeness between a parent and child

'Dad. Dad, wake up,' Alexis said gently, nudging his father.

Jackson Michaels stirred, lifting his head from the crook of his elbow. Alexis surveyed the cluttered study around him. Stephanie always said that the room was an eyesore and wondered how her husband ever found anything amongst it, let alone solved a single case as a senior homicide detective and criminal profiler. 'Organised mess' was Jackson's way of describing it.

Files stacked on top of files, Post-it notes with scribbled reminders were everywhere. A colour-coded investigation board was spread across the far wall, covered in CCTV stills and interconnected with red string, depicting not the secret about Alexis's potential abduction and forgery of his adoption papers but a mundane homicide linked to a drug ring in the outer London area.

Boring.

'Looks like Mum's home,' Jackson rasped, gesturing to the

grainy CCTV footage. The new camera in the kitchen revealed Stephanie preparing Reina's breakfast while she jumped up at her excitedly.

'Sleep in here again?' Alexis asked. He tugged out his earphones, pausing the music that his parents complained he played too loud, and looped it over the neckline of his T-shirt.

Jackson offered a sheepish smile. 'I'd rather work on it here than in the office. Case will wrap up soon, though. Your dad's good at his job.'

Jackson rose to his full height, taller than Alexis by only an inch now, and threw a playful jab at his shoulder that his son deflected with ease.

'You're getting quicker,' Jackson noted. 'Been training recently?'

'Something like that.'

They made their way to the open-plan kitchen and conservatory to find Stephanie pushing Reina off her. 'I wish you'd listen to me the way you listen to your dad. Okay, now you're creasing my clothes. Down!'

Stephanie set down the dog bowl, which Reina instantly pounced on. She pulled free her dirty-blonde hair from its chignon and said to her husband and son, 'An evil stepmother, years of medical school, head of cardiothoracic surgery, and raising two smelly sons, but it's *this dog* that's causing me the most stress. You're meant to be on my team, Reina.'

Jackson wrapped his arms round his wife from behind as she washed her hands. 'I thought I was on your team?' He planted a kiss against the nape of her neck before taking the hair band from her.

'You're just as smelly as the boys,' she muttered, but Alexis watched as she eased into her husband's touch as he retied her hair, her back resting against his broad chest, her scowl fading into a smile in the window's reflection.

'Where's Jason?' Stephanie asked Alexis. 'And you, go get ready. First day of your final year at school!'

With a squeeze of Jackson's hand, Stephanie wandered over to Alexis and pressed a kiss to his forehead, having to stand on her tiptoes to reach him. She took his face in her hands and stared at him intently, analytically, in a way that made him still. When her eyes took in the earphones at his collar, he took the smallest of steps backwards.

'Diagnosis?' he asked, his lips curving slightly.

The worry that lined his mother's face was swept away by a reluctant smile. 'Sleep deprivation. Eight hours minimum, unless you want your immune system, respiratory system, memory consolidation and overall mental well-being to rapidly deteriorate.'

'Doesn't sound like fun.'

'No, it doesn't. And if that doesn't convince you, then might I add that you look ghastly? I can't imagine a certain half-Greek, half-Egyptian girl down the road will want to associate herself with you looking like that.'

Alexis's blush betrayed him. To deny it or argue otherwise only appeared to encourage his parents, and Demi's for that matter, so he went along with it. 'Ha ha, hilarious. Fine, I'll go back to sleep now then.'

'No, you don't.' Stephanie caught him by the ear and pushed him towards the stairs. 'With the grades you're working towards, your father and I are hoping for an early retirement and a month-long cruise. So up you go. Ten minutes until we need to leave. Make sure Jason's ready too.'

'I'm not a miracle worker, Mother. You heard her, Jace,' he called, banging his fist against Jason's door as he passed it. When he heard no response, or any sign of life, Alexis flung the door open, letting the hallway lights wash in.

'I hate it when you do that!' moaned his twelve-year-old brother, shielding his eyes.

'Smells like death in here.'

He let Jason barge past him. Where Alexis was tall, lean and dark-haired, Jason was his opposite: short and blond like his mother with his father's sky-blue eyes.

'Mum and Dad will want to give you the first-day-of-a-new-school speech,' said Alexis.

'I know what they're going to say,' Jason replied. 'If someone starts on me, Mum says rise above and Dad says swing low.'

Alexis shrugged in acceptance. He would've liked to have joined his brother on his first day of school. Alas, Alexis had made alternative plans that were far from mundane or explicable to his parents.

Once in his room, Alexis froze the lock to his door shut. He then placed his hands together and focused on conjuring his proxy until he felt the familiar painless pulling sensation from within.

Blink.

Alexis ignored the whisper of the *Shadow Man* as the proxy slipped free from his own body. He turned away from his proxy to rub at the dark circles that had taken permanent residence beneath his eyes.

'You look like shit,' he told his proxy – an identical version of himself, minus his blue triangular amulet, which could never be replicated.

'I look like you,' the proxy said.

Alexis swept a low bow as if to say 'you're welcome' before studying his reflection. He had allowed his dark hair to grow slightly longer until it became a sea of overlapping waves. Demi said she liked it, that it made him look like a tortured poet, but Alexis thought it only made him look more like Mortem. The bright blue of his proxy's eyes seemed to drown within the black rings, the pointed incisors of its smile looked wolfish, and the hollows of its cheeks made it appear more gaunt than chiselled as it had in the summer.

Alexis stepped closer, inspecting the pale scar over its chest where the *Demon* and Mortem had wounded him.

'Does it hurt?' he asked, feeling the scar on his own shirtless body.

'Not really,' it answered, reaching for the school uniform that Alexis had thrown over his chair the night before. 'Not as much as it must hurt you.'

Alexis nodded. 'I wouldn't want you to suffer for my mistakes.'

He withdrew a sealed box from beneath his bed. Inside lay a brand-new Haven suit, as black as obsidian and as durable as featherweight titanium.

'Big day,' the proxy said, watching him change.

'Choosing our Haven specialities and our first Elemental mission for the High Order,' Alexis replied, excitement cutting through his exhaustion. In the past few weeks he'd thought about it, of course, but he'd come no closer to deciding whether he want to specialise as either a Scholar, Healer or Fighter. Was it overkill to do them all?

'Looking forward to seeing the others?'

Alexis's heart fluttered. 'It's been the longest I've not seen them since we all first met.'

'And you're not going to tell them about the man in the woods or the return of the hallucinatory shadow figure from your childhood?'

Alexis's smile faded. 'You sure know how to kill the vibe.'

He activated the portal device that would grant him direct access to the Haven. A beam of white light shot from its tip and struck the wall, slowing devouring it. It flickered slightly at the edges, likely needing to be recharged. Alexis knew there had been a shortage of portalling devices recently, and he reminded himself to ask Ziya or Incantus for a new one.

'Why am I nervous to go through?' he asked aloud, feeling a flutter of anticipation start up in his chest.

'You wonder if it's changed as much as you have,' said the proxy as it changed into his school uniform. 'The Haven will always be a sanctuary, especially for those who are different.'

Alexis offered the proxy a tight smile. 'You know talking to yourself is the first sign of madness?'

'Maybe you're having a psychotic break after all,' it replied.

Alexis laughed. He brushed the proxy's bedhead and then his own. 'Be good. Look out for Jace. He'll pretend like he won't want to see you around but remind him subtly where he can find you. Stick close to Demi's proxy and just go to the Library in between lessons.'

'Living *la vida loca*,' the proxy replied drily.

'And keep an eye out for anything suspicious. Call me the second—'

Before Alexis could say more, the proxy shoved him into the wall of white, and between one blink and the next Alexis was back in the Haven beneath Stonehenge.

3

ADREF

Adref (adv.) *Welsh origin*
Returning home; homebound

'Alexis Michaels.'

Blaise Ademola grinned at him as though he were a hero returning home from war. Before Caeli could even rise, Blaise enveloped Alexis in a spine-cracking hug with arms more muscular than Alexis remembered.

'The battle's over, man. You can put the weapons down,' Alexis gasped, squeezing his biceps. The hug lingered a beat longer than expected, as though Blaise didn't want to let him go. Alexis returned it just as tightly.

Blaise chuckled and eventually released him, his amber eyes dipping. 'I've mostly stayed between here and Cae's since summer. Working out gave me something to do.'

There was something underlying the words but Alexis let it go.

'Bit intrusive to be waiting in my room, no?' Alexis surveyed his private chamber. Calming bluish hues, the soft rush of water from the fountain that trickled into the arching pool. Everything just as he'd left it in the summer. 'Invasion of privacy much?'

Blaise smirked. 'Hey, I helped the Healers change you when you were in your coma. Trust me, at this point there's no privacy left.'

Thankfully, Caeli shouldered Blaise out of the way and greeted Alexis with a kiss to each cheek. 'Thought we'd have to start our first day without you. Blaise and I got here early this morning so I could settle in and go over the mission objectives with Ziya before tonight.'

Alexis didn't allow his gaze to drift from Caeli's face. Her stormy eyes narrowed, daring him to look for the arm that was held behind her back, as if her hand was carelessly tucked in her rear pocket and not absent altogether.

'Had to set up the proxy for school,' Alexis replied, keeping his tone light. 'I assume you've sent yours in your place too.'

Caeli scoffed and brushed back her platinum-blonde curtain bangs. 'Of course – to ask is to insult. With two of me I hope to achieve my plans for world domination in half the time.'

Alexis saluted her ambition. 'Demi?'

'She's on her way.'

Alexis nodded. With Caeli's and Blaise's eyes on trained on him, he kept his expression neutral before jutting his chin to the door. 'Shall we?'

Their footsteps echoed down the grand white-and-gold staircase that wound round the Haven's cavernous open core. The knot in the centre of Alexis's chest loosened with every step, as if the softly glowing walls of the Haven were absolving him of his stress and placating his anxieties. It was exactly as he remembered: vaulted ceilings, delicate carvings along the marble arches that weaved across the hive in a lattice, and the faint yet undeniable hum of Elemental power.

Home. Alexis felt at home.

Elementals of the Haven they recognised and had fought alongside at the battle greeted them on their descent in a flurry of new robes and uniforms.

'Did I miss the memo on a new dress code?' Alexis asked. Some were dressed in short-sleeved loose robes the same colour as the pale-yellow healing crystals, whereas others were cloaked in gowns of rich purple, their deep pockets bulging with what looked like books.

'Incantus fought to keep the Haven up and running as a training institute after the battle,' Blaise explained. 'Ziya thought it would be good for the different specialities to have different uniforms. Younger kids who haven't yet specialised still wear the combat suits, as do the Fighters. It's been rolled out pretty well.'

They passed under an archway to where Ziya Parashakti stood and waved. She was dressed in semi-formal attire: a grey sweater vest over a white shirt, and her hair was cut short in a curly bob that suited her. 'Hi, guys!'

Just as they were greeting her, Alexis saw the entire Nikolas family emerge from the corridor that led to the student dormitories.

Kallisto, Demi's sister who was a year younger than Jason, galloped towards him on the back of Gibbous. Demi trailed just behind, grinning as Blaise stumbled back in fear of the enormous white dire wolf.

'He is *not* safe to ride!' Blaise shouted.

Kallisto let out a laugh as Gibbous lowered her to the ground. Alexis helped her to dismount as she said, 'He said he'd use your leg as a chew toy if you get any ideas.'

As they laughed at how quickly Blaise went pale, Demi's eyes caught Alexis's. That was all it took to destabilise and silence any whispers from the *Shadow Man*. Her power was in her presence, not just at her fingertips, but in her aura. At her proximity, the smell of her lavender-soaked dark curls and the grip of her arms round Alexis's as they embraced, he felt infused by the unrelenting healing power of the Earth.

'How did we let it go so many weeks?' she asked, finally letting him go.

'The last time we were all together was in Italy after we'd healed,' said Caeli, smiling fondly.

Laughter, sunshine, sand. Sitting on plastic chairs in the garden, playing cards and talking until the stars flooded the skies. 'Do you remember when we caught Cae and Blaise by the—'

'Kallisto!' Caeli exclaimed, cutting him off. 'Your powers of fauna communication must be coming along.'

Kallisto nodded proudly and stroked Gibbous's contented face. 'I've been practising. Mum and Dad said I should start with one genus or family at a time and learn the ways they communicate. I've been working with canines, like Reina.'

'Now that her powers are maturing, Mum and Dad just enrolled her at the Haven,' Demi added, brushing a loose strand of hair from her sister's rich brown eyes that were misted in the centre with a pool of white.

While Kallisto had been born with her vision largely

compromised, her gifts were incredible, rare even for those descended from the Earth Tribe. Where her father, Geb, had influence over flora and her mother, Petra, over rock and stone, Kallisto's powers were some kind of empathic link to nature.

From behind, Geb Nikolas paused his conversation with Ziya and called out, 'Time for your mother and me to go, *habibti*.' Demi's short tawny-skinned father waved at them as Kallisto hugged him. 'Wishing you all the best on your mission with Incantus tonight, *hayati*,' he said to Demi.

'Thanks, Dad,' Demi said, hugging him next.

Alexis stood by himself, listening in to Demi's conversation with her parents while Caeli and Blaise greeted Ziya. He found himself looking at his feet, not quite knowing where to place himself.

'You won't find any angels on the ground,' said Demi's mother Petra. She gently placed two fingers beneath Alexis's chin, encouraging him to look up.

Alexis kissed both her cheeks, ruminating on her words. 'How are you?'

'Wonderful,' she said, and she was the type of person who meant it. 'Everything okay at home? I've not had a chance to grab a coffee with your mum in the last couple of weeks.'

'She's been really busy recently,' Alexis replied. 'But I'm sure she'll message you as soon as she's free.'

Petra crinkled her nose at him as she smiled. 'Take care of each other,' she whispered, her fingers caressing the golden cross she wore at her neck that matched Demi's.

'We always do.'

'*Ela, agapi mou*,' Petra called over Demi to say goodbye and wish her luck. Alexis couldn't help but recall the last time he had heard that term. *My love*. Demi had said it during the battle, mirroring what Alexis had said to her on the quest as she teetered on the border of life and death after being shot by Sinner. Part of him had hoped that something would happen on their trip away after the battle, but he didn't want to force an opportunity. He wanted it to emerge naturally, when they were both ready for it.

Because she was worth waiting for.

4
RAÐLJÓST

Raðljóst (n.) *Icelandic origin*
'Just enough light to find your way'

The amulets glowed faintly at the reunion of the Children of the Elements as Ziya led them towards the classrooms of the Training Academy.

'I missed this,' Blaise said, looking between them. 'It's not been the same without you guys.'

Demi leaned into his side. 'Me too. It felt wrong being apart.'

Ziya led the group silently, not contributing to their conversation. She had been quieter than usual, Alexis noted. After losing her grandmother, Serena Aevum, and the revelation that her mother had been imprisoned inside Mortem's castle for the last decade, Ziya's grief had stolen her excitement. Alexis made a mental note to check in with her soon.

Ziya cleared her throat. 'Term starts today. As you may know, there are three broad fields our Elementals can specialise in after their core training: Scholars, Healers or Fighters.'

'We've seen the new outfits,' said Caeli. 'Very chic.'

'It's a great idea,' Demi added. 'That's why you're the head of the Scholars.'

Ziya's smile deepened.

'We're all really looking forward to celebrating your promotion to Leader tonight,' said Alexis, speaking on his friends' behalf. Demi had arranged a meal for that evening and made sure to invite Valentina too, to Caeli's indisputable displeasure. Alexis was excited to spend time with his friends without a battle waging around them or a mythical fire-breathing phoenix chasing them down the side of a volcano.

Ziya's footsteps quickened after checking her watch. 'Right, lessons start in six minutes and I still haven't briefed you yet, so I'll give you the quick version.'

'If that's even possible,' Blaise muttered, receiving a playful elbow in the side from Caeli and a shrug from Ziya herself, as if to say 'fair enough'.

'Due to your age, power levels and recent experiences, you've been fast-tracked through the core training,' Ziya explained quickly. 'Now you get to specialise within one field, where you will undertake compulsory modules that Akili, Raeve and Taranis deemed essential, or that the new Leaders have since implemented.'

'New Leaders?' asked Alexis. 'I thought it was just you and Incantus?'

'Incantus promoted Olivia Kefi as Leader of the Healers after her inimitable work on developing her own therapy,' Ziya replied. 'Alexis, I'm sure you can testify to that.'

'I can. She's a force of nature.' He meant it. Even if he had lied through his sessions with her to shield his secrets and psychosis, Kefi's ingenious method of manipulating the resonance and temperature of specific emotions fascinated him. He turned to Demi. 'I think you're going to really like her.'

Alexis knew he needed sleep. He knew it because in that moment, beneath Demi's excited smile, he swore he could detect a hint of jealousy in her green eyes.

Blaise nudged him. 'Who's the Leader of the Fighters? Is it Incantus?'

'He can't tie himself down to one field,' Ziya replied. 'He'll continue to oversee them all. He's busy right now, as you can imagine, but he said he's looking forward to seeing you later. Do you remember Oliver Wrought from the High Order, Blaise?'

'The guy who tried defending us?' Blaise turned to his friends. 'He stood up to Secretary-General Kleine, along with Joe's grandmother.' Caeli's eyes dipped at the mention of Joe, but Blaise continued unaware. 'They pushed to send us back-up for the battle, but Kleine blocked it with some bullshit reasoning.'

Ziya said nothing in Kleine's defence. Alexis knew relations between the Haven and High Order had deteriorated since the summer. The portalling device shortage in the Haven was just the latest passive-aggressive jab against Incantus for not accepting their half-assed apology for their absence.

'Incantus says Wrought's a good man,' Ziya assured them. 'Loyal, level-headed, just like his cousin Teller Sagen was. He's since resigned as high councillor of the Erasers and offered us his support.'

'He's all right,' Blaise shrugged. 'Big memory, like Teller. Probably got a lot to teach on different fighting and military techniques.'

'I received all your enrolment preferences except yours, Alexis,' said Ziya.

Alexis winced. 'Still deciding.'

'Term starts in three minutes,' she replied indifferently. She withdrew a silver-plated device from her black trouser pocket and flicked across its screen, identifying the rooms where each class was taking place.

'It was a hard call for me between Scholar and Fighter,' Caeli admitted. 'But I picked what I'm most passionate about. Besides, I'm already a weapon. What more could I learn about fighting?' She blew Blaise a kiss, who groaned.

'All three specialities complement each other,' Ziya said. 'There's theory in battle, research in healing, and healing required in war. You'll still take a few core classes in each, but most of your time will be spent in your chosen field for the foreseeable three years. Four if you specialise as a Healer.'

'Missions need Fighters,' Blaise said pointedly to Alexis. 'Just makes sense.'

'Incorrect,' Ziya and Caeli said in unison.

'Haven protocol requires at least four grads per mission, one per speciality, and a fourth who's often another Fighter,' Ziya added. 'Plus a senior Elemental, usually an operative of the High Order.'

'Okay,' Blaise muttered, growing bored. 'My power's best for fighting. Choose what field suits your element, Al.'

'Not necessarily,' said Demi softly. She smiled at Blaise cheerfully. 'Fire is vital for healing – sterilisation, cauterisation, illumination, warmth. Don't limit yourself, Blaise.'

Blaise didn't answer. Caeli tutted under her breath but didn't push him.

Fighter. Killer. That is all you are good for and all that you want, the *Shadow Man* hissed inside Alexis's head, as cold as ice. He spun instinctively, expecting to find it right behind him, its lips millimetres from the shell of his ear. His friends stared at him, oblivious.

It can reach me here? Alexis had hoped the Haven's light would shield him, that proximity to his friends would silence the voice of his traumatic past. Clearly, it was much harder to chase away a shadow that had no body and a voice that only spoke within his head.

Alexis did his best to make it look like he had been thinking before answering. 'I ... am I able to change if I feel like I've made the wrong choice?'

Ziya groaned. 'Yes, but only if it is not too far into the term. For now, you must choose. Last minute.'

Scholar. Fighter. Healer.

Caeli. Blaise. Demi.

Alexis knew this wasn't about picking between his friends but it felt that way. His choice would determine who he spent most of his days with.

No, think for yourself. What do you want? What do you value?

He thought of Incantus, the man he idolised. Which would he have picked? Alexis wished he could go and ask him.

We shouldn't see him, whispered the *Shadow Man*.

Even more reason to, Alexis thought.

'I think ...'

Since when did I become so indecisive? What do I value? What suits me, my element?

Water was destructive.

Water was healing.

He heard the voice again. *Water is weak. Water is tainted. Water is poison.*

Alexis gritted his teeth so hard his jaw ached. *I have no business healing anyone when I'm still this broken. And if the* Shadow Man *wants battle, then I'll starve it of it.*

Defy the darkness. He would do it at all costs.

Prophecies. Elemental Tribes. The inheritance of power and influence of fate. What Alexis wanted more than anything was knowledge. Truth. While he could pick up on the basics of the other two specialities, he couldn't bring himself to cut off the potential to learn more about the world he had fought and nearly died to save.

Alexis looked at Caeli and decided. 'Scholar.'

5

HEIMAT

Heimat (n.) *German origin*
A place that you can call home; includes a sense of belongingness, acceptance, safety and connection

'Where have you gone?'

Alexis cut Caeli a sideways glance, gesturing ahead. 'The Training Academy,' he answered slowly. 'Concerned for your memory and visual processing skills, Cae.'

'That's not what I meant and you know it.' She brushed her hair out of her eyes before following Ziya into the classroom. 'But if that's how you want to be.'

Alexis crossed the threshold. Twelve others were already inside dressed in purple Scholar robes. He recognised a few and waved at them.

Caeli sat front and centre, tossing aside the bag already on the desk with a gust of wind. Alexis usually preferred to sit towards the back of any room, not because he was any less interested in whatever he was being taught but to avoid being called on to speak.

Your isolation isn't self-imposed, whispered the *Shadow Man*. *The world doesn't want you.*

Thanks for the pep talk, sweetheart. He took a deep breath and plonked himself next to Caeli. Ziya dropped off two sets of robes on their desks before hurrying back to the front.

'I'm worried I'll regret this,' Alexis admitted. He ran his hands over the soft silk of the cloak before draping it over his shoulders and tying it round his waist. He had to admit it was extremely comfortable.

'I thought that was it,' Caeli replied, reclining in her seat, not bothering to unwrap her cloak. She swept her hair over the back of her chair. 'You do this thing where you go dead quiet and your face falls flat when you're hiding something.'

Noted.

'See how it goes,' she suggested. 'I might pull my proxy from mortal school and send it to the Fighter sessions if I feel understimulated.'

The corner of Alexis's mouth pulled up in a half-smile. 'I feel we're more similar than we realise.'

Caeli turned to him and gave him a saccharine smile. 'How lucky for you.'

Ziya stood at the front, clutching a heavy-looking leather-bound book to her chest. Her owlish eyes scanned the room. 'Quiet, please.' Her voice was barely audible over the chatter. She rose on her tiptoes and tried again.

Caeli raised her hand and snapped her fingers. In an instant all conversation was silenced. Muffled words rebounded against the silence barrier she had encased round the Scholars until they noticed they couldn't hear one another.

'She said, *sit*,' Caeli said coolly, her own voice reverberating around the bare-walled classroom. By the time she released the barrier, the Elementals had all found a seat and were looking towards Ziya expectantly, including the scowling girl whose bag Caeli had discarded.

'Thank you,' Ziya whispered to Caeli.

Alexis smiled to the others on Caeli's behalf, realising that being seen as Caeli's ally might make forming other friendships harder. He turned back, hoping that no one would throw gum in his hair.

'Welcome, everyone,' Ziya said, filling her voice with excitement. 'I'm Ziya, the new Leader of the Scholars. Most of you have passed the Haven's core training at different rates, so let's introduce ourselves with a fun fact!'

Alexis groaned inwardly. It was exactly as Taranis had made them do during his first session. Nothing was worse than a forced icebreaker. He could never gauge what he should offer.

Hi, I'm Alexis and I have a dog. Or: *hi, I'm Alexis and I've inherited my psychopathic father's ways and tried to kill my therapist when I was a child because of 'the voices'.*

You're aren't wrong, the *Shadow Man* noted.

Thankfully, the twelve other Scholars' fun facts were largely limited to their powers or what they were keen to study. A stocky boy with long dark hair said he wanted to join the High Order's Council of Magical Relations, whereas a short girl in a hijab, Safina, shared that she had the power of dream manipulation. The girl whose seat Caeli had stolen introduced herself as Kyra and had transferred from the Coven Academy in Cyprus, whereas a tanned boy sat by himself in the corner muttered that he had transferred from the Sanctuario and had only picked the speciality because he didn't like people and he hoped he wouldn't have to speak to anyone.

'Thank you for your honesty, Mateo. Erm, Caeli?' Ziya prompted, hoping to lift the mood again.

Alexis nudged her, stirring her from vandalising her pad of paper with another drawing of a miniature tornado. 'I'm Caeli Doran. Daughter of the Air. Special interest: undecided.' She pressed the end of her pencil to her chin. 'Waiting to be inspired.'

'I'm sure you will be,' Ziya said. She had set down the large tome and had her arms folded behind her, mimicking how Incantus often presented himself. 'You'll get to pick a field of research in your third year on anything you'd like, unless it's been restricted by Incantus or the High Order. Lastly, Alexis ... did you want to introduce yourself? Although everyone probably already knows you too!'

Alexis concealed his cringe as best as he could as he stood and completely avoided looking at Caeli, whose hyperfocus and mock wide-eyed interest threatened to make him laugh. He stepped on her foot beneath the desk, making her curse under her breath.

'Nice to meet you all. I'm interested in prophecies ... since, you know, there was that big one about us that you might've heard about.' A few chuckled, which was good because if his joke had fallen flat, he'd have to kill everyone in the room to save himself from embarrassment. 'Honestly, I feel behind compared to you all, so I'm ready to learn whatever Ziya has planned.'

Public speaking activates the same nerves as combat, Alexis noted as he returned to his seat.

'Thanks, everyone,' said Ziya. 'Now that we're all

introduced, I thought I'd take you to where you'll be spending most of our time.'

'We won't be in here?' Safina asked.

'Thank the First Borns,' Caeli muttered.

Ziya rolled on the balls of her feet. 'We will for formal assessments and if ever we have external speakers, but for the most part, now that you're officially Scholars in training, you can visit the part of the Haven exclusive to us.'

There was a hum of excitement as the class rose to their feet and followed Ziya out. As they walked, Caeli shrugged on her purple cloak. 'Not my colour, but I love the way it flows. Where do you think we're going?'

They were ascending the bridges that crossed the hive. 'To get Ziya this excited? Has to be a library.'

'I hope so,' said Caeli, her fingers crossed.

'You know what, Cae, when I first met you, all stylish and sassy and a bit of a mean girl, I never would've thought you'd be as big a bookworm as me,' Alexis admitted.

Caeli smiled. 'Pretty girls read.'

They entered the Elder Sanctuary, where the white walls of the Haven's hive faded to cool lilac. Alexis remembered nights spent here with Teller Sagen, enraptured by the mischievous Elemental's stories of the legendary Quinate.

As Alexis and the other Scholars settled round the fountain of the angel whose wings formed its tiers, he let his hand trail through the water. The last time he was here was the day before his quest, when he had asked Teller to look into his past to see who his birth parents were. Teller had died before he had the chance defending Incantus and the Haven from Mortem.

'Sagen?' Caeli asked gently, noticing Alexis's sad smile.

Alexis nodded. 'Miss him.'

'He was an icon.'

'Why are we in the Elder Sanctuary?' asked one of the Scholars, a Welsh boy called Quinn who Alexis recognised from the battle. He smiled at him in greeting from afar and got a wave back.

Ziya stood before them, her eyes glinting with joy. 'Few know this, but the Elder Sanctuary is actually one of the largest of all the sanctuaries in the Haven. People think it's only for those Elementals who opt to retire here, but for those who specialise as a Scholar, we get access to one of the most extensive Elemental libraries in our world.'

Caeli glanced at Alexis to see him smirking. 'Called it,' he whispered.

'You're practically an oracle,' she muttered back.

Ziya explained that many of the books had been donated by authors or families, having been deemed too dangerous or valuable to exist elsewhere. 'It's essentially our version of the Library of Alexandria – it actually contains some of the books recovered from the fire there.'

The cohort leaned in, rapt.

Ziya approached the angelic fountain. 'To enter you'll need your cloaks. The portal is protected by wards, a password and a key that you are forbidden to share with anyone who isn't a Scholar.' She bowed at the stone angel and whispered, '*Littera scripta manet.*'

The statue moved, its wings spreading, unfolding the tiers it had formed until water trickled down its face. Alexis and

Caeli shuffled back as the two great stone-feathered wings formed an arch, and in the space in between a flat lilac portal shimmered into existence. Glowing runes engraved the stone rim, reminding Alexis of the archway that led to the Garden.

'I love being an Elemental,' he whispered.

'Your cloaks are your keys,' said Ziya. 'So who wants to go first?'

While the other Scholars began to arrange themselves into an orderly line, Caeli stalked through without a second's hesitation. Alexis smiled and followed her through the angel wings.

On the other side, past the mirage of purple, was perhaps the most wondrous sight he had ever seen.

The hum of magic greeted him, a low, almost imperceptible vibration that fused with the heavy scent of ink and ancient paper. Polished floors were streaked with veins of gold and silver that ran through the wood like rivers of starlight. Pillars of glittering obsidian climbed the walls while winding staircases spiralled at twelve intervals around the oval floor, leading to countless levels, each adorned with hundreds of bookshelves and thousands of books. The central floor space was patterned with spirals of cubicles where Scholars read and wrote, a table and cushioned seat inside each one, dividing it up into a maze of reading nooks.

'I'm in heaven,' Caeli whispered, awestruck. It was the happiest Alexis had seen her in a long time.

The witch, Kyra, bumped into Alexis from behind. 'Sorry,' she said, before she too fell silent, stunned by the sight. One by one, the other Scholars entered, equally breathless. Lastly, after Mateo came in, his eyes sparkling with wonder, Ziya arrived.

She stood before the banister that overlooked the ground floor and pointed to the golden inscription at their feet. '*Lectori salutem.*'

Alexis knew its translation and smiled.

Greetings to the reader.

6

MONACHOPSIS

Monachopsis (n.) *Greek origin*
The subtle but persistent feeling of being out of place

Alexis had hoped that the rivalry between Caeli and Valentina would have mellowed over the course of the summer. It hadn't. From the moment they had met – when Valentina had undermined Caeli, lured them into a Shadowless trap and, most critically, flirted with Blaise – it had been hostile between the two, even while fighting on the same side of a battle.

'I can't stand you,' sneered Caeli, throwing her fork onto her plate.

Valentina shrugged. 'Then stay seated. I'd much rather speak with Blaise anyway. He's far easier on the eyes.'

How Valentina could remain so casual, so unbothered, as the storm that was Caeli raged before her was nothing short of admirable. Or foolish. Alexis stifled a smile.

They had just wrapped up their first Scholar session with Ziya. Five hours in the Library, a brief lunch and a tour that barely scratched the surface. The ancient librarian, a hawkish woman who appeared to rival the First Borns in age, was all glares and warnings, and made clear the consequences of book damage. Yet Alexis, and the other Scholars seemingly, found the atmosphere enchanting and stayed long after their introductory lessons ended.

'So,' said Demi, clapping her hands with a tremendous amount of enthusiasm. A bit much even for her. 'How was your first session? Ziya, I bet you blew them away.'

Ziya adjusted the collar of her shirt. 'Did I do that thing where I speak too quickly?'

'You did amazingly!' Alexis assured her.

Ziya blushed and tried to hide it, but Valentina gently lowered her hand, as if there was nothing to be embarrassed about.

'You really were,' Alexis added. 'Right, Cae?'

Caeli barely glanced up from a hushed dispute with Blaise. 'Huh? Oh yeah. Great, Ziya. Really informative. Not overjoyed about the hundreds of pages of reading we now need to catch up on. Good thing these pockets are enchanted to fit them all.'

Alexis hummed in agreement. 'I might move permanently into the Library. I wish you guys could see it.'

'I've never even stepped into a mortal bookshop,' said Blaise, scoffing.

Ziya beamed. 'Teller and I used to spend hours there. Taranis too! It makes Incantus's bookshelves look tiny in comparison.'

The hive buzzed with post-training chatter. Elementals strolled in casual clothes or were seated at round tables dressed in autumnal burgundy and gold tablecloths. Training bots bustled around to clean up any mess sporting hot-pink aprons – Ziya's sister's idea, apparently.

Valentina had been waiting for them when they arrived,

perched elegantly in all black, a silver blade holding her long dark hair in a bun that she touched whenever she and Caeli clashed.

'Lexi says you get to do a huge research project in your final year,' Demi said to Caeli, working overtime to keep the conversation flowing. 'Any ideas so far?'

Alexis swooped in to assist her. 'I'm still considering the other specialities for now, but if I stick it out here, then maybe something on prophecies. How they're discovered, interpreted, whether they're truly immutable or if free will plays a role.'

'What about you, babe?' Blaise asked Caeli. He leaned over and began cutting up her roast chicken until her glare told him to stop.

'Thinking of researching the Elemental Tribes actually,' Caeli answered. 'We came from them, or at least our ancestors did, but no one's engaged with them for generations.'

Valentina snorted quietly.

Caeli powered on. 'I'd like to see what kind of powers they have. There must be a reason they're so revered yet isolated.' Another snort. Caeli's eyes narrowed. 'Do you have something to say or are you choking? I do hope it's the latter.'

Valentina blinked slowly as if she was engaging with a petulant child. 'Unlikely that you'll find any explanation for their regressive ways, especially the *Dorans* of the Air Tribe. They weren't exactly known for loyalty, wisdom or selflessness.'

Alexis felt Caeli stiffen beside him. 'If you have something to share, say it now,' she said icily.

Valentina sat back in her chair. 'No,' she said whimsically. 'Something tells me it'll play on your mind more if I don't.'

'Neither you nor anything you say plays on my mind,' Caeli countered.

Valentina raised an eyebrow but offered no verbal reply.

This wasn't how Alexis had hoped the meal would go. Valentina clearly enjoyed pushing Caeli's buttons, although he couldn't figure out why.

You know them as little as they know you, the *Shadow Man* muttered. For once, Alexis found himself agreeing.

Blaise broke the silence. 'Best choice I made was specialising as a Fighter.' He picked at the food on Caeli's plate, which was largely uneaten. 'Classes are huge and I'm not that fussed about the modules on military formation techniques or the history of conflict between whichever nation or species, but the practical stuff's worth it. Wrought's no Raeve but he's solid. You'll see for yourself when you inevitably make the right decision and join us, Al.'

Alexis smiled as the girls rolled their eyes. Just as he was about to ask Demi how her day had been, Blaise leaned across the table to Ziya. 'Tell us about this mission Incantus has assigned us tonight. Is it a hard one?'

'Incantus will explain it better than me,' Ziya said. 'He was apprehensive to pull you out so soon into the term, but he and the High Order really need your support in chasing down the last of the Shadowless who escaped the battle. I think he's missed you too. Taranis and I designed your new suits so that they utilise the powers of the Erasers. Wearing them makes you forgettable to mortals. It's quite ingenious.'

'What if mortals see us using our powers?' Alexis asked, thinking of his family.

'I forget that your training in the Academy was solely for the quest,' said Ziya, shaking her head as if she had made a mistake. 'The Maya force cloaks us behind an illusion so that mortals can't accurately process what they see. And if they do, if they have some Elemental blood, then the Erasers will be deployed to cover it up.'

Valentina turned to Ziya as if she was about to disclose a secret. 'Did you hear about that incident in Japan, must've been about two years ago? The thousand-year-old kitsune that bewitched a whole town?'

Ziya gasped. 'No!'

'I'll tell you later,' said Valentina, bumping shoulders with her. Alexis observed the two young woman sat before him, glad they had found one another. Valentina seemed to be bringing Ziya out of her shell and Ziya elicited a softness that he'd rarely seen from Valentina.

Demi helped a training bot clear plates from their table, smiling and thanking it each time. 'I keep hearing people talk about the autumn equinox,' she said, unclipping and pocketing her golden hooped earrings. Unlike the others, she hadn't changed into her Haven suit. 'Is there an event going on?'

Ziya's eyes lit up. 'The Fall Ball!' Her excitement radiated out in waves of energy just like her late grandmother's powers, and the others leaned in, caught up in her field of gravity.

'What's that?' Alexis asked, smiling even before he knew why he should.

'To signal the time when the night becomes longer than the day, Teller always organised a huge party that lasted into the early hours of the day of the equinox. It's an utterly magical affair; some say it's even more fun than the summer solstice feast. In the Haven we also honour those who graduate from their specialism training. People weren't sure if it was going to go ahead this year with Teller gone, but Incantus told everyone that it's never been more important to host it, to commemorate all those we lost in the battle and go into the autumn and winter hopeful. It's a masquerade this year and the colour scheme is the Children of the Elements, so make sure you get in early at Seamless Seamstress for your outfits and masks.'

Her enthusiasm caught like wildfire. Caeli and Demi excitedly discussed dress ideas, as Ziya pointed out the boutique in the plaza on the bottom floor of the hive where her sister helped out.

'Guess we wear suits,' Blaise said to Alexis. 'Although nothing would look better than my birthday suit.'

Alexis grinned. 'Damn it, I was planning on wearing a lacy gown with a thigh-high slit,' he said, throwing up his hands in mock disappointment and receiving a moan of excited pleasure from Blaise. Across the table, Alexis caught Demi's eyes and saw them twinkling as she watched him laugh freely.

'Zi,' Blaise called, interrupting the girls' conversation, 'do we need a date for this ball?'

Alexis flushed. He could feel Demi's eyes lingering on him, but by the time he returned to meet them her gaze had dipped.

'As you're the guests of honour, you're expected to open the night's festivities,' said Ziya, 'so yes.'

'Fancy being my date?' Blaise asked Caeli, flexing his bicep as he rested his elbow on the table.

She made a face of consideration, her nails casually stroking the bulge of his arms. 'Hmm ... well, I guess I could.' Her eyes narrowed in challenge. 'You'd better be a good dance partner, Mr Ademola. With all eyes on us, I don't want you embarrassing me.'

Blaise smirked. 'You know I perform well under pressure.'

Demi and Alexis exchanged looks. *Get a room.*

But then Valentina pulled a cigarette from her purse and leaned in towards Blaise. Despite Alexis's silent pleas, Blaise ignited his finger into a small flame that Valentina cradled with both hands. She took a long drag, her eyes moving innocently to Caeli, as she exhaled a puff of smoke.

Caeli stared in disbelief. 'Any rational train of thought clearly missed your station because what the hell do you think you're doing?' She fanned the smoke away, then waved a gust of wind at Valentina, sending her cigarette flying. 'Touch him again and I'll steal the air from your lungs.'

Valentina made an effort to look round at the nearby tables who had turned their heads at Caeli's outburst. 'Doesn't it embarrass you to live so publicly?' she asked calmly, her attention no longer drifting to Blaise but focused solely on Caeli. 'To be the car crash everyone slows down to watch?'

'Val,' Alexis said warningly.

Stay quiet, hissed the *Shadow Man* gleefully.

Caeli scoffed. 'As opposed to you?'

Demi frowned. 'That's enough, Valentina. No more games or jabs. I will not sit by as you tear down another girl for choosing to live her life differently.' Her tone was uncharacteristically stern.

Valentina reclined in her chair. Caeli, however, was not finished. 'Why are you still here? Don't you have somewhere to crawl back to, you know, from before Mortem hijacked you and made you his mindless slave?'

Valentina didn't flinch but Alexis saw it land.

'That was too far,' Demi said quietly.

Caeli itched her wrist vigorously beneath the table. 'What I said was half as bad as what I thought. She should remember that I bite next time she thinks to patronise me in front of everyone.'

'I think it's time to go,' Demi decided, tilting her head in apology to Ziya. 'It was really lovely until ... just then. Come on, Cae. Incantus said to get to the lab for eight.' She took Caeli's arm none too gently.

Caeli cast a backward glance at the table as she got up, her right arm tucked into the pocket of her Haven suit. 'Sorry, Ziya, but I knew inviting *her* would be a mistake.'

Blaise hesitated but soon followed them. Alexis watched them disappear, realising no one had waited for him.

They don't truly care about you, said the *Shadow Man*.

Piss off, Alexis shot back.

He lingered with Ziya and Valentina. 'Sorry about that. Caeli crossed the line.'

Valentina waved it off. As she did, Alexis caught a glimpse of the dragon-shaped scar on her inner wrist. She covered it the moment she noticed he'd seen it and spoke breezily, 'It's human nature to gossip. I've heard much worse. Besides, I was asking for it.'

'Why do you provoke her so much? Ever since you first met,

the two of you have had it in for each other. If things were different, you'd actually get along quite well.'

Valentina tossed down her napkin. 'I like seeing how far I can push her, to see how much influence I have over her, that's all. Now, if you'll excuse me, being underground is making me uneasy. Zi, I'll be by the Lakes.'

She bowed with grace, like someone who had been taught how to do it properly, and left.

Ziya stayed behind watching Alexis as though he was a book for her to devour.

'Ziya, you're staring.'

'Sorry,' she said quickly, eyes dipping. 'I haven't heard from you much and I didn't know if it was because of what I told you I saw. You using your shadow powers against Mortem, or because I mentioned that your parents might not have adopted you legally ... I promise I haven't told anyone. Not Tina or Incantus or even Parvati.'

She knows too much about us. Eliminate the risk.

Alexis shuddered. *Us*. One person. 'No, we're good – *I'm* good. Don't worry. All good. All fixed.'

Ziya looked relieved and didn't think to question him further. She joined him as he walked towards the first golden bridge of hundreds that crossed the hexagonal-shaped hive. 'Thank the First Borns. I've been worried for weeks that you were mad at me. So what did you find out about your parents? What did they say?'

'Ziya, I love you, but let's pretend I never asked you to look into that, okay?

She nodded, drawing to a stop as she tried to conceal her

blush. 'Good luck with your mission,' she said, offering him an encouraging smile. 'I know you guys will do great.'

As Alexis made his way to the laboratory at the top of the Haven alone, he didn't register the route or the people he passed. He was preoccupied with arguing with the *Shadow Man* who warned him to stay away from Incantus.

He'll learn our secrets. He'll see us for what we are. He'll kill us for it, like he did his brother.

'There is no *us*,' Alexis growled.

Someone glanced at him.

Alexis shoved earphones in and found his playlist of white noise. He turned up the volume until the intense frequency thrummed in his ears.

But it wasn't loud enough to drown out the voice.

At least I won't abandon you. Unlike your friends.

As Alexis walked alone, he feared it might be right.

7
ASPECTABUND

Aspectabund (adj.) *Latin origin*
Letting or being able to let expressive emotion
show easily through one's face and eyes

'Where are the other two?' Alexis asked, spotting Demi standing alone, far from the edge of the hive's spiralling golden staircase. He tugged out his earphones and heard Caeli and Blaise's argument echo faintly from above them.

Demi gestured upwards. 'Giving them space to argue. You know me, I'm not a confrontational person so hearing people fight makes my heart race. I don't want that energy around me.'

Alexis nodded, wondering if Caeli and Blaise would ever find peace. Was it in their nature? Fire and storm – that's who they were at their core, that was the way they had always been.

'That and ...' Demi wrapped her arms round herself. She still hadn't dressed into her Haven suit.

'You don't want to come on the mission,' Alexis said softly.

Demi's jaw flexed as she thought. 'I don't know if I can,' she murmured, then corrected herself. 'I know that I can; I just don't know if I *want* to. We fulfilled the Prophecy, Lexi. Mortem and any trace of the darkness is gone. We lost so much making sure that happened. Why risk more when any other Elemental can go on this mission? Why us?'

The *Shadow Man* sneered. *Such cowardice.*

Rage sparked behind Alexis's eyes. *Say that again and I'll rip you open with my bare hands.*

Demi's voice pulled him back. 'Don't look at me like that. I've earned the right to say no. I thought you of all people would understand.'

She turned away but he caught her hand. 'Demi, I didn't...' He struggled to find the words, but the taunting laugh of the *Shadow Man* was throwing him off-kilter.

'It's not fear that's keeping me here,' she clarified, her bright green eyes hardened with resolve. Her hand reached for her chest, touching the scar that lay between her amulet and crucifix. 'It's guilt. During the solstice my powers caused destruction. Earthquakes, mudslides, shifts in the tectonic plates around the whole world. My powers killed people. *I* killed people. After what I did to Dr Sinner...' Her voice broke. 'Forgive me for not wanting to do it again. That's why I want to be a healer, to put good out into the world and not leave it a darker place.'

You *were the one who killed Sinner*, murmured the *Shadow Man*. *And it felt good.*

Demi stared up at him, waiting – daring – for him to respond.

Alexis dared. Another time he might've met her with kindness and acquiescence, but he knew that if Demi continued to avoid her fears of her powers and of the Elemental world altogether, it would only grow. It would spread to infect everything she associated with it, including him.

'Demi, you have a heart of gold, but don't let the destructive *potential* of your element make you forget the life and strength it provides. That *you* provide.' His voice softened as her gaze devoured him. His throat tightened. 'I'm not going to facilitate your demise. Your power is your strength, and I'd rather you be mad at me if it meant you remembered who the hell you are. I care about you too much to watch you give up.'

Alexis was half-expecting a slap across his face. Instead, Demi closed the distance between them and hugged him tightly round the waist with a force that squeezed the air from his lungs. He stood frozen in the warmth of her embrace.

'I need something to put my faith into,' she whispered, the top of her head pressing against the scar at his shoulder, her breath against his neck. 'I was hoping it could be you.'

Alexis held her, shielding her, and himself, from the shadows that lingered in his mind. 'I don't deserve it,' he whispered, his voice buckling under the weight of the pressure. How could he be responsible for her faith, her happiness, when he had neither himself?

But she was as resolute as ever. 'Then it will be a mistake I'm glad I made.'

For her I will try, Alexis promised himself. He didn't let go until she was ready.

Demi wiped her eyes and offered him a smile. 'Guess I need to get changed.' She stretched out her hand for him to take, another anchor mooring Alexis to this world, to her.

Together, they walked towards their rooms.

'You asked everyone else about their day,' said Alexis. 'How was yours? Did you enjoy your first Healer session?'

'I really did. Blaise makes it seem like being a Fighter is the only worthy path, but there's nothing shameful about being a Healer. Fighters may have won us the battle but it was the Healers who saved us from it.' Alexis gestured to his body as if he was proof of that, which made Demi's mouth tug into a smile. 'It's going to be intense, especially when we start doing shifts at the Healing Sanctuary, but I've never felt more passionate about anything. We're learning about physical and psychological healing, but I think I'll specialise in the latter.'

They passed the dozens of illustrations of Elemental history that marked the walls, depicting the Women of the Elements birthing the Gems and the First Borns' sacrifice. Eventually, they reached the point at which the corridor split into four short staircases, leading to the Children of the Elements' rooms.

'And you were right about Kefi,' Demi said, letting his hand fall from hers, as she turned to face him. She took slow steps backwards towards the wooden door with the symbol of a downturned triangle that matched her amulet. Alexis couldn't stop himself from following her, her eyes portraying an invitation she didn't say aloud. 'She's amazing. Positive, inspiring, knowledgeable . . . a force of nature.'

Alexis smiled, trailing behind her, a step below. His heart thundered as he looked up at Demi through dark eyelashes.

'You are the only force of nature I'd ever want to weather,' he said, his mouth turning dry.

Demi made a small sound as her back touched the door. Alexis moved closer, close enough to see the pulse in her throat, the golden flecks in her eyes, the individual strands of her dark hair. He drank it all in and wondered what she noticed about him. The curve of his Cupid's bow or the edge of his jaw as it ticked in hesitancy. The desire in his eyes or the slight parting of his lips.

She need only speak and he would follow her inside. Let Caeli and Blaise go with Incantus on the mission. Hell, let the world burn. He would curse it all for her.

Demi's throat bobbed as she swallowed. 'The others are waiting for us,' she said, her voice barely a whisper.

'Let them wait.'

'Incantus will be mad.'

'Let him be mad.'

Alexis pressed against her, his suit doing little to hide his desire, his want. Demi inhaled sharply, her hips tipping traitorously towards him.

Then the door clicked open.

Alexis felt a rush of cold air fill the space Demi had just occupied as she stepped back into her room, short of breath. She took stock of him, looking him up and down, before she bit her lip and shook her head. 'Wait for me there,' she ordered, the waver in her voice betraying her.

Alexis rested his head against the doorframe, smiling. 'Sure?'

'Yes,' she said, her cheeks flushed. 'Wait there, Mr Michaels. I'll be out soon.'

'Okay, Ms Nikolas. I'll wait for you.'

As the door shut, Alexis leaned back against it, letting out a long sigh. His smile lingered as he whispered to the air, 'I always have and always will.'

8

DERN

Dern (adj.) *Germanic origin*
Secret, hidden, dark; hidden feelings

Alexis heard Incantus Arcangelo's voice before the laboratory door opened. He and Demi entered, keeping a safe distance between them. The lab hadn't changed since the very first time Alexis had seen it: part clinic, part government bunker, with a giant screen above the sealed tunnel that led to Stonehenge.

'Hi, Gibbous!' Demi said as the wolf trotted over. Alexis scratched behind his ears while Demi crouched to hug him.

'It would have been perfect if Valentina hadn't been all over Blaise,' Caeli snapped mid-argument. 'Not that he seemed to mind.'

Blaise rolled his eyes. 'I was being polite.'

Caeli made a point in rolling her eyes back at him. 'Why is she still here, Incantus? The Haven *trains* Elementals. She already looks trained – didn't you see her at the battle?'

Incantus's tone was calm but firm. 'Ms Doran, the Haven is a home for all who need one. It's not your place to question who stays.'

He turned to Alexis and Demi, his arms open. Up close,

Alexis saw the toll the past few months had taken. His moonlit hair had thinned and dark rings underlined his pale blue eyes. His all-white Haven suit hung looser on his frame too. Giving up his immortality to save Alexis had cost him his health, his vitality, but his eyes still glowed with a familiar light.

Don't touch him, the *Shadow Man* warned, forcing Alexis to halt a couple of feet away. *He'll sense the darkness you used and the secrets you hold.*

No, he won't. But still Alexis didn't step any closer.

'I was worried you'd lost your way,' said Incantus, folding his hands before him.

'It was easy,' Alexis replied with a smile. 'All I had to do was follow the light.'

'How have you been?' Demi asked, still hugging Gibbous. 'Ziya mentioned the High Order's interfering again with the running of the Haven and Sanctuario.'

'They're trying to, but thankfully they're focusing their efforts on hunting any Shadowless who escaped the solstice whereas I've been trying to locate Mortem's castle along the arctic plains, if it even remains. I promised Serena I'd find her daughter. No luck yet.' He sighed.

'You'll find her,' said Alexis. He thought of Serena and Ziya, spending the last however many years believing Aadya to be dead, only to be told that she'd been a prisoner of Mortem all this time. He couldn't fathom Ziya's grief at losing her mother again and now also her grandmother.

'I'm sorry to pull you away from the Haven on your first night,' Incantus said, resting an arm on Gibbous's back. 'I would've preferred to have gone alone or let the High Order operatives handle this alone, but Blaise insisted you were all keen to get back to the action?'

'Yes,' Blaise agreed, only now sharing this with the others. Alexis raised an eyebrow. 'What? It'll be like old times.'

'By supporting the High Order with tonight's mission, Meredith Coin – the deputy secretary-general – and I, hope to convince Kleine that we aren't a threat to him and still respect his authority. It should hopefully help mend things, especially following the ... complications that arose from using the Gems' full powers during the battle.' He clapped his hands together, not allowing them to linger on the destruction they had unwittingly caused around the world. 'Now, tell me honestly, are you ready for this mission?'

Blaise, Alexis and Caeli agreed without hesitation, but Demi stayed silent. Incantus tilted his head at her. She hesitated, then said, 'I still get nightmares. They vary but they're always about the same thing. My powers betraying me ... Mortem ...' She swallowed hard. Even Gibbous looked like he was silently wincing, Mortem's name flaring the grief that consumed him at the loss of his brother, Crescent, who had died defending him. 'Last night I dreamed I was buried alive. The night before, I caused a mudslide, killing hundreds of innocent people. He's always there, laughing.'

Incantus nodded with understanding. 'Does anyone else experience the same? Nightmares or flashbacks.'

Caeli squeezed Demi's hand. 'Yeah.' She looked at Blaise who didn't seem surprised; Alexis realised they must have discussed it already. 'I'm falling through the sky. I'm not ...

powerful enough to fly. Blaise is the one who pushed me, but Mortem is waiting for me on the ground.'

'Burning alive,' Blaise added, staring at his hands. 'These guys leave me to burn alive. Only Mortem stays, waiting to collect my ashes or whatever. I stop trying to escape by the time he arrives.'

Alexis hadn't expected the others to still be haunted by the events of the solstice. Blaise and Caeli had each other, Demi had her family and her faith. He found no comfort in knowing they shared his pain. Eventually he found his voice, feeling the others' eyes on him. 'Drowning. And obviously the Nero one. Mortem isn't there, but I feel his presence.'

Saying it aloud didn't help. The *Shadow Man* crept closer in his mind, whispering doubt. Still, he was grateful not to see Mortem in his dreams. If he did, he wasn't sure he'd ever sleep again.

'These dreams,' Incantus said, scratching his stubbled jaw, 'are likely your minds processing the trauma, showing you what you most fear: darkness, betrayal, Mortem.'

Caeli looked at Alexis. 'Why doesn't he dream of him?'

'Maybe he's no longer afraid,' Incantus suggested. 'Maybe he faced that fear already inside the projection of Stonehenge.'

'So by going up against him alone, you took away our chance to face him,' Blaise seethed bitterly. 'Thanks, Al.'

You did it to protect them and they throw it back in your face, spat the *Shadow Man*, its tone the sound of nails scraping against a blackboard.

Blaise blinked hard, surprised by his own outburst. 'Sorry,' he mumbled.

Alexis nodded, brushing off the sting, but Blaise's words stayed lodged in his chest.

'How do we stop the nightmares?' Demi asked Incantus.

'I recommend appointments with the Healers once a week,' he suggested. 'And try exposure work – using your powers to remind you of your control over them.'

'This mission's perfect for that,' said Caeli, rallying them. 'I've been working with the Healers and Fighters who have been helping me adapt my fighting style, post-limb loss.'

'How is it going?' Incantus asked, smiling encouragingly.

'Getting there,' said Caeli, offering him a small smile back, a silent thanks for organising her new support. Alexis knew that the Haven was accustomed to supporting Elementals living with long-term injuries, and he felt a blossoming warmth at the thought of Caeli reclaiming her lost confidence.

Incantus brought his hands together. 'Then let's go. The High Order's sent the co-ordinates and the mission briefing, which I will inform you of en route. Since you haven't graduated yet, I'll be supervising. I'll be glad of your company and to flex my powers on something more than switching on and off lights. Your weapons are already in the car. When you're ready, make your way to the podiums.'

He pulled a sleek silver tablet from his pocket. Four wide disks floated down from the ceiling to the ground. 'I'll join you shortly. I need to inform Coin we're setting off. Head to the car park, please,' he instructed.

The four Elementals stepped onto their disks. In seconds they shimmered with light and vanished, teleporting to the fields surrounding Stonehenge.

9

GOETIC

Goetic (adj.) *Greek origin*
Like or pertaining to black magic

The Haven's white walls dissolved into a night sky, light fracturing into darkness. Alexis blinked to adjust as chill wind bit at his face, and he couldn't tell if the thought *'much better'* was his or the *Shadow Man*'s.

Beside them stretched the quiet A-road, the commuter traffic long gone. In the distance Stonehenge loomed, thrumming with a power only they could feel.

'Should we have connected to our Gems?' Caeli asked, eyeing the land that only months ago had been drenched in blood and littered with bodies. They had taken a long time to cremate, and the land still hadn't recovered fully.

'There's a reason Incantus said not to,' Demi replied, looping her arm through Caeli's. 'Either we don't need them or he doesn't trust us with them.'

'I didn't mean what I said before,' Blaise muttered to Alexis as they trailed the girls towards the car park. 'I don't know why I said it.'

He meant it.

'It's fine,' Alexis said automatically. 'Everything okay with Cae?'

Blaise shrugged. 'Yeah. We're fine one minute then arguing the next. She still hasn't forgiven me for her hand, I think. And she also keeps going back and forth about asking her mum about her dad, whether she lied about him leaving. A lot's going on there.'

Alexis listened quietly. 'And your parents? Heard from them?'

Blaise scoffed.

'You can always stay at mine,' Alexis offered.

Blaise nodded but said nothing.

They caught up with the girls at the near empty car park just as Incantus arrived, unlocking a battered black taxi.

'I'd rather get the Tube,' Caeli said, as they piled in, pumping from her pocket-sized hand sanitiser. 'As long as it's not the Bakerloo line. It's saying London is two hours away,' she noted from the passenger seat, pulling up directions.

'Then we'll take a shortcut,' said Incantus, pressing a button on the dashboard.

A glowing white portal unfolded ahead of them, shooting out of the headlights. Alexis braced himself as the taxi passed through the wall and entered London. Glowing skyscrapers crowded the skyline, the empty roads around Stonehenge traded for the congested bustle of the city.

'Isn't that a time-saver?' Alexis said, rolling down the window to watch the portal fade behind them.

'With portalling devices scarce, we're forced to rely on some of our more dated technologies and donations from previous students and allies,' Incantus replied. 'Now, let's begin.'

'What job would you do if you weren't an Elemental?' Blaise asked absent-mindedly, sucking in a breath as they cut in front of a red double-decker bus.

'Can we focus?' Incantus groaned, glaring at him through the rear-view mirror.

'Deep-sea diver,' Alexis said.

Blaise smirked. 'Firefighter.'

'Wildlife conservationist,' offered Demi.

'Pilot,' Caeli added. 'Or prime minister. Or a researcher.' She tapped a perfectly manicured finger to her chin. 'Perhaps all three.'

Incantus sighed, then pressed a series of buttons on the stereo, making his and Caeli's seats rotate to face the back.

Blaise let out a high-pitched yelp as Caeli reached back for the steering wheel, only to find it driving by itself.

'Now I've got your attention,' Incantus began, smiling to himself. 'You know our history aligns with the mortal world. In the 1940s the two nearly collided thanks to the Lightbringers.'

'Stepping on your toes with the name, Incantus,' Blaise quipped.

'Lightbringer refers to Lucifer,' Demi explained. 'The fallen angel. Devil.'

Incantus cracked his fingers. 'Before Mortem and the Shadowless, there was Apex and the Lightbringers, although in his own narrative Apex considered himself a hero, a true bringer of light to our people. He believed the High Order had shamed our kind by keeping our existence secret.'

'Where have we heard that before?' Alexis mumbled.

'There's an important difference between Apex and Mortem,

however. My brother was driven by hate and fear. He sought control and tried to achieve this by imprinting us all – he only borrowed this ideology to gain followers. Apex, on the other hand, was driven by an uncompromisable love for our kind. He believed Elementals should reclaim our place as the apex beings and even share our abilities with others.'

'So what happened?' Caeli asked.

'Apex built his army. He kidnapped Aadya Parashakti as a child, Ziya's mother. She was perhaps the most powerful Elemental after those named in the Prophecy of Light and Darkness. As both Aevum and Parashakti, she could exchange, amplify, silence, even grant powers. He meant to use her to empower mortals. When that failed, he turned to rogue witches to brew potions that infected mortals with demonic energies.'

Alexis leaned in, hanging on Incantus's every word. This was why he had chosen to specialise as a Scholar.

'But if Apex wanted to share our powers with mortals, why would he then turn them into demons?' asked Demi, loosening her seat belt as she cracked a window open. 'Wouldn't that make life harder for us? Wouldn't these then have to be defeated?'

'Exactly,' said Incantus, pointing to her as if she had just solved a riddle. 'Chaos. By creating these demonic creatures he provided an opportunity for the rest of the mortals to see us as their guardians. It would collapse the High Order and make Apex a saviour. It truly was an ingenious plan, one that almost worked.'

'How did he fail?' Blaise asked.

Alexis noticed the tiniest hint of a smile on Incantus's face.

'The Quinate?' Alexis asked.

'Correct,' said Incantus. 'We discovered what he was doing and put a stop to him.'

They sped past a traffic light. In the distance Alexis could feel the motion of the River Thames meandering through the heart of London.

'What's this all got to do with today?' Caeli asked.

'With Mortem gone, what remains of the Shadowless likely follow Vultress, one of his most devout servants. She was the wife of Mortem's first protégé Plague, who went missing years ago. He was a foul creature, even worse than his twin Sinner, and she's just as malevolent and powerful.'

Alexis cast his mind back. Where had he heard the name 'Vultress' before? 'Raeve once told me her cousin became a dark witch and sided with Mortem. That her?'

Incantus's expression darkened. 'It is. She wasn't sighted at the Battle of Stonehenge. We believe she was sent out to target and eliminate powerful Elemental bloodlines that could've resisted Mortem's imprinting, which she's continuing to do even after his downfall. The High Order have been working tirelessly to round up the last of the Shadowless to make them pay for their crimes and prevent them from causing any more harm, but it's proving difficult. I fear that with Mortem dead Vultress has become an even greater terror – a beast unchained.'

'How does that bring us to London?' Alexis asked, glancing at the twinkling lights of the skyscrapers as they whizzed past.

'During the Second World War, St Paul's Cathedral was used as an arsenal,' Incantus explained. 'Beneath the crypt, the High Order and High Coven, whose alliance was uneasy at the best of times, built a secret lab to counter the toxins Apex made. That's why the cathedral survived the Blitz – the dome's circumference is the same as Stonehenge's sarsen circle, shielding it with powerful wards. Clergy still guarded the remaining toxins and antidotes ... until last week, when all communication was lost and there was a spike in demonic activity.'

Demi fingered her crucifix. 'Do you think someone broke in?'

'No Elemental would be foolish enough, not even Vultress, but she could use dark creatures to do her bidding. There is a new breed: shapeshifters who wear the skin of those they kill. There's not an official name for them yet, but I call them Renderers.'

'Sounds like a heavy metal band,' Blaise muttered.

'Through them I hope to reveal her whereabouts before she kills again or get her hands on the toxins. If she does, even the Erasers or the Maya force couldn't conceal the havoc she could wreak in her Sire's name.'

'So tonight we find any of these Renderers and kill them before they take the demon-turning toxins back to Raeve's cousin?' Caeli asked as the taxi began to slow down. 'Why can't the rogue witches like this Vultress woman – awful name, by the way – just make new ones?'

'Good question,' said Incantus, unbuckling his seat belt. 'Brewing such destructive potions requires bloodshed. War. The summer's battle might have been enough, but the originals are far more potent, even just a drop. If Vultress gets her hands on them, it could tear both the mortal and Elemental community apart. This mission is classified. Only a few can be trusted, which is why I asked you. We must stay discreet.'

The taxi drew to a halt beside a momentous domed structure. Alexis craned his neck to see the spire atop the dome piercing the night sky.

'Welcome back to the Elemental world, my children,' said Incantus, his eyes twinkling. 'Your first mission begins now.'

10

SUCCIDUOUS

Succiduous (adj.) *Latin origin*
Ready to fall

St Paul's Cathedral stood tall and imposing, its features illuminated by the orange glow of the street lamps. The five Elementals gathered before it, wind tugging at their hair as they retrieved weapons from the boot. Caeli passed them out, Blaise's double-edged axe with its throwing blades embedded round its shoulder, Demi's vine whip and her curved dagger, and Alexis's sword, split down the middle into equal parts of steel and bronze. He crossed them over his broad back in an 'x'.

Caeli gave Incantus his broadsword before drawing her own double-edged spear.

'What about your bow and arrow?' Blaise asked, sliding into her place to reach into the trunk.

'Can't exactly fire it, can I?' She waved her right arm that she'd covered at some point with a grey-leather half-sleeve.

He slung her quiver over her shoulder anyway and secured it to her back. 'As if you need a bow to fire it,' he muttered, tossing it away.

She smiled and kissed him lightly in thanks.

'*Resurgam*,' Incantus read aloud the words from beneath a phoenix carving. 'I shall rise again.' He motioned to Caeli, Blaise and Demi. 'Perimeter check. Use your Elemental senses for any traces of dark or demonic activity. Meet at the stairs of the west front.'

Alexis and Incantus headed the other way.

He doesn't trust you out of his sight, muttered the *Shadow Man*, but its voice was barely a whisper because of Incantus's proximity.

He values my company. More than can be said of you, Alexis retorted.

'How are you feeling?' Incantus asked. 'Nervous? Excited? It's always hard to tell with you.'

'A mix of both,' Alexis answered. He kicked at the dry leaves of gold and red, scattering them across the ground. 'These Renderers . . . are they bad?'

'Yes.'

'Good. I've got some rage to burn.'

Incantus glanced his way. 'Anything you want to talk about?'

Alexis considered confiding in his mentor: about the return of the auditory hallucinations, the secrets about his family and the people stalking them. Even his uncertainty about his power of darkness. He still had no shadow. Did that mean his shadow powers had survived the solstice? Alexis hadn't put it to the test, not since the final moments of the eclipse. But then he'd been consumed by grief and fury upon learning that he had been the one to kill his birth mother. If there was anyone Alexis wanted to confide in, it was Incantus. Only he was strong enough to shoulder the burden.

But that was what it was: a burden.

You've taken away his immortality, now you want to inconvenience him further? How can you claim to care for him at all?

'I'll be okay,' Alexis said, hoping he'd believe it too. *I'll ride the wave as I always have. I'm a strong swimmer.*

'If you insist. I won't pry.' Incantus studied him closely. His expression softened, showing the new lines that now aged his face. 'There's so much pain and suffering in the world and in your past, Alexis. Don't let it live inside your head too.'

Alexis smiled. 'Is that a quote from you or Sapientis Aevum?'

Incantus clanged his sword playfully against Alexis's. 'Trust me, your mentor is far more inspiring than mine was.'

'Oh, I don't doubt that for a second. I do have one question, though.'

'Just the one?'

'You might have heard that I chose to become a Scholar. Did I choose right? What would you have picked?'

'The best Elementals are experts in all three.' Incantus winked. 'Besides, there is no *right* choice. Pick what drives you.'

'What if they all do?'

'Then do them all. You have a lifetime to learn; in fact, you have *many* lifetimes. But for now how about you try out a Healer session with Kefi and a Fighter session with Wrought and then make your decision?'

Alexis grinned. 'Sounds like a plan. You been all right, though?'

Incantus tilted his head side to side. 'For a hundred years I've been told by anyone who meets me that my purpose is to destroy the darkness and fulfil the Prophecy. I guess ... now that we have, I feel a little purposeless. My existence is no longer needed.'

Alexis punched his arm, making him wince. 'You'll always be needed,' he said, and Incantus smiled.

A grand staircase loomed, beckoning them to tall wooden doors and two bell towers that bordered them. Soon Caeli, Blaise and Demi returned.

'I thought I was supposed to be the paranoid one?' Caeli said with a roll of her eyes.

'I just can't get over how no one is noticing us right now,' Demi marvelled, turning every time a pedestrian walked past them, oblivious to their existence. 'Then again this city's probably seen people in weirder get-up than this. Taranis really outdid himself.'

'They were Raeve's design first,' Incantus noted. 'He finished them to honour her.' He turned to his students. 'Let's make the Leaders proud.'

They ascended the steps. At Incantus's touch the great doors opened and they slipped in unseen.

Inside, the cathedral was aglow with candlelight. The domed ceiling arched above them and the walls were vibrant with paintings and mosaics that exploded with colour between detailed statues.

Alexis looked up in awe, before noticing Demi whispering a prayer, her eyes closed, her lips pressed against her crucifix. He gazed at her even though she couldn't see him, and didn't look away until he heard a strained voice speak.

'May I help you?'

A small elderly nun shuffled down the South Transept, her footsteps failing to echo as she approached.

Caeli yelped and used Blaise's body as a shield. She cast Demi an apologetic look. 'Sorry, nuns really freak me out.'

Incantus smiled at the woman. 'We're the brothers and sisters from the Church of Raphe. Reverend Papageorgiou asked us to come. It regards what is buried in the crypts.'

'Just one moment,' said the nun, and bowed her head before parting.

'Call me Brother Blaise,' Blaise grinned, arms spread wide. Caeli laughed and tried to cover his mouth. 'Here with Brother Alexis and Sisters Caeli and Demi.'

Alexis laughed too until he noticed Incantus's hand tighten on his sword. 'Are they here?' he asked, reaching for the swords on his back. 'She saw us so I'm assuming she's Elemental ... or something else.'

Demi crouched low, the whip unravelling in her hand. With her head tilted she said, 'Well, unless the clergy are coming for mass, there are at least half a dozen people coming up the stairs now.'

Moments later, a procession of robed priests and a convent of nuns spilled out from the staircase, their outfits tainted with splatters of blood and another substance, something thicker, darker.

One of the priests stepped forward, his papery white skin pulled unnaturally taut, his neck twisted at an awkward angle. 'Our employer warned us that you were coming.'

Alexis found himself frozen still as he watched the order dissolve before his very eyes. Not quite dissolve, rather ... mutate. Their bodies twisted violently, shedding flesh to reveal slick tar-coloured skin. Lips rolled back to expose fangs and a series of spine-snapping cracks rang out as bat-like wings the shade of acid burst free, shredding apart the last of their stolen skin.

'Don't like that!' Blaise declared, his axe igniting into a roaring flame.

'Vultress sent you to welcome us – how kind of her,' Incantus said coldly, stepping in front of the students. His sword glowed with power as he pointed it at the creatures. 'Will she be making an appearance? Her presence was so very missed on the battlefield. Serena wanted to be the one to end her, but I'll gladly do it in her honour.'

A nun, or a being who had once been a nun, hissed a response. 'She paid well for us to retrieve the potions.' At the mention of it her fellow Renderers revealed a tiny vial that sat pocketed within a flap of skin along their torso. 'And she promised us that if the Children of the Elements were to come, their bones would be ours to feed on.'

Suddenly, a metal plate on the floor exploded. A Renderer shot out through it, lashing its tail against Demi, sending her hurtling into the high altar. She collapsed to the floor, unmoving.

And then all hell broke loose.

11

ORIFLAMME

> Oriflamme (n.) *French origin*
> A symbol or standard that inspires
> confidence, devotion or courage

The remaining Renderers launched into the air with a symphony of snarls and shrieks.

Alexis darted forward, adrenaline flooding his veins, swords slicing towards the first creature. Seconds before its blood could stain his sword, it dived out of the way, soaring skywards.

Fire flashed past him, bursting against another, but its wings quickly doused the flames. Caeli soared into the dome, her spear spinning as she intercepted any who tried to escape. Incantus remained in the middle, battling two at once with practised ease, his glowing blade splitting open a creature's belly before Blaise's flaming axe severed its wing.

Caeli threw a gust of wind and launched a creature towards the golden altar. Before it struck, its body was ripped in half from behind, falling into two piles. Dagger in hand, wet with its blood, stood Demi.

'Those were innocent people!' she shouted, trembling with fury. 'They did nothing wrong!'

A scream rang from above. Alexis glanced up just in time to see Caeli get booted into the balcony that ran round the dome. The Renderer who had kicked her slammed onto the balcony after her, advancing on where she lay.

Caeli threw her spear to her other hand, planning to catch it as she'd done a hundred times before in training, but the spear skimmed past the gloved end of her forearm and fell to the ground, missing Blaise by no more than a hair's width as it stabbed into the marble. His foot caught it, sending him toppling just as a Renderer pounced.

'Blaise!' Alexis bellowed.

Blaise made no attempt to move, not even as the claws of the Renderer swiped towards him. Alexis's blade seared through the monster's talons just in time.

Snapping back into focus, Blaise erupted into flames and launched upwards. Alexis followed, carried by water vapour.

Above, Caeli fought viciously, surrounded by a spinning ring of arrows. 'Don't touch me!'

Before Alexis and Blaise could join her, two more giant Renderers entered the dome, splitting them across the narrow balcony. Blaise's grunts echoed from the other side, spurring Alexis on.

Let me play, the *Shadow Man* whispered.

'I don't need you,' Alexis muttered.

He clashed with inhuman agility against the Renderer before him, trading blows and dodging the venom it spat from its fanged mouth.

'*Enough.*'

The Renderer froze mid-motion. Ice crystallised over

its wings, stilling it in an instant. Trapped and panicked, it shattered its bones trying to break free. Alexis granted mercy with a clean decapitation and its head toppled over the railing where it hit the ground with a sickening squelch.

Incantus and Demi were fending off a group of them below, the tall, muscled older man standing back to back with the shorter dark-haired girl. Incantus was faring far better, and there was one main reason why. Alexis flung himself off the balcony and his feet slammed a Renderer to the ground when he landed. He silenced its screeches with a swift horizontal slit across its throat.

'You're not using your powers,' he stated breathlessly, glancing at Demi as she lashed her whip out at the two Renderers enclosing.

'Not if I don't have to,' she replied. She gagged as blood splattered her. 'Jesus.' She then glanced at the huge mural of Jesus Christ and bowed her head in apology.

Suddenly, the Renderers screeched in unison. Wings beat furiously as they raced towards the oculus in the dome's ceiling as though being called away.

'Don't let them go!' Incantus shouted, but it was already too late. Glass shattered as three escaped through the dome. Caeli barely formed a barrier in time to block the falling shards from impaling them. The Renderer Blaise had been battling abandoned post and also disappeared through the oculus.

Three Renderers remained. Incantus, ebbing with white light, pressed forward, faster, fiercer. The Children of the Elements exchanged looks across the cathedral, unsure what to do. A gust of wind then hurled Caeli's spear into the air, and she caught it mid-flight as she soared after the escapees.

'Don't you dare!' Blaise yelled, but she was already gone, her long hair billowing behind her like a shimmering silver mane as she slipped through the broken panes.

With a fiery blast, Blaise shot up after her like a comet.

'Go – help them,' Incantus ordered to Alexis and Demi. As another Renderer surged from the crypt, he tossed aside his sword and rose into the air, aglow with divine fury.

Demi went to take a step towards him.

'Have you forgotten who I am?' Even overwhelmed, there was a shine to Incantus's eyes. The most powerful Elemental in history, the great defier of death, glowed like an angel sent down from above. 'I'll destroy what's left in the laboratory after,' he said through gritted teeth. A beam of light shot from his hand into the face of the Renderer closest to them, enabling their exit. 'You know your objectives. Don't let a single drop escape.'

Alexis grabbed Demi's arm. 'Come on. He's got this. Pray for them, not for him.'

With a final look at their mentor as he fought against four of the giant monsters, somehow smiling as he threw them away one by one, Alexis and Demi dashed through the doors of the cathedral and into the London night.

'That way,' Demi said, pointing to Blaise's fiery trail that streaked westwards. 'Over the Thames!'

They hurried across the plaza, heading for Millennium Bridge. The Renderers soared low over the river in the distance, their hulking silhouettes skimming the water. Blaise and Caeli pursued, streaks of fire and silver illuminating the night sky.

Demi looked at Alexis. 'You're thinking what I think you're thinking, aren't you?'

Alexis nodded, his eyes on the river below them.

'You promise to catch me?'

'Don't I always?'

Without hesitation, Alexis lifted Demi and hurled her into the River Thames.

12

SCIAMACHY

Sciamachy (n.) *Greek origin*
A battle against imaginary enemies;
fighting your own shadow

'On second thought, I wish I'd taken a bus,' Demi groaned, standing on the surface of the river, her feet soaked with filth.

Alexis landed beside her. With a flick of his wrist the tide surged, propelling them forward as if they were surfing.

'The bus is on the ground and it's cheap,' Demi muttered, grabbing his torso for balance. 'Sure, it's dangerous at night, but I've got a dagger at hand to protect myself.'

Alexis made the ride a little bumpier, grinning as she was forced to hold him tighter.

Above, Caeli was in close pursuit. In the distance the giant wheel of the London Eye and Big Ben rapidly approached along the banks of the river, and the Renderers were only picking up speed, ascending higher into the sky.

'Stop the first one before the bridge!' Alexis shouted, his voice just about reaching Caeli. She halted mid-air, splaying her hand. A wave of wind rushed from behind her and swept up in front of the first Renderer. The winged creature slammed into the invisible barrier, its bones cracking upon impact before it got swept up in a small whirlwind.

A loud pop echoed overhead, as though a firework had exploded over Westminster Bridge. Blaise had caught the second Renderer by the throat in a burning grip and silenced its screeches within seconds.

'Get ready to land,' Alexis told Demi as the last two dived beneath the bridge to avoid Caeli's cyclone and Blaise's bonfire.

Not a second later Demi was propelled into the air. She landed hard on Westminster Bridge, cracking the pavement. Cars screeched to a stop or swerved out of the way to avoid her as the pedestrians nearby fled.

She leaned over the railing and lashed her whip, catching the third Renderer round the neck and yanking it onto the concrete. Blood spurted black into the river.

Beneath the bridge, Alexis listened to the commands of the Shadow Man. *Stop holding back. Make a name for yourself. Remind the world who we are.*

With a bellow he summoned the Thames into the sky, a towering wave that climbed so high its peak surpassed the bridge behind it.

In a swinging motion Alexis launched it against the fleeing creature, killing it instantly and suspending its body in water.

We're more powerful together, don't you see?

Alexis's breathing was ragged, his throat scorched. His amulet pulsed weakly but the deed was done. He rose to join the others on the bridge as Demi stabbed her kill through the chest. Together, they threw their victims' corpses into a bonfire

Blaise had conjured, reducing them to ash and destroying the toxins they had stolen.

'Don't you ever learn?' Blaise growled at Caeli. 'You went alone again!'

'I had to act. I can't count on you, can I?' she snapped, jabbing him in the chest.

'Enough!' Demi shoved them apart. 'Sort it later. People are beginning to notice us.'

Pedestrians screamed as they fled the scene but a couple remained and stared – too clearly. Alexis could tell. The Maya force or their suits hadn't fooled everyone.

Would the Erasers get here soon enough to clear it all up? What if someone had recorded them; would the new suits shield that?

Caeli raised a glimmering mirrored dome, concealing them inside.

'Look!' Demi pointed to the far end of the bridge.

Two more figures dropped into the fleeing crowd. Not Renderers. Priests.

The Elementals immediately gave chase.

'They've probably morphed back into humans,' Alexis said as they went deeper into the city, doing his best to ignore the dawning feeling of panic. 'Hiding in the crowds. Where's the busiest area closest to here?'

'London Waterloo,' said Caeli through gritted teeth. She turned in a circle before throwing her hand in the direction of the huge railway station. 'One of the busiest train stations in the country.'

They sprinted past the whirring sirens of the police and fire brigade, searching for the bare feet of the robed priests.

Exhaustion clawed at Alexis but he ran harder. He couldn't fail Incantus.

What a squander of his immortality that would be.

They burst into Waterloo station and with an unspoken agreement filed out in search of the disguised demonic creatures. People milled under the giant four-faced clock that hung at the centre of the station. Alexis scanned the crowd, searching the balconies and escalators, wondering where he would hide if it were him on the run. His eyes fell on the entrance to the Underground.

'There!'

The priests were barrelling down the escalators, barging people out of the way. Alexis and his friends raced after them, Alexis hauling Demi through the gates after him when she paused. 'You don't need to tap in,' he told her.

'I'd better not get charged,' she muttered.

The platform was packed when they reached it, making it hard for them to stick together.

'Can you see them?' Blaise asked.

Alexis stood on tiptoes to scan the crowd that seemed to move as one, cramming themselves into the train as the doors hissed open. In the far distance screams began to echo from all around – followed by the sound of swords clashing in his ears. The unyielding heat of the sun was against the back of his neck, burning his sweat-soaked skin, drying out his mouth until his breathing became difficult. Alexis swept the hair out of his eyes to see that his sword was dripping with crimson. He couldn't remember whose blood it was. In fact, he couldn't remember how he had even got there.

Where am I?

People were staring at him, all wearing the same face. One he mildly recognised. His breath caught in his throat and he realised all too suddenly who it was. The imprinted man he had killed with his bare hands. The one who had murdered Joe. He could even feel his sticky blood on his fingertips.

'Lexi!'

Demi. Her voice was an anchor. The heat of the sun faded and the screams of battle were traded for the bleeping of the train doors.

'They're getting in,' Caeli yelled, tearing towards them.

Get it together, Lexi. Pull yourself together.

Alexis shook his head and leaped into the carriage, hoping that when the train took off, the hallucinations would stay on the platform, unable to follow. Demi froze opposite him, her eyes growing wide. He could see the panic within them. Her fear of being buried alive. Should he get off to stay with her?

But Caeli grabbed hold of her arm and dragged her inside just as the doors sealed.

'*Mind the gap,*' said the automated voice as the train rumbled into darkness.

13

VIRULENT

Virulent (adj.) *Latin origin*
Poisonous and destructive; hostile

Alexis was grateful for the unspoken rule on the London Underground: to mind your business. Every passenger in the carriage paid little attention to Alexis as he struggled to steel himself, too focused on their own books or music or broken conversations with friends. He couldn't see his friends, but he knew the girls were ahead and Blaise was in the carriage behind.

Alexis pressed a thumb to each fingertip, grounding himself the best way he knew how, and took unsteady steps down the carriage. Caeli's silver hair caught his eye as she leaned down to speak to Demi who was crouched on the floor.

'We've got to get people out,' Alexis murmured when he reached them; the Renderers couldn't have gone far, even if still in disguise.

Demi suddenly gripped a pole, her knuckles white, panting as she stared at a fixed point on the ground.

Alexis moved to her, taking her shoulders. 'Demi?'

She didn't look at him when she managed to gasp out, 'I think it's a panic attack.'

Caeli, looking both worried and defensive, glanced between them. 'How was I supposed to know she was going to have a breakdown?'

Blaise appeared behind them. 'Dee?'

Demi didn't respond, her eyes wide, and Blaise squeezed her shoulder. 'You stay with her, Al.'

'What about the civilians?' Alexis asked. He crouched before Demi, nodding reassuringly as he encouraged her to inhale slowly through her nose. He spoke to Blaise without turning his attention from her. 'You have to clear them before you engage.'

Blaise didn't turn. His voice was completely devoid of any emotion when he said, 'That's not our mission. They're going to die eventually anyway.'

Demi clawed at her chest. 'I can't . . . I can't breathe.'

Alexis sat directly opposite her as Caeli stood by awkwardly. 'They're in the carriage ahead,' she told him. 'I'll try and get people away.' As she followed after Blaise, she began shouting frantically. 'There's a rat! It's filthy! Move back.'

'Demi. Hey, Dem, focus on me, love,' Alexis said, shielding her from the dozens of people who began shoving past to get away. Alexis caught a glimpse of Caeli just before she disappeared behind an invisibility screen. 'You're okay. Breathe. Breathe for me.'

'I feel like my . . . heart is going to explode,' Demi whispered. 'I'm so sorry. I can't . . . stop it.' She squeezed her eyes shut and tears leaked down her cheeks.

'You're going to be okay, my darling.' He tilted her chin up and pulled down the zip of her suit to expose her throat and chest.

In the distance there was the pop as the carriage door at the far end opened.

'Bring yourself back down,' Alexis instructed Demi. 'Open your eyes and tell me what you see. Can you read the stops?'

Demi crushed Alexis's hand in hers.

'B-Bakerloo line. Embankment. Charing Cross ... Piccadilly Circus.' She exhaled through her nose. 'Oxford Circus. Regent's Park.'

A crash echoed from ahead as Caeli's wall of mirrors shattered. The Renderers had abandoned their human skin as they morphed back into tall winged creatures.

'You're doing so good, darling,' Alexis told Demi. 'Keep focusing on what you can see and feel around you.'

Caeli's spear jabbed a Renderer away from a terrified trapped woman.

'I have to go,' Alexis told Demi.

'G-go,' she muttered, pressing her fingertips to her thumbs, mimicking his calming trick. 'Help them. I'm sorry.'

'Don't be.'

She is weak.

'Shut your fucking mouth,' Alexis hissed to the *Shadow Man*.

Demi's gaze snapped to his, but she didn't say anything, and he could only hope she hadn't heard him over the whirring or thought he had been talking to her.

The train slowed to a stop, where the doors slid open and a flood of passengers poured out. In the transitory stillness Alexis darted into the next carriage, just as the two Renderers slammed Blaise through a Perspex barrier. Blaise slid down, bleeding from the side of his head. He made no effort to get up, his movements unhurried as though he had given up.

He is lazy.

Caeli spun and hurled her spear with incredible accuracy. Its point pierced the Renderer's chest, pinning it to the back wall of the carriage. She turned to check Blaise, but that was all it took. The second Renderer grabbed the spear and cracked it against Caeli's head, sending her sprawling down the aisle.

She is reckless.

'Cae!' Blaise shouted, dragging himself towards her.

Make them suffer. Make them pay, the *Shadow Man* chanted.

Alexis swung his sword, luring the second Renderer forward while the first writhed on the floor. Their blades clashed, the train's sudden motion throwing them off balance. Alexis kicked it away and launched a flurry of ice spikes from his palm, impaling its hind leg.

Make them hurt the way we do. Make them all hurt. The *Shadow Man's* voice echoed throughout the carriage as though it had come from someone real, someone physically there.

Alexis charged. The Renderer snarled, its wings raised to protect the stolen vial. He sliced through it, splattering black blood on the nearby seats.

Again.

Alexis lashed out again. His blade sank into its belly. He kept his sword there as it screeched, and grew talons of his own, claws of dark ice that he raked at its face, again and again as if digging a hole.

Good boy.

Alexis's stomach dropped.

His breathing seized.

Because this time, the voice wasn't in his head any more. A figure stood over him, its body composed entirely of shadow, its hand reaching for his face.

Alexis stumbled back. The *Shadow Man* disappeared without another word, vanishing from the rattling train as though it had been nothing more than a trick of the light.

'Alexis!' Blaise shouted from somewhere nearby, just as the fallen Renderer Caeli had impaled struck Alexis in the chest. The blow didn't tear his Haven suit, but his injured shoulder flared; it felt like huge spiked balls were rolling through his nerves.

The Renderer advanced as he dragged himself backwards, its claws twitching in anticipation of severing his head.

Then between one blink and the next, the Renderer was traded for something far worse.

The *Shadow Man* stood before Alexis. It lowered itself over him, drawing closer with every sentence. *She is weak. He is lazy. She is reckless. And you . . . you are doomed.*

Then, for the first time since it had plagued him as a child, Alexis glimpsed its face, and let out a scream.

A screech exploded down the carriage and the train trembled. Sparks burst past the windows as the train tilted, scraping the side of the tunnel. The *Shadow Man* vanished, replaced by the Renderer that was thrown off its feet.

One by one the tall metal poles broke off from the ceiling, curling at its own will to trap the Renderer like a bull behind an iron gate.

A voice rang out. 'God may choose to forgive you for your

sins. I'm just introducing you to Him.' Demi stood at the other end of the carriage, her hair whipping in the wind. She balled her fists and the window shattered inwards, the train wall crumpling around it like paper to crush the Renderer. Its shriek was lost to the scream of moving metal.

The Children of the Elements crawled onto the few seats still free of black Renderer blood as the train rolled to the next station.

The doors beeped as they opened. *'This is Charing Cross. This is a Bakerloo Line train to Elephant and Castle. Please stand clear of the doors.'*

A woman waiting at the platform looked up from her phone and froze, speechless at the sight of the bloody teens. The train doors beeped again before closing. She was still staring at them as the train moved on.

'That was subtle,' Caeli muttered, her head in her hand. Her voice trembled with self-loathing as she shrugged off Blaise's attempt to check on her.

'How's your head?' Demi asked her, her own breathing still shaky. She had clearly exhausted herself, having manipulated not just the earth but the metal too. She didn't look at Alexis, not really. She glanced to check if he was okay, then avoided him.

Did she think he had been talking to her earlier? Did she see him smile while torturing the Renderer? With the *Shadow Man*'s bloodthirst sated for now, Alexis was left alone to deal with the sickness that curdled within his stomach.

'It's fine,' Caeli said, picking at her blood-flecked hair. 'It wouldn't have happened if Blaise hadn't given up.'

'Oh, shut up, Cae,' Blaise snapped. 'I can't be bothered with you and your obsession to do everything your way. You love what you can control and that's not me, so I'm done.'

'What do you mean "you're done"?' she said, whirling in her seat. 'You love to make me out to be some sort of control freak.'

'You are! You have to be in charge all the time. It's exhausting.'

Caeli scoffed and flicked her hair back from her face. 'I'm not going to apologise for having an opinion; you knew that about me when you signed up for this relationship. At least I put effort into things aside from fighting, as if we haven't had enough of that in our lives already.'

Blaise waved his hand dismissively as he incinerated the last of the Renderer's bodies. He'd never been one to back down from a fight, but it seemed like he had none left in him any more. 'Let's be done with it then,' he muttered.

'*Fine*,' Caeli snapped.

'You don't mean that,' Alexis interjected, desperate for them to find a common ground. 'We failed pretty spectacularly here, all of us, but we're alive. Let's not—'

Blaise shot up, eyes glowing red. 'Don't tell me how to feel when you just mutilated that demon like you enjoyed it. Stop thinking you're better than us, you psycho.'

Blaise's comment was like a slap to the face. 'What? I don't—'

But we are. Better than all of them.

'Yes, you do,' Blaise spat. He lounged back in his seat, his jaw clenched impossibly tight. 'Always bossing us around as if you know what's best. Why? I'm the oldest. I'm the strongest. You're not in charge, Al, even if Incantus is your uncle.'

'Someone has to be,' Alexis retorted. 'And it sure as hell isn't you.'

'Lexi,' Demi warned, but he pressed on.

'You know what your problem is, Blaise?'

'Didn't ask.'

'Right, because I'm sure the world is waiting for your permission to speak.'

Demi got to her feet. 'Cut it out.'

Blaise sneered. 'Here it is. The real you.' His eyes held a fire that burned to look at, but Alexis couldn't bring himself to submit. Then came the killing blow. 'Let's let the son of Mortem tell me what's wrong with me.'

The air all but abandoned Alexis's lungs. His throat constricted. He didn't respond; he couldn't. Because in that moment he wanted nothing more than to kill Blaise. To show him exactly what the son of Mortem could do.

Demi and Caeli both exploded at Blaise. Regret flashed in his eyes, but it was too late.

Something irreparable had shattered. Something that couldn't be fixed.

Regent's Park was mostly deserted as they waited for Incantus after Caeli had called him. He didn't sound happy when he hung up.

Caeli and Alexis sat on one bench, Demi and Blaise on another. Demi tried talking to Blaise, but he shut her down quickly.

Alexis said nothing. He should have been thinking about Blaise, about the collapse of their friendships – the only friends he'd ever had – but instead he found himself thinking about something else entirely. Someone else. The *Shadow Man*. Not just that it had appeared again, not even that it had looked more real than before. What terrified Alexis most was the realisation of what the *Shadow Man* was. Of who it was. Whose shadow it had taken the shape of, even when he had been a child.

The person who was haunting him, even after his death.

Mortem.

14

PIKÍT-MATÁ

Pikít-matá (adj.) *Tagalog origin*
Eyes shut; doing something with eyes shut

Incantus met them at the corner of Regent's Park. They clambered into the taxi silently, passing out healing crystals. Demi reported they had destroyed the last of the Renderers and the vials of the toxins. Incantus had demolished the lab beneath St Paul's Cathedral, but the scolding came swiftly.

Perhaps scolding wasn't a strong enough word.

'I have never witnessed such poor communication!' he roared, his grip on the wheel white-knuckled. 'It makes me wonder how the hell you survived the quest on your own! Acts of power so grand that I was convinced you were *trying* to expose our kind.'

'Have there been any reports yet?' Caeli asked meekly.

'It's too soon to tell. The High Order initiated a telecommunication blackout. Deputy-Secretary Coin said one of the largest deployments of the Erasers *ever* has gone out, disguised as government officials or the police, to clean up ... *our* mess.' His eyes flicked between them, only now noticing their silence and downcast glances. His tone softened. 'Even so, the mission was a success. You should be pleased we stopped the potions from getting into Vultress's hands.'

No one celebrated. No one smiled.

Incantus was sharing in their failure. It provided Alexis with no comfort. A small part of him enjoyed being told off, knowing he deserved it. Incantus easing off was just another indication that they couldn't be trusted to handle their own punishment.

By the time they returned to Stonehenge, it was nearly dawn. Only Alexis stayed awake, sitting in the front seat, needing distance from the others. He'd spent the entire journey staring out of the window, surveying the thick clouds of grey that were threatening rain.

'We're home, children,' said Incantus.

As he illuminated his hand to stir them, Alexis peered in the rear-view mirror. Demi sat between Caeli and Blaise. Asleep, the couple had unconsciously leaned towards one another, their hands meeting over Demi's lap. Awake, Caeli pulled away instantly, as if Blaise's hand had burned her skin.

'Any nightmares?' Incantus asked.

They all shook their heads.

Ziya was waiting for them in the lab, but Incantus excused her before she could ask a barrage of questions. After ordering Caeli to the Healing Sanctuary for concussion checks, he left with a weary sigh to reply to the dozens of messages left by the High Order.

Demi offered to stay with Caeli but she refused gently. 'Go home. Get a hug from your parents and take tomorrow off. I'm sure Kefi would understand.'

An awkward silence fell. Alexis glanced at Blaise, hoping he would say something.

He doesn't deserve our kindness, the *Shadow Man* whispered.

Alexis flinched, turning to check where it stood. Thankfully it was nowhere to be seen. Not yet.

He thought of his family and of the figures lurking around his house over the summer. Waiting. Watching. Should anything happen to his parents or brother while he was absent, he'd never forgive himself.

'I'm going home.'

Blaise looked like he wanted to speak but said nothing. Instead, he followed Caeli, mumbling an offer to join her in the sanctuary, but Caeli snapped that he no longer needed to pretend to care about her any more and could finally move on with Valentina without her getting in the way.

Wordlessly, Alexis and Demi passed through a portal and emerged just beyond the treeline of Protegere Forest. They kept to the shadows, walking in silence towards Demi's house at the end of the cul-de-sac.

'Thanks for walking me back,' she said softly. 'And for helping me on the train.'

'Demi.' He reached for her hand, but she tucked it beneath her armpit, shivering. 'I don't know what came over me earlier. It was like—'

You can't tell her. It would only make her think us crazier than she does already.

'I think we all just need sleep,' Demi interrupted. She pressed a palm to her chest where Sinner's arrow had once pierced her. She had trusted him to catch her when she fell from the top of the waterfall. Would she trust him to do the same now?

Demi released a shaky breath. 'I used to wonder if God would ever forgive me for what I had done. Now I wonder whether I could ever forgive Him for putting me through this over and over again.' Alexis's eyes fell to his feet, unsure of what to say. 'We're not ourselves. I can't blame you for encouraging me to come or blame Caeli for dragging me onto the train. I can only blame myself for doubting that healing takes time and for thinking that I could somehow rush nature.'

Alexis wrung his hands behind his back. 'I'm so sorry.'

Demi nodded slowly. 'We'll be okay, Lexi,' she said, turning away. 'We *are* okay. I'll see you soon. Please get some sleep.'

She opened the door, welcomed by light and warmth. Her parents were early risers, and he saw their bedroom lamp flicker on.

Demi turned to wave to him from the doorstep.

But her shadow ... it followed her a moment too late.

Alexis blinked. A trick of the light, surely. Before he could figure it out, she closed the door, disappearing from view.

No one is more alone than the boy without a shadow.

Too tired to resist, Alexis didn't silence the *Shadow Man*. He climbed the gates of his own home, trying to avoid setting off the alarms. He was almost over them when he heard something behind him.

Not the wind. Not the scattering of leaves.

A presence.

Alexis spun. Someone – no, several people – stood behind the treeline, shadows in the darkness, figures of the night.

Without thinking, without caring if they were Elemental

or mortal, Alexis hurled a stream of water at them. The closest figure, a slighter shadow, ducked impossibly fast. The stream cut just above a head of shaved red hair, splashing onto the forest floor. The person, a woman, *laughed* as she vanished into the forest, the others following.

This time, however, Alexis would not let them get away.

He tore into the dark forest after them. He wanted answers. Needed answers. He didn't know what he would do if he caught up with them, but he couldn't think of that yet. First he had to find them.

They are escaping. We can't let them get away! the *Shadow Man* screamed, its figure reappearing in between the trees beside him as he ran. *You know what remains within us. You know it still answers our call.*

Alexis did. Somehow he always had.

The powers of shadow. Still there, stored beneath the surface of the water. Still his.

He hadn't dared to call on them, not even on the mission. But this was for his family. For his mother. His father. Jason.

Alexis stopped running. He closed his eyes and *gave in*.

He plunged beneath the surface and submerged in that dark forgotten ocean that lay writhing beneath, into that part of himself he had spent so long trying to bury. Yet once there, the darkness didn't obey his command.

The *Shadow Man* laughed with cruel excitement as Alexis's thoughts
    faded

                into

                              nothingness.

He was gone. Alexis was gone. Pushed out of the light and into the shadows.

When he opened his eyes, it was the *Shadow Man* who saw out of them. When he moved, it was the *Shadow Man* who guided his steps. And when he caught up with the pale man who had stood outside his house last summer, it was the *Shadow Man* who plunged a hand of onyx-tipped talons into the stranger's chest.

And crushed his heart.

15

WHELVE

Whelve (v.) *English origin*
To bury something; to hide; to turn

Somewhere, far beneath the surface of his consciousness, Alexis was drowning.

Not in water, but in tar. In death and darkness. The blackness dragged him down, thick and unrelenting, just like in his nightmares. Through his own eyes he watched the man he had impaled fall to his knees, choking on blood.

Is this what it's like to be imprinted? Was this how the Leaders and Valentina felt, trapped within their own bodies while another determined their actions?

But Mortem was dead. The world was safe from ever being imprinted. Alexis had *seen* him burst into shadows, vaporised by the combined power of the Children of the Elements and Incantus. So how had the darkness survived?

Unless ... it had endured through *Alexis*. Kept safe and protected within the ring of Stonehenge. The darkness that had always been inside himself remaining.

Now he had set it loose.

The darkness didn't obey him any more. It consumed him.

The *Shadow Man*'s voice echoed through his lips. 'The light can't reach you here. No one is watching. Why are you still pretending?'

But Alexis *wasn't* pretending. Deep within the tar, he fought against the blackness that consumed the eyes he'd seen the world with. Eyes he'd laid upon Demi.

He thought of Valentina. How she had resisted, how she had warned them despite being imprinted. She endured. He would too. He had to.

Swim, never sink.

Alexis staggered backwards, falling against a nearby tree for support. He clutched his amulet to find it glimmering somewhere between obsidian and sapphire. His eyes then fell upon the man he had killed. He couldn't look away. He took responsibility for what he had done, even though it broke him.

Screams of defiance rang out from the *Shadow Man*, the shrill sound reverberating in Alexis's head and perhaps the entire forest. But Alexis clung to the image of Demi, of holding her, kissing her. That memory burned brighter than the dark. Gradually, the black seeped from his eyes. The blue returned to his amulet.

Alexis returned.

Breathing heavily, he felt the *Shadow Man* shrink back to a dull murmur at the edge of his attention. Just a whisper. For now.

Then a twig snapped.

His head whipped around, his eyes scanning the darkness.

There, standing between the trees, was the woman with shaved red hair. She stared with a predator's calm, unbothered by the corpse, by Alexis's savage kill, by the shadows he'd wielded.

Something about her unblinking expression chilled Alexis to the bone, but he didn't give her the satisfaction of cowering. He straightened his back, rising to his full height, and faced her. The act seemed to infuriate her, and the white of her bared teeth glistened in the shadows.

'You'll fall,' she said, her voice like gravel. 'Your family will fall. I'll have my vengeance for who was taken from me.'

Then she vanished.

Panic hit Alexis like a wave. With the danger gone, the weight of it all caught up. He dropped to the ground, his heart pounding in his ears. He pressed his thumbs to each of his fingertips to try and ground himself. *Not now*, he told himself. *Work first. Fall apart later.*

The corpse needed to be disposed of.

Wiping away tears, Alexis moved methodically. The man had no ID, no phone, no keys. Just a dagger in his waistband that sliced Alexis's palm when he found it.

He examined the blade. *What mortal person carries a dagger?*

Just as Alexis was about to return it, he heard the rustling of leaves behind him. It was quiet at first, distant. The wind?

But the noise grew louder. Wilder. A great ripping groan, as if the very trees were being uprooted from the earth. A path was opening up in the forest in front of him, a cluster of trees bowing wide to allow someone through. Alexis looked down at his bloodied hands, at the body. Trepidation gripped him.

What would Demi think of him? If what had happened with

the Renderers in the Underground hadn't convinced her that he was no different to Mortem, then this would.

'Demi?' he called out weakly, the bloodied dagger still in his hand.

The trees parted and someone stepped into view.

Bronze-skinned, stocky build, a face he recognised.

'Uncle Geb?'

Demi's father stared at the corpse, at Alexis.

'Alexis,' he said, his voice rough with dread. 'What have you done?'

16

LASSULUS

Lassulus (adj.) *Latin origin*
Worn out; having one's strength exhausted by toil or exertion

Geb Nikolas scanned the area before his chestnut-brown eyes narrowed at the pool of blood.

Alexis shook his head and muttered, 'We're alone.'

'Are you okay?'

Alexis wanted to tell him the truth: that he was far from okay, so much so that he wondered if he would ever be okay again. Instead, he said, 'I'm fine. It's not what it looks like. They've been stalking my family, watching our house. They want something from us. I don't know what it is, but it's something to do with my parents. I chased after them and then –'

Geb put a heavy hand on his shoulder. 'You were protecting your family. I don't need to know the rest. Step back. I'll deal with it.'

The tree nearby creaked and split open under Geb's command. Its branches wrapped round the corpse and fed it into the trunk before sealing shut, gone within seconds.

Alexis washed the blood from his hands, grateful when the water ran clear from his amulet.

'Will anyone be able to find him?' Alexis asked. It surprised him how detached his voice sounded.

'He is not the only body buried in these woods,' Geb replied. With a gentleness that came from raising two daughters, he steered Alexis away, guiding him back towards Valerian Lane.

'How did you know to find me? Did Demi tell you I ran off?'

'Demetria was asleep the moment she got into our bed. We've always kept an eye on you and your family, Alexis. Even during the solstice, Petra animated and sent forth the gargoyles to look after Demi, while we stayed here in case we were needed to protect your family, as we have done since we moved onto the lane.'

'Under whose orders did you stay?' Alexis asked.

Geb caught his eyes. 'Incantus Arcangelo.'

Geb had strong facial features, Alexis noted, from the bridge of his nose to the square of his jaw. Although he was a whole head shorter than Alexis, he carried himself much like Demi did, with a silent, sturdy sureness. Alexis had always thought Demi had taken after her mother, with their green eyes and golden-toned skin, but, studying Geb, he could see their resemblance.

Geb elaborated, 'I'm sure Incantus has already told you that he feared Mortem sent out the Shadowless to target any threats that could have resisted his imprinting.'

'How would my parents be a threat to Mortem? They're not even Elemental.'

'Because they're important to you,' Geb clarified. 'If his imprinting worked, then your parents and brother may be the only people left that could bring you out of his control. Even with him gone, what better way to hurt you than by hurting them?'

Alexis nodded slowly. 'If my parents knew the cost, they might've let me drown in that tsunami.'

Geb's arm dropped. 'Is that truly what you think of them?'

Yes.

'No,' Alexis said quietly.

As the trees began to thin, the street lights of Valerian Lane glowed ahead. Alexis could see his house – silent, sleeping, oblivious.

'Who was that man?' Alexis asked, casting a glance over his shoulder back to the forest. 'What do you think they want? Are they Shadowless?'

'I don't know,' Geb replied. 'But this isn't the first time someone's come after you though. Another came before, many years ago.'

Alexis stilled. 'Who? What did they want?'

Geb said nothing, but Alexis remembered what he had told him earlier. These woods had more than one body buried there.

'I had to keep Demi's destiny from her for years,' Geb said, gazing at his house. 'When we told her, we held her and cried together, and by the time we stopped, we felt closer than we had ever before. I won't take that opportunity from your parents. Let them tell you whatever it is they're keeping from you, when they are ready.' He offered him a sympathetic smile. 'Your house is warded against any person who seeks to harm someone inside, but I'll keep watch tonight.'

'I don't know how I can thank you for this.'

Geb shoved his hands into his pockets. 'Keep this from Demi. She takes on everyone's pain. If you want to repay me, help my daughter and keep her safe from this.'

We are no good for her. We are no good for anyone.

Wherever the *Shadow Man* was, whether it hid in his mind or somewhere within the shadows of the forest close by, it was right.

Alexis tried swallowing, but a lump had formed in his throat. He could only nod before they parted.

'You're home late,' said his proxy, stirring as he slipped through the window into his bedroom. It inspected him through the dark. 'You look like you've been crying.'

'I'm going to shower,' Alexis muttered. 'I want to feel the water. I want to feel clean.'

Stripping out of the Haven suit, he stashed it and the dying portal device under his bed. On the way to the bathroom, he paused by Jason's room. His younger brother lay asleep, a comic book still open on his chest, hair tousled like a halo. Reina stirred at the foot of the bed.

'Thank you for guarding him, princess.' Alexis adjusted his brother's pillow then slipped back out.

After checking on his parents, he finally stepped into the shower. Water rained down, but the puddle of tears he'd expected didn't come. Nothing came. In its absence was a dullness, a cold, heavy vacancy within.

What is so fundamentally wrong with me that I can't be happy? he thought as the chasm of loneliness embraced him like an old friend.

Later, looking at himself in the mirror, the *Shadow Man* whispered again. *Blink.*

He ignored it, barely, and synchronised with the proxy in silence before crawling into bed, wishing for a sleep deep enough to bury him, wanting nothing more than to disappear from this world, just as his shadow had.

17
MUTTERSEELENALLEIN

> Mutterseelenallein (adj.) *German origin*
> 'Mother's soul alone'; to be utterly and extremely alone
> and lonely, that no one could even find you or reach for
> you, neither your mother nor any soul around you

'Stop! Please stop! Why are you doing this?'

They didn't listen to Alexis's cries. He ran barefoot through the forest, the cold bite of seawater rising round his legs as he fled into the tide. But even beneath the waves he couldn't escape them – his friends. Stripped of their amulets, their faces blank with judgement.

You're poisoning us all, said the creature who wore Demi's face.

We're better off without you, said Caeli.

Blaise's breath was hot against the side of Alexis's face. *You're better off dead*.

A final set of footsteps drew near. His voice was like a blade, conjured with a vehement hatred that couldn't be disguised.

You are the angel that fell from light and bathed in the shadows, said Incantus, a scythe of blinding shadows rising into the air. *And now we will finally destroy the last of the darkness*.

The blade came down and the scene changed. One

nightmare traded for another, then another, until Alexis no longer knew where one started and the other ended.

He awoke gasping to the sound of whimpering and a sickening splatter, clutching his amulet and drenched in sweat. The sky was still dark outside, an oppressive blanket of obsidian. He cracked his eyes open, fighting a migraine, his brain pulsing like it was under siege.

'Reina?' he called out weakly, squinting through the darkness. She didn't respond, her whimpers growing fainter.

He smelt it before he saw it. Metallic. He turned over his hands to see them sticky with blood, lines snaking down his forearms. Horrified, he flung back the covers.

Reina's ripped collar and clumps of bloodied fur lay in a pool between his legs.

Look what you've done, whispered the *Shadow Man*, its breath cold against the nape of his neck. *You're no better than your father. At least he could control it.*

A scream tore from Alexis's throat.

'Lexi!'

Jason burst into the room, flooding it with light. He threw himself onto Alexis, grabbing his shoulders. 'What's wrong? Are you okay?'

Alexis couldn't speak. Couldn't move. Couldn't see the *Shadow Man*.

His eyes fell to the bed, but where seconds ago it had been covered in blood, now it was all gone. His legs were bare, covered only with a sheen of sweat, as were his hands. Even the metallic tang was gone.

There was a bark. Seconds later, the door was shouldered

open with a splintering sound, ripping free the top hinge. Jackson stormed in, handgun at the ready, Stephanie right behind him. Reina appeared between their legs, alive, growling at Alexis as if *he* was the danger.

Stephanie slipped past Jackson and rushed towards Jason, pulling him away from the open window. 'What happened?'

Reina barked at him, but Jackson snapped his fingers, silencing her.

Alexis looked between Reina and his lap, his mind struggling to configure the two images. He had seen her remains, he'd felt the cold slickness of her blood and heard her whimpering.

Jackson strode to the window and gazed out, scanning the back garden.

'Boys, tell me now,' Stephanie said. 'Did you see anything?'

Alexis shook his head. He shoved his knuckles into his eyes and rubbed them until spots of yellow and black collided, before opening them again to examine everyone.

Jason looked between them, blinking. 'I heard Alexis scream. I think he had a nightmare. Dad ... why do you have a gun?'

'Lexi, darling, is that true?' asked his father, ignoring Jason's question while he tucked the gun behind his back and out of sight.

Alexis had let his parents believe his nightmares had ceased over a decade ago, along with the hallucinations, but there was no denying it now. 'Kind of,' he said, his throat hurting as he spoke. 'I think I had a night terror. Must have been because I had a stressful day at school.'

Reina flinched from his touch as he reached for her, her tail between her legs, cowering behind Jackson.

Stephanie bent down to stroke her. 'It's okay, Reina. It's just Lexi. He didn't mean to scare you.'

'Why do you have a gun, Dad?' Jason asked again, rubbing sleep from his eyes.

'I thought maybe someone was breaking in. I've been working on a child-trafficking case . . . not too far from here . . . Maybe it's made me a bit paranoid.'

Alexis didn't buy it for a second.

'Near Protegere? I don't want to be trafficked!' Jason declared, as if it was up for debate. He frowned. 'But wouldn't the house alarms go off if someone tried to break in?'

Alexis spoke on his parents' behalf. 'Of course it would, Jace.'

Stephanie spared Alexis a look, her face unreadable, before she wrapped an arm round her youngest son's slumped shoulders. 'Come on, darling. Let's get you back to bed.'

'Night, Lexi,' Jason muttered, disappearing with his mother, muttering under his breath that the only thing worth kidnapping around here were the Nikolases' animal statues in their garden.

Jackson stayed and perched at the foot of the bed. 'If the nightmares come back . . . or anything else,' he began, carefully picking his words, 'then we can get you meds. Or we can book you in to see someone – tomorrow even. Or I could get Mum back in here; we both know she's much better with her words than me.'

Jackson beckoned Reina over. She warily approached, her ears pinned as Alexis lowered his hand for her. She sniffed it before licking it. Alexis reclined and caught a glimpse of his father's gun as it poked out behind his back, the metal gleaming in the moonlight.

He is lying to us, trying to keep their secrets. We cannot trust him, muttered the *Shadow Man*, almost as though it didn't want Jackson to hear it.

'I'm fine, Dad,' said Alexis. 'Just stress.'

Jackson nodded slowly. He checked the window to make sure it was locked before bending down to pick up the half-broken door. He pointed a finger to the busted hinge as though he was making a note to fix it.

He leaned against the doorframe just before he left. 'I may not say it enough, but your mother and I are extremely proud of the young man you've become, Lexi. I know at times like these, it's easy to think you've made no progress, but remind yourself of all that you have gained since then. Friends, confidence, strength, education and an unshakable drive to succeed. Should the *Shadow Man* come knocking around again, hit it with that and a swift "left, right, goodnight".' Jackson threw light punches in the air, and Reina's tail wagged as she stood on hind legs beside him to play.

The smile that spread across Alexis's lips was so genuine it hurt. 'And you say Mum is better with words.'

Jackson chuckled. 'Sleep well, son.' He scooped Reina into his arms and shut the door behind him as best he could.

But Alexis didn't sleep. He lay beneath the covers, suffocating under their weight as though he was in a straitjacket. Thoughts and memories and fears polluted his mind for hours, locking him out of slumber.

'Please don't come so soon,' he begged the darkness, wondering if it could hear him and take pity on him.

But he could feel it settling in again. The sadness that arrived with the shortening of days, the changing of the seasons. That deep, hollow numbness that no sunlight could penetrate. The weight within made it more difficult to smile, more tiresome to move. To want. To be.

It was different this time and Alexis knew it. This was more than depression. It was the prodromal stage of relapse. And he was running out of time to stop it.

He tapped his fingers against his thumbs, for even after all this time, it was this technique taught to him by the psychiatrist he had tried to murder as a child that was most effective in calming him. The memory of that day and that period of his past tormented him the most.

Would it have been different if Dr Dash had stayed? If someone had helped? Did I lose my shot at recovery before I was even old enough to understand what was wrong with me? Did I dig my grave as a six-year-old? Will I ever be able to get out?

Olivia Kefi was good, perhaps the best Healer Alexis could hope for, but he didn't want to involve anyone at the Haven. He didn't want his private life or history to plague his new life, not more than it already had. It seemed an arbitrary distinction, illogical even, but the *Shadow Man* had already taken so much of his present. He needed someone who understood his past.

By the time the sun rose, bringing with it the nightmare of Nero, Alexis had made up his mind.

He needed to see Dr Dash.

18

KOI NO YOKAN

Koi no yokan (phr.) *Japanese origin*
'Premonition of love'; the feeling upon first meeting someone
that you will one day fall in love with them; the instinctive
sense that a future romantic connection is inevitable

Caeli Doran couldn't breathe.

The Daughter of the Air, the harbinger of storms, could not breathe.

'So first you break up with me in front of our friends and now you're going to ignore me?' she demanded, glaring at Blaise's back as he stalked in front of her towards the dormitory levels.

The slight slump of his wide shoulders was the only indication that he had heard her.

'*Blaise!*'

'I'm tired, Cae,' he mumbled. 'I can't be bothered to fight with you any more. Don't make me say something I'll regret.'

The cold dismissal stung more than any insult. She shoved him, hard.

Ignore me now, she thought, seething, but didn't dare say the words. Caeli vowed to never beg for a man's attention, but their respect? That she would demand.

Blaise stumbled then whirled on her, fire crackling in his amber eyes. 'Don't.' He took a few steps back from her and exhaled. 'You don't get to put your hands on me just because you're upset.'

The softness with which he spoke made her falter, shame cutting through her anger at what she was doing: hurting him because she was hurt, spiralling, not daring to reach out for anyone to catch her from falling because she'd learned not to trust them to pull her up. So she responded the only way she knew how, returning down that familiar route of self-destruction.

She lifted her gloved right arm that ended at her wrist. 'I can't put my *hands* on you.'

Blaise flinched, and that told Caeli all she needed to know. Her eyes fell to the floor so that she didn't have to watch him leave. This time she didn't follow.

Instead of going to the Healing Sanctuary as ordered, Caeli took one step off the edge of the spiralling staircase and dropped. She landed hard on the ground floor, harder than she'd expected. The impact sent pain knifing up her legs and her spear clattered somewhere far away.

Caeli curled in on herself after ripping off her gloved sleeve and cradled her arms in the centre of the empty Haven.

I've ruined it. I wasn't enough. Powerful enough, patient enough, good enough. Not enough to succeed tonight and not enough to make him stay. Why am I never enough to make them stay?

Her grief was inconsolable, overbearing. It wasn't just about Blaise or her hand. It was about everything: the kind blond boy she'd slept with before his final day, the sister she couldn't save, the father who didn't stay. Her strength. Her beauty. All gone.

She was so tired of mourning.

I'm not enough, or maybe I'm too much.

Neither thought proved comforting.

'Doran?'

Caeli stiffened. She didn't need to look to know who it was.

Valentina emerged from the stone archway that had once led to the Garden. Her raven hair was tied back and the soles of her boots were caked in mud. 'Are you okay?'

Somehow that infuriated her. Caeli scowled. 'Do I look like I'm okay?'

Valentina's gaze sharpened, shifting from unfamiliar softness, perhaps even kindness, to her typical guarded boredom. 'No,' she replied. 'You look like you're on your knees crying in the centre of the Haven for anyone to see and take pity on.' Her eyes narrowed. 'You look pathetic. Get up.'

A red portal blinked open beneath Caeli. She fell through it and was vaulted from its partnered end high up into the air. Her arms waved as she caught herself just before she slammed into the ground.

Below, Valentina moved towards the central sparring arena, portalling benches and tables away to clear space.

Caeli's pulse drummed at her throat and she soared towards the stage. 'You don't get to order me around,' she snapped, storming towards her. She lifted her chin to meet Valentina's gaze. Whatever she saw in them, a curiosity or a challenge, she wanted to smack out. 'Don't forget that *I* was the one who helped you first on the quest.'

'Do you ever wonder why?' Valentina replied, leaning forward. 'Why *you* felt it? Why *you* got through to me and not Alexis?'

Caeli fumed. 'Tell me then. You seem to know it all.'

Valentina smirked as she shook her head. 'I'm not like your friends. I'm not going to submit to your whims just so I don't run the risk of upsetting or offending you. You've had the wind knocked out of you, but it's not my job to give it back. You have to fight to reclaim it.'

She swept Caeli's legs from beneath her before she even realised she had moved. Caeli hit the ground hard, rage flaring in her chest.

She flipped onto her feet and jabbed at Valentina, who dodged before it could connect. Valentina beckoned her to try again and Caeli obliged. Valentina knocked her fist aside and shoved at her chest with both hands, heaving her away.

'How do you hope to be as good as you were before, *better* than before, if you're imposing further challenges on yourself?' Valentina chided.

'Because things are different now!' Caeli shouted, waving her right arm. Admitting it aloud cracked something open inside her.

Valentina's tone softened. 'Does that make you weak?'

No.

Caeli wasn't going to let Valentina tell her how to grieve her disability. She wouldn't let Valentina ignore it or undermine it, but she also wouldn't let herself be defined by it. And she wouldn't let anyone else but her find a way to overcome it either.

'It just means I need to find a way to adapt,' said Caeli, 'to make space for myself in a world that won't adapt for me.'

The way Valentina was gawking at her was throwing her off-kilter, clouding her mind from thinking straight. *Why is she looking at me like that? Why does it set my skin on fire?*

Caeli hurled gales at her, hoping to sweep away her confusion, but the cloud of questions remained and Valentina vanished through a portal. The torrents exploded the heaped benches where Valentina had just been while she reappeared high above on one of the hive's golden bridges.

Caeli soared up after her, but flew too fast into another red portal and crashed onto the huge spiral staircase.

'Dorans were always the strongest of their Tribe,' Valentina called as Caeli struggled to her feet. 'They would say the winds obeyed their every *thought*. Not their hands. Don't make their betrayal of the Tribe worth even less.'

Caeli's jaw ached where she clenched it. 'How do you know that?' she demanded.

'Do your own research,' Valentina replied, then kicked Caeli off the bridge.

Caeli spiralled through the air. She raised her arms. The gales from her right arm weren't as sensitive to her command as her left, but they still obeyed. They held her afloat until she landed on a lower bridge.

'There you go,' Valentina said, stepping out from a portal beside her. 'Maybe you're not as hopeless as you've been beginning to act.'

'What kind of sadistic psychopath goes around hurting people with disabilities just to force them to fight for themselves and then mock them the entire time?' Caeli spat. Enraged, she slammed her shoulder into Valentina's chest. Valentina grabbed hold of Caeli's left wrist, and the girls fell backwards off the bridge.

Together, they plummeted.

Caeli writhed to free her left hand, but Valentina didn't relinquish her grip of it, preventing her from using it to summon the air.

Caeli let out a grunt as she hurled her right arm back, willing the wind to submit.

A billowing gale swept from the end of her arm, halting their fall inches from impact and throwing their bodies against each other. Their gazes found one another again, the fight in them traded for shock.

Caeli heard a laugh, and it took her a moment to register that it belonged to her. It was a sound she hadn't heard in a long while. The winds still answered to her call. It didn't mean that her hand was magically healed – it never would be – but it was the first time that Caeli believed what the Healers had been telling her all this time, that she wasn't any less powerful than she had been before. The air keeping them suspended proved that.

Valentina was staring at her again, her eyes wide with wonder and admiration, as she held Caeli close against her slender frame.

It was suddenly hard to breathe, as if Valentina was stealing the air from between them. Caeli didn't know why her body heated the same way it did around Blaise just after he showered or when he came back from training, when his muscles were pumped and slick with sweat.

Caeli swallowed the dryness of her throat, fearing the foreign sensation that rang through her body. *What is this?*

The girls dropped to the floor, the wind dispersing. Valentina rolled once and stood, but Caeli was already marching up to her.

'What the hell is your problem with me?' Caeli demanded, her confused frustration twisting into anger. 'I thought you were jealous of me for being with Blaise –'

'I'm not jealous of *you*.' Valentina's voice fell quiet when she spoke again. 'I'm jealous of *him*.'

Caeli shook her head, causing strands of thin silver-blonde hair to fall before her eyes. 'Why would you be jealous of him?' she asked incredulously.

Valentina's gaze finally met Caeli's, and something clicked.

'I thought you hated me,' Caeli murmured, her cheeks radiating with heat.

'I *do* hate you,' Valentina hissed, her eyebrows knitting together. 'I hate everything about you.' She spoke with conviction, almost as if she was trying to convince herself. 'I hate how disingenuous you are. How easily you quit. You had a shitty thing happen to you and now, what, you let it define you? You're going to wallow in your pain and injustice for ever until someone else, your friends or your *boyfriend*, sweeps in to pick you up?'

Valentina took a step back from her, her chest heaving. She raked her fingers through her hair before her eyes snapped back to Caeli's. 'Be a storm. Be destructive. Be incomprehensible and uncompromising and relenting. I hate you because there is so much more you could be, and you're choosing to make yourself smaller to fit into the eye of the storm when you should be the tempest that surrounds it.'

For the first time in a long time, Caeli's mind fell quiet. No overthinking, no second-guessing. It was an unfamiliar sensation, the lightness, the freedom, and it had come because Caeli knew she didn't need to explain herself. Not to Valentina.

Caeli didn't attempt to analyse the emotions that stirred within her chest. She didn't stop to consider when and where they had taken root and what it meant. She didn't pause to mentally write out a list of pros or cons as she stepped forward and closed the last few inches that separated them.

Caeli thought of nothing as she stood before Valentina. The two of them breathed the same air, and days and weeks and months of tension that had woven cords between them now tightened, forcing them closer.

'Why do you care?' Caeli asked softly.

Valentina's gaze dropped to her lips. 'Why do you think?'

Caeli realised then what it was about Valentina that had made her hate her. She should've realised the truth about the inexplicable, undeniable feelings that Valentina conjured within her sooner, feelings that Caeli could no longer deny.

Caeli didn't know who moved first. Whether her hands gripped the back of Valentina's neck or Valentina pulled her in by the waist. All she knew was the kiss. Hungry, desperate, life-altering.

Caeli felt her chest expand and her lungs fill with more than just air, and, with that, she could finally catch her breath.

PART II

19

WINTERCEARIG

Wintercearig (adj.) *Old English origin*
'Winter-sorrowful'; feeling a deep sadness
comparable to the cold of winter or old age

'Lexi, why aren't you up yet?' Jason's voice carried past the half-hanging door. Watching him struggle with it amused Alexis, who stayed buried beneath the covers. 'We're going to be late. Mum needs to get in early for a surgery.'

'I'm not well,' Alexis mumbled. 'Tell Mum I'm too sick to go in today.'

Jason entered the room despite Alexis's objections. His gentle touch on Alexis's arm, though brief, comforted him more than he expected. It even silenced any stirrings of the *Shadow Man*.

'I'll tell her. Hope you feel better.'

The peace didn't last long. Stephanie charged in, pressing a cool hand to his neck. 'Have you been sick? Diarrhoea?'

'Good morning to you too, Mother.'

She readjusted her engagement ring so that the huge diamond faced inwards, and swept the back of her hand beneath Alexis's messy curls to his forehead. 'You haven't got a fever; if anything, you are running a little cold. Any more nightmares?'

'No,' he lied.

She pulled back the curtains to let in the grey morning light. Alexis groaned and rolled away. 'Some mums trust their kids, you know. They don't do full medicals just to let them skip school.'

Stephanie threw back his duvet before clicking her fingers. Reina leaped onto the bed, pinning Alexis with playful nibbles. 'Some mums aren't doctors,' she said, her eyebrow arched impossibly high. Despite his intention to not smile that day, Alexis reluctantly gave in. 'Some don't enable their children's bad manners. Some don't love their children enough to make them get up and seize each and every day, even if they'll be hated for it. When have I ever been like "some mums"?'

He'd planned on bunking off his Scholar lessons at the Haven to catch up on the reading Ziya had assigned, before checking out Dr Dash online – that was if he was even practising as a psychiatrist any more and whether he took on children as old as Alexis. Oh, and if he would want to meet with Alexis again, considering that the last time Alexis saw him was when he had killed Sinner with a blade of shadow.

All water under the bridge, Alexis hoped. *Better be a big bridge.*

Yet Stephanie Michaels had always been a hard woman to fool and harder still to defy.

Alexis relented. '*Fine.* You win.' He gave Reina a quick kiss and shoved her off him.

'Good,' said his mother, turning on her heel, her blonde hair swishing in its high ponytail. 'Your dad's out all day on a case, and I've got a complex transplant for the world's sweetest grandmother.' She pinched her lower lip between her fingers, one of her only telltale signs Alexis recognised as anxiety. 'God, I've not felt this nervous for a surgery since I was first-year resident.'

'We'll get the bus,' Alexis offered.

Stephanie hesitated. They had insisted on driving them this year – to make sure Jason was adjusting well and to spend more time together, they said – but Alexis pushed. 'There's a stop at the bottom of Valerian Lane. I'll make sure Jace looks presentable, don't worry.'

'Okay, fine,' Stephanie agreed reluctantly. 'Come straight home after. Always running late this family.' She tutted, ducking beneath the hanging door with Reina following her.

'Mum?' Alexis called. 'You're going to smash it.'

Stephanie's lips pulled up into a smile that reminded Alexis of how beautiful she was. 'Thank you, darling. Be good. Lock up properly: windows, doors, alarm system. I should be home for dinner.'

Jason was waiting at the door. 'Next time, put your forehead on the radiator before you call her.' He shot a look over his shoulder to check she was gone. 'Works for me.'

Alexis grinned. 'Your tie's awful. Come here. We have a reputation to maintain.'

Jason rolled his sky-blue eyes. 'Have you seen yourself recently? You look like death warmed up.'

'And what does that mean exactly, Jace?'

Jason shrugged. 'Dunno. But you look ugly.'

'Don't start lying now, Jason. You aren't very good at it.'

'Unlike you,' he replied, his dark eyebrows shooting up accusatorily. The front door downstairs slammed closed, followed by the sound of a car ignition as Stephanie pulled out of their long gated drive. 'If they ask, I'll tell them you were in school with me.'

In spite of all their bickering, it was these rare moments of companionship, of kindness, that solidified their bond as brothers. Alexis knew he should probably send out his proxy, but he couldn't bring himself to offer any more of himself up. He watched Jason from the window until the bus pulled away. He then returned to bed and was asleep almost instantly.

An indistinct number of hours passed before Alexis awoke to the sound of Reina barking to go outside, freeing him from dreams of angels fighting demons. The sky had dimmed to a watery grey, making him curse as he checked the time. Only an hour until Jason returned, and he hadn't been productive.

His whole body ached. He wished he'd brought some healing crystals with him. Next best thing was reheating leftovers as he began searching for Dr Dash's number.

It was as Alexis was flicking through his mother's phone book that he finally came across it.

Dr Carl Dash.

His name had been crossed out in thick black ink but Alexis could make out the digits underneath, the pressure from the pen testament to his mother's desperation years ago, seeking help for her newly adopted child who cried of shadows that whispered to him to do bad things.

He stared at the number, his heart pounding, regretting having eaten.

'You can do this, Lexi,' he told himself. 'First step to getting better.'

He glanced out of the window at Reina chasing pigeons. He thought of Blaise and realised that, despite everything, he missed him deeply.

Shaking his head, he focused. *The number's probably dead. Or changed. Or he's dead. Would he remember seeing me kill Sinner? Incantus said the portal would've wiped any witnesses' memory, right?*

The *Shadow Man* was surprisingly quiet and Alexis resisted the urge to taunt it in case it returned. He steeled himself and then dialled.

It rang and rang and rang.

'Knew it,' he murmured, ready to hang up.

'Hello?'

Alexis froze.

'Who's calling?'

Alexis forced himself to swallow the lump that had lodged in his throat, but still nothing came out.

'I'm hanging up—'

'Wait! My ... my name is Alexis Michaels. You may not remember me, but years ago—'

'*Alexis Michaels*,' the man repeated, his voice grave. It was as if he had just awoken from a long sleep and been thrust into reality. 'I remember you.'

Alexis's stomach lurched as the memory of that day flashed in his mind. The blood, the bucket, the commands of the *Shadow Man*. Compared to what he'd done since, it was child's play.

Dr Dash let out a low hum from the back of his throat. It almost sounded like he was standing right there next to Alexis, back again with his little notebook and his rolled-up shirtsleeves, asking to play with the figurines Alexis had once called his friends.

'The boy with the amulet,' Dr Dash said slowly. 'The boy who was doomed. Tell me, Alexis, was I right?'

20

TĒCTUS

Tēctus (adj.) *Latin origin*
Covered, concealed, hidden

Classical music blared through Alexis's earphones as he raided his father's office. Stephanie's playlist of gentle piano pieces – Einaudi, Debussy, Yiruma – filled his ears. He imagined her listening to the same music as she cut open someone's chest to save their life while he rummaged through his father's files to uncover whatever secrets they were keeping from him.

Alexis hadn't told Dr Dash much over the phone. He knew about patient confidentiality, but that could be broken if he was a risk to himself or others. With an in-person appointment scheduled for a few days' time, Alexis would hold out on the important things until then, and so he only shared with Dr Dash his vague doubts about his parents. When Dr Dash recalled the air of secrecy that had surrounded the Michaelses when he first met them, how cagey they had been when he had asked them about Alexis's adoption, the knot in Alexis's chest loosened. Maybe he wasn't crazy after all.

Reality-checking. Alexis remembered the technique from his infrequent therapy sessions with whichever psychiatrist lasted the hour. If his parents were hiding something, he needed empirical evidence.

Breaking in wasn't hard; he'd used a key made of ice to unlock the office door. The CCTV monitor on the desk was still recording, giving him a view of the front drive and inside the house. Reina lounged near the door, gnawing a chew toy. A small part of him, call it his morality, argued that he should respect his parents' right to privacy just as he hoped they would respect his. Alexis turned up the music to drown out that thought.

But after half an hour of searching, Alexis slumped at the desk, empty-handed and frustrated. He'd found nothing concerning him, just old cases. His father, it turned out, really was as good as his reputation. The 'corpse whisperer', his team had called him, a brilliant profiler, solving murders from the barest threads of evidence. Alexis could've spent hours, days even, poring over each case, but there wasn't enough time.

He rubbed at the paper cuts on his fingers, scowling at the desk. What had he hoped for? A photo of Stephanie and Jackson Michaels abducting him?

'They're good people,' he told himself, resting his head against the back of the chair. 'They love me; they chose me. They're nothing like my birth parents.'

You would not know, hissed the *Shadow Man*, slicing through his defences. *You cannot blame Mortem for wanting you dead after you killed your mother.*

Alexis cranked the volume up again.

I wonder, the *Shadow Man* continued, its shrill voice sending blades of ice skidding down his spine. *Will you do the same to this one?*

'Shut up!'

Without a second thought Alexis threw his head forward and slammed his forehead into the edge of the desk with a loud crack. Pain exploded across his brow as the wood splintered, and blood began dripping down his face from the deep cut at his hairline, but the agony was worth the *Shadow Man*'s silence.

The door to Jackson's office swung open and Reina came bounding in, sniffing the air before licking his face. Alexis blinked through tears. 'Thank you, princess.'

As he reached down to grab his fallen earphones, something beneath the desk caught his eye. A plastic file had fallen loose from a tray that had been screwed under the desk. It must have become dislodged when he hit it. He pulled it free, one hand pressed to his bleeding forehead.

His name was on the top page.

Let's finally uncover the truth, hissed the *Shadow Man*, as Alexis ran his fingers along the edges of it once back in his room. There weren't many pages, and he hoped that meant it contained nothing important, but his trembling hands betrayed him.

The first sheet was his adoption certificate. Most details were familiar: the assumption of Latino ethnicity, matching Incantus and Mortem's olive complexions, although Incantus could do with a few weeks in the sun. The adoption had taken place in Australia after the mega-tsunami that devastated much of Oceania and South America. He'd been around five years old when they found him, but no official records existed. No DNA matches, no dental history, no birth date. His parents set his birthday as 22 February – the day they met him.

How did we end up there? the *Shadow Man* murmured, its breath chilling Alexis's neck as if it was reading over his shoulder. *Where were our real parents? How did we get away?*

Alexis turned the page, shutting it up. Two photos fell onto his lap. The first was of him as a child. It was probably the youngest he had ever seen himself. His blue-and-black-ringed eyes looked up with innocence, and his amulet dangled loosely from his neck, the pendant sitting at his belly. Stephanie's sun-bleached hair glowed as she smiled while he hugged her legs.

In the next photo Jackson held Alexis while Stephanie, visibly pregnant with Jason, laughed beside them, holding a key to what would become their home on Valerian Lane.

The radiance of their smiles stirred something in Alexis. He pressed the photo to his chest, an indelible source of warmth.

Alexis didn't recognise the handwriting on the next page. It looked like a doctor's notes.

> Adoptive parents report nightmares, hallucinations, references to a faceless figure, the 'Shadow Man'. No memory before adoption. High anxiety, strong attachment to parents. Calmer around brother Jason. Early signs of psychosis/bipolar/schizophrenia. Will likely need extensive therapy and medication, although too young to prescribe.

Alexis stared at the notes until they burned into his mind. He remembered the countless psychologists, the coping mechanisms, the endless doubt. Yet this doctor, who he knew to be Dr Dash, saw him more clearly than the others. Alexis wondered now if his parents ended each therapy run prematurely out of fear he might remember something he shouldn't.

The *Shadow Man* cut through Alexis's tender shield with ice-cold blades. *Their secret's cost us everything.*

He pressed the photo of his family harder against his chest, but its powers also seemed to have been severed. Alexis turned the page. What followed were dozens and dozens of his childhood drawings, each illustrating the same thing.

The *Shadow Man*.

You can never be rid of me, it said – a promise, a threat. Alexis threw the pages behind him as if to hurl them into a past that could no longer reach him, but the *Shadow Man* remained. *We will always be together.*

One page was left in the file.

It was a photograph of an investigation board tangled with coloured strings and Post-it notes, instantly recognisable as his father's work. In the centre was a picture of young Alexis, his eyes looking trustingly into the lens. He traced the lines that connected him to the photographs of other people with his finger.

One thread to his adoptive family. Another to question marks labelled: *Birth mother and father, identities unknown, presumed criminal. At least one survived the tsunami. Motive to reclaim son.*

Our adoption couldn't be legal, Alexis thought. *They vanished for a reason. This was why.*

A third thread led to a grainy CCTV footage of a hulking man. The note read: *Kidnap attempt. Likely employed. Deceased.*

Alexis frowned. *Deceased. How? Did Mortem send this monstrous-looking man?*

His eyes landed next on the final connection on the board: a lone question mark. No image, no name. Just the word '*Guardian*'.

Alexis stared blankly, exhausted. Who was this 'Guardian' connected to everyone? A protector? An ally? Incantus? His birth mother?

They have kept all this from us, the *Shadow Man* whispered. Its cold fingers dug into Alexis's jaw, turning his head to the side. *Kept us in the dark. Lied to us. Failed us. Killed the man who tried to rescue us. And for what? For us to turn out like this?*

Its mocking laugh grew louder, amplified by the shadows of the room as the day suddenly dipped into night.

Alexis clenched his fists. 'Stop laughing at me.'

They won't silence me any longer, the *Shadow Man* replied. *It's time you remember who I really am.*

Alexis searched frantically for his earphones. 'Please leave me alone. I –' He stifled the sob that threatened to make its way up his throat. 'I don't deserve this.'

You deserve worse, came the reply.

This time, when it spoke, the sound didn't come from a voice spoken inside his head. It came from a figure. A shadow without a face, a monster given a body. And it was standing in the corner of his room.

Alexis squeezed his eyes shut. 'It's not real. It's not real,' he whispered. 'It's just in your head.' He tapped his fingers to his thumbs desperately. 'It's not real – stop crying.'

But the laughter grew as the *Shadow Man* approached. Alexis felt its presence looming, its hand poised above the scar at his shoulder, inches from his skin.

You will never be free of me.

Alexis steadied his breath. 'My name is Alexis Michaels.' He wasn't prepared to give up on himself now. If this was a breakdown, then he was teetering on the edge. He wasn't yet ready to let the *Shadow Man* overthrow him, to let himself become lost in the darkness. He had to focus on what was real, on what he knew to be true.

'My parents are Stephanie and Jackson. I have a brother called Jason. We live at twenty-seven Valerian Lane. I am seventeen years old.'

The sinister laugh of the *Shadow Man* deepened into a growl.

Keep going, the fighter within him whispered, the part that had always defied the bullies. It was the part his parents had instilled and nurtured within him. It was the part of himself he was proud of, the part he now clung to.

'I am a son. A brother. A friend. An Elemental.'

The *Shadow Man* blurred. Its voice waned. *Our time will come*, it promised. *And when it does, the people who tether you here will be the first to go. She will be the first to go.*

'I am not evil,' Alexis whispered, realising just how much he wanted to stay. 'I am not a burden. Not a mess. Not a psycho.'

He thought of Demi.

Demi, Demi, Demi.

Her light, her laugher. She was a tonic, his cure.

'I deserve to be loved. I deserve to be happy. I deserve to live.'

Haven't I earned the right?

His lips barely moved as he spoke once more. 'I deserve to be in the light.'

When Alexis opened his eyes, the *Shadow Man* was gone, nothing but a faint whisper in the back of his mind again.

Outside, the clouds spilled their contents and it rained for the first time in weeks.

21

KALOKAGATHIA

Kalokagathia (n.) *Greek origin*
A combination of the good and the beautiful in a person

Alexis jumped up as the door to his room creaked open on a single hinge. Remembering the exposed file on his desk, he rushed to hide it.

'Oh, sorry, darling,' came his mother's voice. 'Did I catch you doing something?' There was a pause. 'Actually, I think it's best for our relationship if I don't know.'

Alexis scrambled the pages into his backpack, avoiding looking at them directly. Half opening the door, he steadied it so it wouldn't collapse on him. Stephanie stood outside in one of her comfy loungewear sets, her blonde hair tied back into a loose ponytail. Reina circled her legs excitedly.

'How was work?' he asked, leaning against the doorframe to block her entrance. 'How was the transplant?'

'Well, it went well.' She blinked slowly and pressed her fingers to the crease between her eyebrows. 'She almost bled out, but I was able to slow the haemorrhage and we performed the rest of the surgery successfully. I'm absolutely shattered.'

'I bet you were magic in there,' Alexis said, making her smile.

Stephanie leaned in as if sharing a secret. 'I really was,' she said. 'You feeling better?'

'Fine,' he lied. 'Still have a headache, though.'

'Are you going to let me in?' Before he could come up with an excuse, she slipped beneath his arm into the room, tickling his armpit as she went by.

'Invasion of privacy,' Alexis mumbled as he watched her sit cross-legged in the chair by his desk.

'I wanted to talk with you, Lexi. It's important.'

Alexis shouldered the stiff door closed and sat on the bed, his heart thudding at the same rate as the rain pelting against the windows.

'Is everything okay? Is Dad okay? Where is he?'

'Dad's fine,' she replied, tickling Reina's upturned belly with her feet. 'I spoke to him on the way home. He's visiting his mum.'

Alexis reached over and took a large sip from the glass of water beside his bed, cradling the cold glass between his hands. 'How is she?'

'No change. She's still healthy physically, but of course that's not why she's in the hospital. She apparently didn't say anything this time.'

'Did she recognise him? What does she call him again?'

'Starlight,' Stephanie replied with a sad smile. 'And vaguely, he said.'

'I haven't heard of many cases of dementia in people so young,' said Alexis, shutting the window properly so that the rain wouldn't come in. 'Didn't she have it when she gave birth to him?'

'Apparently so. How she arrived at the hospital with a newborn baby in her arms and a note for his name, just hours after delivery, will always be a mystery. The power of a mother's love.' Alexis's mum swivelled in the chair, her eyes perusing the books on his shelves. After making a single turn, she looked back at him and said, 'It took a long time for your father to tell me anything about her and an even longer time for him to allow me to meet her. To this day she's still officially a "Jane Doe".'

It was hard to picture his father at his age, wondering who his parents were, trying to figure out what had happened to them. Maybe that was why Jackson had become a detective. Maybe that was why he had decided to adopt a child, to save them from a fate he had endured. 'Do you think it was his dad who took her in?'

She shrugged. When she did, Alexis noticed how thin she looked.

The burden of their secret is hurting us all, said the *Shadow Man*. Alexis didn't dare look round, not strong enough to face it should it be standing there.

'Your father gave up looking a long time ago. Besides, his foster families were all mostly good to him. I've always told him that it's better to have no father than to have one and lose him.'

Stephanie looked down, focusing on Reina who had extended her paw for her to shake.

'Still haven't spoken to Grandad Christian?' Alexis asked delicately. He wasn't sure why his mum was talking about their parents, but he entertained the conversation anyway, preferring this to whatever it was that she was skating around.

'Not since Jason was born.' She raised her eyebrows once, almost as if she was dismissing the emotion on the rest of her face. 'That was his own doing. We were so happy for years, just me and him. He'd take me to the beach on Sundays and tell me that every beautiful sunrise was painted for me by my mother. And then he married that wretched woman and tried to get me to stop being with your dad and adopting you. I didn't want him in my life after that. I'm far stronger for it.' She spoke with finality, but her eyes were glossy nonetheless.

'I guess we've all had a rough time with our parents. Is that what you came in here to talk to me about?' Alexis said carefully.

'I know you've always found it difficult.' She looked at him. Without her usual smile she seemed vulnerable, a word Alexis wouldn't ever use to describe her. 'I know there are things you still wish to know. Same with your dad, same with me. But I want you to know that we're not a family because of blood; we're a family because of love. Love is the stitch that ties all broken things together.' She reached across for his hand. 'And, Alexis, you are *my* child.' She squeezed his hand as a single tear ran down her cheek. 'Mine. No one else's. Jason may be my firstborn, but you will always be my first child. I want you to never forget that.'

He tried to dismiss her with a smile, with a shrug, but his eyes had welled up. 'Why are you telling me this?' he asked, clearing his throat when his voice cracked.

She gripped his hand until he met her gaze. 'Because I

know you aren't well, Lexi, and I feel like it's my fault. We've become distant, all of us, with our own busy lives and stresses and jobs. Your father and I are still trying to figure things out and we might not always get it right, but our intentions have always been the same, always with you and your brother as our priority. I want to remind you that you can come to us for help no matter how old you get.'

Don't tell her. Don't trust her with our secrets when she doesn't trust us with hers.

Yet Alexis was able to ignore its whispers this time. He had never considered it before. He had awoken in this world with his parents always being there, always at his beck and call, supporting characters to his narrative, his story. It shamed him to realise that this was their first time at life too, that as he was growing up, his parents were growing old. 'You guys managed to become good parents, without ever experiencing that yourselves.'

The *Shadow Man* had never been easier to ignore. His mother was his safe place. He could tell her anything and she would still be there for him.

'The universe is really testing me right now,' Alexis started, his voice drowned out by the slashing of the rain against the window. 'It's trying to see if I'm going to break and I really don't want to, but I feel like I'm drowning and I don't know if I can hold on any more. I'm in so much pain, Mum.'

Don't!

'The *Shadow Man* is back,' he whispered.

Stephanie's gasp made him flinch. Reina jumped out of the way as she shuffled the chair closer, taking both his hands in hers, stroking them rhythmically as if that would somehow take away the pain.

'I've been trying to not listen to it,' he continued. 'I've been trying not to give it any power. I just want to move on with my life and leave it behind, but it won't let me go.'

'Oh, my baby boy.' That was all that she said for a long time as she pressed Alexis's head to her chest just as she would when he was younger, when he'd wake up crying and screaming from nightmares. 'That ... *shadow*,' she spat the word, irate at the monster that had defiled her son. 'It's a part of you, as much as your arms and legs, as much as any organ is. You have faced it before, fought it and conquered it. Don't run from it now. You will get better again, in time you will.' She placed her steady hands on either side of his face, searching his eyes to ensure he was listening. 'One thing I've learned is that time is the greatest healer, and pain is only the opponent, not the result.'

Stephanie reached into her back pocket. Alexis heard a faint rattle and knew instantly what it was. She handed the box of antipsychotics to him.

He accepted it slowly. He knew his mother had risked everything getting this, not only her medical licence but also her freedom. That was the sacrifice she was willing to make for him. And so Alexis swallowed the tablet. He knew it wouldn't silence the *Shadow Man* – it hadn't before – but it would help with the other symptoms. The hallucinations had only ever vanished after one event, after meeting one person.

'I promise I'll take them properly.'

'I know you will,' she said. She reclined as a long sigh

escaped her, relieved that he had taken the medication without objection. 'Have you heard the proverb "still waters run deep"?'

Alexis recalled Serena Aevum saying it to him the night before the battle. 'A teacher once said it to me, but I didn't get what it meant.'

'A calm and quiet exterior often masks a complex and passionate character,' Stephanie explained. 'No matter how put-together you appear, there's a depth to you that still surprises me, that scares and amazes me. Your teacher must be a perceptive woman. Can't be that wench Ms Mason.'

Alexis smiled. 'It wasn't. It was another one. Ms Aevum.' He was fairly certain he saw a hint of recognition flash across his mother's eyes, but it was quickly dispelled. 'I only knew her a short while, but she was great.'

'Was?' she asked softly.

Alexis bit his lip. Explosions of radiant gold energy filled his mind's eye. 'She passed away in the summer.'

Stephanie reached for his knee. 'I'm sorry, darling. With all that's going on, I hope your friends are here for you. I expected Blaise to be here more now that he's living alone. You two became so close over the summer holidays.'

'We fell out,' Alexis said flatly. 'He said something pretty nasty to me the other day. Threw something I told him back in my face.'

Thankfully, his mother didn't pry. 'Did he mean to hurt you?'

'I don't know. But it hurt anyway.'

'He's probably going through a rough time as well. His parents aren't there to support him. And his girlfriend – Caeli, right? – is still recovering after her crash. He may have not meant to hurt you.'

'You're saying I should forgive him?' Alexis asked, uncertain what he wanted to hear.

'Forgiveness is healing,' she said simply. 'For you more than them. I was harbouring so much anger towards my father for not trying harder with me, but your dad taught me that holding on to hate only poisons you, weighs you down.'

'Dad said that?' Alexis asked dubiously, unable to conceal his own smile.

'In a dumbbell analogy.' She laughed, looking more like herself than she had in a while. 'But the point remains. Sometimes people take out their pain on others because they don't know how to deal with it themselves. Maybe Blaise lashed out because he knew you could take it.'

'Doesn't mean I should be his punching bag.'

'No, it doesn't. But maybe think about *why* it is that he feels the need to punch in the first place. Either way, for the last few years, all you ever needed was one person to be your friend and, as far as I'm aware, she still lives only down the road. Sometimes a person can be just as effective a healer as any medicine. Your father always has been for me.'

Alexis looked down, trying to hide his blush. His mother knew who his heart beat for. She had always known, even before he had.

She kissed his forehead, then pulled the chain of his amulet out from beneath his T-shirt. She smiled as she stroked the blue stone with her thumb.

'All this talk of *time* and I've probably overcooked the

chicken,' she said, heading to the door. 'That's the strange thing with time: it moves quicker when you're not looking.'

'Mum?' Alexis called, holding his amulet. 'You and Dad taught me the most important lesson I know.'

'What's that?'

Alexis smiled at his mother. 'When things go bad, you can either rise or fall. And us Michaelses, we rise. How did I get so lucky to have you as my family?'

Stephanie placed a hand over her heart. 'Oh, my sweet boy, when will you learn? We're the ones lucky to have you.'

22

TURADH

Turadh (n.) *Gaelic origin*
A break in the clouds between showers

'*Littera scripta manet.*'

The angel fountain re-formed into an archway and Alexis entered the hidden Library. He was hoping to avoid Ziya – he couldn't bear her disappointment at him for skipping his classes. In his Scholar robes, he was ready to study.

The Library's grandeur dwarfed him. Most Scholars were at dinner, so he found a quiet alcove and spread out his books. History, philosophy, physics, sign language for the many members of their kind who had permanently lost their hearing in battle, an encyclopaedia of mythical creatures including how best to defeat them, magical theory, divination. Alexis didn't know where to start. This was just half the required reading that he had to catch up on before he started the first-year Scholar modules.

Alexis opted for the book closest to him with a sigh and began to make detailed notes. Conveniently, he recognised much of the history of the Elemental world from the reading he had done in his evenings after training for the quest and from Teller's enthralling stories.

Hours passed in focused silence. His mind settled as he consumed line after line, page after page. Then a voice echoed behind him.

'Yet the Women of the Elements could only create, not destroy, with their gifts, and so they birthed the first of us. Elementals bestowed with a fraction of their powers: the First Borns, and imparted upon them amulets.'

Caeli hovered in mid-air behind him, a thin semi-transparent platform of wind beneath her feet. She drifted round the obsidian pillar and settled into his alcove with tired eyes, her breeze ruffling the pages.

'Photographic memory,' she said, tapping the side of her head with the gloved end of her right arm, not hiding it like she usually did.

'Aren't you lucky?' he replied. 'What did I miss today?'

'I didn't go in either.' She turned the pages of a huge text about prophecies that Alexis was yet to open. 'You seen Blaise?'

The question was anything but casual.

'No, I've been at home all day. You?'

Caeli shook her head. 'Had lunch earlier with Demi when she came in, but I'm pretty sure he doesn't want to see me.' She lifted her chin. 'Anyway, want to study together?'

As they read, Alexis noted how different she looked without her make-up. Softer, her grey eyes lighter.

'Have you read Shade's work on the modern history of the alliance between the High Coven and the High Order?' Alexis asked, returning his attention to the book before him.

Caeli nodded. 'I got speaking to Kyra, the witch from our class. She's actually all right; she offered to share her notes. She's also got a couple of modules to catch up on, so in return I said I'd take on the bulk of reading about the inheritance of powers, since witches and sorcerers don't develop powers the way that we do. She's got no interest in reading the two-thousand-page Parashakti book on it.'

Caeli patted the largest book, which must have been written by one of Ziya's ancestors.

'You said you were interested in the history of prophecies, didn't you?' she said, shrugging off her purple cloak.

'Yeah, but I know the books on it are classified until we're third-years.'

'Sealed by air-tight locks,' Caeli murmured. 'If only we knew someone around here with the power of air.'

Alexis lifted his head to look at her. 'You wouldn't? We've got so many things to cover before we can even start thinking about advanced reading.'

Caeli withdrew a small cloth-bound book from her cloak pocket. 'I've already got my proxy doing some of the catch-up reading Ziya's assigned us. It's not like it can keep up dance or cheerleading any more, so I may as well put it to use. My mother would never think to look at my books anyway.'

Alexis couldn't help but grin. 'All this isn't going to be read in one night . . .'

'Not like you to shy away from a challenge,' Caeli retorted. 'Listen, you look like shit and I feel like it. Neither one of us wants to be anywhere else other than here. Let's see how much we can get through if we do an all-nighter.'

Alexis furrowed his brows at her. 'Are you sure you don't want to have a long in-depth conversation about your feelings?'

Caeli matched his gaze. 'No more than you do.'

With that, they fell into a comfortable silence as they studied, occasionally pausing to discuss something interesting one of them had read. Caeli used her powers to toss sweets into their mouths without touching the books, keeping them going.

'Most Elemental abilities, if they manifest at all, do so around puberty when there is a secondary surge in hormones,' Caeli explained.

Alexis pulled out his earphones – it was hard to concentrate while Caeli dictated to make notes. 'What determines whether or not a person will have powers?' he asked, bored with his current read on the legislation of Elemental law. 'And what powers they'll develop?'

Caeli got back to him half an hour later. 'Not verbatim, because this Parashakti writes the same way that Ziya speaks – don't frown, you know exactly what I mean. Essentially, powers can fluctuate over generations but they usually have coherence: Aevum powers are associated with the manipulation of time and energy, the Sagens' are tied to memory, the Parashaktis' are power-amplifiers or nullifiers, and the Alastors were usually either portallers, teleporters or had the ability to pull objects through space. Bloodline purity increases the likelihood, although that's not a hard-and-fast rule. The author suggests that's why arranged marriages historically aimed to concentrate power, but recent findings have found that someone with even just a drop of Elemental blood in their ancestry may display some power.' Caeli paused. 'Isn't it so bizarre that Ziya has no powers? I'm not saying it makes her weaker or any less of an Elemental – I'm not Ezra – but it's odd, especially since Parvati can manipulate matter.'

Alexis shut his book. 'I read somewhere that an Elemental's powers can sometimes be blocked or triggered by trauma and are often tied to one's emotional state. It's why Demi, the most emotionally expressive of us, is undoubtably one of the strongest with her raw power. I think that's why Akili started our sessions with breathwork so that we could better regulate our emotional and physiological states.'

Caeli bunched up her cloak and rested her head against it. 'With the amount of trauma we've had, I'm surprised I can still blow-dry my hair.'

As the hours ticked on, and it was well towards midnight, Alexis realised that he had made the right call in conjuring his proxy at home to keep vigil. He glanced at Caeli periodically as she fidgeted in front of him. At some point, she had taken off her glove, and her arm lay on the desk between them unapologetically. He didn't comment, letting her be, silently proud.

It was approaching the early hours of the morning when Caeli released an obnoxiously loud yawn, stirring Alexis as he was drifting off.

'I think it's time for bed,' Alexis declared, partly because he didn't want to be wiped out tomorrow, but also because he didn't want to be in the Library when his nightmare wrenched him awake. What if one of the librarians came to shush him? How awfully embarrassing.

'Tell me a secret,' Caeli said suddenly. She scratched at her wrist absent-mindedly. 'I want to trust you with something, but to do so I need you to trust me with something.'

'So that you could blackmail me with it if I ever share yours?'

Caeli shrugged. 'If you've got a problem and you want a hug, you go to Demi. If you want to bitch about it, you come to me. If you want to laugh, go to Blaise. But if you want it fixed, I always thought the best person to go to would be you.'

As far as compliments go, that was the best he could hope for from her. 'What level of importance is this secret of yours? I don't want to trade off something big for finding out who your first kiss was.'

Caeli blanched slightly. *On to something there*, he thought.

'Something no one else knows. Something that would change how people saw you.'

Alexis found himself looking down the rows of tall bookshelves of dark polished wood. *Do I care that much about whatever it is to give up one of my secrets? Am I that nosy?*

Yes. He pondered which secret to disclose. His mind must have been on Demi, because the first thing that came to mind was the secret he was keeping from her.

'I killed Sinner.'

Caeli's eyes widened. 'No. Demi killed Sinner.' More of a question than a statement.

'After you guys went back through the portal with Incantus, I noticed that Sinner was still alive,' Alexis recounted, choosing his words carefully. He didn't want to outright lie, but he was content with omitting key details. 'He survived the fall. Demi's shot was brilliant – it flew straight and true into his chest – but he was a big guy and I couldn't risk him walking away. So I made sure he never did.'

Caeli let out a shaky breath. 'And you haven't told Demi? Even though you know how distraught she's been all this time for thinking she'd done it?'

Alexis's jaw clenched, his gaze falling to the book before him where the lines blurred into an indistinct pattern of black ink. 'There's a lot of things I'm dealing with right now and lying to her is one of them. Call me the king of compartmentalisation.'

'Demi's never been the best shot, has she?' Caeli muttered after a moment, watching him from the corner of her eyes.

'She was that day.'

'Hmm. I wouldn't be so sure.'

Alexis looked at her. 'No ... You?'

Caeli wet her lips nervously with her tongue. 'The arrow was heading for his thigh,' she said quietly. 'I just made sure it landed a little closer to his heart, should he have had one.'

Alexis slumped back in his seat. It didn't absolve his remorse entirely, but the weight of it now felt shared. In a way he had never felt closer to Caeli.

'But that wasn't what you wanted to disclose, was it?' he probed, looking at her through his dark eyelashes.

'I messed up with Blaise,' she finally confessed. 'Big time.'

Alexis's brows furrowed. Their argument and break-up wasn't exactly a secret. The carnage had unfolded for him and Demi to witness. Perhaps she had done something further to damage it?

'What did you do?'

Caeli stood up and began stacking the books, casting dust into the space between them. 'Our relationship has always worked on passion. We argue and bicker and fight to show how much we care. Underlying it all has always been kindness and ... hell, maybe love. But ever since the eclipse, since *this* –' she held up her gloved right arm – 'I feel like he lost interest. Maybe he didn't want me any more.'

'I'm sorry he's made you feel that way,' Alexis offered gently. 'Knowing Blaise, I'd hope that's not it. Maybe he felt guilty for what happened to you and didn't know the best way to support you.'

Caeli made a disgruntled face.

'I'm not telling you how to heal,' he went on. 'I'm the least qualified person to do that, but maybe you should check in with your Healers, physical and psychological.'

Caeli paused from stacking the tomes. At the very top was a book Alexis hadn't collected himself, on the history of warring Chinese dynasties. Ziya hadn't mentioned that when she had discussed the modules they would cover. What was Caeli hoping to learn from that?

Caeli's response pulled his attention back. 'This probably won't make any sense to you. It doesn't make any sense to me either. But if I feel like something is out of my control, even if it's a problem affecting me, some messed-up part of me unconsciously seeks out *another* problem, another fight for me to initiate, just so that I can feel like I'm in control of what's happening. Call me the queen of self-sabotage.'

He understood. 'I don't want to go all Healer on you, but have you ever thought about where that comes from?'

'I know it's going to sound like it's an excuse, a clichéd one at that, and you know how much I hate clichés, but you're the only one who could get what this is like, Alexis. To know that you have a parent out there somewhere who didn't love you enough to stay. It makes you question everything, doubt everyone's intentions and your own self-worth. Now I worry I've just sabotaged the only relationship I can't bear to lose.'

'Blaise told me that you still haven't asked your mother about what happened to your dad.'

Caeli slid the pile of books towards him. She wiped her face harshly before nodding once. 'I'm going to ask her soon. I'm going to figure out who – I mean, *what* – I want. Like the Woman of the Air said, it's good to vent and get it all out.'

Alexis pocketed the books, grateful again for the magical properties of his cloak to accommodate them without being weighed down. 'No storm can last for ever,' he said.

She hadn't noticed him also take the book about the warring dynasties of China from her pile. She would notice soon enough, Alexis was sure, but there was a niggle at the back of his mind that he couldn't ignore. He would say he took it by mistake.

As they descended the Library steps, now amongst the early risers, Caeli thanked him. 'You're a good friend, Alexis. Whether or not Blaise wants me, he *needs* you, so don't be mad at him for too long.'

'I don't plan on it.'

Then came her curveball. 'Why is it that we never got together?'

Alexis nearly tripped.

'I'm obviously a catch,' she explained. 'And no one can deny that you have an ethereal beauty about you that stops most people as they walk past. Yes it does, don't bother arguing with me. Blaise is handsome, no doubt about it, but you're objectively beautiful. Maybe it's your eyes or your aura. Not to objectify you or anything. You also know when to shut up, which is extremely attractive.'

'Cae ...'

She laughed. 'I'm not coming on to you!'

Alexis wasn't sure if he was being pranked.

'I'd never do that to Demi,' she went on. 'I'm just curious. We want the same thing, you and me: to be successful. Whether we're driven by the insatiable desire to succeed or chased by the fear of failure, we have that in common.'

'We're *too* alike,' Alexis answered honestly. 'We'd burn out. You and I are both pessimists, so we flourish when we're with those who draw out the parts of us we're not inclined to show or feel. We keep them grounded, but they keep us dreaming.' He shrugged. 'That, and blondes aren't my type.'

Caeli chuckled, the twinkle back in her eyes as she shoved him aside with a gust of wind. 'I'm everyone's type.'

Just as he was about to depart through the portal, Caeli slipped a small text into his pocket. He could feel the librarian's hawkish eyes watching them as they left, so he waited until he was back in the safety of his own room to pull it out. He turned it over in his hands. Caeli had, at some point in the night, retrieved a forbidden text on prophecies and divination.

Sleep would have to wait.

23

DELUGE

> Deluge (n.) *Latin origin*
> A severe flood; a sudden, very heavy fall of rain

Alexis was five paces from the door of the Training Academy when he heard the unmistakable sound of Blaise fighting.

He shouldered through it, thankful he'd decided to wear his all-black combat suit instead of his Scholar cloak. At least a dozen Elementals were swarming an elevated podium no larger than a few metres wide. At its centre stood Blaise and a curly-haired stocky boy, fighting off the wave of opponents without a weapon to hand.

Alexis had tossed and turned through a restless sleep filled with images of tarot cards, glowing orbs and bloodied hands. He'd woken to find himself standing before his bookshelf, which had been obliterated, his knuckles peppered with splinters. He'd taken it as a sign and decided to channel his restless energy into his first Fighter session.

Violence, clearly, was what was in store. And apparently it was on sale.

Blaise's eyes flicked to him and he did a double take. His face was bruised, his eyes burning a bright amber, his chest heaving.

His companion looked worse: sweating and barely standing, gulping down breaths in between fights.

Alexis stepped forward. 'What the hell?'

The Elementals, of which there were close to three times as many as the Scholar cohort, all turned to look at him.

'Mr Michaels.' A serious-looking man approached. He had an air of authority about him, and the fighting ceased at his command, allowing Blaise and the other boy a moment of respite.

'I've been looking forward to meeting you.' Dark-skinned, jade-green eyes; he had to be the new Leader of the Fighters: Oliver Wrought. 'I've heard so much about you and was dismayed to hear that your talent for battle and strategy were being squandered in pursuit of other specialities.'

He gave Alexis a firm handshake. At his touch, Alexis felt his memory shimmer, as if the images and knowledge he held were shifting into an order that could be accessed and *read*.

Alexis snatched his hand back, remembering that Wrought, just as his cousin, Teller had been, was a memory reader.

Alexis scrutinised Wrought's expression for any sign that he had seen something he shouldn't have. Had he seen Alexis taking his antipsychotic that morning with his breakfast? Had he seen him murdering a man in cold blood a few nights before? Wrought's face remained blank.

'Being a Scholar is not *squandering* any of my talents,' Alexis began, tucking his hands into his pockets. 'And I don't appreciate you trying to access my mind without my consent. It was something your cousin never attempted to do, no matter how curious he was.'

Wrought inclined his head. 'There is honour in all specialities.' Murmurs and snorts of laughter rippled through the crowd behind him, an air of elitism that Alexis hadn't found amongst the Scholars. 'But someone like you, who stood against Mortem and lived . . .'

Alexis saw Blaise's jaw clench.

'In my sessions, our time is split between theoretical learning of military strategy, the history of conflict and practical training. Your friend, Mr Ademola, and Mr Adamson there, were boasting that it is harder to hold down a base against a large number of opponents than it is to take it. Of course, the Battle of Stonehenge is evidence of that.'

'Not that you would know.' It was a low swing and Alexis regretted it instantly. Thankfully, Wrought didn't rise to it.

'In my class, we identify our weaknesses and practise them until they become our strengths.'

Alexis considered his argument. 'Understandable.' Perhaps he would require practice to learn how to respect authority. Alexis would likely truant them if that was the case.

Wrought gestured to the raised podium, where Adamson had recovered and got to his feet with Blaise's aid. 'Care to join, Mr Michaels? I'm keen to observe your fighting technique – how you operate and communicate with a team.'

Alexis swallowed, aware of every pair of eyes that tracked him as he made his way towards the podium.

'Antony Adamson,' said the stocky boy, offering him a tight-lipped smile and a nod as Alexis drew near.

Alexis greeted him in kind, before glancing at Blaise. Neither of them said anything, but Blaise shuffled to the side to give him space, and Alexis slotted between the two, facing outwards. At least Blaise hadn't completely ignored him.

'No weapons. No powers,' Wrought called, settling in a nearby spot to observe. 'The Healing Sanctuary is close by, but you're ordered to avoid any life-threatening assaults. Fifteen minutes. No surrender or forfeit. Begin!'

Three dozen attackers charged. Alexis threw an elbow into one's chest, ducked under a right hook from another and swiped at her legs. He let the instinctive part of his mind take over as adrenaline coursed through his body. Another attacker jabbed a punch into his shoulder, sending a stab of pain down his arm.

Alexis grabbed her and hurled her over his back, muttering, 'Sorry,' as she flew over the heads of Blaise and Antony.

Blaise was using one man as a shield, locked into place with a triangle choke. Alexis smiled. Blaise saw it and grinned back.

'Guys, help!' Adamson called. Three Elementals were dragging him down. Alexis spun and sent a kick into one of their faces, knocking him off, while Adamson reared back and slammed his palm into the other.

Alexis realised that Adamson's build and fighting style were similar to Blaise's, both boys utilising their large frames. Alexis, by contrast, fought elegantly, every assault a flourish, just as he had observed in Incantus's and Raeve's styles.

Adamson returned to the fold. 'Cheers, man,' he offered, bumping knuckles with Alexis.

'Don't worry about it.'

Alexis kept glancing back at Blaise, sensing his pain, his fatigue. A massive opponent landed a blow against the side of his face and blood sputtered from his lips. Alexis didn't think and stepped in between them to take the next punch.

White-hot pain exploded through his cheek. He reeled, dazed.

Blaise snapped. He grabbed the attacker and smashed his head into his own. Alexis blinked away the spots that danced before him and shouted, 'Up and over!'

Blaise dropped to one knee. Alexis stepped on it and was vaulted into the air, wrapping his legs round the attacker's neck and flipping him. The Fighter was sent tumbling back, crashing into three others, while Alexis landed awkwardly on his side.

'Up you get.' He felt the warmth of Blaise's hand cup the back of his neck and a moment later Blaise was pulling him up by his outstretched hand. 'That was a fire move.'

The corner of Alexis's mouth lifted in a half-smile. 'Got ice in the veins.'

Fifteen minutes later, the mat was strewn with groaning bodies. Antony Adamson had fought like a champion but had been taken down by a set of twins who had simultaneously tackled his legs. By the sound of the crack and his scream, something had broken.

Alexis and Blaise remained, standing back to back. They didn't need to talk. Their rhythm was instinctual, an unspoken language. They anticipated each other's movements, adapting and adjusting in perfect tandem.

When Wrought finally blew the whistle, Blaise grabbed Alexis's hand and pulled him into a half-hug. 'I've missed you,' he whispered, a secret declaration for him alone to hear.

Alexis gestured to Adamson, who was now being loaded

onto a stretcher by the twins who were responsible for his injury. 'What about your new best friend?' he teased.

'He's good, but he's not you.'

That was all Alexis needed to hear. He pulled Blaise back into an embrace, not caring about the pain when Blaise crushed him even tighter.

'I've missed you too.'

24

BESHERT

Beshert (n.) *Yiddish origin*
'Destiny'; referring to the seeking of a person
who will complement you and whom you will
complement perfectly; apparent fate of
an important event or friendship

Alexis stayed for the next three hours of Fighter sessions. They received an offensively short break before Wrought sat them down to review footage of their battle. It was less exhilarating than the fight, but gave Alexis a chance to ice his bruised cheek while Blaise monopolised the healing crystal.

Surprisingly, there was no animosity between Fighters. The hulking man, who Alexis soon learned was a powerless Elemental called Henry Gunning, couldn't stop praising him for his technique, and the multicolour-haired woman – Violet Champion – reassured him that it hadn't hurt when he had catapulted her, thanks to her pain-nullifying ability.

They were a chaotic bunch, loud but undeniably fun. By the time Alexis hit the sauna, he was sore in every sense, but it felt good. Besides, after all the beatings, the *Shadow Man* was blissfully silent.

'Bet today's session was more exciting than a Scholar one,' Blaise teased, receiving a few snickers from the others in the sauna.

Alexis, stripped to just his underwear, sat on the sauna's upper bench, heat pressing down on him. The pain, the noise, the battles – all of it dulled with every burning inhale of the dry hot air. Blaise seemed unfazed, his muscular body shimmering with sweat. Gunning and Champion sat below, quiet, struggling to breathe through their mouths.

'You clearly haven't read Orenda's *Many Mediums to Become a Medium*,' Alexis replied, wiping sweat from his brow.

Blaise scoffed. 'Only you would get turned on by reading.'

'And only you would get turned on by brawling and sitting half naked in a sweaty room with me.'

'Well, when you look like that, how can you blame me?'

Champion groaned, standing. 'I'm out before it gets any steamier.'

'You know we've got a tonne of mandatory reading too?' Gunning added, wheezing slightly. He craned his head to look up at Blaise. 'I've got a cousin two years above and she said Wrought's added a lot more theoretical modules to the course. Textbooks on Centauroi–Amazon conflicts and military strategy. Guess he's trying to defy the stereotype that Fighters get their brains knocked out of them.'

Blaise groaned, flexing his massive arms. 'We could read together,' he offered to Alexis. 'Or you could just read for the both of us?'

'I'm pretty sure there'll be picture books to keep you entertained,' Alexis retorted.

Blaise kicked him lightly. 'Cae told me you guys were up late catching up on Ziya's assignments,' he said too casually.

'You spoke with Cae?'

Blaise grinned as he gripped the edge of the wooden bench where he sat. 'We didn't do much speaking if you know what I mean.'

Gunning sniggered before choking on the dry air and descending into a coughing fit, making Alexis and Blaise laugh.

'How subtle,' Alexis noted. 'So you're back together?'

Blaise didn't respond. Instead, he jutted his chin towards the coals in the centre of the square sauna. Alexis took his cue and splashed a small ball of water against them, causing steam to billow into the air with a harsh hiss.

Gunning coughed again and covered his mouth with his hand, before he finally shook his head. 'I'm out,' he gasped, hunkering down as he crawled out, leaving just Alexis and Blaise.

'Whatever you said to her, thanks,' said Blaise. He shuffled to sit opposite him, but his gaze fell on the steaming coals between them. 'We're not back together officially – it's kind of complicated – but it's better than how we left it the other day. We decided we'll take it slowly and see how it goes. I know you and I were . . . not on the best terms, so it means a lot to me that you had my back.'

'I told you that I'd be your family,' Alexis reminded him, crossing his arms. 'Brothers fight. You should see how often Jason and I go at it.'

They fell into silence, watching the hourglass tick past twenty minutes.

'Where do things stand now between the two of you?' Alexis asked, needing something to distract him from the stifling heat.

'Cae said she thinks you're not as into her as before.' He didn't think sharing that part of their conversation violated their rule.

Blaise's back straightened. 'That's not true,' he said quickly, then softened. 'It's just ... she's always been controlling, but it's worse now. I saw her calendar the other day and she had literally blocked out an hour to cry and signed it with an "xoxo".'

Alexis bit back his laugh. Very Caeli.

Blaise snickered too before continuing. 'I don't know if it's PTSD or her sense of humour darkening, but she treats me like a punching bag sometimes, and I don't want to keep fighting with her.'

'Is that why you've been spending so much time here, working out?'

Blaise hesitated, before admitting quietly, 'I've been feeling tired all the time. And lonely.' His voice barely rose above a whisper. 'Some evenings I call on my proxy just to have someone there.'

Alexis's eyes stung at the confession. 'But you've got so many new friends?'

'It's not the same. Sometimes I feel like you'd all be fine without me. My parents haven't contacted me in months, and, honestly, I don't know if they ever will. I just don't know what to do with it, Al. It feels like a pit right here.' He pressed a closed fist to his chest. 'So I train. I break myself to build stronger. It's the only way I can justify being so exhausted all the time.'

Alexis didn't know how to respond. He stared at Blaise through the steam, the heat blurring his vision. He acknowledged the harbouring pain in his own chest that almost felt like tendrils of darkness, forcing them apart, hurling them into a chasm of loneliness.

'I didn't realise you felt the same," Alexis mumbled. "Maybe we've both been trying to heal alone, when we should've come together, just as we did when we faced this whole thing.'

Blaise moved to sit beside him, their shoulders touching. 'I'm sorry for what I said on the train, calling you the son of Mortem.' Alexis shook his head as if to shrug it off, but Blaise continued. 'No, it was out of order. I don't even know why I said it. You aren't like him. Please tell me you know that.'

Alexis's throat tightened. *Just the hot air*, he told himself. 'I do. And I want you to know that even when you feel lonely, you're not alone. Never.'

His mother had been right, as she often, annoyingly, was. Forgiveness provided him with that peace. He felt lighter.

Blaise smiled and reclined. 'Is this the part where we kiss?'

Alexis's own laugh caught him by surprise. 'As handsome as you are, there's only one person I want to kiss, and she's about a foot shorter than you.'

Blaise snapped his fingers in defeat. 'Long dark curly hair, green eyes, the kind of smile that lights up a room?'

The corner of Alexis's mouth lifted in a half-smile. 'That's the one.'

Blaise shot to his feet as though he had just decided to charge into battle. 'Then go to her.'

Alexis also rose. "I will."

They clasped hands tightly, firmly. Two boys who had grown into men. Into Elementals bonded not by prophecy but by choice.

Fire and water. The perfect contradiction, the perfect unity, tied together for an eternity.

25

FORELSKET

Forelsket (n.) Norwegian origin
The euphoric feeling you experience
when you're falling in love

Alexis spotted Parvati and Kallisto in the plaza walking arm in arm with Gibbous at their side, towering over them both. 'Hey, you've got Gibbous as your guide dog!' he joked, patting Kallisto's arm to let her know where he stood. Gibbous cut him a side-eye before huffing.

'He thinks you're annoying,' Kallisto translated with a giggle.

'I gathered. Show me how your powers are coming along,' Alexis asked Parvati, remembering her excitement when she had asked him to do the same on his first day of training.

'I can only manipulate the matter of inorganic objects right now,' Parvati muttered, fishing in her pockets for something.

Kallisto pulled off a dainty but tarnished ring from one of her fingers and handed it over. 'I got it from a market in Egypt and Dad said it's not real gold. Use it!'

Parvati placed it in the centre of her small palm. Before their very eyes, the ring shuddered before it spun on its side, blurring into an indistinct shape. By the time it settled, the ring's bright gold sheen glinted.

'Real gold!' Parvati exclaimed, as she put it back onto Kallisto's finger.

'You're getting better every time I see you,' Alexis praised, giving her a high five, pretending his hand hurt after. Where Ziya was shy and awkward, Parvati was all boldness. He wondered if that was due to her power status.

'Kallisto, have you seen your sister?' he asked, tucking his hands into his back pockets. He had showered and changed into a pair of loose blue jeans and a grey hoodie that he had 'borrowed' from his father.

'She had really bad cramps today so Ms Kefi told her to take the afternoon off,' Kallisto answered, rocking on the balls of her feet. 'I think she's in her room here. Are you going to ask her to the Fall Ball?'

Alexis nodded. Both girls squealed with excitement, startling Gibbous who had begun to doze off while standing.

'They finally updated the portal,' Parvati said, pointing to the archaic stone archway in the distance, the symbols glowing. 'It doesn't go to the Garden any more; it takes you to the most beautiful lake somewhere in Switzerland. You should ask her there! And we can get your outfits from Seamless Seamstress. Maria Sophia's a bit mean, but she's the best, and I'll make sure you get pushed to the front of queue.'

Less than an hour later, the three of them had packed a picnic for Demi, courtesy of Libero's preparations. Sliced meats, cheeses, crackers, a punnet of grapes and a couple of bars of rich salted-caramel chocolate.

Alexis left to find Demi but stopped short on the way to her bedroom. The distinctive sound of Ziya's gasp brought him to a halt before turning the corner. Alexis pressed his back to the side of the wall. He knew he shouldn't be eavesdropping, but his curiosity had got the best of him.

'I had no idea the Qing dynasty still did that,' said Ziya, her voice lowered, sincere. 'I've read about it before, but ... it sounds awful.'

'You can't even imagine it, Zi,' came Valentina's measured reply. 'It was even worse than when Mortem took hold of my mind.'

Was Valentina finally sharing something about her past? Was that why she hadn't returned home?

'I fear I'll spend my life seeking out people who will challenge me, just to feel a sense of accomplishment when I beat them,' Valentina confessed, almost as a whisper. 'I don't want to go after someone who won't love me, who will hurt me, but I'm already doing that now, chasing someone who may not be right for me. Playing with fire.'

Is she talking about Blaise?

Ziya's reply was unexpectedly gentle. 'You are more than what they thought of you. You aren't a victim, Tina. You're a survivor. Those people won't get to you again. Incantus swears he'll keep you and your identity protected. I do too – it doesn't mean much, but I do.'

'Thank you, Ziya,' Valentina said.

The silence that followed was unnaturally long.

Alexis turned the corner just as Valentina portalled in front of him. She quickly covered the scar on her wrist with her sleeve, her face instantly guarded.

'Hey, sorry I didn't see you there,' said Alexis.

Valentina narrowed her gaze. 'You just came up the stairs. Why aren't you out of breath?'

Alexis met her glare, willing himself to not give anything away. 'I fought the four Creatures of the Elements for two days straight, then a day later fought in a battle. I can handle the stairs without losing my breath.' His reply came out sarkier than he intended.

Valentina didn't return his smile.

'Awkward,' Ziya announced.

'I'll see you guys later,' said Alexis, and gave Valentina a wide berth as he passed her. He cast a smile over his shoulder. 'Bye, Val, take care on those stairs now.'

He turned back round, but not before Valentina elegantly stuck her middle finger up at him.

'I'm no gardener, but I don't think you're meant to decapitate the flowers,' teased Alexis, closing Demi's bedroom door lightly behind him.

Demi sat covered in dirt beside the great oak tree in her room, ripping out flowers from their roots. The tree stood like an autumnal sentinel, golden and burnt orange leaves stubbornly clinging to its branches.

She brushed her hair with the back of her hand, smudging dirt against her forehead. 'It's called deadheading. You cut off dying flowers to encourage others to bloom.' Her fingers disintegrated the petals of roses, azaleas and camellias with precision, almost as if she was sculpting it.

'I've got a surprise for you,' said Alexis, a nervous edge to his voice.

Demi raised an eyebrow. 'Uh-huh?' She took his hand. 'Where are we going?'

'First to Maria Sophia's to get an outfit for the Ball, then to the Lakes. Bring your angel cards.'

Demi gestured to her dirt-streaked jumper and asked, 'Should I change?'

'No,' Alexis said, shaking his head slightly. 'No, you look perfect as you are.'

Seamless Seamstress was a small boutique sandwiched between a coffeeshop and a small bookshop in the plaza on the ground floor of the hive, just off from the central dining area and training stage.

'Stop fidgeting,' a woman, likely the seamstress Maria Sophia, snapped from behind the closed front door as Alexis and Demi reached the front of the queue.

'Then stop stabbing me,' replied another woman in a deep Southern-American drawl. 'You know what, I'd rather wear my grandmother's gown. I don't care if she's cursed it.'

Althea Orenda burst out. 'Whoever created the stereotype that witches are hags and crones clearly never met *her*.' She turned to Alexis and Demi as she fixed her medium-length twist-outs. 'My favourite unproblematic duo! Happy upcoming Mabon. I'm manifesting a handsome man and my grandmother's long overdue death, you?'

Demi laughed. 'What's Mabon?'

Althea shut the door to the seamstress's shop with a wave of her hand, muting Maria's ranting. 'It's what we magical folk celebrate on the autumn equinox. Similar traditions to the

Elementals, but we focus on intention-setting for the coming months. It's a powerful day for witches, especially those who draw power from death or darkness.' She raised her hands in defence. 'If you hear reports of any Orendas making sacrifices, please know I will support you in the witch hunt for my grandmother.'

'Noted,' said Alexis. 'How was your fitting? I've heard the customer service is excellent,' he added helpfully.

Althea rolled her eyes. 'Choose your colours for the Ball wisely,' she said, timing her departure to the exact moment that a short leathery-faced older woman appeared with a bright blue scarf tied round her bald scalp.

'Yes, you come in,' she said, pointing at Demi before shuffling back inside the shop. She then glanced at the length of the ever-growing queue and curled her finger at Alexis. 'You too. Quick, I don't have all day.'

The boutique was like a soft marshmallow, walls a cushioned eggshell in colour, with a line of wardrobes spilling threads in every shade visible to the Elemental eye. In the centre was a podium surrounded by a ring of mirrors.

'Style, shape, colour, fit, fabric, shoe?' the seamstress listed, inspecting Demi with sharp eyes as though taking her measurements.

'Pardon me?' Demi asked, trying to recount on her fingers the different questions.

'The Daughter of the Air knew exactly what she wanted.'

Demi blushed. 'Do you have a catalogue?'

The seamstress scoffed as though Demi had just asked her to pee from her finger. 'Undress.'

'I don't—'

'Undress,' Maria barked, waving a hand dismissively at Demi's dirtied clothes. Demi's eyes locked on to Alexis, who made a show of lowering his head and rotating to face the other wall. 'And you,' she added, jabbing a finger into his back.

Alexis shot a glance over his shoulder. Demi had already shrugged off her T-shirt and had it folded over her arms. Maria took it from her and threw it on the chair opposite as though it was covered in faeces. Alexis gripped the bottom of his hoodie and lifted it over his head in one smooth motion, letting it fall to the floor in a heap. He then unbuttoned his jeans and stepped out of them until he was in nothing but his underwear, the bright white lights exposing every sculpted muscle of his back and shoulders, the plane of his lined abdomen, the dip of his hips.

Demi's eyes traced him in the mirror, both of them drinking each other in silently. Heat surged through him as her gaze raked over his body, forcing him to fight the urge to close the distance between them.

Demi muttered replies to Maria's questions while Alexis regained his composure before the seamstress approached him.

'Suit?' Maria asked.

Words abandoned him, flying from his reach like birds in the sky. 'Hmm? Yeah, yes, please. Black, please.'

'No, black is bad luck on the eve of the equinox,' Maria scolded. 'You will wear the colours of your amulets. The Ball is to be thrown in your honour, after all.'

Alexis bit down on his thumb as Maria dropped to her knees

to study the length of his legs. Demi, partially clothed, tried not to laugh at his awkwardness.

Maria finished observing the size of his feet and drew to a stand. She held his jaw in her hands and rotated his head, her eyes scanning his cheekbones and the shape of his brow.

'Dress,' she ordered, releasing his face. She moved to the overflowing wardrobe and withdrew a floor-length white-silk dress for Demi. 'Greens and browns represent health and vitality, blue for peace and stability.' As she spoke, the colour of the dress transformed in her arms, darkening first to a brilliant shade of emerald, then to an icy azure, making Demi gasp. 'Reds or pinks for those looking for love and passion, silver or grey for a desire for wisdom and prosperity.'

The dress drained from vermillion into a metallic sheen. For the first time, Maria looked at them both in the eye, then at their amulets, and smiled. 'I wonder what it is you seek?'

Neither answered.

Maria returned the dress to chalk white. 'I don't do multicoloured,' she scoffed, pulling a face of disgust. 'I'm not having you going out looking like circus animals.'

26

VATICINATION

Vaticination (n.) *Latin origin*
Prophecy; prediction

'Are you sure we were right to let her make our outfits without any input?' Alexis asked, following Demi through the stone archway on the hive ground floor. 'What if she puts me in a hot-pink dress?'

The question fell away as they stepped into the clearing. An enormous turquoise lake stretched before them, ringed by alpine forests and glacial mountains. The water was so clear it mirrored the midday sky, blurring the line between where the air ended and the water began.

Demi exhaled softly, her breath misting before her. 'I miss the warmth of the Garden, but this is just magical.'

The *Shadow Man* hadn't seemed to follow Alexis here. He inhaled the crisp air, savouring the stillness. A picnic basket tied with a white ribbon waited near the edge of the shore, a gift from his newest recruits. 'It has everything you like,' he said, handing it to Demi who squealed in delight.

A rowing boat was docked near the treeline. Alexis wrapped his arm round her waist and lifted her in, laughing as she wobbled.

'If we capsize, I'll kill you,' Demi warned, tucking her hands into her armpits.

'As a Healer, aren't you against that sort of thing?'

Demi tilted her head. 'I'll make an exception.'

Alexis dipped his hand into the icy water and gently stirred the current beneath them, gliding them slowly across the surface. 'How's your training going?'

'Really well,' Demi replied, smiling at the surrounding forests, taking them in. 'Kefi's teaching a mix of physical, psychological and spiritual healing. I spent some time today shadowing Healers in the sanctuary. Surprisingly, I haven't seen Blaise yet, but I'm pretty sure he's who's sending them all our way.'

Alexis grinned. 'I was with him today and I can confirm that.'

Demi's eyes widened slightly in an unspoken question.

'Yeah, we're okay.'

Demi exhaled in relief. 'Good,' she said, unpacking the picnic. 'I was thinking of asking your mum about her experience. I don't know if I have what it takes to be a hot-shot surgeon like her, but she's so inspiring.'

'She loves you, so I'm sure she'd be happy to,' Alexis said, certain that she would jump at the opportunity.

Demi described her classes – anatomy, suturing, healing crystals, early therapy techniques. Alexis noticed her shiver and offered her his hoodie, which she took before nuzzling into the neckline.

'Smells like you,' she said with a shy smile. 'Does it look good on me?'

'Everything does,' he said.

'Are you flirting with me, Mr Michaels?'

Alexis looked up at her through his eyelashes, wrestling with whether to take the leap. To finally act on the feelings that he'd always been too afraid to feel. Her lingering glance was like a silent wish. A dare.

'Would you like that?' he asked. The only thing he could hear was his own heartbeat in his ears as he watched intently for Demi's reaction. 'I've been trying for the last six years, thanks for noticing.'

A beat of silence passed between them before Demi's lips curved into a faint smile. 'Try harder.'

Alexis rose to the challenge. This moment, this lake, felt reserved for the two of them. There were no secrets here, no *Shadow Man*. It was only Demi and Alexis. The earth and the seas. He didn't know how many days, weeks, *longer*, that he had spent wishing that he could just be alone with her. To revel in her company and be the sole focus of her attention, and have her be the recipient of his.

Alexis lowered himself to the bottom of the rowing boat. 'Come here,' he said, cupping her calves. 'You still look cold.'

Demi shifted closer to him, and he held her gently, gazing up at her in worship.

'*You won't find any angels on the ground,*' he said, quoting her mother.

Demi bit back her smile. She dug into her back pocket and withdrew a small cracked deck of angel cards. 'My mum's cards. You asked me to bring them.'

Each card was beautifully illustrated, depicting a celestial being shrouded in a soft glow.

'I read a book on prophecies this morning,' he said.

'Tell me,' she asked, her eyes glittering with interest.

'Some argue that prophecies are stories. The Woman of the Water referred to our quest as one. A story. It got me thinking that perhaps a prophecy isn't always a foretelling of a singular event, but sometimes multiple events in sequence, told only about those who cause ripples in the course of history. Not everything can be foreseen by those with Aeon's Eyes, only the big events.'

Demi tilted her head back to look up at the sky, her eyes closing in a long blink. They were still closed when she asked, 'Are they avoidable? Can we escape our prophecy?'

He paused as the question stirred a memory within him. *'With water washing your roots, you will finally rest.'*

There had been something else the Woman of the Earth had said in Greek to Demi, something about love and death. He couldn't bring himself to translate it fully.

'It's *our* fate,' he answered. 'The actions we take become the events they foresee. We are the ones who write it into existence. Half the power of a prophecy is in believing in it, in accepting and embracing our fate.'

'A self-fulfilling prophecy,' said Demi, returning her gaze to his. 'If someone tells you that you're a bad person over and over, you'll start to believe it, to become it. Maybe that's what happened with Mortem.' She shared a piece of chocolate with him. 'So how does one discover one's fate?'

'Different cultures have different approaches,' he said,

tucking himself closer to her. 'Obviously there are psychics, but their powers, if they're actually legitimate, are usually limited to vague interpretation. Tarot cards, numerology, dream interpretation, palmistry, although that's largely discredited by the book. Norse tradition preferred runes. Astrology is a common approach; that's how they knew when the solar eclipse would fall upon a summer solstice, likely before we were even conceived. Each gives insight but not certainty.'

'Would you want to know yours?' Demi asked. 'If you had the choice. Or would you rather live without the knowledge of what was to come?'

'The former – always,' he said without hesitation.

She ruffled his dark hair. 'Scholar.' She held out the angel deck. 'Angel cards guide you through what's to come, rather than predict. We used them whenever we felt a bit stuck or in need of guidance. You're intuitive, so I recommend you do your own reading and I'll help interpret it.'

'Cae did say that water signs have borderline psychic powers,' he muttered.

'Close your eyes.' Demi spoke softly, easing him in. 'Once you've cleared your mind, set your intention for your reading.'

Alexis drew slow breaths, letting her words wash over him. He closed his eyes as he shuffled the cards, repeating the intention for clarity and guidance.

He wasn't sure if it was the reflection of the lake's surface, but a familiar blue glow bloomed behind his eyes, joined by a warm golden hue that beckoned him closer.

'Once you've connected with the cards,' Demi whispered, her voice sounding faraway yet close, 'draw three.'

Alexis opened his eyes once three cards sat in his lap. Demi pointed to the cards. 'The first card represents your near past, second is your present, last is your future.' They both reached for the first card at the same time, their fingers brushing. For a breath neither moved, until he gestured for Demi to take it.

'Your first card is the "Healing" card, which is in reverse,' she said.

'What does that mean?'

Demi flicked through the small guidebook until she reached the relevant page. 'You may be experiencing a blockage to your healing and recovery. Pain that isn't being processed, physical or emotional. Ignoring it prolongs suffering and delays peace.'

Alexis thought about his conversation with his mother the day before. *'Pain is only the opponent, not the result.'* 'Okay, fine, I'll come to a Healer session with you.'

Demi grinned. 'Hey, I'm just reading what the angels suggested. Your second card is the "Honesty" card. This calls you to face a truth or situation you're avoiding or denying. Does this link to anything you can think of? You don't need to tell me, by the way.'

Too many, Alexis thought, fidgeting.

'There's a couple of things that come to mind,' he admitted, his throat suddenly dry when he noted how intently Demi was gazing at him with so much patience and kindness. He feared he would combust into stardust. 'Things I can be more honest with myself about.'

'Such as?' Demi asked, her body tilting almost imperceptibly towards him.

Everything else, the lake, the forest, the sky, it all vanished.

It was just them rocking in a fragile rowing boat, an unspoken confession hanging in the space between them. He searched her face for some sign, a warning or welcome, and found only her gaze. Steady and warm and terrifying. His mind tried to drag him back to the cards, to the fine line they were treading as friends, but all of it dissolved under the weight of her here now.

He swallowed hard. 'My feelings for you,' he said. The air felt thick, charged. He could feel the pulse in his throat, could hear the soft catch of her inhale. He let the cards fall as he knelt before her, gripping the seat on either side of her thighs, and forced himself to find words to communicate his desire. 'How this entire time, I haven't been able to stop thinking about your lips. Wondering what they would feel like against mine.'

Demi's breath caught, just enough to make him doubt. Then she said, 'And yet you haven't even asked me to the Ball.'

Alexis leaned in slowly. 'Be mine,' he said, he begged, his heart thundering.

'Be your date?' Demi asked, her doe eyes devouring him, her breath warm against his face.

'Be my date,' he corrected himself.

'Yes, Lexi. I'll be yours.'

Alexis slipped his hands round her waist and pulled her closer, their amulets chiming as they touched. The world shrank to the inch between them. The distant cries of the birds, the creaking of the wooden rowing boat, the puffs of cloud in the sky, it all faded away. For all Alexis knew the very Earth had stopped spinning.

'What about your last card?' Demi whispered, her chest

rising and falling with every laboured breath. 'What does your future hold?'

Alexis offered her a crooked smile. 'You,' he answered simply. He held up the last card.

'The "Tower",' she said. Her eyes searched his before they fell to his lips where they settled, sending his heartbeat roaring in his ears. 'Sudden change. Upheaval. Destruction of old structures.' She took a deep inhale, her breath mingling with his, but neither he nor she pulled away. 'Lexi?' she whispered.

He loved the way she said his name. As if he was the only person in this world.

'Yeah?'

'Kiss me.'

And so he did. He lifted her chin and pressed his lips to hers.

A wave surged through him, an electric storm of hunger and peace. Desire and tranquillity. It was as if he had been a starving man and she was the oasis, the fountain he could drink from.

Her hands tangled in his hair, pulling him deeper, burying herself into him as though she was scared he would leave and never come back, the earth she would be uprooted without.

The lake rippled around them and the forest trembled in silent ecstasy.

'Demi.' He said her name between kisses as though it was sacred.

'Lexi.'

He brought her closer into his embrace, finding home within his arms.

'I've wanted this for so long,' she whispered, brushing away tears. 'I wanted to wait until you were ready, until you knew that I was yours and you were mine.'

So had he. It had all been worth it. Every torturous glance, every aching brush of their hands. For the first time in months the *Shadow Man* was silent. His sentence in the darkness was over.

Then a buzz.

Alexis barely noticed it, but Demi pulled away gently. 'See who it is,' she said. She pressed the side of her face against his neck where she could likely feel his racing pulse. 'I'm not going anywhere.'

Alexis reluctantly turned and picked up the phone to see he had three missed calls from his dad. He sat up and pressed redial.

'Alexis? Lexi, are you okay?'

Jackson's voice was raw. There was something in the way he said his name that made Alexis instantly alert. 'I'm fine. What's wrong?'

'Where are you? Are you out? Are you with someone?'

The dawning feeling that something was wrong, that something was very wrong, hit Alexis like a tidal wave. 'I'm with Demi. What is it, Dad?'

There was shouting in the background. A siren. Beeping. 'Good. Stay with her. Go to Geb and Petra's. Now.'

Alexis could only stare at Demi, his mouth drying. 'Dad, you're scaring me.'

'Please don't make me tell you over the phone,' Jackson replied, his voice breaking, shattering something within Alexis.

They're dead. They're all dead. The *Shadow Man* had found him, breaking through the ice and hauling him under.

Alexis extended a hand and the rowing boat rocketed towards shore. The basket tipped and the cards flew into the lake, but Alexis paid no notice.

'Dad, is it Mum? Jason? Please. Tell me. *Tell me!*'

When Jackson spoke, his voice was no longer panicked. It wasn't worried or scared or desperate. It was dull, empty. Broken.

'They were in a car crash. Alexis, I'm so sorry.'

27

ELLIPSISM

> Ellipsism (n.) *Latin origin*
> The sadness a person experiences when
> realising they won't live to see the future

Stephanie Michaels felt like herself again. She had had her hair blow-dried, bought a brand-new white dress and spent her day off enjoying small luxuries. Things had gone ... quiet again. Quiet was good. Quiet was safe.

'Done now, darling,' she said, shutting the car boot on the week's groceries.

'Finally,' Jason mumbled, engrossed in his phone.

'We would've been faster if you'd helped.'

He shrugged, glancing up from his phone to see if his mother found him as funny as he did. 'I didn't want to get in your way. You're so good at doing it yourself.'

She poked the side of his belly. 'I don't know where you and your brother get your sassiness from.'

He arched his eyebrow, a mirror of hers. 'Don't you?'

Trying not to let him see her smile, Stephanie started the engine. As she drove, her mind drifted to Alexis and their heart-to-heart from the night before. Their bond had always been special; she had known that from the first moment she laid eyes on him. To see him slowly deteriorating again brought on a pain no medic could heal. She was just grateful that he could still open up to her.

She handed her phone to Jason. 'Call the school, please?'

Jason stiffened. 'Why?'

Stephanie ignored him until the phone dialled and connected.

Stephanie got straight to the point, knowing the receptionist had a chronic tendency to overshare every minor and major detail of her day if Stephanie ever asked how she was. 'Hi there, it's Stephanie Michaels. My son, Alexis, told me that one of his teachers, a Ms Aevum, passed away over the summer. I was wondering if you had her family's details. She had a really positive impact on him and I would love to pass on my appreciation to her next of kin if that's possible?'

The receptionist's voice carried confusion. 'There's never been a Ms Aevum here at Bishop's.'

Stephanie exchanged a worried glance with Jason. Maybe she had got the name wrong?

'While I have you, Dr Michaels,' the receptionist added, 'Alexis had an unauthorised absence earlier this week. I sent a message home but never got a reply.'

Stephanie felt her stomach drop and missed her turning. Had that been the day she had asked them to get the bus to school? Alexis had promised he would go in. Had he lied to her?

Or, worse, was he hallucinating more than just the *Shadow Man*?

Jason reached for the car's touchscreen, abruptly ending the call.

Stephanie was about to berate him before she spotted something in the rear-view mirror. A black SUV had been tailing them since she had left the car park, even though she had taken a wrong turn and gone back on herself. She might not have paid it much attention otherwise, but the black-tinted windows and lack of a licence plate drew her attention.

Stephanie tugged the wheel sharply to the right, turning down the long road that cut through the forest.

'Home's down that way,' Jason muttered, rotating in his seat.

Stephanie didn't answer. She pressed her foot down on the accelerator and overtook the van in front of her, forcing the car on the opposite lane to brake to avoid crashing into them. The SUV swerved aggressively behind her as it pressed closer.

'Mum, what are you doing?' Jason asked. When he caught sight of her face, of the crease between her brows and the set line of her lips, his concern grew into a panic. 'What is it?'

Never before had they pursued her like this, she realised, like they intended to catch her. Maybe they had grown tired of waiting.

This wasn't just surveillance – they were hunting.

Stephanie caught Jason leaning further forward than he should be able to. 'Put your belt on!' she ordered.

Jason tugged at the belt but it locked each time he pulled it. 'It won't let me!'

A collision rocked the car, shattering the back window, sending shards of glass flying through the air. A yelp escaped Jason as he hit the dashboard. With one hand, Stephanie pressed Jason back into his seat, the other hand white-knuckled on the wheel.

'Call Dad,' she instructed, keeping her voice steady despite the fear rising in her chest. 'And put your bloody belt on.'

'I'm trying; it keeps getting stuck,' Jason grunted, dialling his dad's number.

Jackson's voice rang through. '*Hi, love. I'm on my way home.*'

'Jack!' Stephanie's voice trembled as she leaned over, fear flooding her system at the thought of never seeing him again. 'It's them. They're after us. We're on Old Pine Road, heading to the town centre.'

The SUV pulled up alongside them and rammed into their side. Stephanie fought the wheel, the car swerving between the woodland and the tarmac. 'Put your belt on now!'

'*Steph! Stephanie! I'm on my way,*' Jackson cried.

'Leave my family alone!' Stephanie bellowed and floored the accelerator. She swerved in front of the SUV and clipped its front tyre, sending it spinning off the road. It crashed into the forest with an awful sound and went up in a ferocious explosion.

'Mum!' Jason cried out, but Stephanie remained focused. Relief flooded her.

'Don't worry, darling,' she said. She didn't know how she would explain it to him, but she didn't care about that now. All she cared about was that she would see her husband soon. 'We're okay. We're going to be okay –'

Her breath caught in her throat.

A second SUV was barrelling towards them. Stephanie tried the brakes but the pedal sank to the floor and *nothing happened*. The sob in her chest wouldn't change the inevitable. They were going to crash and there was nothing she could do to stop it.

'Mummy,' Jason whimpered, pulling uselessly at his belt.

Seconds to impact.

Stephanie looked at her son while Jackson called her name desperately through the phone. In that moment, the promise they had made of putting each other first evaporated in an instant.

'A car crash feels like it happens in slow motion.'

That's what my patients say.

Yet for someone like me, someone with my gift, it truly did.

These people had taken almost everything. Our freedom, our safety, our lives. I would not let them take my children.

And so it happened. I still don't know how, but it did.

Time slowed at my command.

Jason couldn't see through it . . . or maybe he could. Maybe he had inherited his own gift – or 'curse', as my father had once called it – and he could see the soft golden energy that wrapped around us, which halted the very laws of nature.

As time stretched out, granting me these extra precious seconds, I unbuckled my seat belt and crawled into the passenger seat. I pressed my body against Jason's and clasped my hands to the back of his seat, locking him into place, my body a barrier between him and the windshield.

'Mum!' Jason's scream drew out until it was consumed by the sound of carnage. I took one last inhale of the scent of his hair then . . .

Time snapped back.

Motion, noise, everything, returned to us in a rush. The cars crumpled, metal folding like paper, and in an instant I was weightless, thrown by the momentum. I flew through the windshield, glass shredding my skin and my new dress.

I slammed onto the crumpled bonnet, my head and chest cracking on impact.

Stillness fell as everything flickered. I lay there, dazed, ears ringing.

It was odd how much time I spent trying to defy death, I realised then. He had become a dance partner, a challenger that sought a worthy opponent, which I was more than happy to be. He would take and I would take back. I thought there was admiration in our battle. Courteous respect for the role of the other. I went to work every day to face him and more often than not I prevailed.

Eight hundred and three lives. That was the number of people I had saved, including my husband and my sons. Perhaps I had overstepped my mark.

Now it was my own beating heart that I felt lurch, my own breathing that became sluggish. Through the haze my eyes found Jason. Bloodied, bruised, unconscious, but alive. His hand rested on the back of my leg, and from his touch I drew strength.

He was his father's son. That had to count for something.

A car door creaked. A woman staggered out from the passenger seat, her shaved red hair crowned by broken glass, her elbow held limply at her side.

She didn't look twice at the driver, who lay unmoving, his head against the wheel. She only stared at me, a crazed look in her eyes.

Good. Keep looking at my eyes. Don't see the shard of glass in my grasp, slick with my blood.

The woman dragged me up by the hair with superhuman strength, bringing my face close to hers.

'You've always known who we are. What *we* are,' *she said, searching my eyes for the truth. I was too tired to conceal it from her.*

'And now I know what you are.' She sucked in the air through her teeth. 'This is for Plague. For taking him from me.'

I swung and stabbed the shard deep into the crook of the woman's neck and shoulder, a killing blow. The woman released a gurgled scream as she dropped me, her hands pressing the wound as blood pounded in my ears.

At first she looked shocked, mortified that she had been deceived. But then that anger turned into something else. The shine of her eyes grew cold, and her gaping mouth widened into a wicked smile as she pulled the shard out.

Not a drop of blood followed it.

Her wound healed in seconds, replaced by a wisp of magenta smoke that dissipated in the wind.

The woman laughed just as I felt something damp trickling down my shoulder. I guess that was where the sound of blood pumping had come from. Gushing lines of red soon painted my dress, pouring from a lesion in my shoulder that hadn't been there a moment ago, which was identical to the one the woman should have had.

'Sire will be most pleased,' the woman said, standing over me like a vulture. 'Your boy is now ours. And with this one –' she glanced at Jason – 'I will continue the twin's work. He will be my new little experiment.'

My instincts screamed to fight, to get up, to protect my children at all costs. To slow time.

Yet I was being naive. It was clear that my time was already up. Golden light crept into my vision, reminiscent of my own power.

I could hear Jackson calling my name through the phone, begging me to answer him. 'Stephanie! I love you more. Stephanie, stay with me. I'm coming! Please wait for me, I'm coming!'

I wanted to answer. To tell him he was wrong. That it was me who loved him more.

But he wouldn't reach me in time to save me, and Jason's hand had slipped away from me.

My last thoughts were of my sons, of my husband, as the golden light swallowed me and took me away. Its warmth was like a mother's embrace, like a sunrise painted just for me.

PART III

28

AONARAN

Aonaran (n.) *Scottish Gaelic origin*
A person who lives in self-imposed isolation
or seclusion from the world

'What do you want?'

Caeli's words were sharper than intended, but Valentina didn't flinch as she perched on the edge of the desk in Caeli's booth. The Library was quiet at that hour, the dinner rush thinning out.

Caeli's proxy, seated next to her, grunted when Valentina sat on the book it was reading, tugging it free and ignoring her.

'How did you get in here?' Caeli asked, trying not to look up. 'Library's for Scholars. I don't see you in a cloak.'

Valentina waved her off. 'I'm a portaller, darling. Don't offend me by doubting my ability. Aren't you going to invite me to join you?'

The question was posed to both Caeli and her proxy.

'No, because I don't want you to,' Caeli said.

'Yes you do,' said the proxy under its breath. It rolled its eyes when Caeli glared at it.

Valentina sat between them anyway, moving a pile of

books to make room, casually scanning their titles. 'What are you—'

'Today's not the day,' the proxy muttered despondently. Caeli wasn't one to shy away from confrontation, but in all honesty neither she nor her proxy had the energy to go toe-to-toe with Valentina.

Not after watching one of her closest friends say goodbye to his mother before the crematorium chamber incinerated her body to ash. The phantom scent of burning clung to Caeli still, no matter how much perfume she sprayed. It was the first time she had seen Alexis all week since his mother's accident. He was never someone Caeli needed to worry about, but the look on his face before he ran from the crematorium had made her chest physically ache, for she knew exactly how it felt to lose a member of your family.

'How was it?' Valentina asked softly, solemnly. 'How is he?'

Caeli just shook her head. 'I'm trying to focus on the things I can control. My studies, namely. I doubt you're here to help.'

Caeli couldn't deny the tension that settled between them. Ever since the night they had kissed, she had done everything in her power to avoid Valentina and any thought of her. Especially since she had agreed to take things slowly with Blaise. She didn't know whether her conflicting feelings for Valentina should matter. And yet Caeli felt that to deny them entirely would be to deny part of herself, a part she hadn't yet had chance to develop and explore fully.

Did kissing Valentina make Caeli a lesbian, even though she had been and probably would always be attracted to Blaise? All her ex-partners had been men; was Valentina a one-off?

No, because Valentina wasn't the first woman Caeli had been attracted to. First, there was Raeve with her tattoos and her swords in her skin-tight silver combat suit . . .

Caeli felt her cheeks reddening and abruptly halted her train of thought. Maybe she was bisexual? Caeli felt a sense of calm at the thought. Either way, she had stayed away from both Blaise and Valentina, and spent her time studying instead, intending to figure it out on her own.

Valentina clearly didn't share the sentiment. She shuffled closer to the proxy, undeterred, not bothering to ask which was which.

'I'm not a fan of altruism,' Valentina said. 'The helpless who rely on the kindness of others are at their mercy. Help yourself, you have the tools.'

'You're not a very kind person, are you?' said the proxy without looking up.

Valentina smirked. 'I think that's why you enjoy me. Unlike you and everyone else, I don't pretend to be something I'm not. I know quite firmly who and what I am.'

Caeli bristled at the implication.

'Elemental Tribes,' said Valentina, pointing at the chapter heading of the book Caeli had spent the last three hours trying to understand. Whoever had translated it from its first language was certainly under the influence all the time. 'What have you learned?'

Good. Studies. This Caeli could focus on instead of how close Valentina was sitting to her proxy, to how electric her body had felt when she had kissed her. How much, despite herself, she wanted to kiss her again.

'The Tribes live in self-imposed isolation, close to where the Gems were found,' Caeli began, graffitiing half a page of writing with miniature tornados as she spoke with her left hand to improve her dexterity. She was the type of girl who read the last page of the book first because she had to know how it ended, so she summarised all she had scanned. 'They worship the respective element and the First Born they descended from. What sets us apart is that the Tribes can only *manipulate* an element – we can *create* it from nothing, just as the First Borns did.'

Valentina nodded absent-mindedly, already fiddling with the proxy's pencil, shooting it through a never-ending loop of appearing and disappearing through the opposing portal faces at her fingertips. 'Why don't the Tribes associate with the mortal or Elemental world?'

Caeli outstretched her right arm and imagined she was curling her fingers to pull at the air. A sweeping gale tugged at the pencil mid-air and she caught it in a hand made from the wind itself. 'Author hasn't said.'

'So, it's you,' Valentina said, her attention settled squarely on Caeli. The fact that she hadn't been able to spot the difference between her and her proxy until then flared Caeli's irritation more than she cared to admit. 'If the author hasn't stated it, think for yourself. No mountain, no view.'

Caeli's jaw ticked as her concentration faltered and the pencil fell. *God, she's annoying.* 'The Women of the Elements told us they could only create, not destroy. That's why they birthed the First Borns to build Stonehenge. Perhaps the Tribes are following in their footsteps and so stay away from our world – a world rife with death and destruction.' Caeli flicked back a couple of pages and traced her finger over the thick papyrus. 'The First Borns' sacrifice wasn't enough. The darkness lingered and would manifest itself in the body of an Elemental. The Tribes vowed to keep their bloodlines "pure" – the author's word, not mine – from mortal blood so a Child of the Element could inherit the First Born's amulet and true power, ready for that time.'

Valentina cheered, tapping the side of Caeli's proxy's head. 'So you do have a brain in there. Must be fun having countless generations dedicating themselves to produce *you*.'

'Any direct descendant could've been chosen,' she retorted, hating how much Valentina got under her skin. With Blaise it had been fun, they stood on equal ground when bickering, but with Valentina she felt like she constantly had to prove herself as an equal adversary. She was beginning to tire of it, even if Valentina's intelligence was something she found undeniably alluring. 'Anyone of my bloodline could have inherited my amulet and been a Child of the Element. It's the timing, or Mortem's interference or *something*, that initiated the Prophecy. I imagine I have distant cousins furious it was me. If only they could see me now.'

Caeli tugged her cloak sleeve over her gloved arm. Valentina's expression cooled. She didn't offer comfort where Blaise would've.

'Does the text say anything about Air Tribe specifically?' Valentina asked, brushing against the proxy. 'About the Exiles?'

'The Exiles?' the proxy echoed.

Valentina raised her thin eyebrows. '*Dorans*. Your ancestors.' Her tone was clipped, her disdain unmistakable. 'Their powers were unpredictable, uncontrollable. The ability to wield storms. They were careless too, and shared the secret of the Tribe with outsiders, shifting the balance between the warring local dynasties, legitimising one over the others. Entire bloodlines suffered irreversibly as a result.'

'So the Tribe exiled them?'

Valentina nodded. 'Gave them the name "Doran", meaning exile, wanderer. They broke the Women's cardinal principle: they had caused destruction, intentionally or otherwise. Some say they fled east, past the Himalayas, and settled in the mountain ranges of Siberia or as far as Alaska. This was many, many generations ago, which may explain why you look more Caucasian than East Asian.'

Caeli's thoughts spiralled. This wasn't a story about a random group of people; this was about her direct bloodline. Her grandparents, her parents. Her mother. She had only ever told Caeli that she had been raised in a small Alaskan town, a cult. Had her father come from there too?

Valentina tucked a lock of hair behind the proxy's ear. Caeli froze, watching the proxy's face, *her face*, being turned towards Valentina's. Its breathing hitched, and Caeli couldn't deny the pang in her heart that wished that were her.

Caeli was an academic, a Scholar. She assimilated knowledge and conducted experiments, all for the purpose of learning. This could be that. Valentina could be her new enquiry into understanding who she was, into unlocking part of her identity she hadn't allowed herself to explore. But guilt curdled in her stomach – not for Blaise, but at the thought of using Valentina as a means to better understand herself. Was that fair to her?

Valentina's lips brushed against her proxy's. Her proxy made no effort to move.

Caeli shot to her feet, scattering pages. 'I can't.' Her proxy shimmered and was reabsorbed into her body, disappearing from sight, from temptation. Its knowledge flooded her, but all Caeli processed was the brief sensation of Valentina's lips.

Valentina didn't move. 'Why not?'

Caeli wished she could compartmentalise her feelings like Alexis, but unlike him everything in her life felt like it was blurring into one. She had to force herself to look at Valentina. 'I'd love to stay and chat but unfortunately I have a breakdown scheduled and I hate to miss an appointment.'

'Caeli.'

'Don't!' Wind burst from her, sending books hurtling down the lined bookshelves. 'Don't "Caeli" me like you know me. Blaise makes me happy. He makes me feel warm and cared for.'

'Sounds like you want him as a father, not a partner,' Valentina cut back.

A dangerous stillness passed over Caeli. 'I shouldn't be the one that has to leave. You should. Get out.'

'Your proxy didn't appear to want me gone.'

You couldn't even tell the difference, Caeli wanted to shout, but she forced her lips closed. If her own mother couldn't tell them apart, how could she expect Valentina to?

The proxy was a soulless reflection, a cold, distant echo.

Is that what people think of me?

'You think this is fun for me?' Valentina asked, her eyes narrowing. Every word was a jab that winded Caeli, striking her in the solar plexus. 'I enjoy taunting you, pushing you, but *this* does not bring me joy. I wish I didn't have these feelings for you, but I do and I'm brave enough to admit it.'

Caeli bit her lower lip so hard she tasted blood. *Blaise, Blaise, Blaise.* She couldn't betray him again. But she couldn't stop thinking about the feel of Valentina's hands in her hair either.

'I can't trust myself to be around you,' Caeli professed. 'So leave or I'll throw you out myself.'

Valentina rose gracefully. 'I thought you were many things, Caeli Doran. A coward was never one of them.'

Caeli didn't waver. 'I am the descendent of generations of defiance. I don't need you or anyone else to define me.'

A wall of cherry red washed over Valentina and she vanished. Then, and only then, did Caeli scream. She reinforced the sound barrier and let a wail of frustration erupt from her.

She hadn't been lying. A breakdown had been scheduled, and she was right on time.

29

MORTALA

Mortala (adj.) *Latin origin*
Unrelenting and deadly; involving loss
of divine grace or spiritual death

'Alexis, it's been twenty minutes and you haven't said a word.'

Alexis forced his swollen eyes to meet Dr Dash's.

'Are you able to share with me how you are feeling?'

How do you think? spat the *Shadow Man* from over his shoulder, circling them while they sat in the living room.

'How do you think?' Alexis echoed, his voice thick, laden with exhaustion.

Reina's head rose from where she lay in Alexis's lap, her eyes searching his. She hadn't barked when Dr Dash came in and she paid little attention to him now. Stroking her fur was the only thing keeping Alexis grounded.

She sighed and settled back down. Alexis didn't need Kallisto to communicate with Reina to know she understood. She felt it too: the sadness, the grief, that had fallen over the Michaels house like fog.

Dr Dash sat patiently on the sofa, his hands folded together, his silver-framed glasses catching the dimming light. Exactly as he had looked all those years ago. Maybe the same light brown sweater too. The shirt must be new, at least – there was no blood staining its collar.

The night is still young, whispered the *Shadow Man* from behind him.

Eleven years later and here they were again. The three of them. Nothing had changed and yet everything had.

'I imagine you are in a great deal of pain,' said Dr Dash gently.

All Alexis could do was nod and continue stroking Reina.

He thought he had known pain. They were long accustomed to one another, in every form and every variant. But grief was different. There was nothing romantic, nothing poetic or endearing, about it. When he had torn free from his father's arms in the hospital to see his mother's unsmiling and unmoving cold body and begged her to wake up, wake up, wake up, he felt no swell of love or wistful melancholy; he felt only agony. After the doctors had told them that they were taking her to the morgue, he had been grateful when they had sedated him before he could tear the room apart.

The morgue was where dead people went. His mother couldn't be dead.

Alexis knew the five stages of grief. Yet that didn't stop him from falling victim to them.

Denial came first, when his father had called. He and Demi had raced to the hospital, both dismissing the idea that anything could truly stop Stephanie Michaels.

Then anger. There was a vacancy, an emptiness to his father's bloodshot eyes when he greeted him at the hospital. The man who was strong enough to break down a door with a single kick dropped to his knees and sobbed into his son's lap, and that had infuriated Alexis beyond reason.

Why is he crying? Why is he acting like she's dead? Why isn't he with Jason? Get off me. Get your hands off me! Where is my mum?

It was only when Alexis threw his weeping father off him that the anger dissipated into something else. It didn't take him long to find the room where she lay. That was when the bargaining began.

Alexis begged her to come back to him, the way that Demi and Incantus had when they had danced with death. As if his love for her was strong enough to haul her from death's greedy clutches. He prayed to all the gods and the devil, to the universe and the Earth. He offered himself. 'Take me. Please take me instead. Erase my existence, steal my breath and my future, and take me instead.'

No god and no law of nature answered his call. The anger returned then with the smashing of glass and breaking of machines before the anaesthetic kicked in.

He woke to find his head resting on his father's shoulder, Jason asleep in a hospital bed nearby. Jason's rounded face was cut and bruised, his blond hair half covering his closed eyes, but he was breathing steadily. That was when the next stage, depression, hit Alexis like a truck.

It stayed. Through Jason's release. Through the blurry limbo of arrangements over the week. Through the funeral, as Alexis stood with his friends. Even now, after Alexis had fled the wake, running six miles home after an argument had broken out between Jackson and Stephanie's father and his hawkish wife.

Now seated on the lounge floor with Reina curled into him, Alexis ignored his ringing phone and the risk that Jackson and Jason might come home from the wake to find him with his old psychiatrist. Thankfully Dr Dash had been able to meet him within the hour, otherwise Alexis didn't know what he would've done.

'Pain...' Alexis's throat tightened. He hadn't shed a single tear during the funeral. Not when the urn sat in front of them. Not when Stephanie's friends spoke of her skill and courage, of her kindness and power.

Power. The word rang bitterly.

He hadn't even cried as Demi, Caeli and Blaise had clung to him in tears. He feared that if he started, he would never, ever stop.

'This pain,' he said slowly, 'feels like blood draining from my body.' He looked away. 'Grief is death by proxy.'

I'm so tired and I don't want to go on any longer.

Dr Dash inhaled deeply as if reading his thoughts. The room darkened around them as the sun dipped behind a thick mass of grey clouds, dulling everything to shadows. 'There is no right way to grieve,' he offered.

The phrase reminded him of Olivia Kefi. Alexis had considered seeing her instead. Or Incantus, who had cancelled a formal hearing with the High Order the moment one of Alexis's friends told him what had happened. Every day he had asked Alexis to see him, but Alexis had declined.

Being away from his family, being in the Haven – foolish, selfish, ignorantly happy – was what had made his family vulnerable.

And what gnawed at him most was the nature of his mother's death. It was so . . . mundane. A car crash. No powers, no fight, no battle. Just . . . gone.

'The grieving process is different for everyone,' Dr Dash continued. 'Especially for something so sudden, so seemingly random.'

'Maybe it wasn't,' Alexis muttered, clutching Reina. 'Maybe it was planned.'

Dr Dash leaned forward. 'What makes you say that?'

'My dad refused the autopsy. He told Dr Ashdown, my mum's closest friend at work, that it was to speed up the cremation, but I know they would've rushed an autopsy for her.' Alexis unbuttoned the top of his shirt to scratch his neck. 'There was another crash half a mile away, where the unregistered driver was found dead too. I snuck into my dad's office last night and found his notes. Apparently Mum's brake line had been punctured. My dad was the first person on the scene, before the ambulances, so maybe he saw something, something about the people following us. Maybe he's covering it up so the authorities don't get involved.'

Dr Dash's eyes narrowed. 'Is that what the *Shadow Man* is telling you to think?'

Alexis bristled. 'No.'

'What about your brother?' Dr Dash asked, changing tactics. 'How is he?'

Alexis rolled his neck. He hadn't left Jason alone for more than an hour except when he was with their father and Demi's parents, who visited daily. Their presence kept the Michaelses afloat, but Alexis would've preferred the solitude. Even from Demi.

'When Jace woke, Dad sent me away, but I hung around

outside.' Alexis scratched at his knuckles until they were speckled with blood. 'He practically interrogated him, asking him over and over what he remembered. It was hard to make out because they were both crying so hard, but Dad sounded ... worried. Like Jace had seen something.'

'And?'

'He only remembered headlights.'

'Do you think he's telling the truth?'

Alexis's brows furrowed. He hadn't considered that. 'He's not like me. He wouldn't lie. Maybe he'll remember more once the concussion fades. He recovered from his injuries quicker than expected, but he's gone through enough already. I'm not going to make him relive it just to prove a theory.'

Dr Dash moved to the edge of the sofa. 'And what about you? Don't you think you have also gone through enough?'

Alexis didn't answer. The *Shadow Man* stood over him now, its claws brushing the nape of his neck. *You deserve it.*

I know.

Alexis's head throbbed. He hadn't eaten, hadn't slept, hadn't taken his antipsychotics either. He didn't care. Reality held no appeal any more.

'What will you do now, Alexis?' Dr Dash asked, closing his notebook.

That was perhaps the easiest question for Alexis to answer.

He didn't want to think about how he'd take care of Jason, how the two of them would survive without their mother to guide them and chastise them, to teach them to see the humour in everything and to have a furnace of passion burning within for anything they set their minds to.

He didn't want to talk about his father, either. Jackson Michaels had been the strongest man he knew, perhaps as strong as Incantus himself, and yet he had been reduced to a shell. A ghost. More than once Alexis had found him awake at night, sitting fully clothed in the living room, as though he was scared to sleep in the bed without her.

His sons had his heart and body, but his wife had had his soul. What would happen to it now that she was gone?

'Alexis?' Dr Dash pressed. 'What will you do now? You can't stay like this for ever.'

The Haven. Demi. My friends. Incantus.

Those were who might heal him.

But the *Shadow Man* wouldn't let him go. It stayed beside him, its coldness, its darkness, latching on to him.

'I can't fathom a world with my mum not in it,' Alexis whispered, finally looking up, tears filling his eyes. 'It's a world without light, without happiness. I begged the world to help me, to offer me just this one thing in exchange for anything, and it ignored me.'

He stood abruptly, making Reina slip from his lap to the floor.

The Shadowless in Protegere Forest. They did this to get back at him, to hurt him.

The *Shadow Man* laughed, gripping his shoulder, knowing what he had just decided.

Dr Dash observed him carefully. 'Perhaps for you, acceptance is not the final stage of your grief.'

Alexis blinked. For a moment, he thought he saw a line of blood stain Dr Dash's collar – but then it vanished in the fading light. Alexis shook his head to clear his mind. Dr Dash couldn't help him, not in the way he needed.

It is not, said the *Shadow Man*.

'It is not,' Alexis echoed, his voice hardening to steel. 'The last stage of my grief is revenge.'

30

FRANGIBLE

Frangible (adj.) *Latin origin*
Easily broken; breakable

Alexis waited in the shadows of Protegere Forest, arms crossed, as a red Ferrari screeched to a halt nearby.

A Ferrari. Really?

'I told you to park down the road,' Alexis hissed. 'Nice car but not very subtle.'

Blaise crossed the street. 'It's after midnight. No one knows it's mine; I only just got it with the money my parents left. What are you doing out here, Al? You must be freezing.' He frowned at Alexis's crumpled funeral shirt, then rubbed his faintly glowing hands against Alexis's arms, spreading warmth through him. 'We were worried when you disappeared after your grandparents showed up. No offence, but they're real dicks for starting a fight with your dad on a day like today.'

Blaise took off his puffer jacket and handed it to Alexis.

'That was the first time I ever met them,' Alexis muttered, recalling his grandfather's look of half pity, half disdain, as if Alexis was the cause of his mother's death.

People need only take one look at us to know what we really are, said the *Shadow Man*, standing like a silhouette beside Alexis and Blaise.

'How are you all? You, your dad, your bro?'

Dr Dash had left barely a few minutes before his father and brother had returned home. Jackson had plated up dinner, but when he set the table for four people, not three, Jason ran to his parents' bedroom and didn't come out for the rest of the evening.

'We're trying to cope in our own way. I'd rather be alone, Jason's been clinging to Dad, and Dad . . .' Alexis swallowed. 'He lost the love of his life. He's keeping it together for our sakes, but it's like his spark is gone.'

Alexis thought back to what Serena had told him the day before the battle, how she had described Darcy Raphe, Incantus's late wife. '*She was his light.*'

Stephanie had been Jackson's.

Blaise opened his mouth to speak, but Alexis cut in. 'I need your help. But only if you promise not to tell anyone. Not even Cae.'

Blaise frowned. 'Of course, Al.'

The *Shadow Man* loomed behind Blaise, but Alexis ignored it.

Alexis's voice hardened. 'I'm being serious, Blaise. What I'm asking is dark, but I can't do it alone. I need you as my best friend, not someone who'll throw this back at me later.'

The *Shadow Man* vanished into a smog of smoke as Blaise stepped forward. 'I promise. What's going on? You're starting to freak me out.'

Alexis jutted his chin in the direction of Protegere Forest. He could sense Blaise's hesitation of the dark, the fear of it was innate for all Elementals. Yet, together, after a moment, they ventured inside.

Alexis's voice stayed low, his steps cautious in the pitch-black forest. 'My mum's car crash wasn't an accident. Since summer we've been watched and now I'm convinced it's the Shadowless. They've come before, years ago when we first moved. Now they're back, more of them, and they're getting tired of waiting.'

Blaise's reply was a string of incoherent questions. 'What? But how? And why? How do you know all this? What could they want with you?' He then swung a punch to Alexis's arm. 'Why didn't you tell me this before?'

Alexis rubbed his arm. 'You had enough going on. If I'd known it would lead to this, to what happened, I ...' He swallowed the ball of lead in his throat. 'I don't know why they're here, but this deranged woman, who I think is in charge, mentioned something about revenge.'

Blaise froze. 'Al ... what are we doing here?'

'This is where they've been hiding. We're here to find them and kill them.'

'This is a job for the High Order, surely?'

'We can't get them involved,' Alexis contested. 'They might investigate my parents.'

'So what? Ziya said the High Order's duty is to protect mortals too.'

'That's not what I mean ... I don't know if it was exactly legal how they adopted me.' Alexis spoke quietly. 'There's too much I don't know about how I could've escaped Mortem. I can't have them digging into my past or my parents. I can't risk it.'

Doubt shrouded Blaise's voice. 'We should still tell Incantus.'

'Later. Right now I'm going to do what I can to protect the rest of my family.' He drew the moisture into a sword of ice. 'So are you with me?'

Blaise responded with a series of thin waves of flame that coiled round his wrists like burning bangles. 'Of course. Your mum ... I only met her a handful of times through my proxy, but she showed me more kindness than my own parents.'

Alexis bit his lip to combat the stinging of his eyes. 'Then tonight we chase the shadows.'

'You should've brought Reina,' Blaise grumbled for the third time, unable to stay quiet.

'I usually do. Don't want Kallisto sensing things through her.'

'Kallisto the dog whisperer,' Blaise muttered.

'Funnily enough, that was what I called Caeli when she started dating you.'

Blaise snickered. 'If I wasn't so tired, I'd think of a comeback.'

Patrolling the forest at night for his mother's killers wasn't normal, but this, joking with Blaise, almost was.

'Dee says you've been avoiding her,' said Blaise, juggling a fireball absent-mindedly. 'I know you haven't been back to the Haven all week, but she said she's come to your house every day and you haven't been answering.'

Alexis rubbed his knuckles into his tired eyes. 'I don't want to feel like a project she has to work on. She's going to make a fine Healer one day, we all know it, but I don't want her to see me like this. To see just how weak, how powerless I feel.'

Blaise stumbled into a low-hanging tree branch and swore

as it cut into his forehead. After severing the branch with a red-burning chop of his hand, he said, 'I get that – not wanting to be pitied, not feeling strong enough – but people's pity shows they care, doesn't it?' Blaise shrugged. 'The Fall Ball is tomorrow night. It might be a good opportunity to spend some time with her there if you were looking to distract yourself.'

Before Alexis could answer, the sharp snap of a twig echoed throughout the forest, amplified in the stillness. Blaise extinguished his ball of flame, plummeting them into darkness.

The sound could be nothing. It could be anything. Everything.

Masked by the trees, a tall figure crept towards them in the far distance, taking slow, careful steps in their direction.

'Incantus?' Blaise whispered.

And then a bark split the night.

Reina.

A bright pale blue light flared from the man's hand, revealing not Incantus, not Shadowless.

'It's my dad,' Alexis hissed, then grabbed Blaise's arm. '*Run.*'

Branches clawed their faces like skeletal fingers as they fled. Reina barked wildly, hunting them down while the intense blue light remained trained on them. Every step was a gamble as they ran in the approximate direction of home. Roots snaked across the path like traps, threatening to trip him up, but Alexis kept hold of Blaise's arm and they caught each other whenever the other slipped.

What is he doing out here?

His father had looked oddly determined before bed – focused

for the first time since Stephanie's death. Maybe he had had the same idea Alexis had.

Like father, like son.

Only he was the hunter and Alexis the prey.

'Why are we running?' Blaise panted.

'There's no good mortal explanation for us being out here with a sword of ice and your hand on fire.'

'How's he keeping up with us?'

I don't know.

Maybe that was what true love was capable of. Gifting superhuman abilities to mortals: strength to mothers to lift cars to save their children trapped beneath, clairvoyance to fathers to predict when their child would fall to catch them just in time.

Shadows shifted and stretched with every step they took. Every sound, every crunch and rustle, felt closer than it should be, and as Alexis's legs burned from exertion, he realised that the forest was no longer quiet. It was roaring, listening, cheering Jackson on to catch them. And it was going to cash in its bet.

Alexis pressed his palms together, his mind clasping at the only solution he could think of. When his proxy was summoned before him, he told it, 'Act like you've been sleepwalking.'

The proxy slowed, dreamlike, devoid of his amulet and weapon. It was swallowed by the dark of the night behind them.

Seconds later, Jackson collided with it.

'Will he buy it?' Blaise gasped, still running, Jackson's torch no longer searching after them.

'He has to.'

They burst out of the trees onto Valerian Lane, bent over, lungs burning. On the horizon the sky had lightened to a smoky violet as the world hesitantly awoke.

'What the hell was your dad doing out there?' Blaise asked, his dark eyebrows knitted together as he wiped sweat from his forehead.

'Probably the same as us,' Alexis muttered, trying to regain control of his breathing. 'I can't believe he came out here. What if someone tried to break in and he wasn't there? What if he found someone *here*?'

Jackson Michaels was a famed detective, a brilliant officer, but what chance did a mortal have against the Shadowless?

After thanking Blaise and inviting him to crash at his for the night, which he politely declined, they parted. Back at home, Jason was asleep in their parents' bed. Alexis lay in his own, restless, until he heard Jackson, Reina and his proxy return half an hour later.

When Alexis finally closed his eyes, darkness seeped into his mind and took shape.

'Please don't. Please! I'll get better, I promise. Don't do this!'

Stephanie and Jackson Michaels didn't seem to hear him. They dragged him by his feet with superhuman strength, their grip grinding his bones. By the front door, waiting for him, was an imposing man shrouded in shadows.

'Mum! Dad! I'm your son. I'm not like him. Don't send me back to him.'

'*You are not our son*,' said his *father*, his body glowing with the pale blue light of the torch he had chased him with. He threw Alexis forward to where his knees cracked against the hard floor. '*You are the devil spawn and I will not have you ruin us any more than you already have.*'

'*You're going back to where you belong,*' said his *mother*, her voice slow, stretching out so that each syllable stung him. She looked just as she had the last time Alexis had seen her, with shards of glass sprinkled throughout her blonde hair, a gaping jagged hole puncturing the side of her neck. '*My last thoughts were of how I wished you had never been born. You did this to me.*'

Finally, the figure cloaked in darkness stood over Alexis. Human features formed across its face. It first morphed into Alexis's own reflection, then it became Mortem. Shadows poured from its mouth when it spoke, soaking into Alexis.

Give in and we will be together. Give in and we will be one.

Alexis woke in terror.

He couldn't take it any more. This was beyond grief. His mother was dead because of his negligence, or perhaps his arrogance. He couldn't let his father or brother meet the same fate. Not because of him. Not when reality was being abandoned, when psychosis and shadow dragged him into its grasp and refused to let him go.

There was a reason it was back. The *Shadow Man*. Alexis had thought that it was because of all he had seen and been through. Maybe that was just a lie he had told to shield himself from the truth.

He grabbed his phone and dialled.

'Incantus?'

'Alexis?'

The *Shadow Man* loomed over him, shaking him in its talons, screaming.

'I need your help,' Alexis whispered, tears spilling down his hollowed cheeks. He felt the *Shadow Man* strike him across the face, but he clenched his jaw and thought of his mother.

'Pain is only the opponent, not the result.'

And then he thought of Demi. *'It hurts to heal.'*

The *Shadow Man* stood no chance against the two most important women in his life. His first love and his true love.

Alexis steadied his voice. 'What happened on the solstice . . . it didn't work. The darkness survived. It survived . . . and I still have the power of shadows.'

31

LIEFDESVERDRIET

Liefdesverdriet (n.) Dutch origin
The sadness, depression or pain one feels about
a love unanswered or love that is gone

'Alexis.'

Incantus embraced him the moment he entered the office, pressing Alexis's head against his chest. At first it felt comforting, until Alexis saw the glow of white light emanating from Incantus's hands.

'Can you sense it?' Alexis asked numbly.

'It's trying so hard to hide from me,' Incantus replied, his glowing eyes closed in concentration. 'Here in the Haven and in my presence it's faint but it's there. I can't believe I didn't feel it before.'

He let go abruptly. Gibbous lifted his head from where he lay by the roaring fireplace, giving Alexis a once-over.

'It's not your fault,' Alexis began, even as the *Shadow Man* scoffed in his mind. 'You've had too much on your plate: rounding up Shadowless, repairing things with the High Order, searching for Ziya's mum—'

Incantus cut him off with a raised hand. 'I am the Elemental of light, and yet I missed the darkness when it was right under my nose. It's not because I've been busy; it's because I've grown *weak*.' He nearly spat the word.

'And whose fault is that?' Alexis asked, his eyes on the worn brown-leather sofas, the dozens of zigzagging bookcases, Gibbous – *anything* but Incantus. 'Whose fault is it that your immortality is gone and your powers have waned?'

'That decision was my own, one that I would make a hundred times over, even if it meant exchanging my life for yours,' Incantus said fiercely. He released a slow, controlled exhale. 'Maybe we are both to blame. Maybe neither. It has always been the nature of the darkness to snuff out the light.'

Alexis sat beside Gibbous where he tentatively stroked him, willing the wolf to see that whatever was inside of him meant him no harm.

'How long have you known?' Incantus asked, watching him intently.

'For a long time I tried to convince myself that it wasn't that. That it was just PTSD or ...'

Don't say it, barked the *Shadow Man*, materialising beside Incantus, his corrupted parallel. *The more we share, the weaker we are.*

But Alexis was done listening to it.

'I wonder if you already know this about me. If you know of my condition, my medical history. My psychosis.' Alexis glanced at Incantus to see if he could read his face. He was doing a good job of keeping it neutral. 'There's been signs of it coming back. I heard it, the *Shadow Man* that used to haunt me as a child, soon after I awoke from my coma. It was auditory only at first, but now it's infected the rest of my senses.' He recalled the sharp sting of its slap when he had picked up the phone to call Incantus. It felt as real as anything else, indistinguishable from reality.

'The *Shadow Man*?' Incantus asked, his head tilting in question.

'That's what I used to call it,' Alexis said with a shrug. 'This figure made of shadow. Imaginative, I know; I was only six at the time.'

Incantus folded his hands beneath his chin. 'It's telling that your hallucinations took the form of shadows long before you knew of this world.'

Alexis hadn't given it much thought. Shadows, darkness, it had always been synonymous with fear and danger. With death.

'I didn't want to believe it was the darkness, that the Prophecy hadn't been fulfilled. But part of me always knew that it had remained after the solstice. The *Shadow Man* and my psychosis, maybe they were always tied to it. Maybe I can never truly be free of it.'

Saying it all in one go was like letting go of the reins of a horse. But Alexis wasn't done yet. 'I used it. When I fought Mortem in the projection of Stonehenge, I called on my shadow powers. Awakened it, which means that it was with me when we were together inside the real Stonehenge. I think that's how it survived the eclipse. Just like before, it escaped the light and concealed itself in the water. In me.'

Alexis remembered the eruption of light that had exploded from Incantus's body as the Children of the Elements clung on to him. Yet, even though his vision had been flooded with white as he fell unconscious, he recalled the coldness lingering in his chest, the wave of blackness escaping Mortem in his final moments, reaching for them. Had it reached them in time?

Alexis hadn't looked at Incantus's face for a long while. When he finally did, his mentor's eyes were shining. 'Did you know?'

Incantus shook his head. 'Olivia Kefi hinted that you weren't honest in your sessions – she could feel the cold, low resonance of deception. Perhaps it wasn't just her you were being dishonest with.'

Alexis thought his tears had fooled her. Clearly he had underestimated her. 'Why didn't either of you say anything?'

'I trusted you,' Incantus said simply, resting his hands flat on his disorganised desk. 'I don't expect you to tell me every thought and feeling you experience, just as I hope you don't expect that of me. It's natural to hold some secrets closer to our chests. I believed that if it mattered, if it was causing you this much pain, you would tell me.'

The *Shadow Man* loomed again, whispering, *He will destroy us for this.*

'Did Mortem, or Nero, ever experience this?' Would confirmation bring him closer to his father? Would it justify Mortem's actions, to attribute them to madness?

'Not to my knowledge. Alexis, I want you to know that it isn't your fault. Any of it. If you hadn't used the shadows against Mortem, then none of us would be alive right now. And with everything that's happened since your mother ...' Incantus crossed to him, kneeling with effort, using Gibbous to steady himself. With his other hand, he clasped Alexis's shoulder.

'Incantus, I need you to destroy it.'

Incantus's chest deflated and his sky-blue eyes lowered to Alexis's amulet. 'I can't.'

'Yes you can,' Alexis protested. 'You're still the strongest Elemental alive –'

'This has nothing to do with strength,' he replied miserably. 'The darkness is part of you. It's not like Valentina and Taranis who were imprinted. It's lived in you from the moment you were born, tied to your very existence. If I tried to rip it out, it might tear you apart.'

'I'm willing to risk it.'

'But I'm not.' Incantus's voice cracked. 'It's intertwined with your mind, your body, just as your powers of water are. If I tried to extract it now, by force, it would leave you a shell of the person you once were. Your heart would beat and your lungs would breathe, but you'd be gone in every other way. I can't risk it. Not again.'

Alexis stared at him. 'You've tried this before?'

Incantus didn't answer. He didn't need to. Alexis recognised the grief that lined his face, the memory that haunted his every smile because of a mistake like this. He didn't need to ask who it was.

The only person he had ever loved. The only person he would ever love.

Softly, Alexis asked, 'Then what do we do?'

Incantus's jaw set. 'We exhaust every other option. There is one who may know what to do ahead of the autumn equinox tomorrow. The one who first spoke of the Prophecy of Light and Darkness. Only he can tell us why we failed at the summer solstice.'

Alexis drew to his feet, suddenly nervous. 'Your mentor?'

Incantus nodded gravely. 'It is time you meet Sapientis Aevum.'

32

LYSSOPHOBIA

Lyssophobia (n.) *Greek origin*
Fear of going insane or mad

The sea breeze lashed Alexis's skin with a salt-laced sting as he and Incantus trudged along the beach in silence. They walked in the shadow of a huge cliff. Grey clouds pressed down from above, mirroring the heaviness inside Alexis. Incantus had said they were heading somewhere along the Jurassic Coast.

Alexis had instantly thought of Demi. 'This was where we were supposed to go on our school trip last spring,' he had told Incantus after they walked through the portal. 'We stopped at Stonehenge because a girl threw up on the coach.' He wasn't sure whether to smile or frown at the memory.

'You would've found your way to us one way or another,' Incantus said, offering him a jacket that was slightly too big. 'You can't avoid your fate.'

Whoever wrote my fate is getting a knife to the throat if I ever meet them, Alexis thought.

'Is the *Shadow Man* with you now?' Incantus asked lightly.

Alexis scanned the vacant beach. 'Nope, all I see is me and you. You must've scared it off.' He leaned closer to him.

'I'm an intimidating bloke,' Incantus said, lifting one shoulder in a shrug. 'I was there, you know. At the ceremony yesterday. The impact your mother had, the number of lives she touched and saved, will resonate forever.'

Alexis looked at the sea that crashed steadily beside them. Where once water had brought healing, now all he felt was bitter cold. He was taken aback by his aversion.

'Why didn't you come over?' he asked. 'I could've introduced you to my dad, told him you were my teacher or something.'

Incantus thought for a moment. 'I didn't want to intrude. I wanted to meet your father and brother more than anything, but that day was not about me.' There was a longing in his voice that touched Alexis. 'I knew you would be okay because you had them and your friends. When you left, I followed you to make sure you got home safely.'

Alexis hadn't sensed anyone following him at the time, but then again, he hadn't been listening. If the Shadowless had attacked him, he wouldn't have fought back. He'd been too lost.

'I've started seeing a psychiatrist,' he shared.

'Is it helping?'

Alexis recalled his decision to substitute acceptance for revenge. Unlike most doctors, Dr Dash hadn't shut him down. 'I guess. Please tell Kefi I'm sorry. For lying. For avoiding the Healer sessions.'

'She is a very forgiving person,' Incantus assured him. 'She'll understand. She just wants to see you getting better, irrespective of who it's with.'

Alexis wasn't sure if he was getting better. For so long he'd hidden the psychosis, the dark, tainted part of himself. He didn't want it infiltrating the new world he had found a home in. If Demi, Blaise or Caeli found out, would they still want him?

A childhood spent with the *Shadow Man* whispering in his ear had established those core beliefs. Alexis wasn't sure if he could ever rewrite them. Yet he had confessed it to Incantus and his world hadn't collapsed.

Alexis wanted to tell him more. About the Shadowless, his father's secrets. Incantus could help. But before he could speak, Incantus halted and looked up at the cliff.

'It was Mortem who used the darkness, not the other way round. He chose that path. Not because of the Prophecy, nor the darkness – which he used as his tool – but because that was who he decided to be. You can choose differently.'

'You believe that?' Alexis asked. 'Or do you just hope? I thought you said we can't escape our fate.'

'Perhaps fate is just the consequence of our decisions,' Incantus murmured. 'We'll soon know why our actions on the solstice didn't resolve the Prophecy.'

'So Sapientis Aevum might have the answers,' Alexis said, scanning the beach. No sign of him yet.

He recalled what he knew about him. Grandchild to the First Born Elementals. The vessel through which the Prophecy of Light and Darkness, and few others, had been foretold. Father to the women-only Aevum bloodline.

'The man is a legend,' said Alexis. 'Yet you never speak of him with affection. Why?'

'*Kindness is a disguise for low expectations,*' Incantus recited, tucking his arms behind his back. 'He wasn't cruel, but he was relentless. Hard, but not evil. He shaped me into who I needed to be and I respect him for that, but I resent him for it too. Some of what he did, what he allowed . . .' Incantus sucked in a sharp breath and released it with a slow shake of his head. 'No matter what his reasons were, justified or not, I cannot forgive him. No amount of time will ever heal that.'

A tutting sound came from behind. 'Ian, haven't I told you already?'

The voice was ancient, the accent unplaceable.

Alexis turned just as Incantus answered, bitterness lacing his reply. 'Time heals all wounds.'

Sapientis Aevum had arrived.

33

ATOTȘTIUTOR

Atotștiutor (adj.) *Romanian origin*
'Omniscient'; all-knowing; someone who knows
everything or has complete knowledge of something

Alexis didn't know what he had expected Sapientis to look like. Certainly not a man in his mid-twenties, young enough to be Incantus's son. He wasn't particularly muscular or tall or handsome. He looked ... ordinary, apart from his eyes, which shimmered with drifting stars, speckled with spots of white and yellow and violet.

Sapientis's lips stretched so that they almost resembled a smile. 'Thank you for finally answering me. The future was unclear whether we'd meet.'

'I am not here for you,' said Incantus curtly. 'I am here for him. Meet Alexis Michaels, Son of Water.'

Alexis shook Sapientis's hand. *Tight grip for an old man*, he thought, noting his intense evaluating stare, searching for any resemblance with Serena, or even Ziya.

'Alexis,' Sapientis said thoughtfully. 'What you and your colleagues achieved on the summer solstice was legendary. For it you will be remembered until the end of Elemental-kind. I see it has come at a cost, however.'

There was an arrogance that underlined his youthful expression, a smugness that counteracted Alexis's tendency to be sceptical of those in seniority. 'Perceptive,' Alexis said.

He had no desire to drop to his knees in awe of the man. He saw Sapientis as the person who thought Incantus would become great only if he broke him, who couldn't even bother to have a relationship with his great-granddaughters or attend his own daughter's funeral. He might demand Alexis's respect, but Alexis had no intention of offering it freely.

Incantus was a pillar of strength beside him. 'We need your help. The darkness within Alexis, which lives within all those born to the water, seems to have survived the solstice. It conceals his shadow and I fear it is growing stronger with the equinox almost upon us.'

Sapientis crouched, one hand stroking the sand of the beach, the other waving for Incantus to continue. 'I'm listening.'

'You know what will happen if I try to remove it after he's spent a lifetime with it,' said Incantus, his jaw tight. 'We need to find another way. I ask you to look into Alexis's future or into the fate of the darkness itself. See if he will ever become lost to it. Then we can learn how to go about preventing this.'

Sapientis said nothing, letting the sand sift through his fingers. As he did, Alexis observed his surroundings with growing unease. Something about it felt familiar, almost as if he had seen it before in a dream.

And then it hit him.

'This coast has seen a lot of bloodshed, and will come to know a lot more in time,' said Sapientis.

This is where it all began, whispered the *Shadow Man*.

'My nightmare,' Alexis said, turning to Incantus. 'This is where Mortem— Where Nero fell.'

Incantus swallowed hard and nodded once.

'The birthplace of darkness,' Sapientis said to himself. He drew to his feet. 'Take us up there.'

'No.' The firmness in Incantus's tone hauled Alexis out of his daze. 'I don't want to.'

'I have never and will never accept weakness,' Sapientis stated.

'Weakness?' Incantus said incredulously, blush rising to his cheeks. 'True weakness was not attending Serena's funeral or the Battle of Stonehenge. We needed you. She needed you.'

Alexis searched Sapientis's face for any semblance of guilt, but all he found was a distant sadness. 'I was needed elsewhere. That field, on that day, would always be the place Serena was meant to die. She knew that and she had come to terms with it.'

Alexis's anger rose, charged by all the deaths Sapientis had foreseen and done nothing to prevent. 'What was more important than fulfilling the Prophecy of Light and Darkness?'

Had he seen Alexis's mother's death too? Was there anything Alexis could have done to stop it?

The laws of time and space had to bend and Sapientis was a coward, he was weak, for not forcing it to.

'The only thing more important than witnessing the resolution of my first prophecy was the discovery of my last,' Sapientis said simply. 'The Prophecy of the Passing Torch.'

Silence settled amongst the three generations of Elementals. It could have been seconds, it could have been minutes. Too many questions were swirling around his head for Alexis to think straight.

'I'm sorry, Alexis,' said Incantus, reaching out to take his arm as his other snatched Sapientis's. 'He will tell us what we need and then we'll go.'

With a burst of white light, they light-jumped to the top of the cliffside, the sand underfoot replaced by the sturdiness of the earth.

Alexis stood at the place that tormented him every single night of his life, unmoored. No blood poured from his skin, but he still felt like his stomach had been hauled into his chest.

I want it all to stop.

He edged closer to the cliffside, ignoring Incantus's warnings, hoping he would fail to catch him just as he did in the dream. The *Shadow Man* roared at Alexis to get back, but that only encouraged him onwards, wanting to do what it so clearly didn't. He could end it all and put an end to his suffering at the place where it all began.

Be with his mother again. Both of them.

Both taken from his world because of him.

Alexis took another step.

A pair of hands clasped his face, and he fell. Not forward through space, but back through time.

It was as though Sapientis was scanning through the pages of a book that was Alexis's life, each chapter written with golden ink. Nero's fall, the ocean flashing his reflection. Yet for the first time, Alexis caught a glimpse of something his nightmare never showed him. Just before the boy closed his eyes, a flash of colour winked from the pendant on his chest. The water amulet, Nero was wearing the water amulet, and its colour flickered between bright blue and pitch black.

The pages flipped forward. Scenes blurred. Gold shimmered.

Alexis was in his bed at home on Valerian Lane, with a sleeping baby lying in the cot beside him. But they were not alone.

A hulking man approached them. Alexis scrambled to stand before his brother, to protect him from this beast that was too big to be human, too vivid to be a hallucination. The giant's hand tightened round Alexis's arm and a scream ripped from his throat.

Suddenly, there was a flash of bright pale blue light and the giant was thrown to the other side of the room. In the place where he had just been stood Alexis's father.

Sapientis moved on just as the giant charged towards Jackson.

More images flashed before Alexis's eyes: a blur of reality and hallucination. He couldn't tell the difference. The *Shadow Man*'s whispers, falling into the Haven, learning that Mortem could be his birth father. Losing Blaise to the volcano, Demi's eyes closing before him, an arrow buried in her chest, Caeli's screams as she stared at the blood gushing from her severed arm. The quest, the battle, the *Demons*, the confrontation inside Stonehenge, and almost every day since, the memory of them tinted darker, dimmer.

Finally, his mother's still, broken body laid out before him, stubbornly refusing to waken.

And then it all changed. The scenes snapped forward like

the recoil of a boomerang and Alexis saw something else. Something that wasn't from his past.

Three bodies lay broken and bleeding around the rocks of Stonehenge. A mass of silver-blond hair. A boy, barely moving. The crumpled body of a girl. Alexis alone stood at the centre, blood up to his elbows, his eyes gleaming black.

Alexis was suddenly dragged away. Golden ink spilled, pages tore, fluttering free as Alexis tried to hold on, to see more, but the book slammed shut.

A woman's voice rang out. The Woman of the Water.

'By the blade of Darkness you will fall, wielded by the one you expect the least.'

Alexis woke gasping, Incantus at his side, pulling him into an embrace as traces of golden light withdrew from his mind.

'Alexis,' said Incantus, searching his face with his white-glowing hands. 'Are you okay?' He turned to Sapientis who had fallen backwards as though struck by a force from the heavens. 'What did you see? How do we destroy the darkness in him?'

Sapientis was staring at Alexis, his infinite star-speckled eyes drawing very still until they looked like black holes. 'You were wrong about the summer solstice,' Sapientis muttered, his voice coming out choked. 'The Prophecy of Light and Darkness is not over. It is still unravelling. But not through Mortem. Through him.'

34

PRETERIST

Preterist (n.) *Latin origin*
One whose chief interest is in the past; one who believes the prophecies of the apocalypse have already been fulfilled

Alexis lay still, the sky above him a blur.

I wonder if Mum knew that day would be her last day, he found himself thinking. Did she sense something in the air that morning? A subtle, almost inaudible frequency that she ignored? If she hadn't, could things have ended differently? Would she have changed anything in those last few hours if she had known?

Alexis wondered if she would have spent so long buying groceries for dinners she wouldn't eat. Would she have woken early to catch the sunrise that her father used to tell her had been painted for her by her mother? Would she have savoured her morning coffee or hugged her sons a little tighter or given her husband one more kiss before leaving and never returning?

Alexis realised that no one knew when their last day was, including whether this day was his. He didn't find himself savouring the beating of his heart or breath in his lungs, though. All he felt was the weight of how cruel it all was.

This is not a death sentence, whispered the *Shadow Man*, looming into his vision. *It is anything but.*

Alexis's voice was barely a whisper. 'How can that be?'

Incantus helped him to his feet, steadying him as he tried to grasp on to the images Sapientis had shown them. The amulet on Nero's body, Jackson shielding him from the intruder, his friends dying around him. And through it all the *Shadow Man* remained.

Darkness is our destiny, it said, turning its vacant face to Alexis's. It didn't sound harsh or taunting. If anything, it sounded pitiful. *Aren't you tired of holding on? The descent into darkness isn't so bad. At least you won't be alone when you fall. We will be together and we will rise with the shadows more powerful than ever.*

Incantus stepped between them, dispersing the entity for now.

'It can't be,' said Incantus, shaking his head indignantly. 'Why hasn't the Prophecy been fulfilled?' His voice grew agitated. 'The eclipse ... it won't align with the summer solstice or equinoxes for centuries. And the children ... they aren't children any more. Blaise is eighteen and Caeli will be too within a month.' He looked at Alexis, searching for support.

Sapientis remained staring at Alexis. 'You always took prophecies too literally, Incantus. One of the few flaws I failed to stamp out of you.'

It's because of me, Alexis thought. *It failed because of what I am.*

'I told you to show me what his future holds,' Incantus pressed, 'so we can stop it.'

Sapientis pulled up his hood against the wind. 'You know I cannot share what the future holds and disrupt the flow of

Aeveternity – not with you, not with anyone. There has been enough ... *disclosure* by the Women of the Elements when they imparted minor prophecies for the Children, some of which are unfolding as we speak. Besides, *this* future is not set. Not yet. What unfolds on this harrowing night, as the hour turns to the day of the equinox, will determine Alexis's fate and the fate of the darkness.'

There's a way to stop it. A way to prevent the vision of Alexis's friends dying at his hand. Yet how could it even be a possibility in the first place? What could his friends ever do to make him want to kill them?

Betray us. Hurt us, hissed the *Shadow Man*.

Alexis shook his head, unwilling to believe it.

What would the great Incantus Arcangelo think of us if he saw what you'll become? How quickly will he try and put us down, just as he did his own brother?

Alexis clenched his fists. As Incantus turned to leave, Alexis asked, 'If you both knew what Mortem would become, why didn't you just kill him?' His second question came out quieter: 'Why not kill me?'

Incantus's eyes weighed heavily upon him, filled with what Alexis was certain would be sadness if he dared to meet them.

'I am the warden and watcher of time, of Aeveternity, but I am not the divine,' Sapientis said simply. He inclined his head at Incantus and spoke slowly. 'I cannot rewrite it. It may be harsh, it may be cruel, but it may also be necessary. Those warned often ignore it. Their fate is their own burden to carry.'

Incantus's grip on Alexis's arm tightened. 'She didn't deserve what happened to her,' he said bitterly, making Alexis realise they were no longer talking about him. Great lashes of wind from the ocean whistled over the clifftop, ruffling Incantus's pale white hair. 'It destroyed her, and nearly me. And for what great purpose?'

Sapientis turned his back on Incantus.

Alexis's blood boiled. *How dare he?* If Sapientis was to insult him, he could take it. But Incantus? After what he had put him through and what he had allowed him to be submitted to? If someone had told Alexis that Demi's death was for the greater good, he would drown the world in retaliation. He dug his nails into his palms to stop himself from pitching Sapientis off the cliff.

Sapientis spoke again as he gazed skywards. 'Darkness is just an absence of light, and light glows brightest when surrounded by it. Without the shadows and the pain it brought you, you would not have become the Elemental you are today.'

'Maybe that isn't such a bad thing,' Incantus muttered. He released his hold on Alexis.

He had barely gone a few paces before Sapientis spoke again, his voice cutting through the wind. 'The blood of the angel and the blood of time runs through the veins of a boy.' Alexis detected rigidity in his mentor's shoulders. 'His conception initiated the first prophecy and his actions on the day of your death will dictate the last.'

Alexis glanced between Incantus and Sapientis, but neither made any move to turn and face each other. *Is this the Prophecy of the Passing Torch? Who was the boy?*

Sapientis continued, 'Only the light of his past can save him from the unspeakable evil of his future. He, the bear and the creator, will endure more loss than any of us and be all the stronger because of it. Strong enough to swim in the river of space and time, life and death.'

With nothing more than a nod to signal he had heard him, Incantus left.

Alexis lingered. Despite everything that had been revealed to him in the last few minutes about his past and his future, Alexis could only think of his mentor. 'Mortem imprinted Darcy Raphe,' he said, more a statement than a question. A few metres separated him from Sapientis, but Alexis felt as though the distance was much greater. 'When Incantus tried to remove the darkness from her, it killed her. You saw it coming and you did nothing. That's why he hates you, isn't it?'

Alexis watched Sapientis survey the beach below them and wondered whether he was seeing into its past, its present or its future.

Finally Sapientis replied, his voice holding no emotion. 'Yes ... and also no.' He made his way towards him, walking as though he had all the time in the world. 'I trained Ian before he became Incantus. He was all I had time for. I ignored my daughters for the herald of light, yet against my wishes, he passed all his training on to his brother. For that, for violating the first line of the Prophecy and for abandoning his brother alone with their father, Incantus blames himself.'

Sapientis's starry eyes settled on Alexis's amulet and he tutted. 'He should have seen it coming, really. Incantus was just as responsible for creating Mortem as everyone else in his life. Including you.'

Alexis didn't know what the final straw had been. The

indifference with which Sapientis spoke of Incantus's pain, the judgement in his eyes at his protégé's humanity or perhaps the disrespect he had shown him. Either way, Alexis snapped. He swung his first with his full weight and struck Sapientis in the face. The thwack echoed across the cliffs as the older man staggered back.

Alexis leaned in, staring at Sapientis now crumpled on the ground, and imitated his tut. He then asked innocently, 'Didn't you see that coming?'

35

DESIDERIUM

> Desiderium (n.) *Latin origin*
> An ardent longing for something lost; a profound
> yearning for someone or something that is unattainable

'You didn't need to do that for me,' Incantus said as Alexis joined him.

Alexis shook off the ache in his knuckles. 'I don't know how you put up with him for so many years.' He glanced back to the cliff but found it empty. 'Thousands of years old and he still doesn't know how to behave decently? What an arrogant, apathetic piece of sh—'

'I fear you've been spending too much time with Ms Doran,' Incantus cut in with a faint smile.

Alexis returned it, realising it was perhaps the first real one all day.

Incantus portalled them back to the Haven just as rain began to fall, the beach giving way to a glowing corridor near the Children of the Elements' bedrooms. Quiet, still.

'Did you want to talk about it?' Incantus asked.

'Do you?' Alexis countered.

'I asked you.'

Alexis leaned against a wall with a faded chalk drawing of the First Borns' sacrifice at Stonehenge, where rays of blue, red, grey and green shoot up into a black cloud above them. He'd once felt special looking at it. Now he just felt empty.

'You told me only you could kill Mortem because of the Curse of Raphe,' Alexis said. 'Whatever it is, perhaps I inherited it too from Daddy Darkness?'

Incantus made a face. 'Please don't ever call him that.'

'With Mortem gone that leaves me as "the darkness". I'm who needs to be put down ... by you.'

Incantus's arms dropped. 'We don't know that. There are a dozen ways to interpret it. You just heard how wrong I got it and how little attention I paid to the final line of the Prophecy.'

'*By oneself is how the other will be slain*,' Alexis whispered, goosebumps sweeping his arms. 'I thought it meant that I had to be the one that had to kill Mortem with the shadows, but now ...'

Something flickered in Incantus's eyes. His gaze dropped to Alexis's amulet.

The *Shadow Man* stirred. *Leave. We have to leave. He intends to kill us.*

Alexis didn't move, but the hallway felt like it was narrowing in on him.

He destroyed his brother. He'll destroy us too if we stay.

Incantus leaned closer. 'We'll figure this out. I promise. I won't let any harm come to you.'

He lies!

Alexis pressed his fingers to his thumbs and fought for calm. *Three things I can see ...* His split knuckles. Incantus's open palms. The illustration of the Elemental Gems

'I implore you to stay in the Haven tonight,' Incantus said. 'Sapientis said tonight is important. Be here when it turns Mabon. You'll be safe.'

There is no safety, spat the *Shadow Man*. *Not here. Who will protect your father and brother when the Shadowless come?*

Two things I can hear . . . Incantus's steady breathing. Distant chatter as the hive prepared for the Ball.

'It might be the perfect distraction for you, to be with your friends,' Incantus offered as if reading his mind. 'I have never seen you happier than with the three of them. Maybe the key to defeating the darkness isn't battle or ignorance but unity.'

One thing I can feel. The grounding press of his fingers to his thumbs.

The hallway opened up, allowing Alexis to breathe. 'It's worth trying,' he said eventually.

Incantus tousled his hair, smiling.

Alexis nodded and turned towards his bedroom.

'Alexis?' Incantus called softly. His eyes, now touched by age, were hesitant. 'Your mother. Did you wish to speak about her? There's something I've been meaning to tell—'

Alexis made a soft noise. *Not now.* Not if he intended to spend the night celebrating. His proxy was at home to guard his father and Jason. Tonight he had Demi. He had promised to be her date – if she still wanted him, that was. After avoiding her for so long, she deserved this. *He* deserved this. And if his mother were here, she would scold him for eternity if he let Demi down.

'Maybe another time,' Incantus said gently. 'I will see you soon. If this Fall Ball is to be anything like the ones Teller used to throw, it will be a night to remember.'

36

CINGULOMANIA

Cingulomania (n.) *Latin and Greek origin*
The strong desire to hold a person in your arms

Valentina rapped her knuckles against Caeli's bedroom door for the third time, promising herself that if Caeli didn't open it within the next three seconds, she'd break it down.

Two. Then she'd throw Caeli across the room.

One. Then—

The door opened. Caeli stood in the frame wearing a loose grey jumper and leggings, her hair in a messy bun.

'You call me here and then make me wait?' Valentina snapped.

Ignoring her tone, Caeli tugged her inside.

Caeli's bedroom was exactly as Valentina expected, aside from the missing ceiling – that was a nice touch. Teleportation lines exposed fractions of it to the sky, revealing burning shades of orange and pink clouds.

'Surprised you came,' Caeli said.

Books were strewn everywhere to the extent that Valentina wasn't even sure which one Caeli was currently reading. She kept her distance. Last time she tried to get close, Caeli's rejection had stung. 'Surprised you called.'

Why am I here? What was I hoping would happen?

Caeli's eyes were fixed on the ring of books surrounding her. She looked exhausted, her aura ... dim.

Valentina crossed her arms. 'You're not getting ready for the Ball? Big night dedicated to you? How could you miss it?'

'I want to finish prepping for Ziya's exams,' she replied. 'And I like to be fashionably late. You?'

The last time Valentina had been at a celebration like this, the night had ended in bloodshed. A lot of it. She still recalled the heavy thick scent of blood and burning that filled the air.

Valentina shrugged. 'Might go later. Not the biggest fan of balls.'

'I've realised,' Caeli murmured, raising an eyebrow.

Despite everything, Valentina laughed. In the daylight she could ignore many things, but tucked away in Caeli's room with nothing to distract her, Valentina couldn't ignore the way her heart rate quickened. Even knowing she was a Doran couldn't shake the way she made her feel. Valentina had always been a vessel for power, used by others, but with Caeli she felt in control. She felt like she had met her match, and the charged feeling she elicited was something she'd never felt before.

'How did you know?' Caeli asked quietly. 'That you liked girls?'

Valentina hesitated. 'I've always known. I wasn't allowed to explore it, but it was always there. In a way it's the truest part of me.'

Caeli nodded as if taking it in. 'I'm not sure who I am or

what I want. It's not just men or women, I think I'm attracted to both.'

Valentina was a woman of poise, of class, and yet standing before Caeli in her bedroom, knowing that she shouldn't be there, knowing that no one knew she was there, made her feel as though her composure was more of a vice than a virtue. It *bound* her. She had always taunted Caeli for her restraint, but perhaps that made her a hypocrite. So Valentina dared to ask the question she knew she shouldn't. 'And is the person you want Blaise?'

Caeli pulled the pencil from her bun and silver-blonde waves came tumbling down. 'I don't want to think about Blaise right now,' she said, stepping out of the circle of books. 'I don't want to think. I just want to test a theory.'

Valentina raised her hand to stop her, speaking aloud the growing concern that had festered since they'd first kissed. 'I'm not here just to be your experiment,' she told her sternly. 'You aren't going to just *use* me. I'm not a conquest or a fetish or a toy to be thrown aside or ignored or abandoned once you're done with me. I deserve many things, but I don't deserve that. I deserve to be considered properly.'

Doubt clouded Caeli's face as she stood still, as though working out an equation. 'You're right,' she said quietly. She released a deep sigh and met her gaze. 'I would never want you to feel used. You ... have awakened part of me that I'm tired of suppressing. I owe it to myself to interrogate my feelings, and it's with you that I want to do that, if you'd allow me to.'

Valentina should have stepped back, but her feet stayed rooted as Caeli slipped off her jumper. Each step forward silenced Valentina's thoughts.

'You are going to regret this later, Doran.'

Caeli looked at her with her grey eyes, the storm in them vacant, seemingly at ease. She wrapped her arms round Valentina's body and whispered, 'Make it something worth regretting.'

Fuck it.

Valentina kissed her. She kissed her and did not stop until their anger, their hatred for one another, combusted into something entirely else. Valentina had never felt more alive. Power surged through her, life returning to a soul she feared had hollowed out long ago.

And she realised that this feeling wasn't one she was willing to let go of again.

37

MARAHUYO

Marahuyo (v.) *Filipino origin*
To be enchanted

It wasn't often that Alexis thought he looked good, but the bespoke suit Parvati left outside his door was extraordinary. A three-piece suit of ocean hues that shifted like liquid silk from midnight blue to a shade of sapphire that matched his amulet. An echo of the ocean's tide.

For the first time in days he styled his hair before putting on the domino mask for the masquerade. It appeared as though Maria Sophia had drawn inspiration from his description of the Creature of the Water they'd battled for the final Gem on their quest. The mask was sleek and sinuous, crafted from lacquered, sharpened scales that glistened between sea blue and onyx. The loose curls of his dark hair fell over the spiralling twin horns that arched from the temples, dotted with dozens of tiny sapphires.

'I deserve to be happy, if only for one night,' he told his reflection before turning away to blink. Tonight he wouldn't be the harbinger of darkness or a grieving son. Tonight he would choose to be happy.

He called Dr Dash to cancel their session scheduled for the evening.

Doubt underlined Dr Dash's reply. 'I really think we should have our meeting.'

'We can reschedule for tomorrow, if that's okay?' He glanced over the book on his bedside table, scanning the pages that Ziya had set them for an upcoming exam. 'I'm sorry for cancelling so late. I'm just tied up with school stuff.'

'Alexis, I strongly advise against this. What if you relapse?'

Alexis shut the book harder than he had intended. He knew Dr Dash was coming from a place of concern, but it was impossible to explain that he need not worry because he was at the safest place here in the Haven, with his proxy at home.

'Thank you, but I've got to go,' Alexis replied. 'I'll see you whenever you next have availability. Thank you and sorry again.'

Alexis ended the call before Dr Dash could protest. Ziya had asked them all to be ready by eight and he didn't want to let her down.

He slammed the door in the *Shadow Man*'s face and padded down the steps to find Blaise.

'Wow.'

It was as if a living flame had been stitched into fabric. Layered robes of his agbada flowed over his muscular frame, woven with aso-oke threads of deep crimson and burnt ember. His phoenix-inspired eye mask arched over his brows and flared out with feathered wings of vermillion, burnt copper and sunburst yellow.

'I didn't think anyone would come close to looking as good

as me,' Blaise said, greeting him with a hug. 'You make a close second.'

'Keep talking like that and I'll be your date,' Alexis teased.

'You should be so lucky. The girls are getting ready in Dee's room. They'll come when they're finished, although it'll probably be the winter solstice by then.'

The two boys walked towards the hive, their strides in perfect sync. Classical music floated throughout the Haven, magically enhanced to reach every level and Sanctuary. It wasn't like anything Alexis had heard before. Instruments he didn't recognise played tunes that compelled his body to move.

But awe overwhelmed him and stole his breath when he reached the Haven's core. Hundreds of twinkling golden and silver stars floated around the lattice of interconnecting marble pathways, and silent fireworks exploded, showering them with autumn light. A sky of deep purple hung above them as the day rolled into night, cast by the projectors above. Vines of ivy and flowers of red and burnt umber adorned the huge spiral staircase, creating the illusion that they were at the heart of the universe.

As Alexis and Blaise walked down the steps, stunned speechless – a feat Alexis thought impossible when it came to Blaise – Alexis noticed that the training arena had become a glittering ballroom, surrounded by a ring of banquet tables that overflowed with platters of food and cases of drinks, perfuming the air with spiced cider and woodsmoke.

'Are those our Gems?' Blaise asked, his eyes darting to the white pillars that towered at the four corners of the ballroom.

The four Elemental Gems, retrieved from the corners of

the world, glowed brightly in the dim light, standing at their respective compass points. They flared brighter at Alexis and Blaise's arrival, signalling their presence to the crowd who swayed to the music of a Fae band. Dresses in shades of blue, red, silver and especially green swirled to face them. They bowed as if they were kings, and the boys bowed back.

Oliver Wrought approached in a suit of blazing orange-red, an homage to his student. 'I believe my late cousin took it upon himself to organise your autumn-equinox events,' he said, taking two drinks from a wandering training bot and offering it to them. 'No wonder he called me after every Mabon to brag.'

Alexis grinned at the thought of Teller Sagen waltzing around the ballroom, outdancing them all until he was the last man standing. 'Do you miss him?'

A sudden glaze filled Wrought's eyes behind his yellow mask. 'The thing about having almost-perfect memory is that it makes it difficult to forget just how much a person meant to you. Even if the Quinate was more of a family to him than his own, he will always be my older cousin, my first friend. I'm sorry if I remind you of him and I'm sorry I'm not nearly as fun as he was.'

'You have nothing to apologise for,' Alexis replied, softening. 'On behalf of Incantus, Blaise and all the Fighters of the Haven, thank you for being here.'

Wrought bowed and departed just as the Gems of Earth and Air sparked. Everyone turned to the top of the hive as two figures descended.

Time slowed. Not in a sudden thunderclap way, but as though a quiet hush had settled over the ballroom just for their arrival. Caeli carefully controlled their descent with a hand composed of wind itself, allowing every guest to take in their appearance in full. But it was Demi who Alexis couldn't look away from.

She looked *magnificent*.

The forest itself had spun her gown. The skirt shimmered from sage to russet, pine to muted gold, with a scattering of leaves stitched down her train. Her bodice was structured like bark as if broken from the Tree of Life itself, and layers of soft embossed velvet traced her curves like winding lianas. Her hair was pulled back in an elegant chignon, with a few soft tendrils framing her face like wayward ivy, laced with golden threads. Twined through her hair were small gilded leaves and tiny ochre stones that caught the light when her heels finally touched the ballroom floor with a click.

Her eyes, hidden behind a mask of ivory leaves and golden and umber threads, instantly locked on to Alexis's.

Applause erupted as Caeli leaped into Blaise's arms, her head tipped back with cries of joy as he swung her around. The sound was pure magic. Yet Alexis heard only his heartbeat. Neither he nor Demi had broken eye contact. It was just her. Just him. And the silent thunderous certainty that the world could end in that moment and he would not care.

Demi took a step closer and Alexis bowed low before her. Even with her heels, she still had to crane her head to look up at him when he rose.

'Am I still yours?' she asked softly.

Alexis released a shaky breath. Her emerald amulet and golden crucifix lay just above the neckline of her bodice, and behind it, against the tan skin of her chest, was the small scar from Sinner's arrow.

'Am I still your date?' she corrected herself.

Alexis took her hand and kissed it. Her skin erupted in goosebumps, every tiny bump like a confession.

'Yes, darling Demi,' he said, watching her eyes twinkle as she smiled, the very same smile that had made him fall helplessly, catastrophically, awfully in love with her. 'You are mine.'

38
RAISON D'ÊTRE

Raison d'être (n.) *French origin*
A reason for existing

The night unfolded more wondrously than Caeli Doran could have imagined. The Haven sparkled with vitality, gowns swirled and laughter bubbled like champagne, almost as intoxicating as the drinks Blaise kept sneaking them, insisting she kiss him for each one.

She did every time, hoping he wouldn't taste the bitterness of guilt on her lips.

'I've missed you,' she said, melting into his strong arms as they danced, the feel of his body so different to Valentina's.

Stop thinking about her, Caeli told herself.

Blaise's brows furrowed beneath his mask, which somehow made him look even more beautiful. 'I've been here the whole time,' he murmured, his calloused hands slipping to her lower back, his fingers tracing her skin.

Her gown was a masterpiece of motion. A single sleeveless layer of near-translucent silk and gauze shifted like mist when she moved. Her gloves, a similar silvery grey, twinkled with hundreds of tiny gemstones. The eccentric seamstress had pulled it off and crafted the dress of Caeli's dreams just hours before the Ball.

Caeli was reclaiming her body, her confidence, and she had no intention of hiding it.

'I guess I've just missed this then,' she replied, her gaze trained on Blaise and Blaise alone. 'Us. Having fun, being passionate, being held by you. I missed feeling wanted by you.'

She wondered if Blaise could feel the weight of the betrayal that sat in her stomach like lead. They hadn't decided they were back together since breaking up after the mission with the Renderers, but Caeli knew that if Blaise had kissed someone else during this time, she would've felt like she'd been cheated on. Part of her also felt like she had betrayed Valentina too, for kicking her out of her room so abruptly before their kiss led to anything further, only to leap into Blaise's arms hours later. If Valentina saw her now, what would she think?

Would she think I used her, just as she feared I would. Have I?

Caeli couldn't deny how good it had felt to hold Valentina, yet at the same time, neither could she deny how good it felt to be held by Blaise too.

Blaise went to run his fingers through her hair. Caeli sent a gust of wind to knock it away. It had taken her and Demi nearly an hour to perfect the waves cascading down her back, adorned with fine silver threads and tiny crystal droplets.

'I've always desired you, Cae,' said Blaise, kissing her. She sank into it, warmed by his body.

Their masks brushed, his like the Fire Phoenix, hers inspired by the gleaming grey scales of the Wind Dragon she'd fought in China, both with a small clear stone that sat just above the bridge of the nose like the Elemental Gems. She felt the Gem of the Air nearby, urging her to synchronise and become Omni with its limitless power, but Caeli had never felt more powerful than she was in this moment.

'Give it a few hours and then I'll show you just how much I desire you,' he said, voice dropping dangerously low, making her legs quiver.

Caeli took a deep breath and looked away to steel herself. Her gaze found Demi and Alexis. The sight of them together was just . . . right. Uncomplicated. Inevitable. 'Why does it look so easy for them, but it's so complicated for us?' Caeli asked Blaise, quietly voicing her frustration.

Blaise smiled softly, allowing her to see that it was something he'd noticed too. 'We're fire and storm, Cae. Might not be easy for us, but doesn't mean we shouldn't fight to make it work.' He pulled her closer and kissed the top of her cheek. 'What are they saying?'

'We should respect their privacy,' she protested weakly.

Caeli met Blaise's eyes and sighed. She lifted a finger, drawing the soundwaves towards them.

'I don't think I've ever seen you look so handsome,' Demi was saying, her drink pressed to her chest. 'I know you've wanted your space, but I've always been here, ready for whenever you are. Tonight we can stay for as long as you want to. Even if we just sit in silence.' She put her drink down and placed her hands against Alexis's arms. 'I go where you go.'

Caeli couldn't see Alexis's face, only the almost imperceptible rise and fall of his wide shoulders from behind. His voice came low and resonant. 'Do you know how often you consume my thoughts?' he asked, and even though the question wasn't posed to Caeli, she still felt her own heart skip a beat. 'The number of times you've saved me without knowing?'

'Alexis the poet,' Blaise murmured. 'Even I'm swooning.'

'He's a dark horse,' Caeli noted. 'Why can't *you* be more romantic?'

Blaise pulled her tighter, his muscles pressed against her body. A silent promise. Perhaps when Caeli had first seen him at the Ball, when she'd leaped into his arms, she had been overcompensating to mask her guilt. But that wasn't the case now.

'Point taken,' she said, her breath hitching.

'Let's stay and enjoy the Ball,' Alexis told Demi, drawing her onto the ballroom floor where the crowd parted for them. 'Then we can go back to the Lakes, where I can summon the courage to tell you what I've been holding on to for far too long.'

Caeli turned away just as Demi's throat bobbed and her eyes shifted in their direction. Blaise was less inconspicuous and was still gaping at them, even after Caeli stamped her high gemstone-encrusted heel on his foot.

The four Elementals drifted closer together, bound by invisible threads to the centre of the ballroom.

'This feels . . .' Blaise began.

'Normal,' Demi finished.

Caeli arched a brow. 'We're at a masquerade ball where everyone is dressed in our honour – what's normal about that?'

'Far too few enemies trying to kill us,' Alexis added, making them laugh.

Blaise whistled over a training bot and handed them each a new glass of a fizzing blue liquid. 'Cheers to us all making it.'

Caeli clinked her glass against her friends'. Tears threatened, but she swallowed them along with the sweet liquid. She didn't want to explain that she was happy, truly happy, and felt like herself again for the first time since losing her hand. Perhaps since losing her sister.

Conversations were soon lost in the music of the Fae. Ziya arrived in a stunning blue saree, monitoring the Ball through her Haven control disk. Demi urged Alexis to dance with her, insisting Ziya deserved to feel special. He only went once Demi promised that their dance would soon follow.

'You're a stronger woman than me,' Caeli admitted to Demi as they watched Alexis trying to entice a stiff red-faced Ziya to dance. 'I wouldn't want anyone dancing with my man, not even Ziya.'

Demi munched on a baguette, her other hand cupped beneath to stop any crumbs from falling onto her gown. She had pushed up her eye mask to pin back her loose curls. 'I don't mind waiting for him,' she said, her grin deepening when Alexis cheered on Ziya as she started freestyling. 'She went to all this trouble to make it the perfect night for everyone else: silent fireworks to not trigger anyone, dedicating time to congratulate the graduates from the summer. She deserves to dance with someone who cares about her.'

'There you are,' came a voice from behind them.

Blood drained from Caeli's face in an instant.

Valentina wore a crimson dress that clung to her like a threat wrapped in silk. *Blaise's colour, how ironic*, Caeli thought. Valentina accepted a hug and a shower of compliments from Demi, but her eyes never left Caeli.

'I assumed you weren't coming,' Caeli said, pulling a *mildly* disgruntled face. She didn't want to crease her make-up.

'Excuse me while I go say hello to Kefi,' said Demi, making her way to embrace the Leader of the Healers who had dressed in a beautiful floral gown the colour of spring. Alexis soon joined them and spoke shyly with Kefi as though apologising for something while Demi parted to speak with a member of the Fae band.

'Are you here with *him*?' Valentina asked, eyes scanning the crowd for Blaise. 'Was the kiss that bad? You seemed to enjoy it at the time.'

Caeli scowled again. 'Don't,' she hissed. 'I-I shouldn't have kicked you out so suddenly earlier, that wasn't fair. I *am* here with Blaise though,' she confessed, feeling a twinge of guilt in her chest when Valentina's eyes dipped.

'I told you not to use me, Doran,' Valentina snarled, her anger failing to mask her hurt.

'I didn't,' Caeli protested, shuffling her away from a nearby dancing couple. 'I'm not.' *I'm not.* 'But I care about him too. I care about you both. I feel so conflicted right now and I'm just trying to allow myself to *feel* and figure it out. I don't want to hurt either of you in that process.'

Valentina tilted her head away from her, blinking tears from her eyes, far too proud to let them fall. 'Looks like you may end up hurting us both while you "figure it out".'

The music of the Fae band suddenly stopped.

'This comes at the request of your Daughter of the Earth,' said a devilishly handsome Fae with huge black wings and eyes the shade of cosmic purple. 'No other requests will be taken, so don't get any ideas.'

A joyful beat rung out from a long-necked lute. Demi squealed when Kallisto dashed to her side, dragging Parvati with her as the crowd began to move in time with the strings.

Kallisto's dark brown dress swept the floor and Parvati's pale blue saree shimmered. Caeli watched with glee as Kallisto linked hands with Demi and the two sisters began dancing, moving in an anticlockwise circle. Demi led the dance, holding up the end of her skirt as she kicked off her heels, shouting something in Greek. It was the same music she'd played earlier when she and Caeli were getting ready.

Parvati watched the sequence of steps and soon took Kallisto's hand, effortlessly joining in, making both sisters cheer. More and more people began to join in, expanding the circle until it took over the whole ballroom floor. Blaise and Alexis dragged Ziya in and sandwiched her between them, cackling as she tripped out of rhythm, relying on them to hold her up.

'What do you want, Caeli?' Valentina asked, her arms crossed over her chest.

Instead of answering, Caeli allowed herself to be whisked away. She slotted into the gap between the Nikolas sisters.

Caeli shook her head to unburden her mind, knowing the answer to Valentina's question couldn't be answered in one night. So she studied the dance instead, focusing her attention on just following the footsteps for now.

'You're a natural!' Kallisto cried as Caeli kept pace as the song sped up. 'It took me years to learn the Kalamatianós.'

'Thank you! Does the dance have a meaning?' Caeli asked.

Demi had a light hold just above the end of Caeli's right arm.

She replied a little breathlessly, 'Greeks dance it at celebrations. It means connection. Joy. Spirit.'

A blaring cheer went up as one last person completed the circle, connecting Althea Orenda with Demi's other side.

Incantus was the only person wearing white – a pale suit, open linen shirt and a mask shaped like angel wings edged in gold and silver and midnight blue.

'Why do I kind of fancy him?' Caeli asked.

Kallisto giggled, squeezing her side tightly. Caeli melted into her touch, reminded of her own sister, who she rarely allowed herself to reminisce about. This time, though, Caeli smiled as she thought of Celina, and wished she could have danced with her too.

The music swelled. Incantus and Demi raised their hands, spinning the circle of dancing Elementals faster. Gibbous had somehow found himself in the middle and barked excitedly, tossing himself in the air to catch the glittering starlight.

Joy spread like fire. Caeli felt it humming beneath her skin, wrapping like a ribbon round every Elemental on the ballroom floor of crushed leaves. Even time seemed content to linger, stretching out the moments before the autumn equinox. This was her family, she realised. Hers and Blaise's.

And so Caeli danced. She laughed.

And fell in love with life all over again.

39

THU'O'NG

Thu'o'ong (v.) *Vietnamese origin*
To love tenderly; to cherish; a deep and sincere notion of fondness and care between family members, friends, or lovers

Alexis's cheeks ached from smiling and his shirt was undone at the collar, his waistcoat and jacket lost to the night after spending the last hour conjuring ice cubes for overheated guests.

The Fae band had played a blend of music drawn from cultures around the world. Levantine dabke followed by Punjabi bhangra, Yoruba bata and Afro-Brazilian samba. Throughout it all, the magical music of the Fae was weaved through, turning the night into one continuous dance.

'It's a video!' said Parvati, ushering Ziya and Valentina over to Alexis and his friends as she pointed a camera at them. Both the elder girls politely declined, but Demi pulled them in, ignoring their protests.

Kallisto also held a camera in her hands beside Parvati. 'Smile!'

A white flash lit up the six of them together.

'Don't touch me,' Caeli muttered through gritted teeth, and Valentina recoiled before silently slipping away into the crowds. Alexis glanced at her, but Caeli was already back in Blaise's drunken embrace, blowing lightly at the side of his sweat-slick neck.

The orchestra stilled as Incantus appeared on the stage. Cheers erupted as he praised Ziya for the Ball. Alexis snatched her Haven command disk so she could soak in the applause, and he and his friends cheered loudly enough that he was certain even those in the Healing and Elder Sanctuary would hear them.

'Tonight is more significant than ever,' Incantus boomed. 'Not only to celebrate new beginnings, but also to honour those who gave their lives to keep the world alight. May we never forget their sacrifice.' He snapped his fingers and dozens of projections shimmered to life, producing portraits that hung in the purple sky.

It took Alexis a moment to realise that the portraits were of the fallen heroes who had died in the long war against Mortem.

Between Ziya and Parvati, an old portrait of Serena Aevum appeared. She looked younger, her fiery hair thicker and face thinner but still wide with joy, not too dissimilar to how Sapientis had looked. Beside her was a bald young Akili Pearce and an undeniably handsome Teller Sagen. They stood side by side, Akili's expression one of mild irritation and Teller's split with a smirk as though taking enjoyment from annoying the muscular monk. Wrought grinned at his cousin and raised a glass to him.

A projection of Joe Coin danced around Althea Orenda who laughed as though he was still there, and slightly off to the side Blaise comforted Caeli as she waved at his smiling face.

One face caught Alexis's eye more than the others, however, the one closest to Incantus. A beautiful woman with dark hair, eyes like melted chocolate, and a smile that for some reason made Alexis's breath hitch in his throat. Darcy Raphe.

She looked familiar. He couldn't remember where he'd seen her before but he understood the way Incantus looked up at her. It was how Alexis's father stared at the empty space beside him on his bed, whispering to the ghost of his wife as if she was still there to tell him she loved him more.

Behind the orchestra, the stone archway began to glow. Recalibrated by Incantus, the portal burst open with white light. Raeve's projection beckoned a figure and Taranis emerged from the archway, followed by hundreds of Sanctuario Elementals.

The Haven erupted into cheers and reunited with the warriors they had fought alongside on the fields of Stonehenge with tears and laughter. Alexis watched as Incantus reluctantly turned away from the projection of four fifths of the fallen Quinate, and embraced Taranis who had been gazing at the hologram of Raeve, grinning as she used the hilt of her sword to flick her hair from her face.

Taranis soon bound over to Ziya and the Children of the Elements, full of energy, cured of Mortem's imprinting, which had held him hostage over the summer. He was dressed in Caeli's colours, a suit of storm-cloud grey and a mask lined with lightning bolts.

He stayed with them a while to catch up and hear how their training was going, before getting drawn into a conversation with Valentina and Ziya about his new project on inter-dimensional teleportation. Soon enough, the three of them were speaking in a technical language that Alexis in his tipsy state failed to follow. It was then, when everyone was busy eating and dancing, that Incantus approached him.

'Go and get the others,' he said, a glint in his eye.

Alexis frowned. 'What have you got planned?'

Incantus raised his mask of angel wings. 'I haven't spent nearly as much time with you lately as I would have hoped. With all of you. It was the five of us in the end who destroyed Mortem. Even if the smallest of shadows remains within you, Mr Michaels, I dare it to show its face when we're all together. Perhaps this will be what purges the last of his powers.'

Alexis nodded, realising that it must have been lonely for his mentor tonight, surrounded by the future he helped build but without the people from his past.

'Where are we going?' he asked.

'The Lake.'

He found Caeli first, dancing with Safina and Kyra from their Scholar class, then Blaise who had been in a drinking contest with Antony Adamson and Violet Champion.

'What did Incantus say?' Demi asked, rosy-cheeked and breathless from dancing with Kallisto.

'He wants to go somewhere. Just us. I'll bring her back,' he called to Kallisto, who pinkie-promised Demi not to tell their parents how late she was still up.

Blaise led the group towards the archway, scooping Caeli into his arms as she was celebrating with the couple from the Sanctuario that she had saved on the battlefield, and followed Incantus through the portal.

The setting sun cast golden and peach-coloured splashes of paint into the darkening sky. The cool mountainous air bit, providing Alexis the perfect excuse to pull Demi into his side.

'I can see the rowing boat,' she murmured into his chest, tucking strands of hair behind her ear after it had come loose from dancing. Alexis followed her line of sight past the lanterns towards the edge of the forest where the small boat was docked.

'I've not been here yet,' Caeli said, trying to sound casual after glancing at Alexis and Demi. She waved her arms before Incantus and Blaise. 'Shall we?'

Alexis caught her wink, telling him everything he needed to know. This part of the night belonged to him and Demi.

As Caeli and Blaise edged closer to the lake, Incantus scooped them both under his arms, carrying them down the wooden pier. They kicked and shouted, but not once did they use their powers to escape his hold.

'I'm not against hitting an old man!' Blaise yelled.

'Drop us, you fossil!' Caeli howled, laughing.

Incantus paused, effortlessly holding them suspended above the surface of the glistening lake. 'Did you plan on going back to the Ball?'

Alexis was waiting for Caeli to spin out of his arms and soar away, determined not to let her hair and make-up be ruined. It took him by complete surprise when he saw her face split into the widest of smiles. 'Fine! Let's do this.'

'What?' Blaise demanded, craning his head to her. He must have seen the twinkle in her eyes, for he reluctantly shook his head and laughed. 'Drop us before you get a hernia.'

Incantus leaped off the pier with them both still in his arms, crashing into the lake with a great splash. Rings of waves undulated around them, and they resurfaced gasping from the cold.

Blaise heated the water as he beckoned Alexis and Demi over.

'I really hope you're not weeing,' Caeli mumbled.

Demi had already kicked off her shoes, but Alexis caught her before she could jump in.

She turned, puzzled. 'Come on, we have to join them.'

'We will,' he said, taking her hand in his. 'But first I think I owe you a dance.'

Alexis led her to the grass and trees. Once in contact with her element, not a foot away from the water's edge, he pulled her against him, and the sound of his friends laughing and splashing each other faded into the night.

'I think this has been long overdue,' he said, as they began to move slowly together as partners.

Demi's hands pressed against his back, holding him close. 'For how long?'

'Since forever,' he answered. Alexis realised that his eyes had been closed. Despite the stammering of his heart, the quickening of his pulse, his mind was at ease, at peace, and for the first time in a long time, he looked forward to tomorrow if it meant waking up to do this all again. 'You've always made sure that no one feels left out. I realised very early on that I needed you in my life. That I owed every ounce of happiness to you.'

Demi pulled back to search his face. 'Why me?'

Why you? There isn't anyone but you, my love.

The air between them felt charged as Alexis's gaze devoured her. 'You walk like the ground will never fail you, silently confident in yourself and in what you stand for. You don't need anyone to give you value, it radiates from here.' He placed a hand over her heart where he could feel it racing. 'I wanted to be perfect for you. Even if I never will be, I'll try for you, my darling Demi.'

Demi's smile softened. 'You don't get it.' She shook her head slightly, her golden earrings swaying. 'You don't see yourself the way the world sees you, Lexi. You think you're undeserving of anything good.'

Alexis dragged his tongue over his lower lip, fighting to hide the impact that her words had on him. This, *her*, was what was healing him. He knew that love and kindness alone couldn't overcome his struggles with his psychosis, but for his insecurities, his indifference for life, Demi was his healer.

'I see you when you look at the sky when it's bright blue without clouds,' she said. 'I see you when you're waiting for Blaise or Jason to laugh at a joke only they would find funny. When Reina comes to you with her tail wagging or when you're telling me about your books. Your face lights up and I swear I can feel the world stop turning.'

Alexis felt his chest tighten as he pressed a kiss to her forehead, watching the water of the lake glisten behind her. A rush of emotion surged to his face, pricking his eyes.

Happiness. Relief. Passion. Gratitude. *Hope*.

The things the *Shadow Man* tried to steal, Demi had gifted back. He wondered how was it possible for his heart to be so full and not explode.

'You're not loved because you're perfect, Lexi,' she whispered, leaning in closer until they were almost sharing breaths, her exhale his inhale. 'You're loved because you're *you*. Besides, I've always thought you were perfect.'

Alexis tilted her chin upwards, as she held her breath, waiting. 'Believe me,' he said, repeating what he had once said a lifetime ago, back when they had promised to each other to wait until the time was right. He couldn't wait any longer. Sometimes people got hit by cars or they lost their minds to darkness, and Alexis couldn't risk that happening before he kissed her once more. 'The perfect part of me is you.'

With that, Alexis leaned forward and kissed her, and for a brief shining moment the seas settled and the Earth stopped turning.

40

CALIGO

Caligo (n.) *Latin origin*
Darkness, fog, mist, vapour, gloom;
inability to perceive mentally

Once all five Elementals had emerged from the lake, they huddled round a bonfire Demi and Blaise had conjured, drying their gowns and suits. Dozens of lit lanterns surrounded them in rings, extinguishing the shadows that should've formed at the bonfire's light, making it feel to Alexis that within the glowing rings, time was suspended.

Is this what I've been missing out on? he thought, feeling like even the colours he saw were more vibrant since emerging from the lake laughing with his friends. For so long the world around him had seemed muted, like he was living an extension of his nightmare. Now it brimmed with energy, especially with Demi in his arms as the fire warmed their faces.

Incantus had removed his shirt and lay stretched back to admire the evening sky. Despite his age and mortality, his body remained chiselled and strong, drawing teasing whistles from Blaise as he covered Caeli's eyes.

Incantus waved his hand dismissively. 'I have just realised

that I am fifth-wheeling,' he declared. 'Forgive an old man for seeking your company. Being with you all reminds me of how it felt to be with the Quinate.'

As he turned, Alexis caught a glimpse of faint white scars along his sides in the flickering yellow light. 'Are those scars?' he asked, surprised someone with his power could bear such marks.

Incantus nodded, turning to reveal a messy lattice of pale marks across his back; barely an inch of skin was free from injury.

'Incantus, who did that to you?' Demi demanded, noting how they had faded with time.

'A whole bunch of people,' he said casually, facing them again. 'Many come from my brother, but most are actually courtesy of my father.'

'Why would he do that?'

'If you asked him, my father wouldn't say that he was an evil man.' His eyes glanced over his students, focusing on Alexis for a moment.

It wasn't until Alexis felt Demi squeeze his hand that he realised that the man they were talking about was his biological grandfather.

'He believed he was doing the angels' work, cutting me open to see if I had the wings of the Arcangelos.' Incantus turned his shirt over to dry the back. 'Worst of all was his power: to proxy himself an unlimited number of times. It often meant that there was more than one of him doing it at a time. After his death, Nero and I used his blood to share his powers with the rest of our people, but made it so that they could only conjure one proxy that couldn't resist being called back to ensure it didn't share the Elemental's power.'

Nearby, at the base of the hill behind them, the Haven's portal shimmered. Alexis was sure he could still hear the music from the Fae band drifting through it. 'Did Mortem also ... suffer?' he asked, although he wasn't exactly sure why. Would Alexis still blame him for turning to the darkness? He thought he would find it hard to imagine his father as some kind of tortured animal, learning to lash out whenever threatened, and not as the all-powerful Elemental that commanded Shadowless armies. Yet surprisingly, the image came with ease.

Incantus's eyes softened. 'Worse than me, especially after I left to begin my training with Sapientis. "*Water has no shadow*," my father would say, fearing whatever darkness could be hiding within Nero. He did everything he could to try and tear it out.' He stared into the flames blankly. 'Nero suffered more than I ever did.'

Alexis thought of the scar that ran from Mortem's jawline down his neck. Had that been from his own father? Had his back looked worse than Incantus's?

Blaise stirred. 'Where was your mum through all this? How could she have let this happen?'

Alexis detected the weight to his question, the accusation. Neglect. It was a kind of abuse Blaise too had experienced. Caeli stroked her hand across his shoulders softly.

'She died giving birth to Nero,' Incantus answered. 'She was a troubled woman for most of her life, however, never much of a mother to me. She could create illusions, blur reality. Sometimes she lost herself in them. The Maya force is named after her, in fact, due to her contribution to its construction in keeping our Elemental world masked from mortals.' A hint of a smile broke through his stony expression. 'She called me "little lux" and even before his birth, called Nero "little nox". I wonder if she truly knew what was happening.'

Demi leaned into Alexis and whispered, 'You okay?'

Alexis nodded faintly, but the stories left him reeling. He had spent his life not knowing where he came from, raised with love by the Michaelses but haunted by a past written into his DNA. Listening to Incantus, he couldn't help but wonder whether this was the origin of his psychosis too. He shuffled closer to Blaise, pulling Demi with him, craving the comfort of their presence.

Incantus offered them a smile. 'If there's one thing I have learned in my many years, it's that the family we share blood with is one thing – a gift for some and a burden for others – but it's the family that we *find*, the family we *choose*, who love us most truly.'

The portal flickered behind them. Ziya burst through, paused to scan the dark lakeside until she located them, then tore in their direction, barely bothering to sidestep the burning lanterns surrounding them.

Incantus was instantly on his feet, detecting her panic. 'What is it?'

'The High Order just called,' she panted, her round face glistening with sweat as her saree pooled on the ground at her feet. 'There's been a sighting of Renderers.'

'What else?' After years of teaching and guiding her, becoming more of a father to her than her own, Incantus knew her well.

She swept her saree back over her shoulder, revealing the golden Aevum brooch that Serena had left for her, an 'A' encircled within a clockface made from wings with twelve indentations. She cleared her throat, but it wasn't enough to shake the waver in her voice. 'Every Aevum woman has been murdered by Shadowless under Vultress's orders.'

Alexis shot upright, cold horror surging through him. He remembered Serena's sisters from the funeral – distant and pompous maybe, but powerful beyond measure. *How can this be?*

'Ziya, are you okay?' Demi asked reflexively.

'Are they coming for you and Parvati next?' Alexis followed up. He knew the Haven was impenetrable, but that didn't ease his anxieties.

'How is that even possible?' Caeli asked, looking between Ziya and Incantus.

Alexis felt Incantus's gaze settle on him. Sapientis had mentioned that the next great prophecy concerned the son of time and the angels. Whoever and whatever it was, perhaps Vultress was working to prevent such a fate from unravelling.

'Is Vultress *that* dangerous?' Blaise asked doubtfully.

'She's an extremely powerful dark witch who practises demonic magic and can transfer any injury she sustains to the person she's looking at,' Incantus answered quickly, pulling on his shirt and hastily doing up the buttons. "So yes, she is."

'Taranis is already in the lab setting up a portal to go with you to where the Renderers have been spotted, and presumably where she is too,' Ziya told him. She then let out a shaky breath. 'I'm sorry, Incantus, but Secretary-General Kleine ... he had something else to say.'

She shuffled on her feet uneasily, her gaze moving past Incantus to rest upon Alexis's arm wrapped round Demi's side. She stared at it for a moment before Incantus cleared his throat, bringing her attention back. 'Kleine and some of the other high councillors want to investigate you. They're questioning your judgement for appointing me as a Leader and for trusting Taranis to run the Sanctuario so soon after he was imprinted.' Ziya wiped a tear of frustration from her eyes, smearing her mascara. 'They're sending their own operatives to the Renderer disturbance, and have asked you to open a portal to the High Order so they can bring you in for questioning.'

Blaise scoffed. 'That's insane!'

Incantus's disappointment was quiet, heavy. 'And if I don't comply?'

Ziya rubbed at her chest and spoke to the ground, reciting what she must have heard. '*Then he'll be arrested on suspicion of murder, obstruction of justice and conspiracy to aid the Shadowless to overthrow the High Order.*'

Anger bubbled in Alexis's chest. 'How dare they!'

'Fools!' Demi spat, gathering her hair into a hasty ponytail. 'If you have to stay here, let us go instead. We'll take down the Renderers.'

Blaise and Caeli echoed her, offering to join Taranis or Wrought, whoever they sent.

Incantus's voice was firm. 'No.'

'What?' Caeli challenged. 'We can use our Gems, become Omni—'

'I said, no. There's a reason she's picked tonight. All forms of dark magic are stronger on the eve of Mabon, strong enough to break even the most intricate wards and protective enchantments. You've been drinking, you have no idea what we could be walking into, and I can't risk the High Order doubting you too. I'll be fine. Stay in the Haven until tomorrow. No questions. Promise me.'

Alexis met Incantus's gaze, reading what he didn't want to say aloud. His friends' presence here was keeping the darkness within him at bay. Alexis being in harm's way might tilt the dial the wrong away. 'We will,' he promised with a nod.

'What about Kleine's threat to arrest you?' Blaise asked.

Incantus's eyes glistened with defiance. 'He's deluded if he thinks his authority has ever extended to the Haven or to me. If he intends to summon me, tell him to wait until after I win another battle he's too afraid to fight in himself.'

Incantus took Ziya's hand and light-jumped away, leaving the four friends standing in stunned silence.

'I want to be him when I grow up,' Caeli proclaimed, huffing out a breath of air. She then sat back down near the bonfire, reaching her arms out to its warmth.

'Incantus said to go back to the Haven,' said Demi, gathering up the damp skirt of her gown.

'Looking like this?' Caeli gestured to her ruined hair and make-up. 'We can wait until the Ball dies down a bit. Why do you think he wants us in the Haven tomorrow, anyway?' The question, while asked to them all, was accompanied by a look to her fellow Scholar.

'I don't know,' Alexis said quickly. In Incantus's absence, unease had crept in. It was as if the whole lakeside had become darker, the wind sharper, the fire colder.

'When the Sanctuario need to return through the portal, Zee will come and get us,' Blaise said, forcing a smile as he fed the fire, but Alexis saw the fear behind it. Blaise wanted the night to stretch just a little longer, and Alexis didn't want to take that away from him just because he thought the shadows of the forest were shifting.

Demi linked her arm through Alexis's. 'Incantus will be fine,' she said, her faith absolute.

Alexis willed himself to believe her. But what he didn't realise was that the strange chill, the whisper of paranoia that rose inside him, wasn't entirely his own.

The *Shadow Man* was back, and it was standing right behind him, a silent reminder that even the most beautiful sunsets faded to darkness.

41

UHKAAVA

Uhkaava (adj.) *Finnish origin*
Threatening; ominous; an intention to harm

Valentina stood alone in a shadowed corner of the ballroom, her frosty stare enough to scatter any slow-dancing couples who drifted too close. Though the Ball was undoubtedly one of the better events she'd attended, large crowds still unsettled her, especially when parted from her Jian swords.

Solitude had once comforted her as a child, a shield from judgement and whispers about her disgraced lineage. But tonight Valentina only felt the absence of what had been hers mere hours before: the press of Caeli's body, the heat, the way her fingers had stroked her skin like wind on water. Now all that remained was the lingering scent of her hair and a hollow ache in her chest.

A voice hauled Valentina from her memories.

'Tina!' Parvati skipped over with Kallisto in tow, a camera swinging from her neck. 'Have you seen Zi?'

Valentina, unsure when she'd consented to the younger girl nicknaming her like Ziya did, kept her voice low. 'She got a call from the High Order. Went to get Incantus. I'm pretty sure they just light-jumped to the laboratory.'

Parvati didn't seem nearly as interested in the message as Ziya had been. 'She said to give her back the cameras when they run out of space. Kallisto's is full and I've taken loads of videos all night. When will she be back?'

'I'm not sure.'

Valentina liked Parvati as much as she could like any twelve-year-old. She reminded her of herself when she was younger: bold, confident, talented, a great Fighter in the making to complement her sister the Scholar.

'We don't mind waiting with you,' Kallisto offered, clearly assuming she was lonely. She wasn't wrong, but she was mistaken if she thought Valentina minded. Fewer attachments meant fewer wounds when they inevitably left.

Stupid girl, Valentina said to herself. *How could you let yourself fall for her? How could you let yourself be used by her?*

And then, quieter: *why am I not enough for her?*

Valentina steeled herself, blinking back tears. She reached for the cameras. 'I'll take them. You enjoy your night before the Leaders catch on and send you to bed.'

Parvati and Kallisto handed them over without objection and parted, while Valentina ventured off to get another drink.

The ballroom was thinning, guests slipping away to more private delights. Valentina conjured a small portal beneath the wine glass of a pretty witch she had seen Caeli dancing with earlier and poured the drink into her own. She wandered away before the witch noticed.

Sipping, Valentina scrolled through dozens of oddly angled photographs Kallisto had taken. She paused at the photo of the six Elementals: Ziya beaming beside Demi, Caeli mid-eyeroll as Blaise and Alexis pulled faces behind her. Valentina barely recognised herself. Her once waist-long hair was now cropped to her shoulders, far more practical for battle, which her old teachers had never allowed.

There was something undeniably warm about the picture. Genuine joy. Connection. A friendship she'd never known. She turned to the videos Parvati had taken. One began with Demi dragging her and Ziya into frame, laughing as light flashed from Kallisto's camera.

Wait–

The glass slipped from Valentina's hand as she gasped.

By the time it shattered, Valentina was sprinting across the Haven, adrenaline coursing through her in thick, thunderous waves. Panic screamed for her to portal, to flee, somewhere far away, but she couldn't. Not while her friends – because that's what they were – and everyone else in the Haven, were at risk.

Because in that moment, caught on video when the camera flashed, there had been six people in the frame.

But only two had shadows.

And the eyes and amulets of the others, for just a fraction of a second, had glinted black back at her – as if the darkness was wickedly greeting Valentina again.

42

NIGHTED

Nighted (adj.) *Old English origin*
Overtaken by night or darkness; blinded by the night

Blaise stabbed at the bonfire, sending sparks into the night. 'I can't believe the High Order are investigating Incantus.'

'It's ridiculous,' Alexis muttered.

'It's not really,' said Caeli. All eyes turned on her. 'Not like that! Just think logically. His brother tried imprinting the entire Elemental population, took down the Haven's Leaders, then, soon after, Incantus makes Taranis – who killed hundreds under Mortem's influence – head of the Sanctuario. How can we or anyone know the darkness is truly gone in Taranis? That Incantus removed it all? That the shadows died with Mortem, whose body – let's remember – was never actually recovered?'

'Because it's Incantus,' Demi answered, as if his name was explanation enough. 'We saw Mortem explode into shadow. The High Order's character assassination stems from jealousy and guilt, not evidence.'

Caeli shrugged. 'Still, it could look suspicious, especially with this Vultress woman being Raeve's cousin.'

'That's only because you have a tendency to look for the worst in people,' Blaise muttered.

Caeli removed herself from his embrace, her eyebrows pulling together in a frown. 'What's that supposed to mean?'

Alexis interjected. 'Incantus will be fine. Caeli's just being—'

'Oh, you don't need to explain how I'm being,' said Caeli, raising her hand to silence him. 'Care to elaborate?'

'Forget I said anything,' Blaise said quickly.

'Just because I can engage in critical thinking, doesn't make me a bad person.'

'I never said it did.'

'You didn't have to. It was implied. See, there's that critical thinking again.'

'Let's not ruin tonight,' Demi pleaded, but Blaise's face remained hard, the reflection of the fire dancing in his tired amber eyes.

'Sorry you feel that way,' he offered weakly.

Caeli shook her head. 'Apologise for what you said, not how I interpreted it.'

Blaise looked at Alexis and said, 'It does my head in how she obsesses over the smallest things and thinks she's so much smarter than me. Sorry I'm not perfect like you, Cae.'

'I'm *far* from perfect,' Caeli snapped, rising, her damp dress hanging limply off her body. A gust of air swept from her, extinguishing some of the nearby lanterns, making the area darken. 'But at least I'm big enough to mean what I say.'

Blaise's jaw tightened, Caeli's jibe having struck a nerve. 'Wrought said the most important thing about being a Fighter is knowing when to pick your battles. Maybe you'd know that if you ever asked how I was.' He shrugged Alexis's hand off his shoulder. 'I'm not going to waste any more of my night with you if you're going to be like this.'

Blaise stormed towards the teleportation archway, knocking aside lanterns and extinguishing their light. Before he reached it, the portal shimmered and Valentina emerged from it, wind whipping her hair and dress as she hurried towards them, camera in one hand, the other clenched at her side. For a moment, Alexis wondered if she was going to strike Blaise, but instead she stopped a few feet before him, just beyond the outermost ring of lanterns.

'You need to come with me,' she ordered, her eyes darting over all four of them. Her long shadow, cast by the light of the fire, stretched out behind her, as her chest heaved and fell with every anxious breath.

'He's not going anywhere with you,' Caeli snapped, flying over to step in front of Blaise.

'You all need to come,' Valentina said, holding up the camera.

'What is it?' Demi asked, joining them with Alexis in arm, barefoot.

Valentina shook her head, her mouth pressed into a serious line. Her eyes flicked towards Alexis in a silent plea, palpable fear within them. It was exactly how she had looked the first time they met her, when darkness had been pulling at the cords of her mind. 'Not here. Just come.' She reached out for Caeli, who recoiled.

'Don't touch me.'

Valentina's nostrils flared. 'It's not about earlier, for the *First*

Born's sake. If you want to pretend the kiss didn't happen, fine. Choose him. Just co—'

'What?'

Caeli spun to Blaise, whose face had drained. 'You did what?' he asked, his voice eerily calm.

'I-I,' Caeli stuttered. 'We – I never ... It wasn't –'

Blaise's gaze slid over hers to Valentina. 'Don't lie to me, Caeli.'

Caeli's eyes dipped and Blaise's chest fell.

'I'm sorry, Blaise,' Valentina said softly, tipping her head towards him. Her eyes then landed on Alexis and Demi, knowing her best chances were now with them. 'Please just trust me and come back to the Haven. You've been—'

A torrent of air rocketed into Valentina, silencing her midsentence. She was catapulted away, disappearing from sight before she could utter another word. The camera struck the ground where she had been standing, cracking as its screen blinked out as the last of the lanterns' were blown out, leaving only the bonfire to illuminate the area.

'Cae!' Demi shouted.

But Caeli had already turned her attention to Blaise, her eyes welling as she tried to get him to look at her. She sucked in a gasp. 'Blaise, babe, listen, it was a mistake. It was just once. Well ... and the night of the mission.'

Blaise made a small noise.

'We'd just broken up!' Caeli continued. 'I saw her and we started arguing and I got in her face then ... I don't know what happened; she just kissed me.' Her voice cracked. 'You have to understand. I thought you were leaving me for her.'

'What's your excuse tonight then?' Blaise asked lightly, humourless.

'We never agreed we were back together!'

Blaise scoffed. 'And yet we spent the whole night together. Was your time with her before or after I held you and you kissed me and told me you missed *me*?'

'It was a mistake! I was just so scared of losing you that part of me thought it would be easier to sabotage it myself.' Tears streaked Caeli's face and she didn't attempt to wipe them away. 'I didn't mean for either of you to get hurt. I don't know what I'm doing. It's like I'm wandering around in the dark, trying to find the answer to how I'm supposed to be feeling.' She reached out for him, but his hand burned bright, forcing her back.

'You're only sorry that it got out,' Blaise said coldly. 'I—' His voice broke and he tore his gaze from her, settling instead on the darkness of the forest. 'I can't even look at you.'

Demi moved from Alexis's side to go over to Caeli, letting her rest her head against her shoulder. With her other hand Demi tried to reach out to Blaise, but he pulled away.

'Don't.'

The bonfire was spitting behind Alexis, ash and fumes billowing out as though it was burning something toxic, something dangerous. He squeezed Caeli's shoulder, then moved past her, stooping to pick up the camera Valentina had dropped. He hoped she had managed to portal herself somewhere safe. What could she have seen to make her so frightened?

He switched it on. The screen flickered, then died, useless in his hands. He turned back to the fire, dismayed. He was about to go to his friends, when a thought crossed his mind. Valentina had been looking down – not just from embarrassment, but as if searching. Searching for their shadows.

The final moments of the solar eclipse flashed before Alexis as he realised what had made one of the bravest people he knew so petrified. He recalled blackness pouring out of Mortem as he screamed. Alexis remembered the sensation of being struck by something breathtakingly cold a fraction of a second before Incantus had erupted with light.

'Guys,' Alexis said hollowly, 'we need to get back to the Haven.'

Blaise opened his mouth to speak, but Alexis pointed to the ground where their shadows should have been. Demi looked, then Caeli. Blaise finally followed their gaze – just as Demi gasped, 'We've all been imprinted.'

43

MAUERBAUERTRAURIGKEIT

>Mauerbauertraurigkeit (n.) *German origin*
>The inexplicable urge to push people away

The *Shadow Man*'s laugh echoed across the glacial mountain range as Alexis stared at his friends: Demi clutching her amulet and crucifix, Caeli frozen mid-breath, Blaise searching the ground for where their bodies should have formed a dark silhouette of shadow instead of containing it within.

All this time? Alexis thought. *How could I not have seen it in us all?*

The *Shadow Man*'s taloned hand cupped his jaw and turned his head away from his friends. *The shadows answer to us. Together we can decide what we do with them. We don't need them dragging us back.*

'What does this mean?' Demi asked tightly.

'That a piece of Mortem lives on in us?' Caeli wiped away her tears. 'That on some level we will be or already are acting on his behalf, like Valentina and the Leaders were?'

Blaise scoffed at the mention of Valentina but said nothing.

'But why haven't any of us ... turned then?' Demi asked. Her question was directed at Alexis. 'The Prophecy's already been met, hasn't it?'

'*The shadows answer to us,*' the *Shadow Man* had said. Not just Mortem. Did that mean Alexis could command his friends too? Could he undo this?

Do we want to?

Alexis turned to see Demi tugging Caeli towards the archway. She went willingly but her eyes hadn't left Blaise; his were still lingering on the embers.

'Incantus said the equinox is a powerful time for dark wielders,' Demi urged. 'It's barely an hour from now. We've resisted it until now, but we might not be able to tomorrow. We have to assume the Prophecy's still in play and trust that we'll be safe in the Haven. Maybe that's what's kept it at bay from taking us over all this time.'

Caeli broke away from Demi's grip. 'Wait.' She sheepishly approached Blaise. 'We have to go. We can talk more inside.'

Blaise whipped his head towards her and in a flash, the embers reignited into wicked flames. 'I'm not going anywhere with you.'

'Don't go with me then!' Caeli retorted, throwing up her arms. 'Just come inside. It's not safe out here.'

'The further away I am from you, the safer I am. You bring out the worst in me. I knew something was off since the summer solstice – I felt it in my chest, right here – but you were too busy cheating on me to notice.' Blaise shook his head, furious with himself. 'All I've done is stand by you.'

'Hate me all you want. You can't hate me more than I hate myself.'

'I can try.'

This is what it wants, Alexis realised. *Incantus wanted us together and the shadows are trying to drag us apart.*

He stepped forward, shaking off the *Shadow Man*'s iron grip. 'Blaise, stop. Caeli felt terrible about it, but we're falling straight into Mortem's trap by letting ourselves be torn apart. Like Demi said, if the Prophecy's still in play, then the darkness might try and make a break for it once it becomes the equinox. That means there's still a chance that all Elementals could become imprinted if we're turned and inside Stonehenge, which is exactly what Mortem intended during the battle. The shadows have only been in you guys for a short time – Incantus should be able to extract them from you once he's back.'

But Blaise had stopped listening. 'You said "felt" – past tense. You knew?' He looked at Demi, but her head was tilted to the earth in shame. 'You all knew and didn't tell me?'

'It wasn't like that,' Alexis started to say. A spray of red-hot cinders spat from the bonfire to stop him from coming closer. 'I had suspicions. I'm sorry, I should've come to you, but I promise I was just trying to do the right thing.'

Blaise laughed bitterly. 'Alexis Michaels, the guy who thinks he knows everything.' He dug his knuckles into his eyes to clear the tears of betrayal. 'You know nothing. You only care about yourself.'

'Blaise,' Demi warned.

After everything we've done for him, this is what he has to say for himself? the *Shadow Man* hissed, its voice coiling like a snake round Alexis's neck.

'I should be inside, but instead I'm out here trying to convince you – trying to keep *you* safe,' Alexis argued back. The fire was burning more ardently, causing clouds of grey smoke to billow, but Alexis didn't want to give Blaise the satisfaction of stepping aside.

'Because it's your fault!' Blaise roared. 'You nearly got yourself killed in that battle just so you could have all the glory. You didn't tell us your plan to use the projections. I could have helped you. Maybe if I did, Incantus wouldn't have sacrificed his immortality to save you. Maybe that would've stopped Mortem from ruining all our lives.'

Alexis reeled, not recognising the boy who took slow steps towards him as though he was his opponent and not the person who had always fought by his side, even when the world was pitched into shadow and death. Blaise's words cut as deep as any sword. 'But no, you wanted to fight Daddy alone, so you could have all the victory. Now look at us. Imprinted. This is on you.'

Alexis couldn't respond. Was it true?

We should have let Mortem kill them.

Demi stepped in. 'Enough! You're out of line and you know it. This is no one's fault and it's not helping. Don't make me drag you to the Haven.'

'Fire burns wood, Demi,' Blaise growled.

'Fire can't burn when buried underground,' she countered, forcing Blaise to look at her.

'That would mean you'd have to use your powers,' Caeli muttered. 'Something you've been too scared to do since summer.'

Demi whirled on her best friend, stunned. 'What does that have to do with you?'

The wind had picked up, whipping Caeli's hair across her face. 'It doesn't. But we started as equals, going down this path at the same time. I respected you for it, for having some drive. Then you got shot and stopped trying. You gave up.'

'Shut up, Cae,' Alexis snapped, but she waved him off.

'I was just trying to cope,' Demi whispered.

'We all were!' Caeli tore off her glove, exposing her right arm. 'Look at me! Look what happened to me.' She pointed her arm at Blaise, training her gaze on him. 'I lost it defending you.' She turned to Alexis. 'And I was in that position because *you* abandoned us when we needed you most,' she said, shoving Alexis's chest. She bit back a sob before turning to Demi. 'And you rid me of the chance to avenge myself, then did nothing but cry about the blood on your hands.'

The ground quaked beneath them, making the lake's surface ripple. Demi's voice cracked. 'I wanted to grieve, to heal, rather than pretend my pain didn't matter. *You* needed to go out on that mission and I put your needs above my own and went with you, but don't for one second think that that was what I wanted or needed.'

Caeli had no reply, but Blaise wasn't done with Alexis.

'You think you're so special because Incantus is your uncle. You and Dee think it gives you the right to tell the rest of us what to do. Deep down, though, you're more messed up than any of us. How do we know that you're not fulfilling Daddy's dying wish? That Vultress and the Shadowless don't now answer to *you*?'

Alexis's hands curled into fists. 'Because I lost my mother to them!'

'And whose fault was that?' Blaise roared, and the bonfire exploded.

Alexis threw up his hands to block it, but the flames licked his skin, just as a wall of water rose to shield him and Demi.

Fight back! the *Shadow Man* screamed.

Alexis drowned out the fire. Steam rose like smoke, masking Blaise's face.

'*You were responsible for the deaths of both your mothers. No wonder Mortem wanted you dead. Jackson probably does too.*'

Alexis hadn't seen Blaise speak, but he heard Blaise's words, spoken with his voice, resound in his head just the same. Clear as day.

The *Shadow Man*'s reply came as confirmation of what Blaise had said.

Let's give him what he deserves. Together.

And so Alexis raised the lake and attacked. The ice-cold water crashed into Blaise, dragging him into the air, keeping him suspended, drowning.

Alexis could hear Demi and Caeli screaming at him, but the *Shadow Man* screamed louder, its hand drawing closer to Alexis's as he held Blaise in place.

This is power. Imagine a world where no one dare defy us.

Shadows grew around Alexis. They tore themselves from the body of the forest, answering his call, scratching at the surface of the frozen river of his mind. His psychosis, his breaking point, would shatter with it the moment the shadows broke free.

That's it, said the *Shadow Man*, its hand closing round his own. *Now let me take over.*

Alexis gasped, snapping awake as he realised what was happening. The water dropped, releasing Blaise, as he staggered away from the *Shadow Man*'s touch.

Demi and Caeli rushed to Blaise as he coughed up water, but he shoved them away. He crawled to his feet. 'Leave me . . . *alone*,' he rasped. He surveyed his friends, or the people that had once been his friends. In the darkness, the faint red glow of his amulet was swallowed by shadows. 'You never wanted me around. Any of you. I'm done with you all.'

He turned to Demi. His eyes narrowed when she rejoined Alexis and slid her hand into his quivering one.

'Your boyfriend, the one you think is so perfect, so good, is a cold-blooded murderer and a liar,' Blaise said.

Caeli shook her head, and Alexis knew precisely the blow Blaise was about to deliver, for it was a weapon, a promise he had entrusted to Caeli that she had so easily passed on to Blaise.

'You weren't the one who killed Dr Sinner, Demi,' said Blaise, his voice like ash. He paused, letting the moment fracture. Demi turned to Alexis, hope dying in her eyes as her hand slipped from his. 'Alexis did.'

44

CAVOLI RISCALDATI

> Cavoli riscaldati (phr.) *Italian origin*
> 'Reheated cabbage'; the attempt to revive
> a long-finished love affair

'The child who is not embraced by the village will burn it down to feel its warmth.'

As Blaise disappeared through the teleportation line, Caeli Doran froze, realising there was a cruel truth to the African proverb. He was going back to the Haven, but she had to explain herself. She couldn't let him think she didn't care about him.

Caeli scrambled to her feet, limping to the teleportation line, one heel still strapped onto her foot. She refused to let anything more be taken from her against her will – to lose anything more than she had already lost. Including Blaise. Valentina was still here somewhere, but she could handle herself, whereas Blaise was out there with darkness corrupting his mind. Besides, Caeli couldn't face Demi and Alexis. The disappointment on Alexis's face, the betrayal and devastation on Demi's, was enough to make her chest ache. Anger and shame twisted within her like a vortex and if she didn't get away, she would explode.

'Get yourselves back to the Haven,' she told them. She

ignored Demi calling her name and vanished through the portal, landing in the glittering warmth of the Fall Ball. Except now it felt like nothing more than an orchestrated ridicule. *Look at what you had*, she thought. *Look at what you've lost.*

She scanned the space, searching desperately. 'Blaise, where are you?'

Caeli hoisted up the bottom of her dress and rose into the air. Maybe she had lost Blaise and maybe she deserved to. But if the darkness was most powerful on the equinox, then she had to make sure she was with Incantus. Only he could stop her from becoming imprinted. She could count on Demi and Alexis to do the same, but she couldn't trust Blaise to think logically when this angry.

Caeli spotted the Fire Gem in the corner of the ballroom. *Of course. If Blaise feels powerless, he'll go to what makes him feel strong again.*

She soared over the dwindling crowds towards the towering marble pillar that housed a monochromatic white sculpture of a volcano, the Gem of the Fire at its crater. Blaise hovered at its capital, fire curling round his legs.

'Blaise, stop!'

'If I become Omni, I'll be strong enough to fight the darkness,' he said, his eyes failing to meet hers as he scooped up the Gem.

'Or you'll just be infinitely more powerful if it takes over,' Caeli countered. Her own Gem called to her from across the ballroom, but she resisted. She had to be smart. There was no other opponent; the opponent was herself, and she couldn't risk giving the darkness more power.

'Don't pretend to care about me, Cae,' Blaise spat, dropping to the floor, drawing the attention of a small crowd of Elementals who were mistaking the confrontation for a performance.

'Liking Valentina doesn't mean I care about you any less,' Caeli said, touching down. 'Look, maybe I never forgave you for what happened to my hand and maybe you neglected me because I wasn't the girl you signed up to be with.'

Blaise's eyes glimmered coldly. 'It wasn't my fault. *You* broke us up, not me.' He slammed the Fire Gem against his amulet and power blazed through him. 'I hope you burn in hell for it,' he hissed, columns of flames twisting round him, obscuring his eyes, which smouldered like fiery coal. 'If you try to follow me, then I might be the one to light the spark.'

In a blink, he vanished in a blaze of fire and ash.

Caeli stood alone, watching the embers wink out. She didn't know how he'd managed to teleport, perhaps it was a new power he had unlocked in his Omni state, but she was too upset to consider it. Her friends were gone, her dress clung to her like a dirty rag. The weight of their falling out made her retch and spill the contents of her stomach on the floor.

He promised he would never leave me.

Caeli pressed her palm to the end of her arm and conjured her proxy. She couldn't figure out why she had done what she'd done, and there was no one else who could either, so she asked her mirror image, 'Why did I do it?'

'Because you wanted to,' the proxy said flatly. 'Because you want them both.'

'I didn't want to hurt either of them –'

'Yet you did. You didn't *want* to want her, but you've never been good at resisting temptation. And you couldn't live without Blaise, but you feared being with him would leave you always questioning, *what if?* At least now you'll know if it was worth it.'

Caeli reabsorbed the proxy. She had to leave. The Haven was suffocating her. The memories, the guilt, the pain.

The Prophecy said that the fate of Elementals would be decided at Stonehenge, on a day equal to or longest from night. It said either a world of light or darkness would be lain and that by one the other would be slain. If darkness was poisoning her, perhaps staying away from Stonehenge could prevent its rise, even if that meant leaving the safety of the Haven.

She summoned a portal with the device intended for her proxy. She would go home instead, back to the woman *she* had raised. Caeli didn't know what would happen to her, but she would confront her mother at last. She'd had enough of not knowing all the answers.

But as the portal closed behind her, the darkness inside sighed in relief.

For Caeli had done exactly what it wanted.

45

ATYCHIPHOBIA

> Atychiphobia (n.) *Greek origin*
> Fear of failure; fear of not being good enough

'I didn't kill Sinner?'

Moonlight caught Demi's face, contorting with betrayal. There was no spinning it. Revealing Caeli's involvement wouldn't help. All that was left, after months of lying to her, was the truth.

'No. I did,' Alexis admitted, lowering his head.

'You saw how that broke me ...' Her tear-filled gaze fell to her hands. 'You saw how I tormented myself. You – you held me as I wept, thinking I'd condemned myself. You said nothing as I considered abandoning the Elemental world as punishment.'

Alexis swallowed the sob that tore up his throat when Demi's voice cracked. He wished she would yell, hit him, anything but this cold devastated disappointment.

'I'm so sorry I lied, Demi. I wanted to tell you, but I was petrified you'd think less of me for it. I-I couldn't lose the faith you had in me; it's the only thing that's kept me going.' He took a step towards her. 'I never meant to hurt you.'

Demi recoiled. 'Do you know how much that hurts? To trust

someone with everything, your fears and faith and nightmares, with your *life*, only to find they don't trust you back? It feels . . . it feels worse than being buried alive.' She turned away from him as though it hurt to look at him. 'I thought I had killed for you. I *did* kill for Caeli, thinking I had nothing left to lose. Both times it's caused me nothing but sorrow.'

The *Shadow Man* hovered over Demi like a phantom, shaking its head. *All she sees in you now is your father.*

'I did it for you,' he said weakly, hoping that would make it all okay.

Demi whirled back to him, her wide eyes a dangerous green. 'You may have killed for me, but you lied for *yourself*. You were meant to be my rock, but now you're the very reason the earth feels like it's falling from under me. The goodness of your intention is lost when all I feel is the harm of your actions.'

'I'll do anything to make it up to you,' he pleaded, wishing she would return to his side so that the *Shadow Man* could stop encircling her. Bathed in the dark of the night, Alexis was certain that should it swipe at Demi, she would bleed. Or perhaps that revealed just how far gone he was. The delusions were beginning to take hold. Alexis wasn't sure how much longer it would be until the light was lost to him for ever.

She had to know it was for her. Surely that meant something? 'I'm sorry for lying, but I'm not sorry I killed him. I'd do it again in a heartbeat. Demi, I'd kill anyone to protect you – drown the world to avenge you.'

'You're asking me to forgive you,' she said softly. 'Don't also ask me to make you feel good about what you've done.'

Alexis's chest deflated. There was nothing more to say.

Nothing could absolve his conscience for the pain he'd caused her. He tried to block out the *Shadow Man* who laughed at the dissolution of the Earth and the seas, for it had been right all along, and he had been a fool for believing otherwise.

Then Demi did the one thing that could silence it. She stepped towards Alexis and took his hand. 'This is not how we end, Lexi.' Her words were entrenched in pain, but if there was such a thing as a tether to reality, an anchor to the light, it was her. 'But I can't be with you right now. I need to find Valentina and see if she's okay. She risked her life to warn us. She's one of the only people to have resisted Mortem's power, maybe she can tell us how to resist too.'

'Demi, it's too dangerous with the darkness inside you,' Alexis protested.

She shook her head. 'See if Incantus has left yet. If he has, then get Ziya or Taranis to lock us all in the White Room until he returns.'

Alexis recalled the small hidden chamber within Incantus's office that had housed the Elemental Gems. It was the only place on Earth that would have been spared from Mortem's imprinting had he succeeded on the solstice, perhaps the safest place in the whole Haven.

Demi's decision cut deep. She didn't want to be near him – or couldn't trust him to hold on and resist the darkness for much longer. Likely both. Alexis wasn't sure which was worse.

'We can get through this, okay?' she said, cupping his face. 'Blaise, Caeli, you and me. I won't let this be how the darkness wins.'

Alexis could only nod and share with her his mantra that had kept him alive and fighting all this time. 'We didn't come this far just to come this far.'

The last time he had said it aloud was to Incantus on the battlefield, when the golden ribbons of Serena's life force had encompassed them and the last of the sun's light had been lost to shadow.

Alexis watched Demi go, picking up a lantern as she walked into the dark forest in the direction Valentina had been thrown.

We can't go back, urged the *Shadow Man*.

It was the only reason Alexis knew he should. He stumbled through the archway, through lights and music, up ivy-laced stairs towards the laboratory, fingers tapping his thumbs, resisting the Water Gem's call.

He reached the doors of the lab – but froze.

He heard a voice from inside. Ziya's. 'I'll delay the High Order. I'll say you heard about the raid and left with Taranis before I could pass on the message. I'm not good at lying, but I'll try.'

Alexis heard Gibbous's heavy steps as he paced, likely circling Incantus as he finished putting on his white combat suit.

'They'll probably bring a telepath,' he said. 'Don't perjure yourself. Just say I'll answer questions when I return. Has Taranis signalled from the other side yet?'

'Not yet.' A beat passed, where Alexis tried to swallow the pulse thundering in his temples. 'Incantus, the High Order will come to their senses. You're the best person to teach us, to lead us.'

I should go in and tell him before he leaves, Alexis thought, wondering why he was eavesdropping when he and his friends needed Incantus's help. But his legs wouldn't move. It was as if the *Shadow Man* knew something was coming, something it wanted Alexis to hear.

'You all idolise me,' Incantus said, his tone falling dark, contrite. 'You think I'm a good person, a father to you all.' He released a shaky breath. 'Mortem asked me what everyone would think if they knew the truth about me.'

What is he talking about?

'Incantus, you don't have to—' Ziya began.

But whatever secret plagued Incantus, it seemed like he could no longer bear its weight alone. 'He knew I couldn't love a child born from darkness, couldn't look at him without thinking of Mortem – not even when he was just a child. Does a good person plan to kill a baby boy?'

Alexis's lungs seized.

'Do I still sound like a good person, Ziya?' Incantus asked. 'To hate a child at first sight because of his father?'

If Ziya replied, Alexis didn't hear. The floor tilted beneath him, leading him away from the laboratory. The man he loved like a parent hadn't loved him back. Worse, he wanted him gone.

Somehow, even though he was far out of earshot, Alexis heard Incantus say one last thing. It was the shove that pushed him off the edge.

'If I had just killed Alexis as a child, we'd all be spared from the burden of knowing him. Maybe it's not too late to correct my mistake.'

With that, Alexis's mind finally cracked.

46

PISTANTHROPHOBIA

> Pistanthrophobia (n.) *Greek origin*
> The fear of trusting people, usually due to
> painful past experiences and betrayal

When a mirror shatters, it makes a noise. The same can't be said for the mind. When the mind breaks, when the line between what is real and what isn't fractures into a thousand pieces, it does so in silence.

Incantus's words struck Alexis like a weapon, wedging deep, past Alexis's battered armour and into his chest, forcing the air from his lungs and the strength from his legs. He didn't question how he'd heard Incantus so clearly, as though spoken directly into his head, echoing against the walls of his skull until it was all he could hear.

Go, before he kills us, barked the *Shadow Man* in a voice that sounded more like his own than Mortem's.

Alexis ran.

Shadows grew and growled, snapping at his ankles. Tendrils of darkness crawled up his arms, refusing to slow no matter how much he tried to wipe them away.

Alexis clasped his amulet and summoned a wave, dousing himself. The cool water shocked him into clarity, but while it dissipated the shadows that plagued him, it couldn't wash away the stench of rotting flesh.

Alexis sucked in a rattling gasp and staggered forward, relying on muscle memory. He didn't know how long this lucidity would last. The Ball's fireworks of gold and silver were already darkening, exploding to the thunder of Mortem's laughter as if he was right there next to him.

Gem of the Water – that's the only way to make the hallucinations stop.

Alexis nodded, grateful for the *Shadow Man*'s assistance. He thought it would have been his friends and Incantus who wouldn't ever leave him, but he was a fool for distrusting the *Shadow Man* for so long, for forcing it into the darkness while he paraded in the light like a fraud.

Go now!

He bolted down the stairs, haunted by the rotting Nekro he'd slain, the faces of the dead crying his name. The imprinted man he'd killed in the battle as revenge for Joe, the Shadowless in Protegere Forest. And countless others, names he'd never bothered to know.

Hands grabbed him from behind. He broke free, stumbling backwards. He would have toppled over the side of the hive's handrail if not for the figure who caught him.

'It's me! It's Valentina.'

Her features came into focus. Sharp. Urgent. Replacing the Nekro that had just been behind him.

'Val?'

She placed her hands either side of Alexis's face, stilling him. 'You're having a psychotic break.'

He gasped. 'H–how do you know?'

Valentina pulled Alexis away from the edge and into an empty corridor. 'I knew someone once who had schizophrenia. I know the signs.' Her eyes dipped, and Alexis noticed the cuts that marked her face where Caeli had thrown her at the lake. 'I've been watching you, wondering if you were heading that way too. I think it's happening.'

She's been spying on us, the *Shadow Man* hissed.

'You've been spying on me,' he said.

She stepped closer, as close as she'd ever been to him, and she didn't for one second glance away as she spoke. 'I know what it's like to have something sinister inside your head telling you what to do. I nearly got Demi killed for it. That was without psychosis further derailing me. I honestly don't know how you're still holding on.'

The memory of the waterfall, the arrow, Demi bleeding on the grass as he and Caeli and Blaise sat around her, hit him like a blow. Pain, so much pain. Maybe it was easier to succumb to the familiarity of the darkness rather than fight for a light that only blinded him whenever he got close.

I told you. You aren't powerful enough, said the *Shadow Man*. Its silhouette towered over Valentina. *Only with the Gem can we stop it all.*

'I don't know what's happening to me, Val,' Alexis whispered. 'I don't know if it's the darkness or my mind or if it's one and the same.'

'I need to take you to Incantus.'

He spun out of her embrace. 'He's going to kill me. I'm not going back there.'

'He's the only person who can help.'

She's lying. They all are. They all want us dead.

'Trust me,' Valentina pleaded.

'Trust you?' he snapped, ignoring the way her thin eyebrows drew together. 'Why should I trust you?'

'Alexis, you need help. I'm trying to help, please let me. If you know another way, tell me.'

Alexis shuddered, overwhelmed by the crescendo of voices in his head. Yet beneath the chaos, a small voice hadn't given up saying the same thing. *Go home.*

'Incantus isn't here,' he muttered. He steeled himself, fighting to see past the shadows until it was just him and Valentina in their tattered outfits. 'I can feel his absence in the Haven. M-my meds are at home. I brought some, but I lost my jacket. I need to get them.'

Valentina chewed her lower lip. 'I don't think it's safe for you to leave. I just dropped off Demi at her room to search for the others. You should all stay here, regardless of whether Incantus is here or not.'

Alexis took her hands in his, fighting for her to believe him, knowing that she was his only way out. 'The *Shadow Man* is begging for me to stay, to connect with my Gem. If I stay, I'll lose. But if I go home, I can take the meds and fight to hold on.'

They all want us dead. They will hunt us down until they destroy us. We must destroy them first.

Alexis hurled water at the *Shadow Man* behind him but it

vanished just before impact. The torrent struck the wall instead, its spray soaking them.

'When Incantus returns, tell him to come to my house,' Alexis went on, clawing at the skin around his eyes. 'To save me or kill me, whatever it takes to fulfil the Prophecy in our favour.'

'Alexis...'

'Whatever it takes.'

Alexis could hear sounds he knew shouldn't be there. Battle cries and rushing water. Colour drained from his vision, just as it did during his nightmare. Yet he could still make out Valentina.

He saw her nod begrudgingly before a spherical portal opened at her fingertips. 'How can I trust you?' she asked, holding the swirling gateway open.

Alexis met her eyes. She stood firm, even as everything else twisted round him, her portal behind her. It reminded him of their first meeting. Back then, she was just a girl with no name except the one she gave them. A stranger with a past she did not wish to share.

But she was a stranger no more.

'You can because I know who you really are,' Alexis said. 'Who you were. I noticed the scar on your wrist months ago, the dragon and the pearl burned into your skin.'

She clutched it instinctively.

'I looked it up,' Alexis continued. The shadows had fallen still as if they too wished to listen, and faintly he could hear what must be the melodic violin of the Fae in the distance. 'The scarification is a ritual for the Qing dynasty, a ceremonial practice for outsiders to marry in to show their devotion. The last time it was done was about a year ago, when the prince married a princess of the Tang family, one of the oldest portalling families in the world. Months later, the temple was destroyed, the prince was found severed in half, and the princess vanished.'

A single tear slipped down Valentina's cheek.

'She hasn't been found since,' he went on softly. 'I heard Sinner, then Serena call you by a different name, the princess's name: Lì Nà Jìng.'

Valentina's eyes shut tight, and her head dipped forward. Her silence was answer enough.

'That's how Mortem captured you, wasn't it?' he asked, his breath rattling in his chest. 'Maybe both families sold you out, wherever you were hiding. You scorned them both, and neither came to fight with us against him on the solstice.'

Valentina's voice was barely audible. 'Who have you told?'

The place where Valentina's eyes had once been were now dark red pits and the long body of a scaled Chinese dragon slithered between the sockets. 'No one,' he promised, trying to blink the image away. 'To me, you're Val. I don't care what you did before. You fought off the darkness better than anyone else and that has to mean something.'

Valentina allowed him to take her hands, and he could tell she was steadying him as much as he was her.

'You don't know what it was like there,' she whispered, her hair spilling over her face as she shook her head. 'You may have learned my identity, but you will never know what I went through. I did what I had to to survive.'

Slowly, the infinite tunnel began to fold in on itself, an end drawing in sight just past the threshold. Alexis knew that she was one of the few portallers who could travel to places she had never been to before, who could search the world through her mind's eye of it. Through his touch, through his mental image of his home, he hoped that she would be able to deposit him there.

Valentina stepped away and inclined her head towards the swirling vortex. 'We are not victims of the darkness, of our past and our pain.' She didn't bother to wipe away the tears that streaked her cheeks; they were not to be ashamed of. 'We are survivors. Hold on to the thought or memory that brings you warmth and happiness and light. Hold on to it with everything you've got. It's the only defence you have against him.'

For Alexis, that light was his mother.

He wrapped himself in the thought of her, not of her absence and of its paralysing pain, but of her presence. The ease with which he could open up to her and the comfort that she never failed to provide him with. Even in death it was as if she was still with him now, holding his hand to remind him: '*Us Michaelses, we rise.*'

It was a hallucination the same as any other, but one Alexis was glad to find himself in.

'Be safe, Alexis,' said Valentina. 'Don't let it win.'

'We won't,' Alexis promised, the hallucination of Stephanie Michaels at his side.

Together, mother and son walked through the portal – and went home.

47

TOSKA

Toska (n.) *Russian origin*
A dull ache of the soul, a sick pining, a spiritual anguish

'Caeli? Honey, is that you?' Celeste Doran peeked into her daughter's room. 'I didn't hear you get back from your prom.'

She froze. Caeli, soaked, stood clutching a small cardboard box taken from beneath Celeste's bed. Its lid lay discarded, revealing a faded photo of a tall smirking man with stormy eyes like Caeli's, a thin silver bracelet, and another photo of Celeste in the hospital holding a newborn Celina.

Celeste hurried in, her arms open, but Caeli didn't move.

'What happened? Why are you wet? Where's Blaise?' Her eyes dropped to the box. It took her a moment to register that it was being levitated in the air by swirling winds that emanated from the end of Caeli's arm.

'Who am I?' Caeli asked, her voice as empty as her chest was hollow.

Celeste's eyes drifted to her amulet. 'You're my daughter,' she said carefully. 'You – you have a gift.'

'I know that,' Caeli snapped. 'I abandoned any attempt to figure out if you knew what I was long ago; I want to know *why* I'm like this. Why I'm incapable of being happy and hurt the people I care most about. I've now realised it's because of *you*.'

Celeste gasped, her hands going to her chest. 'Don't say that. Did something happen with Blaise? We can fix it.'

'I can't fix it!' She clawed at her hair, tearing out clumps. Celeste moved to stop her, but Caeli turned away. 'And you certainly can't either.'

Tears fell. Caeli let them.

'I did the best that I could to raise you,' Celeste whispered.

'Raise me?' Caeli's laugh held no humour. 'I raised myself. Everything I've got in this life is because I earned it, in spite of you and in spite of him.' She threw the photo of her father through the air.

'If he could have been here with us, he would have.' Celeste bent down to retrieve the photo, stroking a thumb across his face.

'I deserve to know,' Caeli said. Her mother met her eyes, knowing that there was no way she could evade the question any longer.

With a steadying breath, Celeste spoke. 'Your father and I were raised in a mountain village in the middle of God-knows-where, with people that worshipped the sky. When I was eighteen, my parents arranged to pair me with a man I'd never met, from the other side of the world. But I was already with your father ... in secret. Looking back now, I think we must have been in some kind of a cult.'

Caeli hugged the box tighter. 'So what did you do?'

Celeste brushed her perfectly blow-dried fringe out of her

eyes. 'We ran away. Hiked for days and escaped. Your dad was a little older than me and seemed to know where to go. He had a gift too, far stronger than my shaky influence of sound. He could make people not see us. We snuck onto a plane. Just before take-off, he went to the toilet ... and he never came back. That was the last time I saw him.'

'Why would he leave you?'

Celeste shook her head slowly. 'I don't know. We spent our first night together the evening before. It wasn't until months later that I realised that I was pregnant. I like to think he left because he feared my other suitor, the ones my parents had arranged, would find us easier if we were together. But, Caeli, what we had was real. If he could've stayed for you, he would have.'

Caeli was furious for letting herself cry, but she could no longer suppress the emotion. 'How do you know?'

'Because he was the one who chose your name.' Celeste clasped her hand over her mouth to swallow her sob. 'Kǎi-Lì. Triumphant. Beautiful. If we ever had a daughter, that should be her name. I changed the spelling to Caeli later, to help us blend in here. But it means from the skies, from the heavens.'

Caeli's legs were threatening to buckle beneath her, but she locked them into place. 'Why didn't you just tell me instead of letting me think I was a mistake?'

'I convinced myself that I had been brainwashed and none of it was real. I realised that wasn't the case when you were born. A white-haired man and an Indian woman came to the hospital and gave me your amulet. I knew they were gifted like we were. They told me to live a normal life, so I did. I took their money – it would last me a few years – and I tried to forget it all.'

Caeli instinctively felt for the piece of the Air Gem that hung from her neck. That had to have been Incantus and Ziya's mother, who had come to inhibit her powers to stop them from developing until Stonehenge drew her back to the Elemental world to settle the Prophecy.

'What about Celina?'

Celeste reached for the box and Caeli allowed her to take it. 'A customer's husband,' she admitted, her shoulders slumping. 'He wanted nothing to do with her or me once I told him. Cae, you helped me survive the most difficult times in my life. You were always so independent, so perfect. So, so clever. We didn't need anyone else.'

Caeli shook her head. 'No ...'

'Yes!' Celeste insisted, rising to her feet. 'It's always been me and you against the world. Best friends. You didn't need your father; you barely needed me, even after Cel died.'

'*No!*'

Wind exploded from Caeli, knocking her mother into the bedframe. Books tumbled, the desk tipped.

'No,' Caeli repeated, staring down at her mother. 'That's the lie you tell yourself to excuse you for being a failure.' Some part of her knew she should stop, that she was being cruel, but whether it was the darkness inside corrupting her or something else, Caeli continued. 'I was a child. Of course I needed a mother. But I learned early that my needs had to come second. That *I* had to be second.' Her voice broke. 'Do you know how much I still blame myself for what happened to Celina?'

Memories flooded back to her. Her sister's blue face, the silence. Her mother's scream that shattered the windows. Caeli had given up her childhood to hold their world together in the years that followed.

'I've spent my life buckling under the crippling need to be perfect – a need *you* imposed on me. I should've been figuring out who I was. Now I'm nearly an adult and I have no idea who I am and what I want. That's what your co-dependency cost me.'

'Caeli . . .'

But she was already climbing out of the window. She didn't know where she was going, only that she needed to fly before she lost the ability for ever. The cold air stung as she shot into the air, not caring if anyone was around to see her, ignoring her mother's cries. Nothing but blackness existed above her, but the part of her that had always feared the dark now called towards it. Winds howled into her as a tempest brewed, but she took little notice.

I cannot blame the storm for blowing. I can only blame myself for stepping outside when I knew the forecast.

Caeli flew higher and higher as though the darkness of space was something she could touch. She needed no air to breathe. She could reach it if she wanted and be free of the constraints of this life and this world and all the demands it had placed upon her. Demands to be hard but kind, to be soft yet enduring, defiant and compliant.

Her scream was lost to the storm.

But what she didn't realise was that it was a calling, a signal.

A burst of fire shot skywards like a flare, stopping just as it reached her.

'Blaise?' she gasped.

Blaise's face was unreadable in the darkness. Moonlight revealed his silhouette, the slant of his broad shoulders and the edges of his jaw, but it wasn't bright enough to show her the amber glow of his eyes that she had fallen in love with.

'Why are you here?' she asked.

'You're not happy to see me?' His voice was calm, not angry.

'Of course I am. There's so much we need to talk about. I want you to know that I never meant—'

He raised a hand. 'What I said earlier, I didn't mean any of it. I'd burn down the world just to be with you, Cae.'

Caeli couldn't believe his words. His anger had been so raw no more than an hour ago. Could he really forgive her so easily? Had he realised they needed to stick together in order to survive this, just as they always had? Caeli's doubt all too easily fell away as relief flooded her, threatening to spill the tears that pricked her eyes before the wind could steal them away. She reached out to touch his face, but he pulled back.

'I want to forgive you,' Blaise said, drawing closer until they were sharing breaths. 'Fire can't burn without air. I want us to be together again. I want you to come with me.'

His flames were cold against her skin. At his proximity, at the thought of losing him for ever, Caeli realised that she would do anything to ensure she was not left alone in this world to fend for herself. 'Come with you where?'

Blaise smiled. 'I'll show you.'

With that, Blaise took hold of her hands and pulled her into the moonlight. The silvery glow revealed the onyx of his eyes and the cold vacancy of his amulet, no longer alive with fire but corrupted by darkness.

It hit Caeli then that the Woman of the Fire's prophecy had finally come true.

'Your fire will be the first to go dark.'

'What about Demi and Alexis?' Caeli asked, her resistance winking out like a candle in the wind.

'If they don't join us, they'll burn with the rest,' said Blaise.

He pressed her arms together. Erupting from her body came her proxy. Blaise held it effortlessly in his arms, showing Caeli what could be hers if she went with him. Companionship, love, to be held up, instead of being the one always burdened with carrying the weight.

'You think you want control, order,' said her proxy in Blaise's arms, its reflection a twisted version of her. 'But what you really want is chaos.'

'Blaise, please . . .' Caeli whispered.

Yet it was as her mother had said. Caeli was clever and so she already knew it was too late. This was the only thing that could silence her mind. The only peace.

So Caeli Doran closed her eyes and let herself be swept away.

She couldn't see Blaise's expression shift. She didn't see the blackness of his eyes falter as a small part of him, the real him, tried to break free from Mortem's grasp to urge her to hold on. It didn't matter by then. She had already surrendered.

Darkness engulfed her, turning her eyes and amulet as black as the shadow she no longer cast.

In her final moments, Caeli understood. To ensure the

darkness's survival, to consolidate it in her mind for ever, all she had to do was make it to Stonehenge on the dawn of the autumn equinox. She was the vessel through which Mortem could execute his plan from beyond death.

Only two of the Children of the Elements remained unturned. If they didn't submit, then Mortem's orders were simple.

It was darkness. Or death.

48

CWTCH

Cwtch (n.) *Welsh origin*
An embrace; a safe place provided by a loved one

Alexis had hoped Valentina's portal would take him straight home, but it only got him to the front gates on Valerian Lane. He and the hallucination of his mother trekked up the drive, climbing through the bedroom window he always left ajar.

His proxy bolted upright in bed, its book falling shut without a bookmark. *As if the day could get worse.*

'What the hell happened?' it asked.

Alexis shook his head. He didn't have the time to explain. He needed his medication.

'Alexis...'

He grabbed the proxy's hands and reabsorbed it, ignoring the influx of its memories.

'I'm going to be okay, Mum,' Alexis muttered, hoping she would believe him. She didn't reply.

There is no hope in fighting, the *Shadow Man* said from his other side with a sad tut. *There is no hope in resisting. A wolf doesn't question its nature to hunt. Why should we?*

Alexis ignored it to rifle through the drawers. Pens on his

desk grew into long dark talons that threatened to slice his hands open. He flung the books off his shelf in frustration and then tipped out the contents of his school bag when his mother pointed at it. Still no meds.

There was a scratching at the broken door. Reina pushed in, tail wagging. Within moments Alexis's mind had twisted her into a decaying red-eyed hellhound that could have been one of Dr Sinner's Hybrids.

Dr Dash. Alexis dug out his phone and dialled his number. He was the only one that might be able to settle his mind, to keep him stable.

'Alexis?'

'I know it's late but I need help. I can't find my meds. I can't—'

'You never told me you were on any medication,' Dr Dash said after a beat.

Shit. He'd have to explain how his mother had smuggled his prescription from the hospital. He looked at her, to where her silhouette flickered like static, as Reina – or the demon that had replaced her – encircled her. His pillar of light would soon be lost and once she was he would have no defences left against the shadows.

'Please,' Alexis begged, shooing Reina out of his room and slamming the broken door closed. 'I'll take anything. Tablets. Injections. Just *help* me before—'

'Some people can't be saved, Alexis,' said Dr Dash, his voice empty. 'Maybe this is your punishment for what you did.' Dr Dash's words forced Alexis to an abrupt stop: his breathing, his heartbeat, even his racing thoughts.

Alexis shook his head, even though Dr Dash couldn't see him. *Not you too*, he thought. *Don't give up on me too.* 'No . . . I've paid for what I've done. I-I deserve to be in the light.'

Alexis wasn't sure if it was the *Shadow Man* or Dr Dash who had laughed at him, but it hurt all the same.

'I've tried my best to help you,' Dr Dash continued, misery dripping through his voice. 'But nothing I do will be enough to scrub away the sins from your past. The sad reality is that not everyone is capable of recovery, and not everyone deserves it.'

'I know I don't, but I want to!' Alexis cried. He looked to his mother – but the *Shadow Man* now stood where she had been.

Alexis pressed the phone against his chest, but he could still hear Dr Dash's reply. 'Do you remember what I called you upon our first meeting?' he asked pensively.

Alexis remembered.

Doomed, the *Shadow Man* echoed.

'Lexi?' Jason's voice from behind him rinsed away the *Shadow Man*.

Alexis wiped at his face and steadied his voice so as not to scare him. He gestured to his hand, but the phone he had just been using was no longer there. He must have dropped it. He didn't bother to look for it.

'Are you . . . hallucinating again?' Jason asked delicately, pushing the door wider to step into his room.

Alexis pressed his lips together and nodded. 'My meds, have you seen them? I usually keep them in my room. Or maybe Mum's medicine cupboard downstairs?'

Alexis went to move past Jason, back out onto the landing.

'I thought you flushed them about an hour ago,' said his brother.

Alexis caught himself against the doorframe. 'What?'

Jason bent over to stroke Reina as she came to sit at his side to look curiously between them. 'Just after Dad left. You said they didn't work any more.'

It took Alexis a painfully long time to realise that Jason must have been talking about the proxy. Why had it got rid of his medication? Had it been acting on behalf of Alexis or on behalf of the darkness?

He searched the proxy's memories, but the image failed to resurface.

Panic swelled inside Alexis's chest, threatening vomit if he dared to take a deep breath. His reason for leaving the Haven, for leaving Demi – to get his medication to numb the psychosis and regain his grasp on reality – was now gone.

Has the Shadow Man *played me?*

Just then, Jason grabbed his arm. The voices faded, shadows quieted.

'Jace . . .'

Jason hugged him and everything settled. Maybe it was Alexis's love for him that grounded him. Come to think of it, Alexis realised that his hallucinations, his nightmares, even the *Shadow Man,* was always weaker when he was with Jason. Maybe the darkness couldn't reach him when he was close to something so pure.

'Have something to eat and some water,' Jason suggested, leading him downstairs. Reina joined them on the sofa as Jason forced Alexis to take a sip of water. She spread out across

Stephanie's blanket, the one she used after long hospital shifts, when she was too tired to make the stairs. She was never there long – Jackson would always come to carry her to bed.

'I keep thinking that I'm going to wake up,' Alexis admitted, staring at the muted superhero film Jason had been watching. 'That this is just another nightmare and I'll wake up and see Mum again.'

Jason buried his face into Reina's fur. 'I do too. If only I'd helped her with the shopping . . . maybe she'd still be here. We'd still be a family.'

Alexis pulled him close. 'Don't think that for one second. It's not your fault, Jace.' Alexis only then realised how late it was, with his father nowhere to be seen. 'Where's Dad?'

'He went out for work stuff a couple hours ago, didn't he?' Jason said.

He left us? What could be so important that he would leave his sons at home at night when he knew there were people after them?

Unless he was in the forest again searching for them?

'You're you again.'

Alexis turned to Jason who was staring at him, his head slightly tilted.

'What do you mean?' Alexis asked.

Jason shrugged, the top of his rounded cheeks reddening. 'I don't know how to explain it. Sometimes you're you and sometimes you're not.' He fed Reina a biscuit. 'It started after that school trip you and Demi went on at the start of summer. You came back and you were . . . different. *Dimmer*. Thought something might've happened that you didn't want to tell me.'

Alexis's proxy hadn't fooled him. Not completely. Alexis recalled Incantus explaining how they lacked the crucial part that made them human, that made them Elemental. Maybe it was the soul. How was Jason able to detect the differences when sometimes even Alexis couldn't?

'Does – Did Mum and Dad think the same?'

Jason shrugged again. 'Who knows? If they did, they wouldn't tell me. No one tells me anything.'

'It's infuriating, isn't it?'

Jason nodded. 'But it's like when Mum covered my eyes during scary parts in films, or when Dad leaves out details in his stories. It's only to protect us.' A sigh escaped his lips, allowing his chest to deflate. Through his overgrown dirty blond hair, his eyes flicked to Alexis. 'Like when Dad lied to the police about the people who crashed into us on purpose.'

'I thought you said you didn't remember anything?'

Jason frowned. 'Bits are coming back. I remember the smell of burning. A woman trying to pull me out of the car. Then Dad showed up and chased her away. He held me and Mum in his arms until the ambulances came, but it was too late for her.'

Alexis's throat tightened.

Jason blinked hard. 'I know there's stuff from before the accident that no one's telling me about. You've all been acting weird. I may be dumb, but I'm not stupid.'

Despite everything, Alexis smiled. He nudged his arm, taking a moment to look at him, to truly look at him. 'People are wrong to underestimate you, Jace. You're a lot smarter and stronger than everyone gives you credit for.'

'I know.' Jason turned his attention back to the television, a grin plastered across his face.

They stayed like that, Reina nestled between them, Jason, despite his best efforts, dozing off with his head on Alexis's shoulder. Only Alexis remained awake.

Somewhere, hopefully in the Haven, he pictured Demi Nikolas praying. He too prayed. For her to hold on. For Incantus to return. For his torment to end, by light or by death.

Lastly, he prayed for his father's safe return. The night was almost up and Alexis wouldn't allow the *Shadow Man* to take him anywhere until he finally learned the secret that had cost his mother her life.

'*They know who we are. They know what we've done. Alexis can never find out.*'

'Tonight, I will,' he promised himself.

49

SCIAPHILIA

Sciaphilia (n.) *Greek origin*
A preference or inclination for darkness; a love of shadows

Reina barked as a key turned in the front door. Alexis hushed her to avoid waking Jason, but her excited paws skittered against the floor as their father entered, clad in black, wearing leather gloves, a duffel bag slung over his shoulder.

'Hi, my princess,' Jackson whispered to Reina.

'You're home late,' Alexis observed, noting the mud caking his shoes.

'Lexi, I didn't think you'd still be up.' Jackson smiled tiredly. 'Is Jason sleeping?'

Jason stirred against Alexis's shoulder. 'What time is it?' he mumbled.

'Almost midnight,' Alexis answered.

Jackson came over and tousled Jason's hair, Reina still dancing around his legs. 'Past your bedtime, young man.'

As Jackson bade his younger son goodnight, Alexis slipped into the conservatory, far from Jason's ears. At that hour, the glass walls revealed only darkness and his own bloodshot reflection.

Jackson joined him a moment later and closed the door behind him. The duffel bag clinked as it hit the floor. Reina must have gone upstairs to get into bed with Jason.

'Are you okay, my boy? You look unwell. Have you taken your meds?'

Alexis caught sight of the reflection of the *Shadow Man* in the window. It was standing by Alexis's side.

He cannot lie to us both, it whispered.

Its presence brought Alexis a surprising sense of comfort. 'Where were you?'

Jackson removed his gloves and washed his hands in the kitchen sink. He didn't scrub them as viciously as Stephanie did, Alexis noticed. It was such a minor detail, but the grief it conjured was powerful enough to make his eyes burn.

'I was out,' Jackson replied measuredly. He studied his son across the room. 'What's wrong, Lexi? You seem upset.'

'You left us alone when you know there are people after us.' He might as well get straight to the point.

Jackson rested his elbows against the island as he towelled his hands. 'What do you mean? No one's after us.'

Shout at him.

'Stop lying!' Alexis snapped.

Jackson didn't flinch, but his gaze hardened. He looked more like a detective now than Alexis had ever seen him look, but Alexis had no intention of being the subject of his enquiry.

'Stop hiding things from me,' he pressed, mirroring his father's stoicism. 'You've been doing it all my life and I'm sick of it. I know what's been going on. I know a lot more than you think.'

'About what?'

'About me. My adoption. The people who killed Mum.'

Jackson's eyes darted to the side as if listening to something unseen. Wordlessly, he rounded the island and took a seat at the glass dining table opposite Alexis. He rested his hand on the back of the chair to his right, the one Stephanie usually sat at if she had dinner with them, and pulled it back slightly.

Jackson looked up at him and said, 'Tell us what you know.'

You are a sinner, said the *Shadow Man*. *Everyone is a sinner.*

Alexis left, returning moments later with the file from his father's office. He took a seat opposite Jackson and flicked it open as though it were a cadaver ready to be examined, his finger pointing to the page like a scalpel to skin. He scattered the sheets across the table: legal papers, his drawings of the *Shadow Man*, Dr Dash's notes, the image of the investigation board.

'I know you forged my adoption papers,' he began. 'That we disappeared for nearly a year after you found me. I know someone came looking for me years ago and wanted to take me back. I remember it ... vaguely. And I know that the people who work for my birth father have been watching us for the last few months and are the reason Mum died.'

Alexis spoke steadily, ensuring he avoided any mention of the Elemental world. He had so desperately wanted his father to admit to it all, but the moment he had mentioned his mother, Jackson's eyes had lowered and filled with tears faster than he could blink them away. After that, despite whatever the *Shadow Man* was saying, Alexis only wanted to hug him.

'How do you know all that?'

He underestimated us. They've always underestimated us.

Alexis crossed his arms. 'You can't drug me up and hope I don't ask questions.'

Jackson pitched forward in his seat. 'We've never done that,' he protested. 'Everything we did was to keep you and your brother safe.'

Great job you've done there.

'You owe me the truth.' Alexis fought against the *Shadow Man*'s suggestion to shout again, to be aggressive, to make his father feel some semblance of the pain he had inadvertently caused him. But Alexis didn't want to fight any more. He just wanted answers. 'No more lies. No more secrets. I don't care how dark it is; I deserve the truth.'

Jackson's head tilted to the side as if the ghost of his late wife was speaking to him. Alexis didn't think it was particularly healthy for his father to daydream about her, but that was exactly what he had done. Jackson released an awfully long sigh, his gaze returning to Alexis's. 'We'll – I'll tell you.'

He extended his calloused hand across the table.

Alexis didn't take it, his own too sweaty with fear.

Jackson withdrew and took a breath, shuffling the papers in front of him. 'Your mother and I eloped to Australia without telling anyone where we were going. That February, the day after we got married, was when the tsunami struck. It was one of the largest recorded in recent times and it hit much of Oceania and South America. We joined recovery efforts, your mum with the medics, me with the police. I know you've watched documentaries about it, but to see the wreckage, the carnage in person, is something no video or story can ever do justice to. It was ... horrific.'

Jackson released a shaky breath. He reached across the table to examine the image of the investigation board. 'Then Stephanie and I were taken.'

Taken? Alexis leaned in.

Jackson pointed to the question mark that connected Alexis, him and Stephanie, and the unphotographed birth parents. The 'Guardian'.

'By who?' Alexis asked.

Jackson scratched his stubble as though it was a question he had asked himself many times over the past eleven and a half years. 'We awoke tied back to back in a ruined building. A man was there, but I couldn't see him.' Jackson's hands balled into tight fists. 'He said he meant us no harm, but if I wasn't sedated by whatever he had given me, I would've ripped his head off. Your mum calmed me down. I think she might have caught a glimpse of him and for whatever reason it put her at ease.'

'What did he want?' Alexis's throat had gone dry at the thought of his mother and father tied up somewhere, but he couldn't bring himself to get a glass of water, petrified that his father might clam up again.

Jackson rested his hand against the empty seat beside him. He stroked it gently. 'He told us to find a boy in the wreckage, one wearing a triangular blue amulet. Said his father was a criminal who had trafficked and murdered. That if his people found the boy first, he would be in grave danger. I asked why he didn't just take the boy to the police, but he said they couldn't be trusted. Steph asked where the mother was, but the man said he didn't know, that she was likely dead.'

Jackson's eyes filled with tears. 'He freed us and disappeared before I could get a decent look at him. Stephanie stopped me from going after him when we heard a baby crying. A little boy, no older than four or five. Starved, scared, stranded.'

Jackson reached out, his hand gripping nothing but air, but he pressed his other hand against his chest and fought to finish speaking. 'This man, whoever he was, was looking out for you. When you opened your eyes, a mixture of colours I've never seen before, I knew that you needed us too. We couldn't walk away.'

Alexis stared at the mystery figure on the board, his guardian.

Incantus. It had to be. He had lied by saying he had never met his parents. Why had he picked them of all people? Alexis knew he had to be raised away from the Elemental world due to the Prophecy, but why had Jackson and Stephanie Michaels been the mortals tasked with raising him when Incantus knew first-hand just how much danger they would be in should Mortem find them?

The *Shadow Man* joined them at the table. *He's always lying to us.*

'So you took me?' Alexis asked, struggling to think of a response in line with what he was supposed to know. 'Just like that? Based on the word of a stranger who didn't even tell you his name. How did you know he was telling you the truth?'

'We didn't at first,' Jackson replied, collecting himself. 'We kept you with us for a few days, debating what to do. And then they came.' He shifted in his seat. 'Dressed in cloaks, searching the hospitals for a boy with a blue necklace and eyes like the ocean and night sky. It didn't take me more than a minute to know what kind of people they were, Lexi. You're looking at a doctor and a detective ...' Jackson paused, wrongfooted by Stephanie's absence. 'You were raised by two people who have spent their entire lives working to make this world a better place, to help and heal the people in it. We had to keep you safe from them. So when they came to search our hotel, we knew that they had somehow found us ... and we fled.'

Jackson sniffed harshly and wiped the tears from his cheeks. He spoke flatly now, detached. 'We went into hiding. Quit everything. Travelled the world with the money we had, just the three of us. We talked about settling somewhere under different names so that no one could find us. I always liked Italy, but here's always been home and I couldn't leave my mum alone any longer. We hoped after nearly a year, we would be safe. We moved to a quiet village outside London with the lowest crime rate, Jason was born, and you *finally* started talking. Things were good. Mum finished her training. We were happy ... until the following December, when someone broke into our home.'

Alexis remembered what Sapientis had shown him. Pale blue light, a hulking figure in the dark. A memory or a hallucination?

Jackson wrung his hands in his lap. 'This person, this *beast*, said he was taking you back to your birth father and that we'd live if we didn't resist. I didn't believe him, and even if I did, you were *our* child and we wouldn't let him take you away from us. That's when the fight broke out. One thing led to another and he was on top of me and ...'

Alexis stared at his father, having known for a long time where this was going but unable to believe it unless he heard him say the words. 'You killed him?'

'No.' Jackson's eyes dropped and he released a breath. 'Your mother did.'

Alexis's stomach turned as if the world had suddenly tilted. His mother, a *mortal*, had killed Plague? Mortem's lieutenant, an infamous dark Elemental? Was that why Vultress had gone after her?

'We had a choice,' said Jackson resolutely. 'Be good people or be good parents, and we chose to be good parents. I buried him deep in the woods, expecting more to come. For more than a decade, no one did. Until a few months ago when they finally found us again. At first they kept their distance, but still I begged your mother to let us pack our things and go. She refused, saying we had built a life here and that she was tired of running. I-I could never say no to her. My life's biggest regret is not taking us all away. If I had, she'd still be with us.'

Tears stung Alexis's eyes as he watched his father crumple. The noise wasn't like anything Alexis had ever heard before. It tore open a wound in him that he knew would never fully heal.

His mother. His stupid, reckless, murderous, brilliant, loving, unstoppable mother.

She was never really our mother, though, was she? She dug her own grave.

Alexis flinched at the *Shadow Man*'s words. Somewhere along the way, he himself had faded, and in his place was a person made up of nothing more than betrayal and pain and trauma and lies.

'Say something,' said Jackson quietly, tentatively.

It was devastation or fury, and the *Shadow Man* chose the latter.

You're murderers.

'You're murderers,' Alexis repeated.

'We were trying to protect you,' Jackson explained, but it fell on deaf ears.

An undercurrent was stirring within Alexis. It was picking up speed, growing dangerous, threatening to drown him unless he went along with it. He had to bunch his fists and press them against his legs to ensure his powers didn't erupt from him in a flood. 'You lied to me my whole life, kept me caged in this house. No consistent therapist, no friends. Just medication to keep me numb. And, you know what, even now, I could probably get over it all. I could forgive you for taking me and for killing that guy. But lying to me all this time?' He almost laughed, but he knew there was nothing truly funny about it. 'I always thought I was messed up, ruined from birth, but it was because of you.'

'We didn't know what we were doing, Alexis!' Jackson shot up, his hands slamming the table so hard that Alexis thought it would shatter. 'I've never done this before. I've never been a parent! I've never *had* a parent!' He gesticulated wildly. 'Everything I do is for this family. I give and I give from a well I never had the luxury of drinking from and still it's not enough.' Jackson slumped back into his seat. 'I know I should have been better. I will spend my life knowing that until my last breath, but I will also die knowing that I *tried*. I tried to break this cycle of neglect and abandonment; we both did. We may not have been perfect, far from it, but we did the best we could. I don't want your sympathy, Lexi. I just want you to know that we were doing what it took to protect you.'

'I wasn't worth it!' Alexis swept the file off the table, casting the papers up into the air. Papers that were somehow meant to summarise his life, but which didn't come close to documenting his pain, fluttered like failed promises. 'I wasn't worth putting your lives in danger. Everything that's happened was all for what? For *me*?' His throat closed up and he had to choke out his next words. 'What about Jason? You keep saying he'll be fine, that he's indestructible, but he's just a kid. He doesn't know what's going on, he doesn't know if he's safe, he doesn't know what's real and what's just in his head –'

Alexis caught himself, realising he was no longer talking about his brother. This wasn't just about his parents and their secret that had cost Stephanie her life, but about everything else too. That he was a cold-blooded murderer. That he could be the one to cover the world in eternal darkness and steal the shadows of all Elementals if he chose to. Fighting with his friends, Incantus wishing him dead. Unable to sleep without being haunted by nightmares. Unable to stay awake without being haunted by hallucinations. Surrounded by nothing but darkness, a fog that couldn't be lifted.

He got to his feet, knocking his chair over. 'By trying to save me,' Alexis said very plainly, 'you've put your real son at risk.'

'You're our real son too,' Jackson said, reaching for him.

Alexis moved away from his father's touch. 'No. I'm not. I thought I was. I tried to convince myself I was. But I'm not your real son and you aren't my real parents. I got Mum killed and Jason hurt. It's no wonder Dr Dash gave up on me again.'

Jackson frowned. 'Dr Dash?'

'I've been seeing him since Mum died and even *he* thinks

I'm a burden. I tried to convince him I wasn't, but he's right. I wasn't worth saving.'

Jackson rounded the table so that he was standing before his son, his hands on Alexis's shoulders. His face was pale. 'Lexi, what are you talking about?'

Alexis met his gaze and registered that something was wrong. 'Dr Dash ... He said—'

'*Lexi.*' Jackson shook him slightly. He winced from the contact as though his hands were burning iron, but he didn't move until his father spoke again. Not until he delivered the final blow.

'Dr Dash has been dead for eleven years.'

Alexis staggered as Dr Dash materialised behind Jackson. He wore the same suit he had worn the other day, that he had worn all those years ago, but this time, blood was spilling down his shirt from the slit across his throat.

A thunderstorm rumbled in the distance. Between one flash of lightning and the next, Alexis stared at Dr Dash. 'How?'

The *Shadow Man* answered his question at the same time as his father did.

You killed him.

50

KADOTA

Kadota (v.) *Finnish origin*
To disappear, vanish; to get lost, be missing; to fade

We are the child of darkness. Of the angel of death. That is who we've always been.

'I killed Dr Dash.' It wasn't a question. 'And you covered it up.'

Jackson's chest deflated. 'I buried him in the forest too.'

Alexis frowned as the shadows laughed at him. 'I-I remember seeing him leave?'

Jackson gently shook his head. 'By the time we got to you, he was already gone. You couldn't have known what you were doing.'

You did.

Jackson's voice was tentative. 'We'd hoped you wouldn't remember.' His eyes searched Alexis's. 'Have you been hallucinating him?'

'I need to go,' was all Alexis could bring himself to say.

The *Shadow Man* wrapped an arm round his slumped shoulders, guiding him out. He didn't resist. If Jackson called after him, Alexis didn't hear. He could only hear the *Shadow Man*'s whispers, telling him isolation was the only option.

Shame crashed down on Alexis. Every conversation with Dr Dash, every piece of advice, was nothing more than a lie conjured by his own collapsing mind.

How long have I been falling? Alexis wondered. *What else have I made up?*

He reached Jason's door and could hear Reina scratching to get out. As he opened it, he caught a glimpse of Jason's blond hair as he stirred.

The *Shadow Man* jerked him away. *Do not poison him too.*

Between one blink and the next, Alexis found himself in the bathroom facing the mirror: bloodshot eyes, exhaustion that hollowed his cheeks and drained the colour from his face.

Blink. Let it in, child. You have nothing left to lose. Accept your nature, your darkness. Accept yourself.

'I didn't come this far just to come this far,' Alexis whispered to himself.

The *Shadow Man*'s cold breath was at his ear. *You should never have come this far.*

His gaze fell to the amulet glowing faintly on his chest. Blue. Still blue. The only light left.

'Water,' Alexis murmured. He turned the taps, filling the bath with scalding water.

Still clothed, Alexis slid in and submerged. There was so much noise in his head. His thoughts tangled with the *Shadow Man*'s until he could no longer tell who was speaking. Time dissolved. Alexis didn't know how long he remained underwater, but he heard the distorted sound of his parents' voices.

'*We should have left him to drown,*' said his mother.

Alexis surged up, gasping. 'Mum?' He wanted to beg her to return, even if she hated him, but he could no longer hear her voice, as though it was lost beneath the surface of the water.

Alexis thought his element would help, but he had forgotten that that was where the darkness liked to hide. All too late he realised his mistake as he blinked at his distorted reflection on the water's rippling surface.

A figure burst through the surface of the water, shattering the liquid mirror. The *Shadow Man*'s icy hands locked round his throat and dragged him under.

The edges of the bath faded until Alexis could see nothing except the vast emptiness of a dark ocean, an abyss so deep that no light could reach.

Swim, Alexis. Swim! But his limbs were too heavy, the pull too strong.

The *Shadow Man*'s voice rippled through the depths. *All these years together and you never thought to ask me my name?* Dark water began to seep through Alexis's lips, forcing him to inhale. *Is that because you feared the answer?*

The *Shadow Man*'s voice – no, *Mortem's* voice – echoed around Alexis like an invisible current. It flooded into him with the shadow of water. *Your time is over. I can finally be free of you.*

Before Alexis's eyes, the *Shadow Man*'s true face finally began to form. No longer a silhouette but something solid, something familiar.

The last thing Alexis Michaels saw before darkness claimed him, before his eyes and amulet turned black, was that all along the *Shadow Man* had never been Mortem.

It had always been himself.

PART IV

51

CRYPTOZOIC

Cryptozoic (adj.) *Greek origin*
Living hidden or in darkness

Jason Michaels rubbed his eyes as he entered the conservatory, catching his father whispering, 'I failed him.'

Yet only Reina was in the room.

'Dad? I heard shouting. What happened?'

Jackson turned away from him, kneeling beside the dog. His voice was strained. 'Nothing, my boy.'

Jason didn't believe him, not when he was talking to no one again. Did his father now have what Alexis suffered from? Jason placed his hand on his father's slumped shoulder. 'What did you and Lexi argue about?'

Jackson stood slowly, his face barely visible in the dim light. 'We'll be okay.' He picked up the ornate flea-market clock Stephanie insisted be kept on the dining table. 'It's after twelve. Go back to bed,' he said, returning the clock to the table.

'Is it about your case?' Jason persisted, shuddering from the cold, wet spray that swept in after Jackson unlocked the back door to let Reina out into the pouring rain. 'Did Lexi have a go at you for taking it on? He looked really bad earlier.'

Jackson ran a hand through his hair. 'This has got nothing to do with you.' He kissed the top of his head as he passed. 'Please let Reina back in before you go up.'

'But it's dark outside.'

Jackson snapped. 'I'm exhausted, Jason! Just do what I say for once.' He caught himself, his face beginning to soften, but Jason had already turned away.

'Everyone in this house has bloody anger issues,' Jason mumbled once he had gone. 'The man who wants me to be a detective doesn't like me asking questions. My bad.'

The back door rattled in the wind, making Jason startle as minutes ticked by while he waited. The automatic light hadn't turned on and he could barely see Reina when she suddenly began barking. Jason squinted into the pitch-black garden and called her, trying to see what she was barking at.

That was when his breath seized in his chest.

In the darkness, Jason saw the outline of a man.

A scream tore through the silence of the Michaelses' house, ripped from Jason's throat. Terror flooded his body, but his legs refused to move, rooting them to the stop. The man outside tapped his fingers along the conservatory windows as he drifted towards the open back door, smiling slightly.

Jason's instincts screamed at him to run, but he couldn't leave Reina. What if the man hurt her?

Jason lunged to the door. In the garden, at least a dozen cloaked figures emerged from the shadows, revealed by a crack of lightning. One by one, as if signalled by the moon, they began to move towards the house.

'Reina!' Jason bellowed over the storm. His heart hammered

so violently that he could feel his chest vibrating with each pulse, but he clung to the doorframe, searching for her.

He saw the glint of her metallic collar as Reina pelted towards one of the cloaked intruders, her teeth sinking into their arm as she forced them to the ground. Reina scurried back and snarled at the others as they continued to advance, blood dripping from her jaw.

Jason glanced back at the man on the patio. If he didn't leave now, he might not reach his dad in time. How had the security system not gone off? How had his father or brother not heard him by now?

Jason stepped free from the safety of the house and cried one last time, 'Reina!'

She turned, her attention snapping to the man approaching Jason. She bounded towards them and flung herself at the man just as he grabbed Jason. Her jaws clamped on to the hand of the intruder, who yelped as she began yanking him back to the patio, away from Jason and the house.

The man swore through gritted teeth. With his other hand he snatched her by the collar and spun. With a sickening crack Reina slammed into Jason, sending them both sprawling inside.

The man took his first step into the house, blood dripping from his hand.

Reina struggled to stand guard, growling. The intruder raised a black dagger –

But he hadn't seen Jason snatch up his mother's antique clock before Reina had collapsed into him. Jason launched himself at the man and swung with a roar.

The clock smashed into the man's temple. He crumpled, falling outside.

'Don't you touch her!' Jason bellowed and slammed the door shut so harshly that the windows wobbled in their frames. He locked it just as more cloaked figures pressed against the glass, their faces contorted with frustration. 'Quickly, Reina.' Jason scooped up her trembling, rain-soaked heavy body to drag her away.

'Dad! Lexi! Help me!'

Why aren't they coming? Where are they?

Footsteps thundered above, and there was a crash from his parents' room. Jason set Reina down and rifled through the cutlery drawer until he found a bread knife, then bolted for the stairs, but before he got close, the front door suddenly imploded in a cloud of dark magenta smoke.

From the mist, a sharp-faced woman with shaved red hair stepped into the hallway.

Her eyes locked on to Jason and he recognised her instantly. She had been in the car. The car that had crashed into his mother's.

Behind her, a second intruder waved a hand. A moment later, Reina was sent skidding across the floor as though struck by an invisible force. She collided against the wall with a hard thud and fell still.

Jason screamed again.

He ran for his father's office where he knew there was a hidden panic room. He had barely reached the door before a thick purple-red chain coiled round his wrist, yanking him to the floor.

'Get off me!' he shouted, slamming the shackles against the wall.

The second intruder looked at the red-haired woman. 'The brother. What do you want us to do with him?'

She wriggled her fingers at Jason as if they were old friends. 'We don't need the other two.' There was something about her eyes, a lack of humanity, a thirsty madness, that made Jason far more fearful of her than of the man who had thrown Reina with his mind. 'Sire will not miss what he never possessed. Let us wipe out the last of the Aevum bloodline. Kill him.'

She smiled at Jason and added, 'Say hello to your mummy for me.'

Jason stared as the man unsheathed a long curved dagger. Somewhere he heard his father screaming his name. Then another voice spoke to him, soft, kind, familiar. Near.

It whispered to him, 'It's going to be okay, my boy.'

Jason could have sworn he felt his mother's hand tighten around his.

Aevum bloodline. His mother's voice. People with powers. It was all too much to process and there was not nearly enough time.

Jason could only scream as the blade sank towards his chest.

52

ANGELIFY

Angelify (v.) *Latin origin*
To make into or like an angel; to imbue with the
properties of a powerful, protective divinity

'I miss you so much,' Jackson Michaels murmured to the empty room. He removed the gun from his waistband as he perched on the edge of the bed to remove his shoes.

'What did I tell you about putting guns on the bed?' came the familiar voice.

Jackson felt hands slide over his chest from behind. The muscles of his chest relaxed at her soothing touch. 'Sorry,' he muttered, and tucked the gun into the top drawer of the bedside table. He turned round to where his wife sat behind him, shimmering softly with a pale blue glow. 'I so desperately wish you were here, Steph.'

The undead spirit of Stephanie Michaels caressed his face. The feel of her was almost real, almost true, but the spark of life was something not even Jackson with his abilities could imitate fully.

'If only I had got to you sooner, I would've been able to save you both,' he said, kissing her palm.

'You saved our son,' Stephanie replied. Her body glimmered where Jackson held her, her spirit tethered to him by his powers, visible to him alone. 'That's the most important thing.'

Corpse whisperer. That's what they used to called him, the profiler who could step into a crime scene and know exactly what had happened to the dead, as if he'd somehow spoken to them.

It was a gift he had only ever shared with his wife, although she hadn't been his wife when he had told her. Yet he knew somehow, someday, she would be.

Stephanie wore the clothes she had been cremated in, a designer long-sleeve black dress that covered much of the scars and bruising from the crash. She looked up at him with her brown doe eyes that had never failed to settle his heart and sat on the bed, her weight making no impression on the sheets.

'We didn't make a mistake in saving Alexis,' Stephanie assured him. 'Because that's precisely what we did. We *saved* him, and we've continued to do so every day since, the best way we know how. Don't forget that while he was growing up, so were we. Perhaps we made mistakes in lying to him all this time, but I'm sure you'll be forgiven in time.' Stephanie smiled sadly, knowing the same grace could not be extended to her. 'For time heals all wounds.'

Jackson wiped away the single tear that bled from his eye. He had hoped to speak with Alexis earlier, but by the time he had come upstairs, his eldest son had locked himself in the bathroom, a bath running behind the door.

Even with their gifts, Alexis's fractured mind wasn't something he could heal with the pale blue glow of his hands, nor could Stephanie slow the rate at which he deteriorated with her golden strings of time. That was their combined biggest failure as parents.

'I wish you were here instead of me,' he said. 'Really here.'

His own childhood had been empty. A mother who didn't recognise him, a father unknown. He and Stephanie had tried to do better than they had experienced, but with her gone he felt utterly unqualified to continue.

'You would be so much better at this than I am.'

'I'm with our babies whenever possible,' she said, standing before her husband. She pressed his tired head against her chest where her heart no longer beat and brushed her hands through his hair. 'Even if they can't see me, I'm there, cheering them on, kissing their bruises and holding their hands.' She tipped his head back and pursed her lips into a knowing smile. 'As such, please remind Jason to brush his teeth. I watched him and he only did it for thirty seconds.'

Jackson smiled for what felt like the first time in weeks. He watched her pad over to the windows to look out at the front lawn of their home, wondering how he had been so lucky twice. First, to find her. Second, to have her return to him.

Till death do us part.

Not for us, he thought.

'You should get some sleep, baby,' Stephanie said softly. She turned when she saw something in the window's reflection and her face dropped. 'Behind you!'

Before he had time to turn, hands wrapped round Jackson's throat. He spluttered, gasping for air that wouldn't reach his lungs as his feet were slowly raised off the ground.

Jackson rammed his head backwards and heard a crunch

as bone and cartilage snapped. The figure released him and staggered backwards, allowing Jackson to suck in a breath and turn to face the assailant. His bald, scarred head caught the moonlight as he wiped blood from his nose with the back of his hand. Then he charged again.

Jackson flipped the intruder over his hip until he sprawled on the floor, where he slammed the man's head into the corner of the bedside table until he stopped moving.

'My cream carpets!' Stephanie exclaimed at the growing pool of dark red. 'Watch out!'

Jackson dived out of the way just as a dagger sliced into the space he had just occupied. He snapped a kick to the second intruder's chest, sending her toppling. She went to get back up, but Jackson cracked his knee against her jaw and she collapsed, falling still.

He didn't need to ask who they were. He already knew what they were after, and what he was prepared to do to stop them.

A scream rang out from downstairs, accompanied by the distant sound of Reina's barking over the thunderous rainfall.

'Jason!' Stephanie gasped, her eyes wide. She glanced through the window. 'They've found a way in.'

'I'm going to kill them all,' Jackson muttered, bolting for the door —

Something smashed against his forehead. Exploding waves of paralysing, dizzying pain coursed through Jackson as he flopped backwards, barely feeling the second impact of his head striking the floor. Two more intruders rushed in, one holding a thick black bludgeon that glistened with his blood, the other with fingernails that grew longer with every second.

Stephanie leaped over the bed to stand before him, but the man's claws passed through her body and raked Jackson's chest, splattering blood on the wall beside him. Jackson could barely move, not even to cry out. His thoughts spiralled, the nauseating pain reminding him of the first man who had come years ago, the towering beast whose presence alone made him feel as if he was dying a slow death from every disease, sickness and virus. The man had been a walking plague that had infected and immobilised him. And this pain was doing the very same thing.

Jackson felt a warm breath against the side of his face. 'You do not die today, my love,' Stephanie whispered beside him.

Jason screamed again from downstairs. *What's happening to him? Where's Alexis?*

Stephanie swooped her arm beneath the back of Jackson's bleeding head. 'I'm going to have to wait a little longer for you. Rise and fight for this family.'

As the two enemies pounced on him, something deep inside Jackson erupted. Something wild, powerful, inexplicable. Something Jackson made no attempt to contain.

A brilliant cool blue-white light exploded from Jackson's hands, rippling from a place deep within. The light hurled the intruders against the walls with a sickening splat. They were dead before they even landed, before the light receded back into Jackson's skin.

Jackson gasped from the exertion and got to his feet to retrieve his gun from the bedside table. He knew bullets didn't always work on people who had abilities like he and Stephanie had, how they swerved round them or rebounded off invisible shields, but he couldn't rely on his powers, not when he struggled to control its direction and using it exhausted him so much.

'*Jackson!*' Stephanie called from the stairs, staring in horror at what was going on downstairs.

Jackson tore forward, but got no further than a couple of steps before the windows exploded behind him. He staggered, dazed, just as arms like steel wrapped round him, slamming him into the bedpost.

His vision dipped.

Stephanie vanished, as did the power at his fingertips.

The last thing Jackson saw was a blade so black it seemed to swallow light swing down towards his head.

53

MALEFIC

> Malefic (adj.) *Latin origin*
> Causing harm or destruction, especially
> by supernatural means

Sleep. That was all Alexis needed for the darkness to fully claim him.

He could see it now, Mortem's plan unfolding now through his hands. Mortem's back-up plan had always been the Children of the Elements. Slowly corrupted, they would turn by the autumn equinox, allowing Mortem to live on *through* them. All that was needed to consolidate his reign was for them to be inside Stonehenge at dawn.

The Prophecy of Light and Darkness had never specified the role the Children of the Elements would play in the fate of the world, only that it was their decision to make.

'*Once the four corners rally,*
A world of light or dark will be lain.'

Mortem had ensured it would be the latter.

Yet Alexis's sleep was ripped apart by a scream that pierced the void. The noise called to him as if it was a beacon of light in a storm.

Jason.

No power of the darkness could keep Alexis under when he knew his brother was in danger.

Swim, Alexis, he begged himself. *Swim.*

Alexis surged awake, his lungs burning with life as he broke the surface. His eyes shot open. That was when he saw that he wasn't alone.

There was a man standing over the bath, his dagger glinting in the fading light as it came stabbing down towards him.

Alexis rolled away, narrowly avoiding the blade that plunged into the water with a splash. Alexis didn't have time to think. Instinct took over. He reached up, pressed his hands on either side of the man's head and twisted sharply until –

Snap.

Together, they crashed to the floor, but only Alexis got back up, his chest free from the weight of remorse. There was no time to wait for regret to find him or to falter with hesitation.

He fled the bathroom, dripping wet, and turned the corner to see another Shadowless climb through his open bedroom window. Over her shoulder, Alexis saw at least a dozen more in the garden. Reina's barks split through the thunderstorm and he glimpsed her lunging towards the Shadowless closest to the door to the conservatory where Jason was screaming.

The second Shadowless blocked him from seeing what happened next. 'Come with us now and we might spare their lives,' she said, her eyes brown, clear from the darkness. She had *chosen* to follow Mortem.

'It's your life that won't be spared,' Alexis growled.

She lunged, aiming a kick at Alexis's hand as he reached for the dagger, then again at his face, sending him reeling. Blood filled his mouth and dripped down his chin.

The woman sneered as she crouched and pressed her black-tipped fingers against the carpet. At her touch, a ring of decay spread out, degrading the cream fibres to ash.

'My mum loved these carpets,' Alexis said, seething.

As the Shadowless raced towards him, her hands reaching for his face, Alexis turned his palm in her direction and jerked it back. The water and every other fluid in her body was drained from her in an instant, reducing her to a dried husk. Alexis was gone before her bones had even crumbled to dust.

Water. He still had his powers.

Not for long, hissed the *Shadow Man*.

Just as Alexis evaporated the water that drenched his clothes, he heard a grunt and then a crash from somewhere on his floor. He raced to the landing to see a machete-wielding man advancing on his father. Alexis flew and tackled the Shadowless, locking his legs round his head like a vice, just as he had seen Valentina do in battle. He shifted his weight to the side, flipping him until he struck the ground, the machete clattering to the floor.

Jackson snatched up the machete before Alexis could and cracked its steel hilt against the man's skull.

'Where did you—?' Jackson asked, stunned. His eyes scanned Alexis's body for injury as he fought to stand. 'I-I never taught you that.'

'Self-defence classes over summer,' Alexis panted.

He eyed the other unmoving bodies in the bedroom that his father had somehow handled, receiving only a bruise to the side of his head in return. He couldn't help but feel proud. *Go Dad*.

Then Jackson hauled him into the tightest of embraces. 'I love you. We love you so much.' Jackson stroked the damp hair at the back of Alexis's head. 'We're so sorry for what we did, Lexi. Are you okay?'

How had Alexis let the darkness make him hate them? As if he could ever hate them. In the face of danger, true danger, Alexis realised that the only thing he cared about was keeping what remained of his family alive and safe.

'It's okay. I'm fine.' It was all Alexis could say for now. 'Where's Jason?'

His father snatched him by the arm and pulled him towards the hearth. 'There's a panic room behind the fireplace here,' he said, pulling away a loose tile to reveal a retinal scanner that Alexis never knew existed. As Jackson presented his blue eye to the screen, he said, 'All of us are registered to open it. Stay there. There's another one in my office behind my desk. I'll get Jas—'

There was a contorted *boom* from downstairs followed by Reina's howl.

Jason cried out, 'Get off me!'

Before Jackson had time to realise what he was doing, Alexis had already fled from the room. He slammed the door shut and unleashed a flurry of hard ice to lock it into place.

'Lexi!'

The door rattled violently, but the ice held for now. Alexis didn't think – and vaulted over the banister.

Alexis had only a split second to take in the scene before him. Jason was pinned, a knife inching towards his chest. Beside them was the hawkish woman he knew to be in charge, Mortem's most loyal Shadowless. Vultress.

Alexis's hand gripped the banister and he swung himself forward. He struck the woman with a fierce double kick, launching her into the wall so forcefully that the plaster tore and she disappeared from sight.

The man turned. An inch of his blade was red with Jason's blood, and the sight of it tapped into a fury Alexis had never felt before. He wasn't sure if he shouted, but it took him all that he had to not let a wave of darkness erupt from his body.

The Shadowless swung at him, but he ducked effortlessly out of the way. He spared a moment to inspect Jason. He was alive, unconscious but breathing.

Alexis caught a punch to his cheekbone that sent him spinning. Somewhere behind him, possibly from the conservatory, was a detonation. Within seconds the conservatory was on fire, billowing flames spreading slowly across the room.

'You're just a child,' the man sneered. The dagger shimmered in his hand and its shape bulged, the blade morphing into an axe. 'I missed out on the Great Battle to spy on and steal back a child?'

Alexis summoned an ice-sword. 'And now you're going to die by one.'

He lunged forward. The two blades arched and met in the middle with a clang. The man's axe shimmered again and a second later it shrank to a small blade. He jabbed it at Alexis and its edge nicked his side.

'Name?' Alexis demanded, swinging his sword, forcing him to step back.

'Blade Blackburn.'

Alexis spread his arms wide and conjured a dozen spinning

frozen blades. He took pleasure in watching the Shadowless's face drop. 'Goodbye, Blade Blackburn.' Alexis fired the icicles.

Blade's body thudded to the wall, nailed by the frozen spikes. Alexis melted the ice, letting the corpse drop, its body punctured with a dozen holes that were still too frozen to bleed.

'Mum?' Jason stirred, dazed.

Alexis rushed over, disintegrating his ice-sword at the same time as Reina limped over to join them.

'I heard your voice,' Jason mumbled, his eyes fluttering open.

'It's me, Lexi,' said Alexis, helping him to his feet as Reina licked the side of his cheek.

In the next room, fire was spreading towards the kitchen, sending clouds of smoke to rise and stain the ceiling. Beyond, Alexis sensed more Shadowless waiting to get in. He had to get Jason out of harm's way.

'Help me get you to Dad's office,' he said, taking most of his weight.

'I think I weed myself when I passed out,' Jason muttered, as Alexis steered him away from the dead man's body.

'No different from most nights then,' Alexis replied.

Jason gave him an irritated side-eye. 'I heard Mum. She's here.'

The weight Alexis was carrying somehow got heavier. His heart cracked. 'I feel like I see her too sometimes,' he admitted. Just an hour ago the image of her had been the only thing tethering him to this world as he fled from Incantus.

Jason elbowed his side in frustration. 'It's not like that! I'm not hallucinating. I *heard* her speak to me. I felt her hand in mine.'

Alexis saw the sincerity in his brother's sky-blue eyes and nodded, wanting to believe him. Many a crazy thing had happened that night, but his mother returning from the dead to speak to Jason couldn't be one of them. Still, Alexis smiled and said, 'Tell her I said hello.'

They reached the office, where he propped Jason against the desk while he watched the surveillance of the house. Fire was roaring in the kitchen, rain pelting like steel-tipped whips against the conservatory from outside. The patio was littered with Shadowless who were blasting apart walls of stone and plaster and wood to get in. Upstairs, the hallway to Alexis's parents' room was eerily empty as his father continued to hammer against the door to escape.

A metallic clicking caught Alexis's attention. He turned to see a small retina scanner just above Jason's eye level on the back wall. He didn't recall his father telling him about it until tonight. Maybe Jackson had told the proxy who had kept it from Alexis, or it had been a panic room designed to keep the family safe *from* him, should he ever attack them like he had Dr Dash? Either way, Alexis was grateful as the scanner registered Jason's eye.

Part of the back wall opened outwards and a bright overhead light inside the chamber flickered on. Alexis couldn't see much apart from a small twin bed and a couple of cabinets. There was no time to inspect them.

'Dad's paranoia finally pays off,' Jason marvelled as he hobbled inside, collapsing onto the bed.

'How's your chest?'

Jason grimaced. 'Hurts. How did you get that guy off me?'

'Pure wit and charm.'

Jason stroked Reina delicately. 'I hit one with Mum's clock.'

Alexis couldn't hide his surprise. He bit back a smile. 'Guess Mum was wrong: time doesn't heal all wounds.'

There was a crash from above. Vultress and at least half a dozen more Shadowless were still in the house. With both his sons beyond his protection, Jackson Michaels wouldn't rest until he got to them, but that only put him in grave danger. The Shadowless had defiled the sanctity of their home for too long. Whichever way it ended, Alexis had to deal with it tonight.

Alexis stood. 'Reina, come here.'

She moved to sit attentively at Alexis's heel.

'Where are you going?' Jason asked. He pulled himself up using the bedframe, but he wasn't strong enough to walk without support. 'Don't leave me, Lexi.'

The lump in Alexis's throat was more difficult to swallow than expected. 'I'll be back, I promise. I'll make a run for the main road to get help. I'll be okay. I've got Reina.'

Jason began staggering after him. Despite everything in his body that wanted to stay close to his brother, Alexis swung shut the great bulk of the metal door between them, sealing Jason inside.

Reina was limping less than she had before. She was looking up at him, her tail between her legs but awaiting his order. Alexis kissed the top of her head. 'Good girl, Reina. Brave girl. Now go up to Daddy. Guard.'

He pointed in the direction of the stairs, helping her to understand. Together, they returned to the lounge, where smoke filled the room and the walls flickered from the glow of the flames. Alexis patted Reina's back and she darted upstairs, disappearing from sight.

With no one else about, no family members to protect or conceal his powers from, Alexis unleashed a torrent of water from his hands and headed to the kitchen to extinguish the flames. Through the hissing clouds of steam, a band of Shadowless who had just broken in froze at the sight of him, taking measure of the Son of the Seas, the child of their Sire they had been ordered to retrieve.

'My house?' Alexis asked, running his tongue across his bloodied lower lip. His eyes darkened, more onyx now than sapphire. 'My *home*?'

He deflected a beam of energy shot towards him. Fire raged around them, growing more ardent, climbing the walls, but the Shadowless retreated from *him*, not it.

Why are you waiting? asked the *Shadow Man*. Tendrils of darkness caressed the corners of his mind, begging to be exorcised. *Why are you still clinging on to your humanity when it has already been taken from you? These people seek to claim your life. Are you going to let them or are you going to do as you have always wanted: to drown them in their own blood?*

In the dark of the night, Alexis had no reason to hide who he really was.

'You want me? Here I am.'

Water exploded from the taps of the sink, joining with his own, controlled by an invisible current. He threw the streams into the Shadowless, submerging their heads in a swirling vortex.

Once all eight Shadowless were engulfed, Alexis arched

his back and his powers pulsed again. He strained under the pressure, his muscles burning with cold fire, but blood was on his mind and he was desperate for its taste. When Alexis opened his eyes, through the smoke and the spray he saw blood joining the whirling current.

But it wasn't the carnage that stole Alexis's breath. It was what he saw beyond it.

Three familiar faces emerged from behind the captured Shadowless. They stared at him through the blood and water with eyes as dark and as empty as black holes, watching him, waiting for him. They were people he once knew as friends, now here with the Shadowless to put an end to him and his family.

'I'm going to rip the souls from your corpses,' Alexis growled, and darkness bled into the stream of water and blood, shredding apart what remained of the trapped Shadowless.

Consumed by rings of blue, crimson and black, Alexis felt the shadows call to him, belonging to him, just as water did. It was part of his nature that couldn't be denied, no matter how hard he tried to seal himself off from it.

He finally understood what Incantus had meant. There was no *Shadow Man* here. There had only ever been the two sides of him: the one who dared to step into the light even if it blinded him, and the one who hid in the dark.

If this was what it felt like to switch off his humanity, to give in, how could he convince himself that it wasn't worth it? If he could ensure he never again felt betrayed or hurt or alone, he should take it. Why deny it?

'Lexi?'

The voice struck him like lightning. It spoke to the purest part of him, the part that was vulnerable and human. The part of him that was a Michaels.

Everything fell. Water. Blood. Shadows. His friends vanished before his eyes, as though they had been nothing more than an illusion in the flames.

Alexis slowly turned to find Jason staring at him, his eyes wide, his mouth agape, having seen it all.

54

ACATALEPSY

Acatalepsy (n.) *Greek origin*
The impossibility of comprehending something; the belief that human knowledge can never have true certainty

'Jace.' Alexis stepped towards him, but Jason backed away. His tear-filled eyes flicked to the ring of fallen corpses that encircled Alexis like a grotesque halo.

'I switched the CCTV back on,' Jason said numbly. 'I saw you heading towards them. I thought you were giving yourself up. I know they're here for you.' From his waistband he pulled out one of their father's pistols. The gun wavered in his grip, its barrel pointed at Alexis. 'I was going to come and help you. But . . .' He gestured to the bloodbath. 'What are you?'

The dying remnants of fire clawed at the walls behind Alexis, heat kissing the back of his neck with burning lips, but he didn't move. The talons of the darkness in his mind had receded with his rage like the drawing back of a tide. He glanced behind him, thinking about what had been there, on *who* had been there only a moment ago, and whether or not they had been real.

'I'm an Elemental.' The house of lies he had been raised in was burning down and he had no intention of extinguishing the flames. 'I have the power over water ... and shadows. We protect the world from demons and creatures you've read about, the ones from myth and legend, who come from my world.'

Jason shook his head, sweat plastering his curling dirty-blond hair to his forehead. He still hadn't lowered the gun. 'But how? How did you ...? How?'

'I found out this summer,' Alexis said carefully, edging closer. 'Demi and I went to Stonehenge and met Blaise and Caeli – my friends who came to the funeral. We were taken, or dragged, to the Haven and met a man called Incantus Arcangelo. He told us we're the Children of the Prophecy of Light and Darkness – destined to send the world into or save it from shadow.'

Jason frowned, the gun in his hand wavering. 'But you said *your* power is the shadows?'

Alexis pressed his lips together. 'It is. But he meant my birth father. A man called Mortem. We destroyed him on the summer solstice, but his people are still after me.'

He was right in front of Jason now, his hands raised to show him he was no threat, despite the blood snaking down his forearms. 'Jace, I'm so sorry. Mum, this invasion – it's all because of me. You have no idea how many times I thought of you and wished that I could've shown you the Haven, but we're sworn to secrecy. Even if I had, there's an illusory force that would've stopped you from seeing any of this. We even have proxies to keep up our normal lives.' His brother's face hadn't softened. 'Jace. Jason ... please say something.'

The gun slipped from Jason's hand and landed on the floor with a heavy thud.

'You have powers!' Jason exclaimed, his face shifting from solemn focus to wide-eyed awe. 'That's so unfair!'

The knot in Alexis's chest finally loosened. For a moment there he really thought Jason was going to pull the trigger. Alexis snatched up the gun to see Jason still bouncing on his feet, his hands raking through his hair.

'Can I get some too?' Jason asked, no longer concerned by the corpses that surrounded his brother. 'How did *you* get them? Cosmic blast? Radioactive shark?'

'Not quite,' Alexis said, pulling him from the fire that had already returned to engulf most of the fallen Shadowless, burning their bodies to lumps of charred flesh and bones, destroying any evidence of a supernatural death. He let them burn before extinguishing the flames. 'It's inherited. Even so, most Elementals don't have powers. Sorry, but because Mum and Dad are mortal, you probably don't have any. I could get arrested for sharing this with you. You have to swear to never tell anyone.'

Jason sagged. 'Fine. Does Demi have powers too then? What about Kallisto?'

The mention of Demi triggered what Alexis had seen through smoke and fire. 'Did you see her or my friends on the cameras?'

Jason coughed from the smoke, his voice becoming hoarse. 'Why would they be here? If they were they would have helped us, right?'

Thinking about it, Alexis didn't recall seeing their amulets. Could it have just been another hallucination? If so, how many other moments he was sure he'd seen or heard were nothing more than his own mind deceiving him?

'So what's this Incantus angel-guy like?'

Before Alexis could reply, a crash split the air. Jackson burst through the smoke, Reina at his heel. He froze at the dead body of Blade Blackburn, then at the fire that had consumed half of downstairs, then at his sons.

'Boys!'

Jackson ran to them and hauled them into a crushing embrace. With them at his side, Alexis felt stable for the first time since the falling out by the Lakes, his mind now teetering on clarity rather than instability. For a few short seconds, they were simply three Michaelses, their arms wrapped tight round each other, Reina pressed close.

If he wasn't mistaken, Alexis could have sworn he felt a fourth set of arms join them.

Jackson kissed their heads. 'My brave boys. My beautiful sons. Jason, are you okay?' Jason nodded, tears streaking his face. Jackson checked the bloodied mess at Jason's chest, relieved it wasn't fatal. 'Your big brother protected you, didn't he?'

Jackson took a deep breath before turning to Alexis who had bent over to hug Reina. 'Don't ever run off like that again.'

The corner of Alexis's mouth lifted with the slightest glimpse of a smile. 'Just returning the favour.'

Jackson placed his hand on his shoulder, the weight of it warm and familiar, healing in a way. 'It was never a favour.'

The fumes were thickening, filling the air with a dense grey smoke that swelled in Alexis's lungs whenever he inhaled. He couldn't extinguish the flames now that his father was here. After Jason grabbed the urn of Stephanie's ashes from the mantelpiece, Jackson quickly ushered them out into the slashing rain, a gun at the ready.

'Alexis, take your brother to the Nikolases',' Jackson ordered, leading them to the edge of the lawn. 'Tell them it was a fire and that I've already called the police.'

Alexis shook his head. 'You're not going back in there.'

'I need to make sure that they're all taken care of,' Jackson said. 'Alone.'

'I can help,' Alexis protested, gesturing to the gun he'd taken from Jason.

'I know you can,' Jackson said, cupping his son's face. Alexis knew they were both likely thinking of the corpse at the bottom of the stairs, the one with a dozen holes in it. 'No matter what the world throws at you, you have always endured. But your brother needs your protection more than I do. I'll be fine. I'm not alone.'

He snapped his fingers; Reina barked at his side. The sight of the two of them reminded Alexis of a mortal version of Incantus and Gibbous.

Jason swayed on his feet, clutching Stephanie's urn tight to his chest while his bloodshot eyes struggled to stay open.

'Come back to us,' Alexis said to his father, his voice cracking. 'We can't lose you too.'

'You could never lose either of us,' Jackson replied. He jutted his chin for them to get going as he backed towards the house. 'Love you,' he whispered.

'Love you more,' Alexis and Jason called back.

As Jackson and Reina vanished into the fire, Alexis scooped Jason up into his arms and took off, running through the rain, keeping an eye out for any sort of movement in the bushes. When they reached the front gates, he could see a small figure in the distance, standing beneath a floral umbrella, one arm extended towards them. Behind them, the wrought-iron bars had been bent out of shape as if forced apart by something huge, a crane or possibly a tractor.

Petra Nikolas exclaimed something in Greek and clutched them both, bringing them beneath the umbrella. 'Boys, are you okay? I tried calling when I saw the smoke but no one answered.'

Alexis set Jason down on the grass. Jason tried to speak but was sent into another coughing fit. 'The Shadowless broke in,' Alexis told her openly, ignoring the look of concern she cast Jason's way. 'But how? I thought the house was warded against any kind of intrusion?'

'The equinox would've supercharged dark witches,' Petra explained quickly, her arm still held out towards the house. 'If powerful enough, they could have broken down the protections, especially if invited in.'

Alexis struggled to catch his breath. Every second outside while his father was still in there felt unbearable, torturous. 'Why didn't you help us?'

Petra straightened. 'Me being here is the only reason your house hasn't collapsed,' she said through gritted teeth. Alexis noticed what was sweat, not rain, pattern her forehead as she kept her arm held out in the direction of the house. 'Geb is in the forest stopping more from coming. The First Oath of our Tribe, of all Tribes, is to create and not destroy, just as the Women did. Tonight we broke that oath once again to keep you and your family safe.'

Alexis looked towards Protegere Forest. If he focused hard enough, over the sound of the rain, he thought he could hear the snapping of branches and the occasional cry in the distance.

'I'm sorry,' he said, pulling her closer to shield her from the rain. She smelt like wood and herbs, reminding him so much of Demi that it ached. 'Where's Demi?'

'She's safe at the Haven. She called and told us everything.' Alexis's body stiffened, but Petra held him against her. 'She was sleep-walking and would have connected with the Gem of the Earth and fled had she not boarded her door with the tree before she fell asleep.' Despite everything, a small smile, barely visible, grew on Alexis's face as he pictured her protected by her intuition. 'Ms Kefi is with her, making sure she stays awake until Incantus returns. As soon as I know your father is safe, I'm taking you straight there.'

The last thing Alexis had heard Incantus say was that he wished he was dead, that he should have killed him to be sure the darkness was gone forever. Now Alexis couldn't be sure whether that really was Incantus or if it belonged to another voice of the *Shadow Man*, like Dr Dash.

With each passing minute, he grew more aware that his father hadn't come out of the house. He couldn't wait any longer. Before Petra could stop him, he tore free and sprinted towards the house.

'Alexis!' Petra screamed over and over, but he plunged through the smoke.

Columns of coiling fire surrounded him, blistering his arms as he delved deeper, burning his clothes until he was shirtless. Smoke clawed at his lungs and caused tears to burn tracks down his cheeks. Alexis clutched his amulet and shot bursts of water from his hands, extinguishing sections of the fire jarringly slowly. As spitting clouds of steam enveloped him, he realised it was getting harder to conjure his powers. The shadows were eagerly awaiting his command, stifling his access. Would he lose all connection to the water element before the night was up?

A twisted, triumphant screech cut through the hissing.

Vultress.

Alexis dived after the sound, flames winking out as he clambered blindly through the hole in the wall where Vultress had disappeared.

Something heavy tripped him. He hit the ground hard, smacking his head. The world dimmed, his senses silenced, and he lay there waiting for his mind to stop spinning.

The smoke was thinner here, low to the ground. Alexis opened his stinging eyes and blinked to regain his vision and see what he had fallen over.

It hadn't been a thing. It was a person.

His father.

55

EIGENGRAU

Eigengrau (n.) *German origin*
'Dark light'; the colour seen by the eye in perfect darkness

Jackson Michaels lay motionless, blood pouring from a stab wound in his gut. Too deep, too dark. *Too much blood.*

Alexis couldn't breathe. He could only sit and stare in horror until he noticed Reina, her teeth tugging at Jackson's sleeve, trying to drag him away from the flames. She barely moved him before collapsing, panting weakly.

Alexis crawled to them, pressing his trembling hands to his father's wound, hoping to staunch the bleeding. Jackson's chest barely rose as he took stubborn breaths, his lips quivering, his eyes blank.

'Dad?'

Jackson blinked at him before his gaze drifted again. He wasn't dead, not yet, but Alexis recognised the blade that he had been cut with, the wisps of darkness that surrounded the wound. It wasn't one most survived, not even Elementals. If he had any hope of saving his father, he would need a supreme Elemental healer and more time than he knew he had.

Alexis forced some of the spilled blood back through his

father's severed veins with his powers, delicately manipulating the fluid. He'd saved barely a litre when a woman's voice came from behind him.

'That was a long time coming. Eleven years coming.'

Vultress stood at the edge of the room, watching them like an animal watches its prey. Her clothes were torn in the same spot Jackson had been stabbed, but little blood marked her dress.

'He did it to himself,' she said, smiling wickedly as the fire flickered in her pupil-blown magenta eyes. 'His last moments will be spent in agony – the least he deserves for what he did to Plague.' Her sword shimmered darkly. 'Recognise this kind of blade, boy? Not even he can survive that.'

Alexis clutched his father's hand, begging him to hold on. A soft blue glow pulsed at his wound, a similar hue to Alexis's faintly glowing amulet. Was the blood reflecting the light somehow?

Incantus had said Vultress had the power to transfer any wounds from her body to another, as if she was a human voodoo doll. Did it require eye contact the way her cousin Raeve's paralysing Concilium charm did?

'Dad?' Alexis asked again, pleading for him to respond.

Jackson's sky-blue eyes looked at something beyond Alexis. Through blood-splattered lips, he rasped, 'You didn't ... come this far ... just to come this far.'

Alexis swallowed his sob and rose, turning his back on his father and Reina, who remained loyally at his side, even as the fire threatened to approach them. His rage-filled gaze levelled on Vultress. 'His name was *Plague*?' he said, madness creeping into his expression. Sweat soaked his body, making it glisten when the muscles of his stomach rippled as he laughed. 'Plague and Sinner? Thank the First Borns my mother and I killed them.' He watched her eyes grow even wider with unbridled wrath. 'How embarrassing was it for you to learn that these great beasts of men were taken down by a five-foot mortal woman and a teenage boy with less than a month's training? Seems like there's a pattern with Mortem's protégés.'

Ice bled into a scythe in Alexis's hand, a frozen mirror of Mortem's. He pointed the blade at Vultress. 'Time for you to follow the trend.'

Vultress snarled and lunged. Her sword of darkness swung for his head, but he blocked it just in time with his scythe, which shuddered and almost splintered from the impact. Her knee came for his ribs, her elbow for his jaw. He stumbled back, Reina growling weakly behind him.

'I thought you needed me alive,' he taunted. A torrent of water poured out from his hand like a whip. He lashed it at her, but she dissolved it into a magenta haze shaped like a vulture's curved beak.

'Sire ordered me to kill your abductors and take you to Stonehenge if your mind wasn't already his. He never said in one piece,' she sneered.

Alexis roared and flung himself at her, narrowly avoiding a hex sent his way. He threw her backwards and cracked her head into the wall, hoping to see pain register on her face. Instead, it was his head that burned white hot with agony, so intense that he almost slumped to his knees, his vision spinning dangerously. Vultress smiled as Alexis tried to move away, realising his mistake. He'd made eye contact with her.

Vultress took her sword to her own arm and ran the blade along it before he could look away.

Before Alexis's very eyes, a deep gash opened on his arm, his skin splitting beneath the blade of an invisible sword. Her hawkish birdlike laugh filled the room as Alexis clutched at his arm, but Vultress hadn't finished with him yet. Her taloned nails clawed at her own face, and his cheek tore open.

Her power operated similarly to Raeve's. She wasn't nearly as good with a sword as her cousin, but she didn't need to be, not so long as he looked her in the eyes.

And so Alexis shut his eyes.

Her hiss confirmed the limits of her abilities. Guided by heat and sound, Alexis summoned a wave from above. It crashed over them both, drowning them in force and fury.

They grappled beneath its weight and traded blows in blind violence.

Alexis rose first. He felt for the sword of shadow, his body drawing close to its coldness as if it was an extension of him. He swung blindly and the tip of the blade seared through something soft and fleshy.

Vultress screamed. Magic flung Alexis back, and he spun through the air before he connected with the wall, causing his eyes to fly open.

When his vision adjusted to the light, he saw Vultress half engulfed in the fire she'd staggered into, her robes and body aflame, her stomach bleeding heavily from the gash across her midsection.

Alexis kept his eyes low so she couldn't transfer her pain to him. 'See you in hell,' he spat.

'Look at me!' she shrieked, firing a hex. He deflected it, his eyes fixing on his father who lay far too close to her.

Vultress followed his gaze.

'Look at me!' she screamed, her talon-like fingers reaching for Jackson's face.

'No!' Alexis shouted.

Reina snapped her jaws at Vultress, but the crazed Shadowless didn't flinch. Jackson stirred, head tilting to see what was happening. One second of eye contact and it would become his pain, his death.

'Dad!'

What happened next unfolded faster than Alexis could process. Or maybe it was that everything else seemed to slow down, as though the flow of time had reached a bottleneck, one moment stretching out to the next.

The fire's roar stretched. Reina's barks echoed. Vultress's movements blurred.

The only thing not bound by time was Jackson. Through eyes that took too long to blink, Alexis watched Jackson struggle to his feet with a newfound strength, as though there was someone else there to support him, to grant him speed while everything else around him staggered to a halt. He clutched his stomach, blood spilling between his fingers. He spared Alexis the briefest of looks, an incomprehensible, indefinable look, and Alexis could have sworn that his father's eyes were glowing with the same blue-white light he had seen in Protegere Forest.

Jackson then turned away and tackled Vultress, driving her into the fire. But his momentum was too much and his body entangled with hers. Before Alexis could realise what had just happened, Jackson was gone, engulfed by the flame.

56

CICATRISE

Cicatrise (v.) Latin origin
To heal by the process of forming scars

Time returned to its natural speed jarringly fast.

Alexis sat in the wreckage, Reina at his side, both staring at the withering fire. Like the tears he had been holding back, water erupted from his hands, dousing the flames in a great surge that left steam hissing in its wake.

Through the smoke, Alexis glimpsed two figures on their knees, a man and a woman, their foreheads pressed together. Alexis blinked, waving away the last wisps of grey smoke. His vision swam as the two silhouettes merged and the familiar figure of the woman faded away, leaving only the man behind.

His father.

Jackson's shirt had burned away, red welts scaling his arms and chest. He still clutched his abdomen, yet he managed to look up when Reina barked and leaped onto him.

'I-I thought you'd ...' Alexis stammered. 'The fire ... your stomach ...'

He dropped to his knees. The hole still gaped and bled from Jackson, but the blade's darkness had somehow vanished.

Whether that was due to Alexis or the death of Vultress, he didn't know.

Alexis let himself crumble into his father's arms. He knew they had to go, that Jackson needed urgent care, but in his father's embrace – the father who had raised him and bathed him and risked his life over and over for him – Alexis didn't feel like a warrior or an Elemental. He felt like a five-year-old boy. A boy who had been rescued from the seas and needed parents to love him.

In his arms, for the first time in a long time, Alexis finally felt at home.

His voice came out hoarse and broken. 'I'm sorry for what I said. For how I acted. You are my parents. I know you are.'

'Hush,' Jackson whispered, his weight growing heavier with every passing second.

'Alexis! Jackson!'

Geb Nikolas burst through the charred doorway, his face lined with soot and exhaustion.

'Give me your sweater,' Alexis said. Geb complied, and Alexis worked fast, binding Jackson's stomach as best as he could. 'He's lost so much blood. We need to get him to a hospital.'

If his mother were here, she would have been able to save him on the spot, without the authorities ever knowing. But sirens would come, and the charred bodies would be impossible to explain.

Geb read his concern. 'We take him to ours.'

Together, they carried Jackson out, Reina limping in front. Jackson tried to speak, but Geb told him to conserve his strength and rest his head on his shoulder. They hurried down Valerian Lane in tense silence.

Petra gasped as they burst into the warm, softly lit Nikolas home. She jumped up from Jason's side, where she had been cleaning his face with a sponge while he slept.

'Lay him here,' she directed, clearing the kitchen counter.

As soon as they set him down, she applied pressure to the wound. The blood that spilled onto the worktop didn't seem to faze her.

'We have to call the police,' Alexis said. Behind him, Reina curled beside Jason, asleep in moments. 'For Jason too. Why isn't he awake?'

'I gave him a concentrated extract of valerian root,' Petra explained. 'I've released it into the air from the valerian plants down the lane to keep the neighbours asleep too.'

She dipped beneath the counter and retrieved what looked like a sticky lime-green balm that Geb began lathering onto Jackson's burns. The tourniquet seemed to be holding, and Alexis's Elemental senses reassured him that the bleeding had mostly stopped, but his father's heart beat faintly.

'I can barely feel his pulse. We need a hospital,' he insisted.

'I've already called a senior Healer,' Petra said, dipping out of the room. She returned with pale yellow healing crystals and spare clothes, a loose black-knitted sweater and a pair of trousers, which she passed to Alexis. The second healing crystal she tucked into Jackson's tourniquet, before lightly applying the balm to the burns on Alexis's back. 'The Erasers are coming too.'

Alexis turned. 'What?'

Petra glanced at him with care. 'Trust me, none of us ever wanted the High Order to know where your family lived, but there's no other way now,' she said softly, continuing to apply the cooling balm. 'They've seen and heard too much. The Shadowless must be cleaned up and the truth erased from Jackson's and Jason's minds.'

Whether it was the valerian root or the lack of proper sleep, Alexis was having a hard time keeping up with what she was saying. 'My father didn't see anything,' he protested. 'We don't need the Erasers. I can dispose of the bodies myself. I can bury them in the woods.'

Geb shook his head. 'It is not fair, not to the forest nor to those who can hear their whispers. The High Order must see proof that Vultress and the Shadowless are gone. We will tell them that it was us who stopped them. It's safer for your father and brother to forget and let their brains convince them of a mortal explanation: a house fire, tripping on a knife.'

Alexis knew they were right. If his father woke, how would he explain it all to him? The missing bodies? The impossible fight? Alexis using his powers? Jackson would be better off forgetting. But wasn't that exactly what his parents had done to him his whole life? Kept him in the dark for his safety? It had infuriated him at the time, but he understood it now. Maybe to love, you had be prepared to lie.

But Jason? He had seen into the Elemental world directly. Alexis looked to where he slept beside Reina, wondering if there had ever been a time when they had been closer. He thought of Incantus and Mortem, their bond twisted. He wouldn't let that happen with his brother.

Alexis drew in a deep, steadying breath. 'Let the Erasers come. Let them clean up the mess and erase my father's memories. But not Jason's.'

'Alexis . . .' Geb began.

'He didn't see anything,' Alexis protested, unwavering in his stance. 'He was unconscious and in the safe room for most of it. Tell them he stayed here. Just don't let them touch his mind. If when he wakes up and mentions something about the Elemental world, I'll call the High Order myself. Promise me. Please.'

Petra and Geb exchanged a look, then nodded.

Before Alexis could thank them, Geb placed another crystal by Jackson's side where it glowed faintly.

Petra washed her hands and checked the clock – it was the early hours of the morning. 'Alexis, we have to go to Stonehenge,' she said.

'I can't,' Alexis said, joining her by the sink. The crystal and balm eased the biting pain of his burns, but the ache in his chest was yet to abate. 'That's where the darkness wants me to be at dawn. Vultress said so too. When I . . . was sleeping, I saw what it wanted me to do. This was Mortem's plan all along, to get the shadows to Stonehenge.'

Petra fetched her shoes and a coat from the back door. 'Demetria's pretty certain that the only reason she's fought off his imprinting all night is because of the Haven. It's a miracle you've resisted, but we can't be sure of Caeli and Blaise. If darkness has corrupted any one of you, we must stop them reaching Stonehenge before sunrise.'

'Have you spoken to Incantus?' Alexis asked, stroking his

father's dark hair. He didn't want to leave him, but he appeared stable now and would be safe in Geb's care until the Healer arrived.

Geb nodded. 'Vultress may have sent him away as a distraction, but the area was still swarming with Renderers. We told him what's happened and he's trying to get back now that the High Order have it under control.'

'Have they arrested him?' Alexis asked.

'I'd dare them to try to,' Geb replied. 'I told him what's happened here and he believes it's not just the darkness that needs you inside Stonehenge at dawn. Stonehenge has always been an amplifier of *light*. If you four are still in control there at dawn, Incantus believes you could destroy the shadows within you all – including you, Alexis. Just as you were supposed to on the solstice.'

'But what if by the time we get there, not all of us have managed to resist?'

Petra shrugged. 'He wasn't certain on that.' She handed Alexis one of Geb's coats. 'We don't have a portal so we'll have to drive. If we leave now, we'll make it just before sunrise. Demi passed the message on to your friends. We have to pray they receive it and get there in time.'

Alexis looked back at his father and gently shook his shoulder, hoping he would wake and tell him not to go. What if, as soon as Alexis left him and his brother, the delicate hold Jackson had on stability fell away?

'He'll be all right,' Geb promised. 'Our Healer's the best there is. We'll make sure the damage to your house is seen to. It's lucky your nosy neighbours own a construction company.'

Alexis smiled – it wasn't often that Geb joked. 'Go. Take care of my daughter. Just as I had faith in you on the solstice, I have faith in you now.' He offered him a fleeting but firm hug.

'Thank you,' Alexis said. 'For everything.'

He looked at his brother and Reina, storing the image in his mind's eye before bending to kiss his father's forehead. His skin was warm, which was a good thing. Alexis needed a bit of that Nikolas optimism that all would be well.

'Don't worry,' he whispered. 'I'm coming back. I'm coming back and when I do, I'll be me and everything will go back to normal.'

He followed Petra to her car, clinging to the image of his family like a lifeline, and took off into the night. That image would have to be his protector, his last defence.

Because when dawn came, the Prophecy would be decided one way or another. And if the decision between light and darkness, freedom or surrender, came down to Alexis, he didn't know what he would choose.

57

PHTHARTIC

Phthartic (adj.) *Greek origin*
Deadly; destructive

Alexis checked on the night sky for perhaps the thousandth time in the last few hours. The oppressive black was beginning to lighten; dawn couldn't be more than half an hour away.

Rain fell in sheets but Petra didn't slow. Her foot was welded to the accelerator, weaving through traffic that thickened as they drew closer to rush hour. The radio blared to keep them both awake.

Alexis tucked the now drained healing crystal into his pocket. His burns didn't look so angry, but Vultress's claw marks remained across his face.

'How are you doing, darling?' Petra asked gently, manoeuvring out of the spray from a lorry cruising in front of them.

'I'm fine,' he rasped. 'Thank you again for driving me all this way.'

Petra lowered the volume of the radio. 'I made Incantus – and your mother – a promise that I'd look out for you. I do not break my promises.'

Alexis blinked through burning eyes. 'Thank you.'

'She would be so proud of you.'

A tear tracked down his ash-coated cheek. 'I don't think she would,' he said quietly.

Petra shifted her thick curls over her shoulder so she could see him better. 'As a mother, nothing hurts more than watching your child suffer. It undoes something inside you; it cuts through the heartstrings one by one. The pain is unbearable.' She released a shaky breath, revealing her concern for her daughter who was also at risk of Mortem's imprinting. 'But what keeps you going is the hope that the lessons, the skills, the love you give are enough to convince them it's worth it. That their suffering won't last for ever, so long as they keep faith. That is what you are doing now. That is why she'd be proud. Just as I am.'

When Petra extended her hand, Alexis took it. He didn't care that he was crying. He unburdened himself of the impossible weight of the grief that drowned him.

'I wasn't done loving her yet,' he said, releasing Petra's hand. 'She didn't get to see me grow up and I didn't get to see her grow old. I didn't get to take care of her the way she took care of me. To make her smile and laugh and be happy. We weren't *finished*.' Alexis's voice crumbled, tears burning his eyes. 'I'm scared to live in a world that lets people like her go, but allows people like me to stay.'

Petra let him cry. Her silence allowed him to feel what he had been suppressing: the raw, unintelligible emotion that rocked his body and unleashed rain from the clouds.

'You will go on.' Petra's words were barely audible over the thundering of the storm, but that only made her speak louder. Clearer. 'You will. Because everything your mother and father gave you wasn't for nothing. Incantus's teachings weren't for nothing. My daughter's love isn't for nothing.' She waited until he lifted his head to meet her gaze. He did, ever so slowly. 'Grief is nothing if not an artefact of love. It exists to remind us how deeply we can love. Despite whatever comes at us, shadow, darkness, death, it can never take away what makes us human. So keep your head up, Alexis, because you won't find any angels on the ground.'

A single break in the clouds let sunlight flood the car as though it were just for him, a beam to pull him forward, onwards.

An incoming call flashed up on the car's dashboard and Petra answered instantly. *'Agapi mou*, how are you?'

Demi's voice cut through the static. 'I've got a hold over it, Mamma,' she replied. 'Kefi's keeping me awake and Valentina's on the other side of my door too. Still no sign of Cae or Blaise. How far away are you?'

Petra gripped the steering wheel tighter and accelerated. 'Twenty minutes.'

There was a pause. Then Demi said, 'Lexi?'

'I'm here, Dem. I'm okay.'

Demi's voice wavered. 'Thank God. I wish you hadn't left, that you'd waited for me ...' She caught herself. 'I heard what happened. I'm sorry I wasn't there to help you. But Dad said the Healer came and worked wonders. Your dad's going to be okay, Lexi.'

Petra screamed before Alexis could reply. All too late he

saw the car ahead skidding to avoid a truck that had flipped on its side. Petra slammed on the brakes, but they were going far too fast. The car hydroplaned and smashed into the back of the truck in a matter of seconds.

Alexis threw his arm across Petra's chest. Airbags deployed, bending his arm at an awkward angle as the screech of tyres and tearing of metal exploded all around him.

Alexis had barely recovered from the collision when the car was heaved forward again, slammed into by another from behind. Glass shattered and screams rang out as more vehicles piled in on the bridge they had been driving over. After a minute, everything faltered to a stunned silence.

Alexis beat away the airbag and rolled his shoulder. 'Aunty Petra?'

Her green eyes fluttered open. 'I'm okay,' she groaned as he unbuckled his seat belt to inspect her. 'You?' She glanced at the stereo, but Demi's call had disconnected.

'Fine,' he said, even though he absolutely was not.

A thunderous boom shook the bridge, as if the sky itself was quaking. Petra let out a yelp as Alexis whirled round to look through the cracked windscreen. He couldn't anything beyond the wreckage.

The passenger car door was pinned shut by another car. 'Sorry,' he said, and punched through what remained of the windshield.

At least thirty cars surrounded them, twisting across the overpass. His attention snagged on a section of the safety barrier that had crumpled away. A family SUV teetered over its edge, two tyres hanging off the side. It wouldn't take more than a stiff wind to send it toppling over onto the motorway below.

Screams rang out from behind Alexis. Dozens were fleeing from their cars, abandoning the bridge, running from something.

He turned and saw why.

A swirling funnel cloud tore across the landscape, pulling debris and rain into its rotating jaws as it headed for the bridge.

Alexis felt their presence before he saw them. Just as his amulet had once been able to sense the proximity of theirs, the darkness inside yearned to join the shadow trapped within them.

Alexis hauled himself onto the truck ahead to see what had caused the first crash. That was when he saw the boy and girl with matching black eyes and amulets coming towards him.

58

NĪPAN

> Nīpan (v.) *Old English origin*
> To grow dark; to become darker as the light fades away

'Alexis, get down from there!'

Petra ripped apart the roof of her car with her bare hands and clambered out. Her hair whipped in the wind as the tornado spun towards them, shuddering the overpass beneath their feet.

'We're a few miles from Stonehenge!' she yelled. 'Sunrise is close. Get there before they do! I'll help the civilians.'

Alexis nodded and saw her begin to wrench apart jammed cars, manipulating the steel and stone to clear a path. He returned his attention to his old friends just in time to see Caeli throw her hands skywards. The tornado howled faster, hurling cars like toys.

With a wicked smile, Blaise shot up continuous streams of fire, feeding the storm, igniting it into a burning vortex that showered the sky with ash that fell with the rain.

All across the bridge people were screaming. Whatever the Maya force might be showing them was enough to get them to clear the area. Yet some remained trapped inside their cars.

Alexis looked back at the family car teetering on the broken barrier. He skidded over car tops until he landed at its rear. Without considering whether he was strong enough to haul its weight, he squatted until had a hold on its bumper.

A cry escaped him as he pulled it back onto the bridge, the rain sustaining him. Without so much as a look in his direction, the mother inside jumped free, gathering her three children together before they fled.

'Yeah, you're welcome,' Alexis muttered, trying to catch his breath.

A series of explosions shook the sky. Cars burst into flames in the tornado, spitting streaks of fuming petrol onto the roads below. Alexis had only just formed a thin shield of water before they came raining down.

Blaise and Caeli hung in the air like stringless puppets, strangers in familiar bodies. Alexis had to remind himself that Mortem was the puppeteer as he slowly approached the two people who were once his closest friends, people he had trusted with his life.

'Shocked at what you see?' Caeli called, her grey hair whipping in the wind. They had both changed into their Haven Fighter suits, prepared for battle.

'We're so much more powerful now,' Blaise added, the spinning, burning blaze roaring behind him. 'Join us. See what real power feels like.'

Stonehenge was a speck on the brightening horizon. To have any hope of reaching it before Caeli and Blaise, Alexis would have to somehow catch them off guard. 'This isn't you!' he bellowed, clutching a nearby truck to keep him steady as the bridge continued to shudder. 'Mortem has hold of your minds, but I know you're still in there somewhere. Fight it! Don't let him turn your pain into weakness.'

Caeli laughed at him. There was another explosion from the vortex as it devoured a wind turbine, its propellor spinning wickedly in the air.

Alexis's voice rose in anger. 'How could you come to my house and burn it down with my family inside?'

Blaise flinched and Alexis swore the black of his eyes flickered. 'We didn't,' he whispered.

Before Alexis could continue, the ground trembled. Over the sea of fields, barely visible in the faint morning light, a ripple cut through the earth. Soil exploded as a figure shot into the sky and landed on the bridge beside him.

Demi.

Alexis took her in his arms instinctively and rolled her behind an overturned truck for shelter. It looked like she hadn't slept in days. Her hair had been scraped back from her face and she too wore her Haven Fighter suit. Dark bags lined her bloodshot eyes, yet they and her amulet were still a defiant green.

'Demi.' He said her name as if she was the only person in the world, as everyone else, the people on the motorway, Caeli and Blaise, even the standstill firenado, faded into the background.

She gently touched his cheek, her thumb brushing the claw marks. 'Mum?'

'She's evacuating everyone else. She should be clear.'

Demi nodded. 'And you?'

Alexis could only shrug.

Demi glanced at her friends and the burning, spinning vortex behind them. The sight of both seemed to devastate her. 'I was just with Ziya. She – she doesn't think that it's the four of us that dictates what happens with the Prophecy within Stonehenge. Lexi, it's *you*.' She gripped his arms, making him wince. 'It's your choice as the Elemental with the power of the darkness to decide how the Prophecy ends. "*By oneself is how the other will be slain,*" it said.' Her eyes bored into his. 'As the only living wielder of darkness, *you* determine the fate of it. You alone.'

Sapientis Aevum had said it was no longer through Mortem but through Alexis that the Prophecy was continuing. Alexis hadn't considered it properly at the time, but now, with sunrise only a few minutes away, the importance of the decision before him finally struck him.

And his first thought was not of heroism.

He could have infinite power. Control over everyone.

Demi looped her arm with his, a rock at his side, unmovable and unyielding. 'We have to get you there now. I'll find Mum and distract the others. I-I have to try and heal them.'

Alexis lowered his head. 'I don't think you can.'

'I have to try. You go. Run, drive, just get to Stonehenge however you can.' She tiptoed and pressed a kiss to his cheek. 'I will never lose my faith in you, Lexi Michaels. Whatever happens, you will always be the boy who jumped off the edge of a waterfall to save me.'

With nothing more than a squeeze of his hand, Demi left, stepping into the path of fire and storm. She had to shout to be heard over the roar of the wind. 'Cae, Blaise! I know you're in there somewhere.'

'We're right here,' said Blaise. He wrapped his arm round Caeli's waist and they walked in tandem to meet Demi.

'We're here and we want you to join us,' Caeli added.

'I'm talking about the real you,' Demi protested. The concrete cracked beneath her as she buried her footsteps deeper to keep her footing. Alexis knew he should be following her orders. Even if he ran, he wasn't sure if he would make it to Stonehenge in time. But he was locked into position and could do nothing other than watch Demi as the rain beat down upon her, once again choosing to heal where he would resort to destruction.

Demi opened her arms wide. 'I'm talking to the boy who makes me laugh until my belly hurts and the girl who is my best friend. The girl who was willing to kill a stranger for thinking they hurt me. Who doesn't like physical contact but would stay in the same bed with me because she knows I do. I'm talking to my sister, Caeli, and my brother, Blaise.'

With Blaise and Caeli fully distracted, Alexis was able to creep away, weaving through the wreckage, glancing back whenever he could.

Caeli was shaking her head, her eyebrows lowered as if it physically hurt to speak. 'They're gone. They were weak. No match for the darkness.'

Demi pressed closer. 'You would never submit to someone telling you who you are.' She was only a few metres away from them now, close enough to see the black veins that spiderwebbed from their eyes. 'He is far too strong, and you are far too defiant. Those are the friends I'm here for and I'm not going until I have them back.'

Demi was speaking to the truest parts of them, the parts they hid from the world but let Demi see, because she would accept them without judgement and love them without condition. As Alexis finally fell out of earshot, he could see that she was getting through to them, and the firestorm was beginning to falter.

Alexis reached Petra at the bridge's end, conducting cars with great sweeps of her arms. Metal and stone scraped in response as she barricaded the bridge from access and cleared paths for escape.

She grabbed him by the shoulders and thundered, 'What are you still doing here?' She caught a glimpse of her daughter in the distance and sucked in a sharp intake of air.

At the other end of the bridge, Caeli had dropped to her knees, her hands – one of skin and bone and the other of air – moved to her long silver hair. When she spoke, her voice rippled from the winds itself. 'Dem . . . it's too much. Go now. *Please.*'

An encore of crashing thuds answered her. Trapped debris hurtled down like an asteroid shower as the firenado waned, losing momentum. Caeli was fighting it, resisting the shadows just like Valentina had. Demi's touch might be enough to ground her, just as Caeli's touch had got through to Valentina.

Blaise looked more guarded as Demi came close, his eyes still shining dark as they searched over her shoulder. 'Where's Alexis?'

Almost instinctively, despite being dozens of metres away, Petra shoved Alexis behind her.

'Look at me!' Demi shouted, her arms reaching out for her friends. Caeli edged closer, her right arm rising to meet hers.

Petra ripped open the door of an abandoned car. 'We have to go!' she ordered, blinking away tears as she clambered inside, waiting for Alexis to join her. 'Trust her – she knows what she's doing.'

Alexis stole one last look towards Demi as Petra turned the ignition.

Neither Caeli nor Blaise had retreated.

Then –

A spinning wind turbine fell free from the tornado's vice, plummeting towards the three of them. Alexis called out in warning, his shout tearing the stillness.

The disturbance, or perhaps Alexis himself, the second son of shadows, was all it took for the darkness to regain control over Caeli and Blaise.

A wave of fire and wind erupted from their bodies and the firestorm exploded, hurling out all that it had swallowed. Burning debris roared down over the motorway, fire for rain. The broken propellor soared in Alexis's direction. The spinning blades were likely to miss him but only by a few metres.

Alexis then realised who was directly in its path. Petra scrambled to get out of the car, but she wouldn't be quick enough. She cried his name, *'Alexis!'*

Alexis knew what he had to do. He couldn't save his mother, but he could save Demi's.

And so he threw himself in front of her.

A scream tore through the sky as the turbine struck him, tossing him from the bridge. Alexis hardly heard it as he was flung through the air, weightless for a few beautiful seconds before the pain of both impacts would steal his breath. His powers were all that stopped him being severed in half, but it might not be enough to save him from the fall.

Something swooped beneath him. A gale strong enough to catch him lowered him gently to the bank. He had been spared by a power that could've only come from one person.

Alexis might have tried smiling had the bridge not then collapsed.

The scream had been Demi's. The moment she saw Alexis take the hit for her mother, his body tossed away like a rag doll. The moment her hope shattered.

A pulse burst from her body, stronger than any earthquake, devastating what remained of the bridge, hurling Blaise and Caeli far away.

Just like that, the nightmares of her hurting innocent people came true.

Just like that, Demi Nikolas broke.

And the darkness claimed another of the Children of the Elements.

59

PHILIA

Philia (n.) *Greek origin*
The love between friends

Rubble rained down. Sirens shrieked. Screams tore the air. Yet even after the bridge collapsed, blocking the motorway below, Alexis was granted no time to take it all in.

His amulet pulsed in warning. Someone was coming.

Through the dust, a figure clawed through the debris, flinging it aside in desperate sweeps. Alexis tried to rise, but his chest failed to draw breath properly. Pain infiltrated every nerve. He lay helpless as the familiar figure dug her way to him as if her life depended on it.

'What have I done?' she kept whispering, horror flooding her voice. Demi stepped into view and her mouth fell open. Her knees cracked against stone as she dropped to his side. 'Lexi. *No.* Are you – Can you hear me?'

Alexis could see the green of her amulet darkening as the infection swept across her, poisoning every cell of her mind and body. He strained to lift his head and reached for her.

'You have to get away,' Demi muttered, clutching her amulet

and crucifix, wincing at every tortured and panicked scream. 'Please. I-I can't get it out of my head. Leave me.'

Alexis caught her before she could stagger away. Every blink brought blackness to her eyes, staying longer each time.

'You didn't give up on me, so I'm not giving up on you.' He gripped her face as the skyline lightened around them. 'We've got minutes before dawn breaks, and Caeli and Blaise will be lost to the darkness for ever. I can't make it there without you. Please, *agapi mou*.'

In desperation, he kissed her. Hard. Desperate.

Demi's amulet flickered green in response. He had her for now.

'Thank you,' she whispered.

The reprieve did not last. Howls ripped across the sky. Caeli and Blaise were coming.

Before he could even begin dragging Demi, the ground opened beneath them. At first Alexis thought the darkness had regained its control, that she planned on burying him alive, but then he was lurched into movement. Earth shifted at Demi's command and a tunnel burrowed ahead, before they were propelled forward faster than they could ever run.

Alexis glanced at Demi; her face was twisted in effort, her wet hair plastered to her cheeks as she shifted their trajectory in the direction of Stonehenge.

'Can you manage it?' he asked, rubbing his aching chest.

'I have to,' was all she replied.

Explosions rang out from above. A fireball tore into the ground, sending dirt spraying into the air just seconds after they passed. Demi gasped but steadied her hands, not daring to look back.

As she continued steaming ahead like a submarine in water,

Alexis reached for the rain in the skies. He could feel the blood in Blaise and Caeli's bodies, even the darkness that had drowned their souls. It was too dangerous to manipulate it, not at the speed in which they were travelling, not when it was them. Instead, he raised water barriers to slow them down.

'Almost there,' Demi grunted, her face and hair caked with dirt.

A rolling wave slammed into them, hauling them into daylight. Alexis tried reaching for Demi's hand but she slipped out of his grasp. Dirt scattered as they emerged into the open.

Caeli hovered before them, her eyes gleaming black. Stonehenge was just behind her, the first light of dawn glinting between the rock pillars. 'There is no escaping me,' she bellowed.

'Then let's join you,' said Demi. She launched the earth skywards and slammed into Caeli. The two girls collided with a thwack and plummeted to the ground, rolling to a stop just outside the outer ring of Stonehenge.

Alexis landed and was instantly engulfed in fire. Blaise charged at him, his fists blazing. Alexis tried to absorb the blow with water, but Blaise's full powers in his Omni state overwhelmed him. Alexis went down hard, the air in his lungs beaten out of him.

'You've always held me back,' Blaise sneered. He lashed out a leg that sent Alexis sprawling. 'It's time I got rid of you once and for all.'

Alexis didn't know whose thoughts were powering what Blaise was saying: a manipulation of his own or Mortem's. There was only one of them that Alexis could hope to reach.

'Blaise, you're my best friend.'

Blaise stomped down with a burning boot, but Alexis swept him off balance as it came down. He staggered to his feet, pain stabbing his ribs. 'Blaise, you're my brother.'

Fire roared from Blaise's mouth. Alexis countered with a stream of water, steam hissing between them. Blaise waded through it, hurling a flurry of fireballs his way. 'You are my weakness,' Blaise said through clenched teeth, his eyes squeezed shut as though he couldn't bear to look at him.

Alexis backed away, aware of the assault, of where Demi and Caeli were, of the timing of the sunrise. This was the last chance.

He let down his water shield. It slithered apart, washed away in the rain until nothing stood between him and the boy on fire.

Blaise seized him by the shoulders with burning hands and lifted him into the air, relishing in his screams. 'I will no longer answer to you,' he spat, staring with hatred at the amulet Alexis wore, its colour split equally between black and blue. 'Your soul is mine to destroy.'

The pain was unbearable, but Alexis forced the words out, borrowing strength from a place he thought had been destroyed with his mother's passing. 'We can't escape the shadow that finds us . . .' He stopped struggling. 'But we can face it together. You've got me, Blaise. You've always got me.'

A memory flickered in Blaise's eyes. The fire waned and for a heartbeat, his amulet glinted red. 'Al . . .'

Alexis blasted him with water.

Blaise flew back, his head striking a pillar, and crumpled beside Caeli and Demi.

Alexis dropped to his knees. A wave of nausea swept over

him, dizzying him to the point of blackout. It took all that he had to stagger over to them, gasping.

Demi was on her back, her eyes fixed upon the horizon. 'Hurry,' she whispered, rolling onto her front. He seized Caeli's wrist, then Blaise's. Demi crawled beside him, her fingernails digging into the dirt to drag herself along, while Alexis hauled the other two to the centre of Stonehenge.

Standing there alone, the vision Sapientis had showed him became realised. It was then, as the sun broke the horizon on the day of the autumn equinox, that the darkness inside Alexis made a final bid for release.

It flooded Alexis with every loss, every betrayal. The *Shadow Man*. The hallucinations and the nightmares. His mother's lifeless figure, his father's bleeding body. Bloodshed. Loneliness and lies. A lifetime of torment.

And he could stop it. Alexis could stop the pain by unleashing the power he had been born into. Let it sweep across the world, let it imprint the minds of every person with a drop of Elemental blood. Something within Alexis knew that it wouldn't be Mortem who would be in control of it all; it would be him. He would be the highest power the world had ever seen and no one could stop him.

He could be free, even if no one else was.

But in amongst the dark tides of his life, there was a flash of light. He pictured his parents and the love they shared, the indestructible love that was intermixed with their suffering. His brother. The Haven, the place where he trained and studied, where he had learned who he wanted to be: a Fighter, a Scholar *and* a Healer.

His friends. The sound of their laughter.

Incantus, embraced in his warmth, even when Alexis reminded him so much of the brother who had taken everything good from him.

The memories became a wall that held back the flood of shadows. What would any of it mean, what would it be worth, if Alexis had determined it all to happen?

Maybe a life with no pain was easier, but a life without joy, without freedom, was no life at all.

That was the choice Alexis made. Not a life without darkness, but a life with the true value of light.

And Stonehenge answered him.

A silent explosion of light burst from the stones, bright enough to rip the shadows from their souls.

Alexis hunkered down and reached out to steady himself. He was met by Caeli to his left, Blaise to his right and Demi before him. The four friends held on to each other as the current of light surged through them, as it had on the summer solstice, as it had the day they met and first fell into the Elemental world, a world that couldn't bear to see them go.

The dying screams of the *Shadow Man* were cast out from Alexis's mind, leaving an empty quietness in its place that was far from familiar.

For the first time in his life, Alexis Michaels was free.

60

TOSDACH

Tosdach (adj.) Scottish Gaelic origin
Marked by absence of sound; failing to speak
or communicate when expected to

Four swirling pillars of shadow hovered above the Children of the Elements.

Alexis stared up at the largest, his own, recognising what had haunted him long before Mortem's imprinting. The shadows twitched, diminishing without a host, fading in the dawn, as the rain finally ceased.

'We're free,' Alexis said softly, lungs drawing air, savouring the richness of its taste.

He was the first to turn his back on the shadows. His knees gave out, but before he could fall, strong hands caught him. There was a warmth in them he instantly recognised, a warmth that minutes ago had nearly burned him alive.

'Al ...' Blaise couldn't meet his eyes, staring instead at the scorch marks on Alexis's bare shoulders. Caeli and Demi collapsed into each other's arms, sobbing with relief and regret, exchanging apologies.

Blaise stood awkwardly, still holding Alexis upright,

searching for words. 'I tried so hard to stop him. He – he came for me first, knowing that without you guys I had no one. The things I said, what I did ...' His voice broke, his amber eyes shining. 'You must hate me.'

Alexis didn't reply. He saw Blaise wrestling with his guilt, with all the venom he had spat, whether or not Mortem had twisted it. Blaise must've realised he wasn't saying what Alexis most needed to hear, and added, 'You'd think I'd be good at apologising by now.'

'You've always been a slow learner,' Alexis said, a smile tugging at his lips.

The tension cracked, though Blaise's smile was brief. 'You deserve to hate me. *I* hate me. Hit me if it helps. Just know that I'm so, so sorry, Al. I'll do anything to make it right.' Emotion rushed to Blaise's face, forcing him to choke on his words. He bowed his head, ashamed as Caeli and Demi looked their way.

Alexis took him in, the real Blaise. The one who fought and failed and tried again. Maybe that's what mattered. Alexis had fallen too, had lashed out and nearly succumbed, and had spent a lifetime with the darkness learning to resist his worst urges.

Hadn't his mother once told him that forgiveness healed not only others but oneself? After everything they had been through and survived, to heal and bask in the glory of light without the fear of being blinded by it was something Alexis wanted, but only if he had his best friend by his side.

'I could never hate you,' he said. 'Not for long. No more than I could hate Jace.' He squeezed Blaise's shoulder, forcing him to look up at him. 'I'm sorry too. For abandoning you, for lying. I forgive you, if you'll forgive me.'

Blaise's eyes filled. He pulled Alexis into a tight trembling hug. Seconds later, two more pairs of arms joined them. The Children of the Elements clung to each other in the centre of Stonehenge, four parts of a whole reborn in the place their story began. They would have stayed longer had the cloud of darkness above them not suddenly contorted, writhing as if sickened by the sight.

Caeli stepped towards it, head tilted. 'It doesn't look like it's dying,' she murmured. 'It's . . . changing.'

The shadow pillars warped. The indistinct edges sharpened, forming something tangible, anthropomorphic. Recognisable. Something that shared their faces.

Four figures now stood opposite them, their eyes burning black, a hole in their chests where their amulets should be.

Stonehenge hadn't destroyed the darkness; it had merely extracted it.

Standing before them were their shadow proxies.

61

CAELUM

Caelum (n.) *Latin origin*
The sky; the heavens

'You should have been destroyed.'

It was all Caeli could think to say.

Stonehenge pulsed around them, marking their arena, vibrating with an unfamiliar frequency as it fed the proxies.

Her proxy smiled coldly. 'And yet here we stand.'

Blaise's arms erupted into bright red and yellow flames. 'Not for long.'

A whip of roots pulled from the earth formed Demi's whip, and Alexis shaped a sword of ice from hardened rain.

But they were not the only ones who possessed power. The proxies mirrored their weapons, each forged from shadow incarnations of their elements.

'Mortem using proxies as a back-up?' Alexis said. 'How derivative. I can't imagine how desperate he must be to steal the trick his own son used against him.'

A pulse rippled from the stones, infusing the proxies with unstable dark power. It was then that Caeli understood what had happened.

'Mortem reversed the properties of Stonehenge somehow,' she said. 'At dawn it didn't destroy the darkness; it purged it.'

'But proxies can't live without the host,' Demi recalled.

'Mortem doesn't care about imprinting us any more,' Alexis replied. 'He just wants us gone.'

Caeli had had enough of talking. If it was a fight they wanted, a fight they would get.

She shot skywards, her proxy chasing. Beneath her, Demi's green eyes bored into the black pits of her own. 'The earth is mine.'

'Over my dead body,' her proxy replied, a black whip cracking at the air.

'That's the point.'

Caeli launched herself at her proxy. They collided in the air, thrashing each other with blades of wind and darkness. Below, Demi stomped her foot and the land trembled, opening up gaping fissures that streaked, forcing her proxy to dive aside.

Caeli snapped an elbow to the back of her proxy's head, sending it tumbling to the ground just behind where Alexis was grappling with his double.

'This takes being your own worst enemy to a new level,' he called over his shoulder to her.

Caeli landed to his rear and, despite everything, she smirked. 'I hate how I find you funny.'

Alexis's proxy was catapulted aside by a steamrolling Blaise.

'Thank you for catching me earlier,' Alexis said breathlessly.

Caeli dipped her head. 'I'd say I'm sorry, but that word isn't in my vocabulary.' She returned her attention to her proxy as it drew to its feet. 'However, I'll sit your assignments this term to make it up to you.'

'Deal.' With that, they parted and re-engaged in battle.

Caeli whipped through the air, clashing with her proxy in bursts of wind and black energy. She saw Demi coming towards her, her own proxy entangled in her whip far behind her. She read Caeli's unspoken intention and let her launch her skywards with a gust of wind.

Demi seized Caeli's proxy mid-air and slammed it down to the earth. Meanwhile, Caeli squared off with Demi's proxy.

'How can you hurt me?' said the shadow wearing Demi's face, her voice suddenly innocent, unsuspecting, so much so that Caeli dropped her wind razors. 'I thought I was your best friend, Cae?'

Caeli pointed to the real Demi who was bashing in her proxy's head with a rock. 'You're not. She is.'

Demi's proxy's face slackened. Her eyes glimmered black. 'You mean nothing to anyone. The only smart thing you ever did was give up.'

Demi's shadow proxy placed its hand against one of the nearby monoliths. Upon contact, its aura pulsated with dark power, connecting to an inextinguishable supply. Caeli watched as it grew stronger.

Think, Cae. You're a Scholar; you don't need anyone to figure it out for you.

Evidence. Logic. Intention. Caeli juggled them all.

She looked at the rocks that made up Stonehenge. They hummed in synchrony, reverberating with a cold energy that was focused inwards on the proxies – the opposite direction of the light that had poured out on the summer solstice. If Stonehenge was where the proxies were drawing their powers, maybe it was their lifeline too.

If that was the case, what would happen if the proxies were taken beyond the sanctuary of Stonehenge? It was a shot in the dark, but a theory Caeli was willing to test.

Demi's proxy advanced, her whip raised, but Caeli was done with holding back. She embraced her power and swept her arms wide. Mortem had taken her mind, just as he had taken Valentina's. He had pitted her against her friends, against herself. It was time Caeli reintroduced herself to him.

She pulled on the wind around her and the power within. A chaotic, wild, untamed power that she no longer wanted to control or suppress.

A rolling hurricane thundered from her body. The wind struck Demi's proxy's at full force, and a scream of fury and anguish rang out as it was hurled past the ring's edge. Beyond, the darkness was no longer protected against the rising light on the horizon. The black energy that made up its body disintegrated, devoured by sunlight, gone without a trace.

Caeli sagged from exhaustion, the air in her lungs gone. Demi, the real Demi, rushed over, abandoning Caeli's proxy who lay in a bloody heap on the ground.

'How did you do that?' she asked, cleaning the dust from Caeli's face and hair as she steadied her.

'Their bodies are tethered to Stonehenge,' Caeli replied breathlessly. 'When Alexis chose light, the darkness inside us was trapped in here.' She rose her voice to a shout, loud enough for Alexis and Blaise to hear: 'They can't exist outside Stonehenge.'

Demi hugged her fiercely. 'You smart, smart girl.' She broke away when they heard a grunt of pain. 'Stay here. Finish yours off. I have to help the boys.'

Caeli nodded weakly. Her eyes followed Demi as she raced to collide with Blaise's proxy, extinguishing the black flames it was beating down on Blaise. Caeli turned from them just as Blaise and Demi forced his proxy past the threshold, unable to watch as it screamed and disintegrated.

A sudden gust of air torrented into Caeli, slamming her into a standing stone. Pain raced down her spine, but she swallowed it and forced herself to her feet. She and her bloodied proxy circled one another, grey and black winds swirling around them as they ascended into the sky.

Until a burning presence waded through the vortex.

'Need help?' Blaise asked, taking Caeli's arm.

Caeli's proxy stood no chance. Obliterated by their combined powers, it turned to ash and embers long before its charred body rolled out of Stonehenge.

Caeli and Blaise turned to one another as they touched back down, the winds around them dissipating.

'Blaise . . .'

He shook his head. 'I think—'

A wave of darkness erupted from Alexis's proxy, cutting Blaise off mid-sentence. All Caeli could do was pull Blaise towards her and hold on to him as the tide beat against them at an intensity that stole every thought from her mind, sending them spinning through the air beyond Stonehenge.

The ground met them with a sickening slap. When Caeli finally stopped rolling, she prised open her swollen eyes.

The last shadow stood alone in the centre of Stonehenge, its eyes glistening so black that it stole the light from around it, the same way the *Demons* had.

'You think you can kill me?' Alexis's proxy bellowed, darkness pouring from its hands. 'There is no stopping me.'

Not too far from where Caeli and Blaise had fallen, Alexis lay unmoving. Demi was kneeling over him, her lips moving as she gently sat him up. Even from this distance, Caeli could see the exhaustion that lined his face, the shallowness of his breaths. Yet the thing Caeli loved most about Alexis was that no matter how many times he was beaten down, he got back up.

'Look at you,' Alexis said, his words entrenched with disgust and possibly pity too as he struggled to his feet. He pointed a trembling finger at the horizon where the sun had wholly broken free, casting light across the land, filtering through Stonehenge's black rocks. 'It's well past dawn. You failed, Mortem. Now you're the prisoner. Soon you'll be nothing but a nightmare.'

Tendrils of darkness spilled from Alexis's proxy. They latched on to the stones, connecting with its polluted powers.

'What makes you think this is over?' it asked, staring at the ground.

'You've lost,' Caeli announced. She hauled herself to her knees, then to her feet. 'Do yourself a favour and walk out and end it.'

But the proxy smiled. 'You seem to be forgetting that *I* am not the only one within Stonehenge.'

Caeli followed its gaze, realisation striking her as she remembered what lay directly beneath the ancient ringed structure.

The Haven.

Alexis acted first. The brightest of blue light exploded from his amulet, shooting like a river towards Stonehenge. It struck the edge of the monoliths closest to him with a roar, illuminating the blackness that was tainting them. Seconds later, a green blast rocked into the stones, quickly followed by great rays of red from Blaise's side.

Finally, Caeli hurled all that she could forward, her amulet glistening a luminous grey against her chest. She thought of Ziya and Valentina, the Library. She would not lose her home.

Beneath the combined powers of the Children of the Elements, Stonehenge whirred with an effervescent pulse, the glow of its stones flickering between white and black, light and dark. Somewhere in the centre, Mortem's screams echoed as Alexis's proxy collapsed under the weight of the warring powers.

Then, from the sky above Stonehenge, white light flooded Caeli's vision.

Incantus Arcangelo glimmered as he absorbed the combined powers of the Children of the Elements, turning it to white fire that bled from every inch of his body.

With a final blast, he hurled the incalescent light down upon Stonehenge, purging the darkness. No longer contained within a body, the shadow that had once been inside Alexis vanished. By the time the light had rescinded, Caeli opened her eyes to see that all traces of the shadow, of what remained of Mortem's power, were gone.

62

SERAPHIC

Seraphic (adj.) *Hebrew origin*
'The burning one'; beautiful and pure;
relating to an angel of the first order

A week after the autumn equinox, Alexis sat in Demi's childhood bedroom on Valerian Lane when a message buzzed on his phone.

Outside.

He set down his book on the Elemental inheritance of powers, pulled his jacket from the half-emptied suitcase, and glanced at the room Demi had offered him and Jason after the Michaelses' house fire. Demi hadn't been home much, only her proxy, an utterly ordinary shadow-free proxy, kept up appearances and bunked with Kallisto.

Demi's room was full of life. The earthy-toned walls were covered with photos, the windowsill crowded with plants. It was as close to her as Alexis could be.

Downstairs, early-morning October air drifted into the kitchen. Light grey clouds dotted the sky, pulled leisurely by the wind as though they had nowhere to be and no reason to cry. Alexis was staring through the window towards the edge of the forest when he heard the excited patter of footsteps.

Alexis scooped up Reina when she jumped at his legs. The effort made his chest twinge, but the pain was minimal thanks to the Healers in the Sanctuary.

Jackson Michaels entered a moment later, phone to his ear as he waved at his son. 'Sounds great, Geb. I'll be over in a bit. No, honestly I'm fine. It'll give me something to do besides hogging your sofa.'

'Any updates on the repairs?' Alexis asked after he hung up. He stood opposite his father at the counter where he had been laid out not too long ago, his blood dripping from its edges as his life slipped away. Although the memory of it, and of everything else that night, had been wiped from his father's mind, Alexis couldn't help but wonder if any part of him knew just how close he had been to joining his late wife in the afterlife, wherever and whatever that may be.

'By some miracle, the structure's intact,' Jackson replied, biting into the chocolate-chip banana loaf Petra and Kallisto had made the night before. 'Nikolas Construction's on it. At least your mum's getting the new kitchen she always wanted.'

Alexis admired the urn of her ashes that Petra had placed on the windowsill, overlooking the lane and the forest. Grief had taken up permanent residence in his chest, but the pain had softened. It would never go, but no longer did the memory of his mother bring only sadness.

'I'm sure she's kicking you in spirit form,' he said, retrieving his shoes from the back door.

'Oh, you have no idea.'

Outside, Jason and Kallisto were carving pumpkins, laughing as Kallisto told him a dramatic story. Jason watched, entranced, his eyes and mouth wide in wonder and disbelief. Alexis smiled to himself, grateful that he knew the truth now and also that he had a friend to talk to about it. It was their secret, a harmless one, which they had decided they weren't going to share with any of their parents.

'You sure you're well enough to help?' Alexis asked his dad, channelling his mother. 'You should still be resting.'

Jackson threw mock punches his way. 'Look at me,' he said, slightly breathless while Reina skated around his legs. 'I'm a machine.'

Alexis rolled his eyes. 'You passed out from smoke inhalation and stabbed yourself with a knife you were holding.' It was the lie Oliver Wrought had impregnated in Jackson's mind when he came to oversee the Erasers, while a number of High Order Operatives disposed of the Shadowless corpses.

Jackson frowned. 'Rusty machine, then. You off to the library again? Need a lift?'

'No thanks, I'll take the bus. See you later.'

'Is it a date?' Jackson called as Alexis left.

'Go away!'

'Take Demi somewhere nice!' Jackson's laughter followed after him as he shut the door behind him.

Alexis wrapped his jacket tighter as he crossed Valerian Lane, heading into Protegere Forest. Thin beams of sunlight filtered through the trees, illuminating the forest floor of fallen leaves of red and gold.

A figure waited for him in the distance.

'Sorry I'm late,' said Alexis.

Incantus Arcangelo turned from where he had been looking upon the Michaelses' house, where builders and architects milled about freely. He was wrapped in a pale overcoat, Darcy Raphe's brown blanket round his neck.

It was the first time Alexis had seen him since what had happened at Stonehenge.

'How's your father?' Incantus asked, wind tousling his white hair as his gaze lingered on the Nikolases' house.

'Fine,' Alexis said, then corrected himself. No longer would he use it where it didn't truly fit. 'Whatever the Erasers did, he seems to believe it. He still thinks it was just an electrical fire. An accident. He hasn't mentioned anything about the invasion or even about the Shadowless. Not to me at least.' He let a sigh escape his lips. 'They must've been working overtime to cover up what happened on the motorway too. Almost makes up for the High Order's incompetence. Thank the First Borns they dropped the charges against you.'

Incantus rolled his eyes, a clear indication he wanted to move on. He buried his chin into Darcy's blanket, inhaling whatever scent it still held. 'What of his health?'

Alexis mirrored Incantus with the collar of his quarter-zip. 'Vultress stabbed him with a shadow blade. I didn't think people could heal from that, not even Elementals. Yet all he has is a scar.' He shuffled his feet, approaching the topic he had been dancing around for the past week. 'That night, Geb told me they had sent for their Healer friend.' He noticed Incantus's micro-reaction, an ever so slight raising of his eyebrows. 'When you showed up at Stonehenge, you looked old. At the time

I thought it was just exhaustion from your fight against the Shadowless.' Gently, Alexis reached upwards, his hand stopping at Incantus's sunken cheek. Grey streaked through his hair, and lines etched deep around his eyes. He looked, for the first time in decades, his true age.

Alexis spoke through the lump in his throat. 'Why did you do it? Why did you use your own life force to heal him?'

Incantus pressed his nephew's hand to his cheek, allowing him to feel the last of the power of light that remained.

'Because it was the right thing to do.' Incantus took a breath. 'One of the main reasons you turned out to be so different from Mortem was because of your parents. Mortem knew nothing but abuse, neglect, manipulation. That's what he learned and that's what he became. Jackson and Stephanie saved you from that with kindness and patience. Love was at the centre of all their decisions. It was clear to see in the way they were with each other.' He closed his eyes, his face contemplative. 'It was why I led them to you after the tsunami. After failing to keep you all safe from the darkness and the Shadowless, it was why I healed your father. It was for them, for you, and to pay them back for the burden of responsibility I placed on them.'

Very slowly, Incantus turned from Valerian Lane and began to walk, leaves crunching beneath his feet. Alexis offered his arm and Incantus accepted it. There was strength in him still, a strength that would surpass most Elementals. A strength that would never fade.

'I don't know how to thank you,' Alexis said. 'You gave up your immortality for me, and now your remaining years for him.' He held on to Incantus's arm much tighter now, aware that there would come a time when he would no longer be there.

Incantus was quiet, then said, 'I thought I sensed you when I was in the laboratory with Ziya.'

Alexis recalled the conversation that had sent him spiralling. With the *Shadow Man* banished, Alexis could see how it had manipulated him with the voices of the people he loved most. Incantus wishing he had killed him as a child, his parents wanting him gone, Blaise saying he was responsible for the death of both his mothers.

Alexis now knew those words had never been spoken. But there was no denying what Incantus had initially shared with Ziya – how he could never love a child of darkness and could never look at him without thinking of Mortem.

'We don't have to talk about it,' said Alexis. 'I understand why you said it. All of it. Even contemplating killing me as a baby to prevent all of this. And it's okay.'

Forgiving Incantus, forgiving Blaise and his parents, it was just as healing for him as for them. His footsteps fell lighter, his chest expanded wider with each breath.

Incantus stopped. 'I wasn't talking about you,' he said gently.

He released Alexis's arm, then continued for a few steps alone, guided by the feel of the magic that ran through the forest of secrets.

'Then who?'

For a long time, Incantus didn't answer. The breeze through the trees was all that sounded. He slowly turned, his gaze failing to meet him. 'I was talking about my son.'

Alexis halted. 'You – you have a son?'

Incantus's sky-blue eyes glazed. 'I didn't know he was mine. Not for a long time. I thought he was Mortem's. I couldn't bring myself to raise his child, the child that he forced my wi—' His voice caught. 'That he forced *her* to carry. I wasn't . . . I couldn't do it. Not if he had Mortem's powers but her face. But I couldn't kill him either. Not a baby. Not *her baby*.' Tears bled into the wrinkled creases around his eyes. 'I have a son; he's alive and grown, free from our world, with a family of his own, but I am not his father. Not in any way that matters.' Incantus hung his head in resignation.

Alexis felt the weight of his pain. Once upon a time, a time not too long ago, he would have been desperate to know more. The more you knew, the less shocked you'd be, that was what he had once believed. And although there were still things he did intend finding out, questions he knew he would continue to ask, the painful history of Incantus Arcangelo was no longer one of them.

Alexis stepped closer. 'I'm sorry you had to carry that alone and I'm sorry you never got to meet him. If he's anything like you, then the world is lucky he's in it.'

Incantus looked at Alexis with his head tilted, blinking. 'Thank you . . . for not judging me.' The simplicity of his reply struck a chord in Alexis that reminded him that while he knew Incantus as an all-wise and all-powerful Elemental, at the end of the day, it was still his first time at life. Alexis couldn't expect him to be perfect just because he wanted him to be.

'I asked you to no longer keep me in the dark,' Alexis said. 'And you haven't.'

They walked in silence, embracing the beauty of the forest in autumn.

'Do you think we did it this time?' Alexis asked eventually. 'Do you think the Prophecy has been fulfilled?'

Incantus was thoughtful. 'There's still so much I don't understand about it, not well enough to be definitive. We can only hope that if Mortem returns, you and your friends will still be here to save us.'

With his face inclined skywards, searching for any ray of light through the cracks in the canopy, Alexis couldn't help but see Incantus as his true age, the age his body now reflected – a man who had lived a lifetime that outlasted all those he knew.

'How did you do it?' Incantus asked, his eyes still closed, his face basked in the sunlight. 'How did you defy the darkness for so long?'

Alexis waited until Incantus turned to look at him. When he did, he smiled. 'I just had to follow the light.'

Later, Alexis used one of the newly delivered portalling devices to meet Olivia Kefi. When she asked how he was, he let the tears fall and said aloud, 'I'm not fine.'

Kefi smiled kindly and took his hand. 'And now we can begin to heal.'

Alexis spoke of the *Shadow Man* and of his childhood psychosis. Of murdering Dr Dash and then, a decade later, Dr Sinner. Of the quest, the battle, his mother. Of all the things he had buried for too long, of all the love he still held for her.

That was the day he truly began to get better, because he realised that it was never his mental illness that had held him back, but his ignorance of it. He could not hope to be healthy by pretending it didn't exist.

He was a person with mental illness. A sufferer. A survivor. But he was not weak.

Every day he got up and tried again. That made him a fighter.

Every day he chose to stay on the long road of recovery. That made him a healer.

And every day he learned that it was okay to falter, to lose his footing, so long as he figured out how to find it again. That made him a scholar.

It was something no shadow could take away from him.

Not any more.

Not ever again.

Incantus told Alexis that he would return to the Haven soon, but that hadn't been the case. He had wandered through the quiet of Protegere Forest, steeped in memories of light and shadow, joy and grief, of the sound of laughter and the quiet stillness of death. He found himself back on Valerian Lane, standing before the house that marked a life he had quietly shaped from the sidelines.

At the centre of his thoughts was Darcy Raphe.

Even now, he could paint every single detail of her face. The chocolate brown of her eyes that could level him with a single glance, the defiant curve of her smile that unmade him, the power of her touch that had once unchained his wings.

He had hoped their child would inherit everything from her. But instead, the boy had become a mirror of them both. Even from a distance greater than the street that now lay between them, Incantus had seen reflections of himself. In his resolve, in his quiet strength and his ability to draw greatness from others, in his boundless love.

Incantus wanted nothing more than to meet his son properly, to introduce himself formally. To forge some kind of bond that was half the relationship he had seen him have with his own two sons. And yet after all that had been taken from him, after so many years, it would be a cruelty, not a kindness. So Incantus watched from afar, as he had for forty years. A silent guardian. A witness to a life that, despite its pain, had grown into something beautiful.

There had been one other gift he *had* granted him, however. The name he now used as his last. The mythical archangel: the protector, the healer, the guardian who carried souls to heaven and gave them the chance to redeem themselves. It was a name that, from what Incantus had heard and seen, Jackson had lived up to.

Michael.

63

SOPHROSYNE

Sophrosyne (n.) *Greek origin*
A healthy state of mind, characterised by self-control, moderation and a deep awareness of one's true self, resulting in true happiness

'I think I'm bisexual.'

Caeli watched Demi across the table in the quiet coffeeshop in the Haven's plaza, where they sat concealed from view, awaiting her response. Caeli noted the occasional sideways glances, likely a result of the destruction they had caused the week before, but ignored it. The only person she wanted to talk with was Demi.

Demi's hair fell in dark ribbons over an oversized Haven sweatshirt, her hands clasped around a mug of hot chocolate. 'When did you realise?'

'I guess part of me has always known,' Caeli said, trying to keep her heart rate steady. 'It got harder to ignore after our sessions with Raeve. I didn't know if I wanted to *be* her or be *with* her.' Demi smiled, encouraging her. 'Seeing how open Akili and Teller were about their sexuality made it easier for me to consider, but I never really thought about it. I'd only ever had boyfriends and was never single long enough to think properly about why they never worked out. Then we met Valentina. At first I thought I felt distrust, dislike. She made it easy to interpret my feelings that way. But then ...'

She rubbed her wrist where it itched beneath the table. She wasn't wearing her glove – she no longer felt the need to. The glove had always been to hide that part of herself, and since purging Mortem and the shadows from her mind, she no longer wished to be anyone other than her unapologetic true self.

Demi noticed and offered her hand. 'I'm so proud of you.'

Caeli frowned. 'Why?'

'For finally following the Woman of the Air's advice.'

Sudden tears stung Caeli's eyes. 'You aren't going to ask if I ever fancied you?'

Demi tilted her head. 'You think that little of me?'

'No,' Caeli admitted. It was one of the first times she'd spoken about her sexuality aloud, and it felt more liberating than she'd expected, like she had been a bird caged but now set free. Valentina had wanted an answer from her and Blaise hadn't wanted to know. But it was with Demi that Caeli could speak freely without being rushed to suddenly have all the answers. Rather than shun her feelings or act like they didn't mean anything, bringing them to light granted her permission to understand them better. It was only after accepting that part of her, and learning to take pride in it, that Caeli allowed herself to think of Blaise and Valentina.

'I know I need to talk to them both,' she said. 'I've avoided them all week and that's not fair to either of them.'

'Do you know what you'll say?'

'I'm scared I'll make the wrong decision,' Caeli admitted. 'If

I choose Valentina, I'm throwing away all this love I have for Blaise. It's only ever been him until now, and I can't picture my future without him pissing me off every day and holding me every night. But Valentina pushes me and excites me and gets me like no one else does. She brings out this side of me that I'm beginning to like. If I don't pursue things with her, then what's this all been for?' She sighed. 'Classic Libra – so indecisive.'

Demi gently massaged her wrist, applying pressure in slow rhythmic circles. 'I don't think it works like that,' she said. 'You won't be any less bisexual if you stay with him or choose to be with her. From what I understand about it, it's based on how you *feel*, not who you're with, right?'

Caeli dabbed at her eyes with a napkin, not wanting her mascara to run. 'I worry that when I stop performing, when I stop the act, people might realise they no longer need me.' She thought of the years of servitude to keep her and her mother afloat, the role of leader she took on at school, her inability to ask for help when she was struggling to balance everything she wanted to achieve in life.

'Why would they leave?' Demi asked.

'Because it's the sparkle they're drawn to, not the real me beneath it, the me that's flawed and jealous and selfish and exhausted. Valentina wants me to be someone I'm not and Blaise expects me to be who I used to be. So who do I trust to stick around? The one I've always needed or the one I never knew I wanted?'

Demi leaned in. 'I think you owe it to yourself to take the time to figure that out yourself. The most important question isn't who you want to be with, but who you want to be.'

'I want to be cared for.' Her reply tumbled out of her as if conjured by magic. She spoke freely, truthfully, thinking of what she'd deprived herself of since losing Celina. 'I want to be looked after. Treated and adored and admired. That's all I've ever wanted.'

Demi left her seat and wrapped Caeli in a hug. They sat in each other's arms, gently rocking, letting the sounds of steaming milk and hushed conversations surround them.

'You deserve that,' Demi whispered. 'So if you need to be with someone, be with the person who provides it in abundance.'

Caeli decided then. Silently, resolutely.

Demi must have felt it, because she leaned back. 'Can I give you your birthday present now?'

Caeli wiped her eyes. 'Yes, please.'

Demi withdrew a large box tied with purple ribbon from her tote bag, and placed it in her lap. 'I'll save the card for tomorrow.'

Inside was a pristine prosthetic hand that Caeli's Healers had made for her weeks ago.

'I painted its nails silver like yours,' Demi added, a hesitant smile dancing on her lips. 'You don't need it, you may not even want it, but it's yours if you ever do.'

Caeli blinked back tears for an entirely different reason. 'It's the best present I've ever been given.'

'So it's not me?'

Valentina's disappointment was thinly veiled as she browsed the Library shelves near the star-speckled ceiling of the grand archives. 'I promised myself to never beg for anyone's love,' she continued, scowling slightly, 'but what does he have that I don't?

Besides the obvious. Is it because you don't want to accept the side of you that likes women?'

Caeli owed her honesty. 'You and I are both dragons,' she said. She continued, even though Valentina appeared to be more interested in inspecting the spines of the leatherbound books on their dusty shelves. 'Blaise is a phoenix. You get me, you see me, but with him I find harmony. He balances me and provides a warmth and a softness to my edge.'

Valentina's eyes dropped. 'I could provide all those things too,' she said quietly. 'I've only ever wanted to push you to be your best.'

Caeli took a step towards her. 'My decision isn't because of Blaise. I hated you for your cruel methods, but now I can honestly say I'm grateful. You forced me to pick myself up and you reminded me of who I am.' The air was still supercharged between them when their eyes met. It was something Caeli wasn't sure would ever fade entirely. 'But I have my teachers to push me. My friends push me. *I* push me. I want you to know that this isn't about Blaise. It's about me.'

She placed a hand on Valentina's shoulder. 'I'm so sorry if you felt like I used you, and I'm sorry if I did. You were never just an experiment. What happened between us mattered to me, as do you. You opened my eyes to a part of me that I never let exist and for that you will always have a piece of me, Valentina. Don't think my decision erases that, any more than it erases that part of me that's bisexual.'

Caeli pressed a featherlight kiss against Valentina's cheek. If the portaller was burned, she did a good job at masking it.

'Go,' Valentina said softly. 'I'll be okay. I always am.'

Caeli began walking away.

'Doran?' Valentina called out.

Caeli turned.

'The sky's the limit,' said Valentina, offering her a gentle smile. 'Don't be afraid to reach for it.'

Caeli coughed from behind Blaise just as he was raising his hand to knock on her bedroom door.

He turned. 'Oh, hey,' he said, his mouth pulling up in a half-smile.

'Hi.' She climbed the short flight of stairs up to him. 'Looking for me?'

'I was.' Blaise made space for her, backing up to the wall. 'Can we talk?'

Caeli knew Blaise well enough to know something was off. The awkward shuffling of his feet, the rapid blinking. She knew. 'You don't want to be with me.'

Blaise slowly nodded.

And Caeli exhaled. Her loosened breath unwound the knot that had formed in her chest. 'I was coming to find you to say the same thing.'

Despite making the same decision, Blaise looked somewhat crestfallen. 'You picked her?'

'I picked myself.'

Caeli did want a partner one day who could provide all that she sought: love and tenderness and kindness. But she also now knew that she could provide all that herself, especially while she figured out who it was that she wanted to be.

'It's not about what happened with Valentina,' Blaise clarified. 'Not entirely. It plays a part, but not for the reason you think.'

Caeli suddenly became aware of her arms at her sides and folded them over her chest. 'We've changed so much, Cae. I spent so long doubting if I was right for you, I never asked if you were right for me. I used to fear being alone, but now ... I think I can handle it.'

It became painful for her to continue looking at him. 'I've realised the same,' she said, grateful more than words could express that there was a mutual understanding between them, that they both sought the same thing, even if that thing was no longer each other. 'I used to fear not being enough and now I know I am – based on how I see myself, not how anyone else sees me. I think I want to be on my own to figure out what's right for me, and I see that you do too.'

Blaise nodded. 'Who knows? One day we might find our way back to each other.' There was hope in the words he chose, promise in his eyes. His gaze slid over Caeli's lips, which glistened from the light of their amulets.

If this was the last time she would be so close to him, close enough to feel his breath against her cheeks and see the pulse in his neck, she wanted to savour every second of it. 'For what it's worth, when we were good, we were incredible,' she said.

Blaise's face softened. 'We really were.'

Caeli tilted her head in question and he nodded, inviting her silently into an embrace. She rested her head on his chest as his arms closed round her, holding her tightly against his chest where she could hear his beating heart. In what might be their final embrace, she inhaled his scent and could hear him breathing in hers.

'I'm going to miss you,' she whispered, hoping it wouldn't be as embarrassing if she only said it quietly.

Blaise pulled back slightly until they were facing one another again, still locked in their embrace. 'I'm not going anywhere,' he said. 'I promised you I would always stay, even if we don't work out.'

Caeli swallowed and offered him a small smile. 'So I'll see you at my birthday dinner tomorrow?'

'With balloons, party poppers and a big cake.'

'Victoria sponge?'

'I'm not an idiot,' he snapped, and for a moment they were them again, bickering as they always did.

Blaise lowered his head to her, and she felt his full lips press against her own. Fire filled her bones, providing her with a gentle warmth like a hearth in a home in winter. She knew it was a parting kiss, a goodbye kiss, so she made it last as long as she could before she finally pulled away. It would be all too easy to fall back into their relationship, but she owed it to herself to commit to her decision before she ran the risk of hurting someone she cared about again.

When Caeli returned to her room, alone, she waited for the weight of heartbreak to hit her.

It never came. Instead, there was a sense of space. Her time was hers again. Her efforts, her energy, all hers. She had gifted herself the chance to live for herself, without anyone depending on her, without anyone to guide or take care of. Only herself.

And that was enough.

She was enough. Not perfect, but complete.

In that moment, Caeli realised that while she was still the same independent, self-sufficient girl she had always been, she was no longer alone and without people she could rely on. And that made all the difference.

64

REDAMANCY

> Redamancy (n.) *Latin origin*
> The act of loving the one who loves
> you; a love returned in full

Alexis found Demi at the Lakes just before sunrise, a couple of hours before his first Healer session.

'Didn't expect to find you here,' he said gently.

She turned, her hand falling from the edge of the docked rowing boat they had once shared. In the cold wind of the glacial mountainside, she hugged her arms tighter round her body.

'Why not?' she asked.

'Would've thought this place reminded you of all the bad things that happened here.'

'There were good things that happened here too. I'd rather remember those.'

Alexis saw her in his mind's eye, hair drawn up into a chignon, body laced in a gown worthy of the Woman of the Earth herself, eyes guarded by a mask that only made her more alluring.

She looked expectantly at him, waiting to hear what he had to say.

'You were the only one who never turned,' Alexis said. The wind pulled at his dark hair. With the darkness gone, the heterochromia of his eyes had faded too. It was barely noticeable at a distance, but as he drew closer to Demi, he saw her face soften when she noticed it. 'After all, the Earth is the only element that casts a shadow. No darkness could ever hold out within you.'

Demi's gaze dipped.

'There's something else.' His throat threatened to close, but if there was anything he had taken away from his first session with Kefi, it was that he had to be honest, especially with himself. 'During the quest, the Woman of the Earth said something to you in Greek. At the time, I didn't fully understand it, and when I asked you what it was, you said it wasn't something you planned on listening to.'

Demi's lips parted, but no words came.

'Το να αγαπάς αυτό το αγόρι θα είναι ο θάνατος σου,' Alexis recited, blushing in case he'd mispronounced it. He then translated: '"Loving him will be the death of you."'

The words hung between them. He stared at her, and she stared right back at him. She then stepped towards him.

Alexis moved back and raised a hand. It was taking all his strength to tell her this now, but he would fall to his knees if he had to see her pain and beauty up close. 'I don't know where things were going with us,' he said, massaging his throat to clear it. 'But I'd never forgive myself if something happened to you because of me. I cannot let that be your fate.'

He thought of Incantus and his father, how grief clung to them. He couldn't end up like them. He couldn't allow the world to suffer the loss of a soul as pure as hers just because he needed her to keep him afloat.

'We're not meant to know our fate,' said Demi, steady despite the tears in her eyes. 'We're told we are born to die, but I won't let that stop me from living how I choose. With whom I choose.'

Alexis shook his head. 'I can't risk it. I'm your doom. I will not be the reason you die, Demi. I would sooner die myself.'

He turned from her. His strength had run dry and he had said what he had come to say.

'It's too late!'

Alexis froze, unable to do anything other than stare at a distant point on the lake's surface that reflected the gathering rain clouds.

'It's already happened, Lexi.'

Alexis turned to see her spreading her arms as though relinquishing herself of all restraint.

'You've etched your name into my heart in a way not even death could erase,' she said.

The clouds opened. Rain fell, gentle but persistent.

Demi didn't run to take shelter. She let the rain soak her. 'Death is coming for me, for us all. But I refuse to let the fear of it take what time I have left. So tell me, Lexi, do you love me?'

Alexis's chest deflated in a single exhale. *What a silly question*, he thought. She was the girl who smiled at her own reflection. Who waved at animals and nodded whenever he spoke so he knew someone was listening to him. She was what he needed, what he wanted: the sunlight he feared standing in in case it cast him out or revealed the dark shadows of his secrets.

His voice wavered. 'I'm not well. I-I . . . too easily fall to ruin.'
Demi took a step towards him. 'Then I'll heal you.'
'I may never be free of the darkness.'
Another step. 'Then I'll be your light.'

His resistance was growing futile. The dams were cracking and he couldn't hold himself back for much longer, not if she kept coming towards him, kept staring at him, kept loving him. He had to find a way to stop her for good.

'I have psychosis.'

Demi wiped the rain from her face as though she hadn't heard him right. This was the only weapon Alexis had left in his arsenal to keep her safe from him.

'I hear and see and feel things that aren't there,' he said. 'I lose touch with reality. Even with Mortem gone, the shadows of my mind might return.'

He was wet through to his skin and bones, but he had done it. She had stopped. Her gaze remained fixed on his, her eyes filling as she pieced everything together. Why his family had hidden him away, why he had always worn earphones, why he had reacted to things unsaid.

And yet, despite it all, she took another step towards him. 'Then I will stand by you and hold your hand to remind you that I am real,' she said, her voice hitching in her throat. 'When the shadows manipulate you into looking into the past, I'll be here to remind you that it's only because there is light in your future where it cannot exist.'

And, just like that, the dam broke.

'I love you,' Alexis whispered. 'Σ'αγαπώ,' he repeated in Greek, and then again in Arabic, so that she could hear it in every language she spoke. 'أحبك. I'll learn to say it a hundred different ways in case you ever doubt or forget. You are the Earth, and I am hopelessly, irrevocably trapped in your orbit.'

Demi gasped at the revelation, her hands flying to her chest. *As if there would be anyone else but her.*

Words poured from Alexis like rivers. If they were doomed, let them be doomed together. 'You make me feel whole. My hallucinations never had any power when it came to turning me against you.' He was crying too, but he didn't care, because he loved Demi and she loved him. 'All my life, I didn't know who I was or where I was meant to be. Now I know. I'm meant to be with you, to spend an eternity with you. My every smile, every laugh, every dream, it is for you, my darling Demi. You are everything I've ever wanted and everything I thought I didn't deserve. My strength, my weakness, my power, well before the water or shadows came to be.'

'You are my power,' Demi echoed, her face breaking with the gentlest of smiles.

Alexis took her into his arms. When he kissed her, the Earth applauded in the crashing of waves and the blossoming of flowers.

'I love you,' he said between kisses. He meant it with every fibre of his body, as if it was written into his DNA, carved into his future, her soul meant for ever to intertwine with his. It was a bond that nurtured like a tree and the water, providing shelter, care, providing a home that could never be burned down. Although he couldn't see it, he knew their amulets were glowing, ebbing with a flow of energy that would surpass time or distance, life and death.

'Let us be done with chasing sunsets at the end of our days,' said Demi, cupping his face as the sun rose, flooding them with golden light. Alexis gazed up at it freely, blissfully, blindly, as though his mother had painted it just for him to admire, just as her mother had for her. 'Let's start treasuring the start of them too.'

It was then, with Demi in his arms, where she belonged, that Alexis realised something else. It wasn't necessarily the great displays of light that removed the darkness, rather the everyday glimmers. By acknowledging it, tending to it, refusing to let it fester like disease on a stagnant lake, he was able to show the shadows the door. He would do the work every day to keep himself afloat, because after all this time, he finally believed he deserved to.

If there's one thing I've learned, he thought, *it's that sometimes we must cross paths with the shadow to know the road he takes is not the one you wish to follow.*

'Why is it still raining?' Demi asked, looking up. Alexis tilted his head back, letting the raindrops strike his face, knowing that he wouldn't find any angels on the ground. Not beyond the one he held in his arms.

'It's the good kind of rain,' he said and kissed Demi again. 'The kind that washes all the bad things away.'

EPILOGUE

Four shadows raced against the dawn on the morning of the autumn equinox, fleeing from Incantus. They clung to the darkness of the world as their only salvation.

It had taken days, weeks, traversing icy-blanketed plains under perpetual night until a castle materialised in the distance. It blinked into existence to welcome them before teleporting a hundred miles away again, never to be seen or caught. Through the cracks of the stone walls, the shadows seeped like water, reforming with growing urgency until they reached their destination.

Far below, trapped in the lowest dungeon of the castle, lay a woman still alive. She had felt and heard the dying cries of all those who remained after the summer solstice, Nekro and Hybrids and Shadowless alike. It had been awful, but it had been better than the endless silence that had replaced it.

The silence was an oppressive darkness, a tunnel without any end, not too different to the life she had lived for the last twelve years.

Now she sensed the shadows returning, calling for her powers again. Amplification, nullification, transfer.

Unable to stop it, unable to awaken, Aadya Parashakti could do nothing but wait for the master of darkness to reawaken.

The four shadows hung over the Elemental to whom they belonged. As they flooded into him, his eyes snapped open, revealing rings of both blue and black.

His plan hadn't worked. The Children of the Elements had resisted him. Yet through their minds, he had learned *everything*. About the Haven, about Incantus, about Alexis. Most importantly, he now knew what Alexis cherished above all else, and what would happen to him if she was taken from him.

Not yet. Not today. For his vengeance to be complete, Mortem would have to wait for the winter solstice. Only then would he strike.

And Mortem would do it using the boy Alexis called a brother, the one born to Arcangelo and Aevum, angel and time: Jason Michaels.

ACKNOWLEDGEMENTS

Writing is often described as a solitary act, but nothing about this journey has been done in isolation.

First, I would like to recognise the patients and clients I have worked with in the past. Thank you for providing me with an insight into your lives and allowing me to learn more than any textbook or study could've provided. Thank you to my family members for opening up about your experiences with your mental health journeys, and to myself for being honest with my own. Together, we have ensured this book accurately reflects and represents the reality many of us experience, untainted by glamorised or romanticised notions of suffering. *We didn't come this far just to come this far.* I can't wait to see what we do next.

Thank you to my muse, my love. Every day you inspire me. For the longest time I struggled to write about love and acceptance, but through being with you it has never been easier. You have allowed me to dare to chase the sunsets at the end of every day and look forward to the sunrises too, wherever in the world we find ourselves.

To my whole family for your unwavering support,

encouragement, patience and love. To my little baby, Coco, who has left us to join Monty in the fields of forever, and to Rocky for helping me to mourn while reminding me to love. To my friends, near and far, in person and online on BookTok and Bookstagram – you have guided me through writer's block, encouraged me during moments of imposter syndrome, and cheered me on every step of the way. Thank you for enriching my life.

To my editor, Tierney Holm, and the whole team at Simon & Schuster who have worked tirelessly on building my author career and championing my series. Your insight, support and efforts have shaped this book into something far greater than I could've done on my own. Thank you my agent Safae El-Ouahabi, for always advocating for me and fighting tooth and nail to ensure I get everything I now know I deserve. And to Jennie Roman for your delightful copyedits and Sally Critchlow for your proofread.

To Katt Phatt for another beautiful, Elemental-inspired cover, and Alex Forrest for breathing life into my characters and creating the most stunning illustrations for people to adore.

Thank you to my three authenticity readers: Lauren, Tina and Lucy. You made sure I wrote Caeli's story with care and sensitivity, enriched by your lived experiences. Thank you also to the people closest to me in my life that opened up about these parts of their identities and journeys in the hope that anyone reading this book can feel seen, safe, loved and whole, which is precisely how I feel about you.

To my readers. Oh, how I love you. There's so much to say, but I would end up getting carried away and write another book. I can't thank you enough for all you have done for me. Showing up, recommending my books, celebrating every minor and major milestone. Everything I do is for you. This book is yours as much as it is mine.

With love and light always,

Andy x

ALSO IN THE SERIES

LOOK OUT FOR BOOK 4

COMING 2027

ABOUT THE AUTHOR

Andy Darcy Theo is the bestselling author of the Descent Into Darkness series. The first book in the series, *The Light That Blinds Us*, was an instant TikTok sensation. He is a British-Greek Cypriot with an educational and occupational background in clinical psychology and teaching. When he is not teaching, learning or reading, he is developing this compulsive, character-driven fantasy series, which he first started writing at age thirteen.

Andy can be found on TikTok, Instagram and Twitter: @andydarcytheo and be contacted via his website andydarcytheo.com